BEFORE THE MOUNTAIN FALLS

LUISA A. JONES

This is a work of fiction. Names, characters, businesses, places, events and incidents are either the products of the author's imagination or used in a fictitious manner. Any resemblance to actual persons, living or dead, or actual events is purely coincidental.

Copyright © Luisa A. Jones, 2026

The moral right of the author has been asserted.

All rights reserved. No part of this book may be reproduced or used in any manner without the prior written permission of the copyright owner. This prohibition includes, but is not limited to, any reproduction or use for the purpose of training artificial intelligence technologies or systems.

To request permissions, contact the publisher at rights@stormpublishing.co

Ebook ISBN: 978-1-80508-707-6
Paperback ISBN: 978-1-80508-709-0

Cover design: Eileen Carey
Cover images: Arcangel, Shutterstock

Published by Storm Publishing.
For further information, visit:
www.stormpublishing.co

ALSO BY LUISA A. JONES

The Gilded Cage
The Broken Vow

What We Left Behind

Goes Without Saying
Making the Best of It

To Nic, Claire and Julia, with thanks for a quarter of a century of unfailing support, kindness, and friendship.

"We are all in the gutter, but some of us are looking at the stars."

– OSCAR WILDE

A NOTE ON WELSH PRONUNCIATION

In Welsh, the emphasis is usually on the last but one syllable of each word – shown in bold font below.

The Welsh letter Ch is pronounced in the same way as in the Scottish word "loch".

The Welsh letter Dd is pronounced like the "th" in "the".

The Welsh letter Ll is pronounced by putting the tip of the tongue behind the top front teeth and blowing air along the sides of your tongue. It approximates to a "hl" or "thl" sound.

The Welsh letter W is a vowel, equivalent to "oo".

Aneurin – "An-**nigh**-rin"

Ceinwen – "**Cane**-wen"

Emrys – "**Em**-riss"

Gwenllian – "Gwen-**hlee**-an"

Idwal – "**Id**-wul"

Mabinogion – "Mab-in-**og**-yon"

Moel Carnau – "Moyl **Car**-nigh"

Pant Glas – "Pant **Glahss**"

Sioned – "**Shon**-ed"

Bach – pronounced like the German composer's name [Little/small, also used as a term of endearment]

Bore da – "**Bor**-eh dah" [Good morning]

Cariad – "**Ca**-ree-ad" [Love/darling]

Cawl – "Cowl" [Stew, usually made with lamb or mutton]

Cymanfa Ganu – "Cum-**ann**-vah **Gan**-ee" [Festival of hymn-singing]

Cymdogaeth – "Cum-**dorg**-aith" [Community/neighbourhood]

Dwt – "Doot" rhyming with "put" [Someone small and cute – like the Irish "dote"]

Diolch – "**Dee**-olch" [Thank you]

Eisteddfod – "Eye-**steth**-vod" [Festival of Welsh poetry, music and culture]

Nos da – "Norse dah" [Good night]

Os gwelwch yn dda – "Oss gwel-**ooch** un tha" [Please]

Rwy'n dy garu di – "Royn duh **ga**ree dee" [I love you]

ONE
LONDON, SEPTEMBER 1939

Norma

In all her girlish dreams of her wedding day, not once had Norma Sparrow ever imagined that she'd be wearing a secondhand maternity frock she'd picked up from Watney Market. She'd also – naively as it turned out – never considered that the bridegroom might fail to turn up.

Yet here she was, still sitting on the bench in Arbour Square Gardens where they'd agreed to meet, with the flower in her buttonhole wilting after two hours in the late afternoon sun. She plucked it from her lapel and crushed it. Bruised, the petals fell onto her lap, where her belly proclaimed her disgrace to the world.

"Damn you, Dickie Tucker," she muttered.

It should have been done by now. He should have come strolling along the path like the cock of the walk in a nice new pinstripe suit, flicked his cigarette end into the flower bed, and looked at her with that smirk that told her he knew they were the best-looking couple in the East End of London. He should have tilted his elbow out just enough for her to tuck her hand into it, and sauntered with her into Stepney register office, just her and him and a couple of the staff or passersby to witness the deed that would have given her instant respectability.

Not respectability, perhaps. Not with Dickie for a husband. But changing her name to Mrs Tucker would have saved her. She'd have been secure, her recent misdeeds made irrelevant by a piece of paper and a thin gold band.

Across the park, a couple posed for snapshots with friends and family, all dressed to the nines and grinning as if they'd won a hundred guineas at the greyhound races. Norma swallowed and looked away. Her mouth was so dry, her tongue seemed to stick to her teeth. Her face hurt from the effort of trying to look unconcerned.

Nearby, a clock struck the hour. Six o'clock. No more weddings today.

Norma sniffed, flicked the petals from her lap, and rose with a defiant, sweeping glance around her in case anyone was watching. If Dickie hadn't the decency to at least come and tell her what had been more pressing than his own wedding, then she'd have to go and demand an explanation. But first, she needed to change out of these borrowed shoes.

She tucked her jacket around her and held her handbag across her front while she marched down Commercial Road, chin held high and a bold wiggle in her walk that attracted whistles from tradesmen passing in vans and lorries. She didn't even spare them a glance, but kept her eyes peeled for any sign of her errant fiancé. Disregarding the way the too-narrow shoes pinched her toes, she continued past the row of shop fronts where shopkeepers were pulling down the blinds and flipping the signs on their doors to *Closed*.

At last, with a toss of her blonde curls, she paused at Alma's door and rang the bell. The shop was closed, but Alma would hopefully be at home in her flat above the premises.

Alma was the embodiment of everything Norma wanted to be: not only was she glamorous, married and comfortably off thanks to a successful tailoring and alterations business, but she was also childless. It was a bit late to emulate her boss in that respect, though. *Should have thought of that six months ago, instead of being stupid enough to believe Dickie when he said he'd be careful.*

The scraping of a bolt being drawn made Norma stand straighter and paste her smile on more brightly, just as the door swung open to reveal Alma, black hair immaculately permed and set. The only sign that she was off duty was a pair of pink marabou-trimmed slippers instead of her customary polished heels.

"What are you doing here?" Alma demanded, frowning at the unexpected sight of her employee waiting on the doorstep. "I thought you was supposed to be getting hitched this afternoon?"

"I need to give you these back." Norma gestured towards her feet and held out the matching handbag.

Wordlessly, Alma stepped aside and waved her in, then followed her up the narrow flight of stairs to the flat.

Norma hadn't felt so nauseous in weeks, but there was no point in putting this moment off. It had been made clear that she couldn't continue working for the Goldmans now that her pregnancy was showing. Clenching her jaw, she peeled off the oyster-coloured gloves and handed them over before following Alma into the living room. Under normal circumstances, she'd have paused to take a wistful glance around at the clean, modern wallpaper and stylish armchair where Alma's husband sat to smoke his pipe. But not today. She emptied her purse, lipstick, compact and hanky out of the handbag and tucked them into her pocket.

"You'll ruin the line of that jacket," Alma said, one pencilled eyebrow arching as she accepted the empty bag.

"How else will I carry them home?"

"Tsk. Where's Dickie, then? Don't tell me he's left you in the lurch."

"Looks like it, don't it?"

The disgust in Alma's eyes hurt even more than Dickie's rejection.

"You've got yourself in a right pickle, then, my girl. I'd like to help, but..." She cast that same pursed-lipped look towards Norma's stomach, then shook her head.

Norma swallowed hard. Begging didn't come naturally to her, but without her job in the Goldmans' sewing and alterations shop, she didn't know what she'd do.

"Alma... Mrs Goldman. Can't I work out the back where no one can see me? Having a bun in the oven don't stop me being able to sew, does it?"

"We've talked about this before. We run a respectable business, and you'd be seen as a bad influence. No one wants to send their son or daughter to work with a girl who... And my customers wouldn't like it."

The words fell like an icicle down the back of her neck. Alma wouldn't meet her eye. Six years of loyal service and hard work counted for nothing. By failing to seal her status as a respectable woman today, Norma had blown her last chance to redeem herself.

"Keep the shoes, if you want," Alma said as Norma bent to unbuckle them.

Pity wasn't much use to her, though.

"Thanks all the same, but what will I do with a pair this colour? Until the next time I try to get married, they'll be about as much use to me as a chocolate teapot."

It had been one of her gran's favourite sayings. Gran would have had plenty to say about this mess. Dickie would be watching his back now if she was still alive.

Alma's mouth turned downwards and she rubbed her palms together as if she was itching to be rid of her employee. She'd set her shoulders and was gazing around the room, at the ceiling and out of the window, anywhere except at Norma. Perhaps she found the situation uncomfortable. Ironic, considering it was Norma who was getting sacked for being an embarrassment. If she could only have got that ring on her finger today, she'd have been allowed to continue for another couple of months, and then Dickie would have provided for her. But as things were...

"I left my own shoes in the shop this morning when you lent

me these. Any chance I could have them back now? Then I can be off. Leave you to your nice, comfortable evening." It was hard to keep the bitterness from her voice, even though Alma no doubt thought she only had herself to blame for her situation.

While Alma was downstairs fetching the shoes, Norma reached up to unpin the pretty little hat. It had been lovely wearing a full set of matching accessories, even for just an afternoon. There was no point dwelling on that now, though. What was done was done. She dropped the hat onto the table before powdering her nose and primping her hairstyle in the mirror over the fireplace. She needed to put her armour back on before facing the world.

With her thoughts occupied by what she might say when she caught up with Dickie, the sudden appearance of Alma's husband behind her made her jump.

"Ooh, hello, Mr Goldman. I didn't hear you come in."

"Too busy admiring yourself in the glass."

"Not really. Just tidying myself up." She turned and fixed the bright smile back on. Mr Goldman had a reputation among the girls in the workshop. They all joked about never turning away or bending over in front of him. He had a way of putting his hand in the centre of a girl's back when leaning over her to examine her work, as if he wanted to feel the fastening of her bra through her dress. Norma had never been alone with him before. She'd made sure of it.

Something in his look made her take a step away. Her back bumped against the mantelpiece. With his hands resting on it, either side of her shoulders, there was no avoiding the smell of his tobacco breath fanning her face.

"Here, let me show my appreciation for all your hard work in the shop," he murmured.

Before she could respond, he'd caught one of her hands and was pressing a roll of paper into her palm. Frowning, she opened her mouth to ask why he'd be giving her money, but he spoke first, his words making her fingers curl into fists.

"I hear you've got yourself into a bit of a fix. But you know, Norma, a nice girl like you... I might be able to help you out a bit now and then, if you're willing to help me out in return. You scratch my back, I'll scratch yours, if you know what I mean. It'd be a shame for your... talents... to go to waste."

His face was too close. The only thing she wanted to scratch was his eyeballs, which were angled blatantly towards her bosom as if it was heaving provocatively instead of fearfully. She flinched as one hand moved. Before she had time to duck or side-step, it cupped the side of her breast.

She shoved him away, bile flooding her mouth, shuddering from the way his touch had made her skin crawl.

"You can clear off now." Alma's voice from the doorway was flint-hard as she thrust Norma's old black shoes towards her. "I should have guessed you couldn't be trusted. Little tart."

"But... It ain't what it looked like. I never led him on, I swear."

The look on Alma's face told her there was no point in protesting. She'd never believe Norma had done nothing wrong. People were always quick to assume the worst of her. But for Alma to do it stung badly enough to really hurt. Norma had always looked up to her, modelled herself on her style and aspired to be a brilliant seamstress with a business of her own one day, just like Alma. She'd worked until her fingers were raw, her eyes burned and her neck cramped to prove herself in the Goldmans' workshop. Yet it seemed none of it had meant anything.

With her cheeks flaming, Norma ducked under Mr Goldman's arm. Instinct born of experience made her tuck the roll of cash up her sleeve, out of sight, instead of throwing it back in his face as she wanted to.

Norma had only just finished lacing her shoes onto her feet when Alma propelled her towards the stairs and out onto the doorstep. The front door slammed shut.

Thanks to Mr Goldman and his horrible wandering hands, she'd have no chance of getting her job back now, even if she could get Dickie back in line. Without a job to pay her rent, and with this blasted belly getting bigger, she'd be homeless within a week.

Painfully conscious of her unadorned left hand and with no handbag to conceal her tummy, and no hat or gloves, she felt half-dressed out on the street. Norma was used to being looked at when she was out and usually enjoyed being the object of male attention. Now, though, it would be happening for all the wrong reasons. Now, she wished she could be invisible.

The old, familiar feeling of being unwanted and dirty rushed in, bringing memories along with it that she swiftly squashed down with a skill honed by years of practice. With her head down and shoulders hunched, she hurried as inconspicuously as she could to her lodgings. Tears pricked, but she blinked rapidly and clenched her fists until her nails bit into her palms. She absolutely would not cry. Getting all blotchy wouldn't help her chances of persuading Dickie to face up to his responsibilities. That would have to be her next task.

TWO
PONTYBRENIN, SOUTH WALES

Miriam

Overhead, a floorboard creaked. Miriam's heart skipped and she hastened to the kitchen doorway to listen for footsteps, tucking the book she'd been reading under her apron.

She let out her breath. Emrys must only have been shifting position, not making for the stairs. It would have been unusual for him to come down after he'd knelt to begin his nightly prayers. She generally had a clear fifteen minutes or so to prepare their cocoa. Fifteen minutes she'd been planning to use for some illicit reading.

She wasn't cut out for secrecy, but she knew what her husband's reaction would be if he caught her reading this, and it wasn't worth upsetting the apple cart.

From the stove, the sound of hissing sent her running back to move the saucepan off the heat. She huffed under her breath at the sticky mess and reached for a cloth. It had been silly of her to attempt to read whilst heating the milk, but she had so few quiet moments, and her sister Dolly would need the book back when they met at Contadino's café next week. With a sigh, she slipped the book back into its hiding place behind the jars of preserves on the top shelf of the larder. Emrys and Aneurin wouldn't find it there.

As she hung up the apron that she'd been wearing over her dressing gown and nightdress, she tried not to dwell on the passages she'd been reading when she'd been interrupted. No wonder Dolly had passed her the book so surreptitiously, nudging it towards her under the tabletop in Contadino's and sending her a mischievous wink.

"Have a look at this, but don't let anybody know you've got it," she'd whispered.

Miriam's mouth fell open as she peeked at the slim volume in her lap. *Married Love: A New Contribution to the Solution of Sex Difficulties.* With her cheeks flaming, she spread her napkin over it and glanced around. No one seemed to have noticed.

"I read it in bed, a chapter a night. Poor Ivor didn't know what had hit him. Not that he was complaining, mind, except when I told him he needs to put a bit more effort into wooing me." Dolly gave a throaty chuckle and downed the rest of her coffee.

"Wherever did you get it?" Miriam asked, keeping her voice low.

"I found it in the study at Plas Norton, while I was dusting. I'll have to put it back, obviously, but I'm sure no one will notice if you hang on to it until I see you next. It's not as if Mrs H will be needing it, with her husband dead nearly twenty years. Although I suspect over the years, she's had a couple of... well, let's call them friendships, shall we? On her trips to London, of course. Never in the house."

Miriam frowned. She didn't approve of the idea of Mrs Havard having affairs, but nor did she think her sister should spread gossip. "What makes you think that? You've never been to London with her."

Dolly checked no one was listening and leaned across the table. "When I was unpacking her suitcases once, I found a..." Behind her hand, she mouthed *Dutch cap*.

They'd been forced to change the subject then, to Miriam's

relief, as the young waiter Johnny Contadino had come to check if they wanted more coffee. Once he'd gone, Dolly returned to the subject of the book.

"Perhaps if Mam and Dad had been able to read something like that, it might have helped. From what Mam told me once..."

"What?" Miriam asked.

"Oh, nothing. Forget I said anything." Dolly fidgeted with her napkin, eyes in her lap.

"You're saying there were problems... in *that* side of their marriage?" Miriam wasn't sure she believed that their mother would ever have shared details of such intimate issues, even if they had existed. Their parents hadn't always seen eye to eye, but it had never occurred to her that their physical relationship might have been the cause.

"I don't really know. But Mam said something once that made me think he'd had other women. Or, if not women, then *a* woman."

Miriam suppressed a gasp. "I can't imagine it. Dad's a good man."

"Even good men can be tempted," Dolly replied with a shrug.

"Emrys would never do that."

She wasn't sure she liked Dolly's sardonic expression.

"No, Emrys probably wouldn't."

Still thinking about Dolly's revelations and the subsequent surprises contained within the book, Miriam trod carefully up the stairs with the two cups of cocoa. She remembered her mother's advice to her before her wedding day: *Don't expect too much. We women go in with high ideas of what marriage is, and men can't live up to it.* Was that what she was doing, expecting too much from Emrys by wanting him to show her affection in that way?

It was confusing. On the rare occasions when she and Emrys were intimate, he'd always behaved as if he were inflicting something shameful upon her. She had the sense that he only did it as a concession to her desire for a baby of her own. When they were first married, and she was still caught up in the joy of being a new wife, she'd once admitted that she liked it, that being kissed and touched was pleasant, even exciting. He'd made no secret of his disapproval.

"What kind of woman would confess such a thing?" he'd asked, his voice harsh. He'd rolled off her and retreated to his own bed. The gap between them had seemed a chasm she had no way to cross.

She'd accepted that he must be right, and there must be something wrong with her for the way her body thrilled at being touched and having the weight of his body over hers. For several years now, she'd felt ashamed of herself, too conscious of his disappointment – disgust even – to mention the subject again. But according to the book, it was normal for a woman to enjoy the conjugal act.

Emrys was on his knees, dark head bowed over his hands on his bed. His private prayers were always in Welsh, the language he'd grown up speaking before he ever learned a word of English. Miriam understood little of the vocabulary, but the fervency of his entreaties to the Almighty was clear enough. She loved his voice, even when she couldn't comprehend much of what was being said. The rhythm and depth of it, deep and dark like a seam of Welsh coal. The way he rolled his Rs, as if he savoured the words and delighted in the way they felt in his mouth. The richness of emotion underlying the words made his voice sound like music. When she'd first heard him preaching in Chapel, she'd been moved by the passionate way he spoke as much as by the words themselves. Even now, eight years later, she still felt the same stirring in her belly.

Quietly, she placed one cup and saucer down on the crocheted mat on his nightstand, before sidling past him to her own bed. She hung her dressing gown on the hook inside her wardrobe, then slipped under the bedclothes to sip her own drink while she waited for him to finish his devotions. By the time she finally echoed his *Amen*, her cup was empty and his cocoa had an unappetising greasy film.

He suppressed a grunt as he eased himself to a standing position. His left leg always pained him, and especially when he'd been kneeling for a while. Miriam didn't comment, knowing he hated any reference to the shrapnel wound he'd suffered in the trenches. She'd once made the mistake of suggesting he shorten the period he spent at prayer, or find a more comfortable position, and had been told that a mind focused on the flesh was in opposition to God.

"I hope it hasn't gone too cold," she murmured as he took a slurp from his cup.

"It's fine. *Diolch*," he thanked her.

"I've been thinking," she began, but stopped when she realised that he'd already picked up his Bible and opened it.

"Hmm?" Distracted, he looked at her over the top of his reading glasses with one eyebrow raised, dark brown eyes unblinking.

He was still a handsome man, even with his black hair turning silver at his temples and forehead. She longed to sweep the stray lock back from his brow, but it felt as if there was a distance of more than a few feet of carpet between them.

"Aneurin will be at your mam's until tomorrow evening. We have the house to ourselves. I was thinking that perhaps we could try again?"

A muscle flickered near his eye before he lowered his gaze back to the Bible resting on his lap.

"If it was God's will to bless your womb, I believe He would have done so by now, *cariad*."

She sank back against her pillow, absorbing the words, though she wanted to resist them. He'd given up on her, then. Perhaps it shouldn't come as a surprise, after so many years of marriage and still no child together. He had the consolation of his son, Aneurin, after all, and might not feel the lack of a baby the way Miriam did. But the book had prompted her to think differently. If they performed the act more often, perhaps she'd have a better chance of conceiving. And even if it turned out that she didn't, it would be comforting to feel physically close to him now and then. She was still young enough to want to be desired, and the book had suggested it wasn't wrong to wish for that with her own husband.

Still, she'd have to be careful. It wouldn't do for him to suspect she'd been influenced towards a direction he would disapprove of. And he'd be irritated if she interrupted his Bible reading.

Without another word, she padded to the bathroom to prepare for bed. Simple and spartan though it was, it was Miriam's favourite room. Living in the manse often felt like living in a goldfish bowl. Members of the congregation had an unnerving habit of letting themselves in at all sorts of inconvenient times. The manse was as much Emrys's workplace as the chapel down the road. As the minister's wife, Miriam was frequently called upon to provide comfort to the lonely, to help organise events, and to provide food for meetings and unexpected visitors. But in the bathroom, at least, she could be assured of some privacy.

Having spent her early childhood with only a tin bath in front of the kitchen fire, she would always feel grateful for the luxury of hot running water and a tub in which to soak. Even Emrys never disturbed her when she bathed.

They'd never seen each other completely naked. He changed his clothes in the privacy of the bathroom and always knocked before joining her in the bedroom. It was something else she'd always accepted as normal, assuming he and his long-dead first wife must have been the same. But the book had made her wonder. The book said that the sight of a woman in the bath might enchant a man. It would be quite something to feel that the sight of her had that kind of power over her husband.

After washing her face and cleaning her teeth, she took her time brushing her long, wavy hair until it shone and crackled under the bristles. During the day, she kept it tied back in a bun, her face bare of make-up. Emrys didn't approve of vanity, but even without cosmetics and with her eyebrows left unplucked, she knew hers wasn't an unattractive face. Her reflection in the small bathroom mirror showed her complexion was still smooth, with rosy cheeks under black-lashed, cat-green eyes. She had a slender neck, and good bones, with a figure she would describe as average: neither too fat, nor too thin; not tall, but not short either. She skimmed her hands over herself, feeling the contours of her body and closing her eyes as she pictured Emrys's lips pressing against the hollows at the base of her throat or behind her ears. Tipping her head back a little, she allowed her thoughts to dwell on how his mouth would feel kissing hers, how his fingers would feel making their thrilling journey up her thighs to open her body to him.

By the time she'd returned to the bedroom, he'd lain back on his pillow, his glasses and Bible back on his nightstand beside his empty cup. He'd left the lamp on, and she felt his gaze upon her as she moved past his bed. This time, though, she perched beside him, letting her hair hang like a silken veil as she bent to kiss him goodnight.

Propping her chin up with one hand, she laid the other on his chest, lightly at first, then insinuating one fingertip between the buttons on his pyjama top until it met the warmth of his skin. His own hand came to rest on hers, and she stilled.

"Miriam—"

"I haven't given up hope," she said, cutting him off but keeping her voice gentle, careful to make it an entreaty without any hint of a reproach. "Despair is a sin, you've always told me. I keep thinking of Abraham and Sarah, and how they were blessed with a child long after they'd stopped believing it was possible. Please, Emrys – don't give up on me."

He let out his breath and her heart leaped as he lifted his hand to stroke one of her curls back from her face. Experience had taught her not to appear too eager. In the moment before he reached to turn off the lamp his pupils dilated, turning his eyes hungry and black. She pulled back his bedclothes and squeezed in beside him, spreading her hair over his pillow and reaching her arms out hesitantly to hook them around him, inviting his kiss. As always, the sensation of it made her feel she was dissolving into nothing more substantial than a puddle of yearning. She wriggled, lifting the hem of her nightgown almost shyly, smiling against his lips and then trailing gentle kisses along the roughness of his jaw.

"*Rwy'n dy garu di*," she said, voicing her love in one of the few phrases she knew in his own tongue. She released a sigh when he said it back, then arched in surrender as he touched her most tender place to make it ready for him. Biting back the moan that threatened to escape her throat at the delicious sensations his finger had awoken, she closed her eyes in anticipation of the moment he would push himself inside her. When the moment came, she couldn't help a soft gasp. He started to move, and she clutched his buttocks with one hand, shuffling lower in the bed to press herself more closely against him. She let her mind go, focusing only on the physical sensations rippling through her body, the heat of his breath against her ear and the rush of yielding to desire. Her own release, aided by the pressure of her fingers, came silently and unnoticed as he juddered with his own. In the privacy of the darkness she hid a smile and held his spent body against hers for as long as he would allow.

THREE

Norma

Norma's tongue poked out of the corner of her mouth as she concentrated on turning the key in the front door without making a sound. Hopefully, Mrs Bishop wouldn't hear her sneaking in. Norma had already heard more than enough words of wisdom about how she should have kept hold of her ha'penny and how this was a respectable house. Mrs B had only allowed her to continue renting her room on the understanding that Dickie would make an honest woman of her before the evidence of her sin started showing too brazenly. Now that he'd jilted her, there seemed little chance of being allowed to stay. Her future depended on getting Dickie to put that promised ring on her finger.

Creeping inside, Norma took care to close the door softly, hardly daring to breathe as she tiptoed across the tiled floor past the cage containing Mrs B's beloved twittering finches. Knowing how the bottom stair creaked, she stepped straight onto the one above, grabbing the banister for extra leverage. She was halfway up the stairs when her landlady appeared in the hallway, her greying hair wrapped around curlers and covered by a hairnet.

From the foot of the stairs, Mrs B's sharp eyes examined Norma. "You're back early. I wasn't expecting to see you until tomorrow. Did it all go well?"

Norma made sure her left hand was out of sight and pasted on her most sparkling smile. "Perfectly, thanks, Mrs B." It wasn't a lie, as such, because things *would* be perfect in a couple of days, just as soon as she'd sorted out the mess with Dickie. "I'm just getting changed, then heading back out."

"Taking you out for a bit of grub, is he?"

"Mmm." Norma set a foot on the next step, but was forced to pause when Mrs B failed to take the hint.

"Just so's you know, the new tenant wants to be in by six o'clock tomorrow, so your room will need to be emptied and cleaned before then."

"Really? As soon as that?" Norma's step faltered. Her knuckles whitened on the newel post at the bend in the stairs.

"Can't have it standing empty, now that you won't be needing it, can I? He seems a nice enough young chap. Bit older than you. Works in a butcher's shop, but he's promised me he'll have a wash before he comes back here after work. I've told him in no uncertain terms he'll have to give the bath a good clean after using it, and I won't be doing his laundry. Course, I won't say no if he can get me some cheap cuts of meat now and then. Especially with the chance of war on the horizon. If it's anything like the last time, we'll be glad of any extra grub we can get."

Unable to speak, Norma merely nodded.

"Will you and your feller both be coming back here tonight? Only, my guests like things to be quiet. Discreet, if you know what I mean." Mrs Bishop flicked at an imaginary speck of dust with her handkerchief, wrinkled cheeks aflame.

Norma knew exactly what she meant, but widened her eyes with an appearance of innocence that belied the size of her belly. "I promise if we come back later, we'll be quiet as mice, but I'm not sure what's happening yet. He might have booked us in somewhere posh, for all I know," she added airily, to keep up the impression that everything was in hand.

"I'd better not keep you from packing a bag, then."

At last she had the excuse she needed to bolt upstairs. Her hands shook as she let herself into her room. As soon as she was safe inside, she fished inside her sleeve and retrieved the thin roll of money Mr Goldman had slipped into her hand.

Three reddish-brown notes unfurled in her palm. Thirty shillings. Her mouth twisted. Was that what her favours would have been worth to him? Pride made her want to tear them up or burn them, or give them away to some beggar in the street. But she wasn't in a position to stand on her pride. Though it stuck in her gullet like a lump of half-chewed gristle, the sensible thing to do was to keep the cash.

Opening the biscuit tin in which she kept her sewing tools, she took out her needle case. Two more ten-bob notes were tucked inside. Her life savings. Not much to show for years of hard work, but still.

Looking around the small space with its unfriendly, faded wallpaper and chipped brown paintwork, she made a mental inventory of her few possessions. It wouldn't take her long to clear out.

The most important item was her sewing machine. It was old-fashioned, so old it proclaimed *As Supplied to HM Queen Alexandra* amongst the scrolling gold leaves decorating its black paint. It was also heavy and cumbersome, but she wouldn't be without it. She might have temporarily lost her fiancé; she might have lost her job and be on the brink of losing what had passed as a home for the last couple of years, but as long as she had her sewing machine, she still had hope. Hope of earning a crust in a respectable manner. Hope of still keeping herself clothed in stylish togs that made other girls envious. The machine's solidity was strangely comforting: instead of weighing her down, it anchored her. It was the only link she still had to her gran, the fearsome woman who'd taken her in when she was eight. Gran hadn't been warm or affectionate, but she'd been the only person Norma had ever been able to count on to take her side in a battle.

Most of the clothes hanging in the tiny wardrobe no longer fitted her, thanks to her ever-increasing belly. She'd put off making or buying any maternity clothes, clinging to the hope that somehow, she wouldn't need them. Even her underwear was uncomfortably tight: she'd had to give up on her girdle, and felt bare and exposed without it.

She hated not having a waist anymore. She'd always been proud of her hour-glass figure and the way it attracted male attention. Her looks were the only thing anyone admired about her, and this baby was ruining them. Not only had it cost her her figure, but also her reputation and her job. All because of a bit of fun, a few larks in an otherwise lonely life, when she'd let herself enjoy the pleasure of someone wanting her.

In less than twenty-four hours, it would also cost her this dump of a room. Believing she'd be a married woman by now, she'd given Mrs B notice, and by the sound of it her landlady had wasted no time in finding a new tenant. Tomorrow, if Norma couldn't fix whatever had gone wrong between her and Dickie, she would have to pack up and find somewhere else to live.

Best not to dwell on that now, though. She'd find a way round it. The wedding could be rearranged easily enough. Dickie had always fallen easily for her charms. A little too easily and too enthusiastically, as it had turned out.

Norma wasn't ready to be a mother. Her own had been so awful, she was bound to make a hash of it. When she'd first realised her monthlies were late, she'd tried everything to bring them on. Jumping up and down; hitting herself in the stomach hard enough to leave bruises; gin and nutmeg, and a bath so scalding hot she fainted when she got out. Even Beecham's Pills, when none of that had worked. Still her body had betrayed her. The unwelcome parasite clung to her like a creature from a horror flick, and there seemed no safe way to rid herself of it. In fairness to Dickie, he'd offered her a tenner to pay a Knitting Needle Nora to sort it, but she'd heard stories of girls getting into trouble with the rozzers for that. Worse, she knew of a girl from the hair salon who'd died after getting someone to help her out of the same sticky situation. The thought of it made Norma feel sick. Persuading Dickie to marry her had been a much safer bet. Even allowing for his famously spectacular temper, it was better to hitch herself to his wagon than to put her fate in the hands of some stranger with dirty hands and a hook.

Crossing to the wardrobe, she pulled out her smart little hat with a feather, and her other pair of shoes, glamorous heels that she wore on nights out with Dickie. A spritz of the scent he'd given her made her feel a little fresher. With the items from her pockets stowed safely in her handbag, and her lace-ups shoved under her bed, she was ready to go and find him. Dickie had the power to sort everything out: he didn't deserve to get off scot-free while she lost everything.

The best way to deal with the kind of fear she was feeling now, Norma had learned over the years, was to put on a fearless smile and show she wouldn't be beaten.

Mrs Bishop was lurking in the hallway making kissing noises at her finches. She looked Norma up and down with her head tilted to one side, eyes bright and dark like one of the birds fluttering in the cage behind her.

"You alright, duck? You look a bit pale."

"I'm fine, thanks. Just tired from all the excitement today, I expect."

"Aww, you'll be wanting to get back to your husband, won't you? It's a shame he didn't come back with you. It would have been nice to offer you both my congratulations... Mrs Tucker," she added with emphasis and a simpering smile, as if she'd never looked down her nose at Norma for getting herself in the family way.

"Thanks," Norma said again.

Mrs Bishop beamed a toothless smile. She often took her

dentures out once she'd eaten her tea. Presumably, she'd eaten while Norma had been tidying herself up. Norma hadn't eaten since breakfast.

"You'd better run along now. You won't want to disappoint him by keeping him waiting on his wedding day."

The irony of it made Norma want to scream.

FOUR

Norma

By this time in the evening, Dickie would most likely be in the pub. It took only twenty minutes to walk there. Twenty minutes to work out exactly what she'd say to him – whether to wheedle or to nag, or to laugh it off, or to bat her lashes and pout – but by the time she arrived outside the door of The Boatman, she still had no clear plan.

The river stank in this part of Stepney. As the summer evening cooled, damp air rose to mingle with traffic fumes and odours of oil and decaying matter on the foreshore behind the pub. Along the road, the Limehouse canal basin was busy, the mast of an old-fashioned sailing ship just visible where it stood taller than the roofs of the nearby warehouses. Taller still, the chimney of the power station puffed out smoke. A train chuffed along the railway line, making the ground shake.

As she drew close to the pub, Norma blinked away the grit in her eyes. Like all the buildings around here, the pub's brick exterior was blackened by sooty smog. A faint flavour of rotten eggs settled on her tongue as she sucked in a deep breath for courage and pushed open the door. Inside, a fug of warm sweat, tobacco smoke and ale enveloped her. In the narrow bar area stood a dozen or more dockers, still in their working clothes. Her skin prickled as every pair of eyes turned and fixed on her, appraising, burning into her clothes as if to strip them away. The rumble of deep voices faded momentarily.

"The snug's out the back," the barman growled in the lull caused by her invasion of this masculine space. He wiped the surface of the bar with a rag held in a fist as meaty and hard as a butcher's block.

Ignoring the way her stomach fluttered with nerves, she made for the bar, not deigning to acknowledge the men who parted to allow her to pass.

"I don't want the snug. I'm looking for Dickie," she said.

A thick-set man beside her chortled. "Looks to me like you've already had plenty of that, darlin'."

His drinking companion let out a guffaw that nearly made him spill his beer.

Embarrassment turned Norma's cheeks scarlet, but she faced the men, drawing herself up to her full five feet and three inches.

"I'll tell Dickie Tucker how you spoke to his wife-to-be, shall I?"

The man's porcine eyes flickered, but his companion merely laughed again.

"Can't see him doing nothing about it for a good while," he said.

Norma frowned, confused, then noticed a trio of men coming in. At their centre was a wiry young man she recognised as one of Dickie's friends. Their eyes met, and he gestured to her to follow him back outside.

It was a relief to reach the cobbled street and breathe air that didn't reek of rough men.

Dickie's friend was waiting outside.

"It's Jacko, ain't it? Dickie's pal from work?"

He nodded, squinting through the plume of smoke rising from the fag stuck between his lips.

"He was supposed to meet me today, but he never turned up. D'you know where he is? I thought he might be here."

Jacko took a last drag on his fag end, then flicked it to the ground and crushed it with his heel. "You ain't heard, then? He got banged up."

Norma blanched. "He's in prison?" It couldn't be true.

"Coppers nabbed him last night. Him and Artie Micklewhite was both up before the beak this morning."

"But..." Norma lurched against the wall of the pub for support. "He'll be out soon, though. It's a mistake. Ain't it?"

Jacko rubbed the back of his neck. "Dunno. I wouldn't bank on it if I were you."

"Flamin' Nora. We were supposed to be getting married today."

"Fecking idiot. Him, not you." With a grimace, he gestured towards Norma's stomach. "I take it he's responsible for that?"

Colour rose to her cheeks. "Yes, but... He said he'd look after me. He'd already asked me to marry him, so... And you know Dickie. When he wants something, he's not an easy man to say no to."

"Well, he's left you up a gum tree now, and no mistake."

"He'll get out, though, and then we can still get hitched."

Jacko glowered towards his feet. "Look, Norma. I hate being the one to tell you. A man was found, done over pretty bad. Dickie had beaten him at cards and the feller wouldn't cough up his winnings."

"Dickie gets into fights all the time. It sounds like this one was the other feller's fault. So what's the problem?" Norma paused. "There's something else, isn't there?" she asked, watching as Jacko huffed out his breath, shuffling as if he would rather be anywhere but here telling her this. Her hands had clenched so hard, her fingers cramped. She flexed them, but they curled again at his next words.

"The bloke died," he said. "He was fished out of the canal with his hands tied behind his back and his nose cut."

The smoggy air felt like a pillow over her face.

Norma's legs couldn't hold her up: she sank back against the wall, eyes wide and wary. "You're saying my Dickie is a murderer?"

"I ain't saying nothing."

"You believe it, though. I can see it in your face."

Norma didn't want to believe it. The man she'd had such uproariously fun times with, whose lively eyes had danced with laughter and then burned with desire for her, making her feel like a princess with his occasional gifts of flowers or chocolates or scent. The man who had swept her off her feet and danced so skilfully, charming her with a pursuit so determined it could only ever have ended in her surrender...

The man whose child was growing inside her.

Could he really be capable of such brutal violence? The thought was so awful, her brain seemed frozen, on the verge of shutting off.

"No. No – it must have been an accident. Perhaps the man ran off after the fight and someone else did it. It might not have been Dickie."

Jacko's voice sounded faint; with an effort, she forced herself to listen.

"The police seem convinced it was." He sighed and shook his head. "There was another feller, a year ago. They couldn't pin it on him that time. But this time, there was witnesses, and someone's blabbed. I can't see him getting out."

Her limbs were trembling as if winter had come early.

Jacko patted her shoulder. "Look, I've always had a soft spot for you, Norma. You're a pretty girl. I reckon you'd like to stay that way. If you've got any sense, you won't hang around to see if he gets out. You'll get as far away from him as you can, while you've got the chance. For your own sake, and for the kid." With a final warning look so intense it seemed to burn into her eyes, he turned on his heel and disappeared back into the smoke-filled pub.

Norma set off for the safety of her lodgings, scuttling along the dark streets with her breathing tight and rapid as she willed herself not to panic. She'd got through bad stuff before. But as bad as things had sometimes been, they still hadn't been nearly as bad as being jobless and pregnant by a murderer.

This was a whole new level of disaster.

FIVE

Norma

Norma spent a sleepless night, unable to quieten her mind enough to rest. What should she do? All the way back from the pub, she'd been on edge, seeing violent thugs and murderers in every shadow until at last she reached the boarding house. To her relief, she'd managed to creep inside and slip upstairs to her room unnoticed by Mrs Bishop.

Her mental image of Dickie had been shattered. He wasn't the charming rogue she'd thought she knew. He'd slashed and beaten a man, and dumped him in the canal to drown – if he hadn't been dead already. All over something as trivial as a game. And it might not have been the first time he'd done so. Even his own friend believed him capable of it, and had warned her to take her chance to get away.

Had she loved Dickie? It was hard to be sure. She'd liked him most of the time, more than any of the other men who'd pestered her, wanting to be seen with a pretty blonde on their arm. She'd loved the way people looked at them together, as if she was out of bounds, on a pedestal. Loved his attention. The way he made no effort to disguise his desire. The way he called her his princess and lavished money on drinks and flowers for her. Looking back, it was a shame he hadn't spent it on useful things that she could keep or sell now that he wasn't around. She wouldn't make that mistake with a feller again.

By six in the morning, with summer sun already streaming through the thin curtains, she decided she might as well get up. The sound of the bathroom door opening along the landing prompted her to take a quick bath. She tried not to notice how her body was changing: the blue veins on her breasts and the swelling of her stomach were sickeningly apparent without the benefit of clothes to cover them. While she scrubbed herself, she focused on the cracks in the glaze on the tiles, looking for patterns to shut out the voice in her mind that couldn't help wondering when and where she'd next have the chance of a good soak.

In some ways, she told herself as she got dressed, things were better than they might have been. Yesterday she had lost her prospective husband, her home and her job, but at least she had a bit of money. Money might give her choices. If nothing else, it could buy her time and some new digs.

The most obvious way to fix her current predicament was to get rid of the baby. If she were no longer pregnant, she'd find it easier to find a job and respectable lodgings. Maybe she could even find another man to help her forget Dickie; one who would keep his word and look after her.

But the thought of it gave her a heavy, queasy sensation. Her pulse thudded. Even fifty shillings wouldn't be enough to pay someone reliable to help her out of trouble. She'd heard it could cost as much as five pounds, maybe more. So unless she could find a way to double her money, she'd be limited to the worst kinds of bumbling butchery...

Even if she could go to someone more expensive and skilled, the procedure's aftermath might be more painful and dangerous than the thing itself, and she had nowhere to go to recover. She could end up in hospital, or even in prison like Dickie. She couldn't bear the thought of being locked up.

A prod from inside her stomach made her recoil. It was as if it knew what she'd been thinking. How she hated feeling it move, reminding her how helpless she was. The thing was a little bully, jabbing at her insides, telling her that she couldn't escape it, that even if she could get the extra money to pay for a proper doctor to sort her out, the risks now she was so far gone were too great. She should have taken Dickie up on his offer of cash months ago, instead of being stupid enough to trust his empty promises.

Perhaps she should go and visit him in prison, see if there was still any chance for them to get hitched? But the idea of marrying a murderer was nearly as terrifying as the thought of a scrape job.

The room felt airless. She crossed the few steps over to the window and threw up the sash. Her breath came in gasps and her head swam frighteningly, making her grip the splintered, half-rotten wood of the window frame to steady herself. She'd have to come up with another way to make a fresh start.

As her head cleared, she noticed the sound of singing. It grew gradually louder. A whole crowd of voices singing 'It's a Long Way to Tipperary', and the tramping of footsteps. From along the road, headed by smartly dressed adults, a column of children was marching as if they were on parade. Each member of the long line carried a bag or pack of some sort. Policemen wearing white gauntlets directed traffic to pull aside and let them pass as they made their way down the street towards the railway station.

They must be evacuees. Poor little buggers. Norma hoped they'd find welcoming homes out in the country, wherever they were going. Having had her fair share of foster homes until her gran grudgingly took her in, she knew only too well how unpleasant they could be. Those memories had made her turn down the offer of evacuation when she'd thought she'd have a home with Dickie.

Back then, only weeks ago when she'd believed her life was on track, it had seemed more sensible to take her chances with bombs than to set off for an uncertain reception in the countryside, far away from the only places she'd ever known. But perhaps, now that things had changed so drastically, it might not be such a terrible prospect after all. Perhaps she should find out if it wasn't too late to register for evacuation. Impossible though it was to imagine living anywhere but the East End, it would give her a chance for the fresh start Jacko had recommended. She'd be given somewhere to live; food to eat; medical care. In a new place, where no one knew her or her background... Why, she could be anyone. She could be respectable.

With her mind whirling with possibilities, she knelt on the bare floorboards and pulled her two battered cardboard suitcases out from under the bed, tossing them onto the mattress before flipping open the catches. For the first time since yesterday afternoon, she knew exactly what to do.

SIX

Norma

Norma packed her two suitcases with her belongings: her clothes; her wash bag, hair pins and comb; a single, creased photograph of herself as a child with a ribbon in her hair, her little brother looking misleadingly cherubic at her side; and a bundle of sanitary rags – not that she'd be needing those for a few months. Her sewing tin fitted inside the case of her sewing machine, along with the sharp scissors she'd had to save up for. Her handbag had just enough space for her few items of make-up and her hairbrush. She'd have to wear her winter coat and best hat on the journey, despite the warm late-summer weather, as there was no easy way to carry everything.

Her stomach rumbled at the mouthwatering aroma of frying bacon drifting through her window, prompting her to stand her suitcases beside the bed, then sneak out while Mrs B was busy in the kitchen. After a toasted teacake and a cup of coffee in a nearby café, she felt energised, even excited. Today would be the start of a fresh adventure.

A pawn shop stood fifty yards or so along the road, with three golden orbs hanging above the entrance. Although it wasn't clear whether the broker would have been willing to haggle anyway, or whether her smile and fluttering eyelashes convinced him to reduce the price, within half an hour a thin gold wedding ring graced her left hand. He insisted that thirty shillings was a bargain, and she supposed it was, considering it would enable her to pass herself off as a married woman. She left the shop with her chin tilted at a proud angle. No one would condemn her on sight now. Mr Goldman's dirty money had been put to the best possible use.

She was abuzz with excitement at the prospect of reinventing herself. As she marched back towards her lodgings, she debated the thorny problem of her surname. She could perhaps call herself Mrs Tucker, so the baby could at least have its father's name. But did she really want to link herself to a suspected murderer? The whole point of going away was to start afresh.

There was no need to creep inside Mrs B's hallway now. She mounted the stairs with her hand on the banister, enjoying the way the ring glinted when the light caught it.

Maybe it would be easiest to use her own surname, and simply call herself Mrs Sparrow instead of Miss. But that might make it too easy for Dickie to find her if he should ever get out of prison and decide he wanted his child. As much as she'd miss the fun they'd had on their evenings out, the thought of a murderer coming looking for her was a daunting prospect.

It was a dilemma, alright.

If she called herself something completely different, would she even remember it? And what should it be? What should a woman call herself when she could be anyone she wanted? Ideas whirred in her mind as she flashed a duster quickly around the room, pausing at the windowsill where she had a clear view of a row of pigeons on the roof opposite. She could change her name from Sparrow to Pigeon, but it didn't appeal. Pigeons were dull and plump. She'd want to be a much brighter, cleverer bird, like Mrs B's pretty little finches with their striking colours. Finch would be heaps better. *Norma Finch.* She said it out loud, and found she liked it.

That was that. Miss Norma Sparrow would become Mrs Norma Finch.

After one last check for any stray possessions that might have found their way under the bed, she was ready to leave. Carrying her suitcases in one hand and her sewing machine in the other, she descended the stairs with care, then set her belongings down and delved in her pocket for her key.

"You're off, then," Mrs B remarked, padding down the hallway with her thick lisle stockings wrinkling around her ankles. She frowned at Norma's luggage. "I'm surprised your new hubby hasn't come to help you with your things. They're heavy for a woman in your condition."

"He wanted to, but you know how it is. He's a busy man," Norma lied, offering a rueful smile.

She dropped the key into her landlady's outstretched hand and bid her farewell, stepping out into the street with a light step despite the weight of her luggage. Tipping her chin up to the sky, she squinted at the sunshine. By the time she arrived at the station, her armpits felt moist under her coat and her shoulders ached.

It wasn't hard to see where to sign up: a queue of women, many of them with young children, were waiting. Norma joined the end of the line and little by little moved forwards, willing the clerks at the desk to hurry up. The noise of squalling infants and whining toddlers was grating. All the mothers looked weary and many were short-tempered. Was that what she could look forward to if she kept the baby? Years of feeling frazzled and looking like a washed-out dishrag, lashing out with slaps and sharp words at the slightest provocation? Constantly having to keep her eye on what the kid might be getting up to, to make sure they didn't cause trouble or get hurt? How would she manage with no one to help her and no one to provide for them? And what if the kid turned out to be a ruffian like its dad? Thinking about it made her head spin.

At last it was her turn to speak to the officious moustachioed man who asked for her name.

Despite having practised saying it several times in her room, she stumbled over it.

The man's thick gingery brows drew together and he held his pen above the paper, frozen in midair. His demeanour seemed as starched as his old-fashioned collar.

"You don't sound very sure, Mrs Finch?"

Her harmless ruse to ease her way into her new life suddenly felt like a crime. She swallowed hard.

"I only got married this week," she said, her voice higher than usual. She paused and remembered to give a tinkling, coy little laugh. "I'm still getting used to having a different name." That part, at least, was true.

She pretended not to notice the way his gaze hovered over her stomach. Plenty of people were already in the family way when they got married, after all.

"I don't appear to have your name on my list. Perhaps you registered for evacuation under your maiden name?"

Her upper lip prickled and she put her suitcases down to wipe it. "I didn't realise I'd have to register before today. Can't you just put me on a train? It said in the paper that expectant mothers can go along with the kiddies."

"There are procedures, Mrs Finch. You should have registered for evacuation in advance with the Health Centre, as these other ladies have done."

"Oh, but – I didn't know. Please, I'd be ever so grateful. Can't you just take my details here? I can't go lugging this lot to the Health Centre in my condition; I'm already half dead on my feet."

"You've had weeks to register. You can't just turn up with your suitcases and expect to get on a train today." He shuffled his papers crossly, then scowled as he looked up and saw her chin wobble. "This is most irregular," he grumbled. Nevertheless, she took it as a hopeful sign that he might be softening, as he asked for her address.

"That's the thing, sir. As of this morning, I don't have one. I've got nowhere to go."

"No fixed abode," he said in a more doubtful tone, laying down his pen. "Why have you nowhere to stay if you were only married this week?" His scowl was more perplexed than annoyed.

"I gave my landlady notice before I got married... But things haven't worked out with my husband the way I thought they would."

He blinked.

"He's been sent to prison," she whispered, leaning forward with a pleading look. "That's why I've got to get away. I'm scared they'll let him out and he'll hurt me." It sounded melodramatic, but this part of her story, at least, was true.

She had shocked him. "Don't you have any other family you could stay with while you make arrangements?"

"This is the only family I've got," she told him, pointing to her stomach.

Her own words seemed to pierce her heart like a bodkin. She'd been hating the baby, even wishing it would die so she could be relieved of the burden of it, and yet it was the only living thing that had any tie to her. What kind of monster was she?

Standing there trying to convince this silly man to help her, it hit home that she was alone in the world, with no one to care about her and nowhere to go. The thought was so overwhelming, tears burst out, as wild and unchecked as those of the screaming baby being held by its mother behind her.

The man's mouth fell open. He must be appalled to have a woman blubbing so uncontrollably at his desk. But she couldn't help it. Gulping sobs made her chest heave so powerfully she wanted to throw up over his paperwork. Despite her embarrassment, which grew as he looked around in obvious desperation, her shoulders juddered and she leaned on the edge of his desk, scared her knees might give out under the weight of this sudden torrent of emotion.

To her surprise, she felt the steadiness of arms wrapping around her, and found a handkerchief being pressed into her hand.

"It's Norma, isn't it? Norma from the Goldmans' shop? I thought I recognised you. I'm sorry for your troubles, Norma."

Blinking through her tears, Norma realised the kindly face leaning over her belonged to Mrs Rosen, a customer whose clothes she had often been called upon to alter. She murmured thanks, comforted that one person at least might care what happened to her.

Mrs Rosen addressed the man behind the desk. "Let her take my ticket," she said. "I can go another day. Under the circumstances, I think we can both agree that this young woman needs the seat more than I do." Paying no attention to his protests about the irregularity of the situation, she insisted until he gave in.

Within a couple of hours, Norma was on a train heading west and, for the first time in her twenty years, away from the city.

SEVEN

Miriam

Miriam looked forward to her monthly Saturday lunches at Contadino's café with her two sisters, Maggie and Dolly. Although the three looked similar, with their wavy dark hair and eyes of varying shades of green, their lives were very different.

Maggie, the eldest at forty-three, had been a midwife for nearly twenty years. The long working hours sometimes meant she couldn't join these regular sessions, but today Miriam was pleased to find her already waiting at their usual table when she arrived at the café. For many years Maggie had lodged with her landlady, Venetia Vaughan-Lloyd, a magistrate, town councillor and former mayor of Pontybrenin. Miss Vaughan-Lloyd's house was large, modern, and individual, rather like its owner. Although Maggie rented a room from her, their relationship was on an informal footing. Maggie often prepared their meals on days when their daily help was unavailable, and supported her landlady with a myriad of everyday tasks, as Miss Vaughan-Lloyd suffered from the debilitating effects of a childhood bout of polio.

Dolly lived and worked as a housekeeper in an even larger house in the countryside a few miles from town. She and her husband Ivor ran the household, employed by Mrs Havard and Miss Fitznorton, two half-sisters. Like Emrys, Ivor was a veteran of the Great War, but any resemblance ended there. While Emrys was preoccupied with matters of the soul and the intellect, Ivor was intensely practical. Emrys sought a harvest of souls; Ivor was more interested in nurturing flowers and vegetables. Where Emrys was self-controlled and serious, Ivor was easy-going and looked for the humour in any situation. He was good for Dolly.

Miriam was conscious of the irony of three sisters, whose mother had given birth to nine children in all, having not a single child between them. Only their brothers had children. Unlike Miriam, Dolly seemed to have accepted her childlessness with equanimity. When asking her about it once, Dolly had shocked her by shrugging her shoulders and saying: "Maybe Ivor used all his sperm up in France."

Miriam couldn't imagine ever being able to joke about something so deeply painful. It was difficult even to look at a baby without experiencing a yearning so strong it was like a physical sickness. It was a mystery to her how Maggie coped, working with so many new mothers and their infants. Inexplicably, some didn't want their newborns. Miriam had puzzled over how they could be so ungrateful for the blessing God had bestowed upon them. Despite Maggie's exhortation not to judge them, it was hard to swallow her bitterness. But perhaps this month it would be different. Perhaps this would be the month when her prayers would at last be answered.

Maggie looked up with a smile as Miriam entered the café. "Dolly won't be coming today," she said once they'd exchanged greetings. "She telephoned me earlier to say five evacuee children were billeted at Plas Norton yesterday."

"Five? My word, she'll be busy then. Five children will mean an awful lot of extra work for her, won't it? Whyever do they have so many?"

"Apparently Dodie took pity on them for fear that brothers and sisters would be split up. She's sensitive about that sort of thing, bless her, after her years away at boarding school. And I gather the billeting officer knew the house had several empty bedrooms, so they didn't have much choice in the matter."

The young waiter approached their table. Johnny Contadino, nephew of the café's owner, had come to Pontybrenin to work for his uncle and aunt a few years ago and had soon become popular with their customers. It no doubt helped that he was rather handsome, with his slicked-back black hair, expressive brown eyes, attentive manner and ready smile.

"Can I get you something to eat, ladies? Your usual, or are you in the mood for something different today? We have a very good minestrone on offer, if I can tempt you?"

Three girls on a neighbouring table nudged each other and blushed at his talk of temptation, giggling when he squeezed past them on his way back to the counter.

"Venetia's taken in an evacuee, too," Maggie revealed, stirring her coffee. "I came home from work yesterday evening to find her already settled in with her suitcase unpacked."

"A child?"

"Not in our case. We have one of their teachers."

"Oh. Well... It might be quite nice for you, having another woman in the house. Perhaps she'll help with the cooking."

"Perhaps. It may be easier than having a child to stay, given how tired Venetia is most of the time. I worry about how hard she works. She's been throwing herself into her charitable works with the Women's Institute and helping to raise funds for the Jewish children coming over from the continent. She's in constant pain."

"I'm sorry to hear that. I'll remember her in my prayers."

"Thank you. I would have preferred to host a child, personally, but by the time Vee arrived at the church hall there weren't any left."

"Poor little things, having to travel so far from their homes. I can't understand how parents can let their children go off to strangers like that. If I had a child, I'd never send them away."

"Not even if staying might mean they faced German bombs?

Could you honestly risk their lives for the sake of your own feelings, Mim?"

Miriam sighed. "It must be a terrible dilemma, having to decide whether to keep them with you to face the danger of bombs, or to live with strangers who might not look after them properly."

"More are due to arrive today," Maggie said. "It was tricky finding them all billets yesterday, so I don't envy the billeting officer."

Their soup had arrived, with slices of bread spread with a lavish layer of butter, and they both laid their napkins in their laps and started to tuck in. It was thick and tasty, with generous chunks of vegetables and short strands of vermicelli.

"You've got two spare bedrooms at the manse, haven't you?" Maggie asked as they ate.

"We have, but Emrys would never agree to having an evacuee billeted with us."

"He'd risk a hefty fine, or even a prison sentence, for refusing."

Tearing her bread into small pieces, Miriam kept her gaze on her bowl of soup. She could only hope it wouldn't come to that. Emrys was a man of principle. A man of his word. If he set his will to something, he wasn't for changing. "He doesn't agree with it," she said, so quietly Maggie had to ask her to repeat herself.

"What do you mean, he doesn't agree with it? Do you mean being a host, or the evacuation programme?"

She cast a quick glance around, but no one seemed to be listening. "It's more than that. He doesn't agree with the idea of another war. You know he doesn't. And if there *is* a war, heaven forfend, he doesn't think we should have to host children from England here."

"I don't understand." Maggie looked perplexed.

Miriam shifted uncomfortably. She always felt awkward trying to explain Emrys's views. He articulated them so much more convincingly. "He doesn't want Wales to be dragged into a war of England's making, that's the long and short of it. As far as he's concerned, it's nothing to do with us, and we shouldn't be required to support it by doing things like hosting children from London."

He'd voiced this in much stronger terms, but she couldn't bring herself to use his words. Not in public, and not when Maggie was looking at her with that severe look on her face. She put down her spoon, appetite gone.

"Well," Maggie said, still with one eyebrow raised disapprovingly. "In that case, he'd better pray Hitler pulls his troops out of Poland."

EIGHT

Norma

Norma had been on the train for at least half an hour before she could rouse herself to take much notice of her surroundings. At the sight of fields rolling past the window, lush and green despite the heavy black clouds that threatened a storm, her spirits started to pick up.

Flippin' 'eck, Norma, you've only gone and done it. Thanks to Mrs Rosen's selfless generosity, she'd managed to get herself evacuated from the city, on a train packed full of women and kids.

There was no sense in looking back. She had been allocated to a small group of women, all more advanced in their pregnancies than Norma, if the size of their bellies and their grumbles about their backs, ankles and bladders were anything to go by. The one sitting closest to the window, whose loud voice dominated the conversation, seemed determined to outdo all the others.

"They'd better send me somewhere decent, or I won't stand for it," she said. "What with my back, I shall need a good mattress. And I hope they put me with nice people, not any old riffraff. I have my standards, and I shan't compromise them."

Norma dug in her handbag for her powder compact. After

dabbing at the worst ravages from her earlier outburst, she refreshed her lipstick. She'd slept on enough bed-bug infested mattresses in her time to know how miserable it could be. But right now she'd be grateful just to have somewhere to lay her head. *Beggars can't be choosers*, she reasoned with herself; although technically, she wasn't a beggar now, with her remaining twenty shillings secreted in a pocket she'd sewn into her bra the previous night. There was no telling how long that cash would have to last her, though. The longer she could hang on to it, the better.

Across the aisle, a pretty brunette who looked childishly young sat quietly with her hands twisting anxiously over her bump. Her chin trembled as if she was on the verge of crumpling into weeping. An auburn-haired woman beside her had angled her shoulder like a barrier between them, and the woman opposite was whispering to her neighbour and sending pointed glances her way. The young brunette had removed her gloves, and Norma noticed her left hand was bare.

A shaft of anger drove Norma to action. "D'you fancy swapping seats?" she asked the redhead, deciding she could bear it no longer. "I'm not bothered about sitting by the window, but maybe you'd have more fun watching the rain clouds instead of looking down your nose at that girl all the way." She stood with her hands on her hips until the woman moved, then plumped down into her vacated seat and sent the girl a friendly smile.

"Warm in here, ain't it? My name's Norma; what's yours?"

"I'm Frannie. Yes, it's roasting." Her shy attempt at friendliness was quickly quelled by a poisonous glance from the other women.

"Don't let those snooty cows get you down, Frannie," Norma said. "You never know, what with a storm on its way, the wind might change and then their faces'll be stuck like that for the duration. What d'you reckon?"

Frannie giggled, quickly covering her mouth with her hand as if she'd done something wrong. She delved in her bag and pulled out a greaseproof paper package, then unwrapped it and offered Norma a thick-cut beef paste sandwich.

"How old are you, Frannie?" Norma asked.

"I'm seventeen," Frannie whispered. Tears filled her eyes, but she blinked them away, and Norma sent her an encouraging nod. "I've never been away from home before. Have you?"

"Not this far." Norma thought for a moment, unwilling to reveal too much about her circumstances. "It's an adventure alright, ain't it?"

"I s'pose so. I'll miss my mum, though. Will you miss yours?"

"Mine's dead," she said out of habit, squashing her immediate feeling of guilt when Frannie offered sympathy. It might be true, after all. There was no way of knowing what had happened to her mother after she left Norma and her brother to go to the pub one evening and never came back. All through Norma's years in foster homes she'd heard nothing, even when she went to live with her gran.

For the next hour, she kept Frannie talking by asking about her family and her sailor boyfriend. She deliberately ignored the other women, especially the loud one who kept boasting about how wonderful her husband was. When asked about her own situation, Norma gave as little information as she could. It made her uncomfortable to lie, especially to Frannie, who had been so open about her own circumstances, but she had little choice but to stick to her story now.

She couldn't help wondering how the family who'd soon be hosting her might see her: a brash Cockney blonde with smudged mascara and scarlet lipstick, cheap shoes, and a chip on her shoulder as big as a London brick. Whatever she knew herself to be inside, she'd have to put on a front of confidence to match her assumed surname and marital status. She couldn't afford to let the mask slip if she was to succeed in starting a new life.

The train trundled on through station after station, beneath increasingly leaden skies. Raindrops beaded like gems on the windows before the movement of the train sent them sliding away. Occasional loud claps of thunder could be heard above the rumble and hiss of the engine, and flashes of lightning skewered the horizon. Norma hoped the rapidly deteriorating weather wasn't a bad omen for her stay in the countryside.

At each station, groups of passengers were called to disembark. At Cardiff, Frannie and Norma were told to lug their baggage onto a smaller train to continue their journey on a branch line. Their carriage was noisy with grubby city children who had also made the journey to Wales. After Frannie's name was called at a town whose name Norma couldn't even attempt to pronounce due to an extravagant number of syllables and a perplexing lack of vowels, Norma was the only expectant mother left among the travelling evacuees.

Norma patted powder onto her shiny nose again, her stomach fluttering. They couldn't have too much farther to go, surely? The heat in the compartment was oppressive, the air thick and stale.

The railway ran along a valley, past hillsides scarred with black wounds and lined with row upon row of terraced houses which clung to the slopes. Factories and mine workings breathed out plumes of smoke, and between the towns bleak, tussocky moorland was dotted with sheep and crowned with dark tips of coal waste.

At last, a harassed-looking porter helped Norma off the train, out of the station into a rain-lashed street, and onto a claret-and-cream painted bus. Only a single decker, not the kind of tall red London bus she was accustomed to. Chugging and coughing, the bus conveyed her and a dozen or so wide-eyed children, along with their stern-faced teacher, to a church hall with tall windows and a polished wooden floor. There, they were greeted by the welcome sight of a tea urn and slices of fruit cake.

Norma accepted a cup of tea gratefully, but left the cake for the children, who pounced on it like animals. Hungry though she was, she was too nervous to eat. The butterflies in her stomach were performing acrobatics, her lower back and hips were aching, and her arms felt like they'd been dragged from her sockets after carrying her sewing machine, suitcases, gas mask and handbag on and off trains and buses, and in and out of buildings. Now and then, a stabbing pain shot through her left eye, making her squint, and she felt as if a metal band encased her forehead. Thank goodness she'd worn her lace-up shoes, not her nice ones. Even so, her feet and calves were tired. She longed for nothing more than to lay her head on a soft pillow and claim the oblivion of sleep.

While she watched, people from the town came in to select an evacuee to take home with them, as if they were choosing a new dress from a shop window. Norma noticed that the prettiest little girls and strongest-looking boys were chosen first. Such was the way of things, she supposed, crossing her fingers and hoping as the children trooped out with their new guardians that they would be kindly treated.

Her own experiences of foster homes had been variable. One or two were best forgotten. Her home with her mother might have been bug-ridden, filthy and damp, but there were worse things in life for kids to face than dirt. Even now, as an adult, she felt nauseous at the thought of having to depend on strangers. First chance she got, she'd be getting back to work and finding a place to settle. Whether in this town, or somewhere else, remained to be seen.

Soon, all the children and their teacher had been taken.

A thin man came in, brushing rain from his coat and shaking an umbrella out through the doorway as he stamped his feet on the mat. Norma noticed a clerical collar when he unbuttoned his black coat. He and the billeting officer murmured together, sending looks Norma's way and gathering up their papers. She was the only evacuee left unaccounted for.

The billeting officer approached, stuffing his hands in his pockets and clearing his throat. Behind him, the vicar waited near the door, checking his wristwatch.

"Mrs Finch?"

Norma looked around, then remembered. This would take some getting used to. "The very same," she said, mustering a weak smile. It wouldn't do to get on the wrong side of this chap when he had the power to choose her accommodation. If she didn't co-operate, she might end up in a coal shed somewhere.

"Reverend Appleton needs to close the hall now, I'm afraid. There doesn't seem to be anyone else coming forward, but don't worry. We'll find you a billet before the night is out."

His melodic Welsh voice sounded uncertain, and his frown didn't inspire confidence, but she got to her feet as gamely as she could, swaying slightly as she slipped the string of her gas mask and the strap of her handbag back over her head.

The man bent to take her sewing machine, expressing surprise at its weight.

"After you, then, Mrs Finch," he said, nodding towards the door. "Let's go and find you a billet."

NINE

Miriam

At the dinner table, Miriam's stepson, Aneurin, poured each of them a glass of water. "Another batch of evacuees arrived in town today. I saw the bus pass the office on its way to the church hall," he said.

Miriam glanced at Emrys, whose expression had darkened predictably at this news. He chewed on his lamb chop as if it had turned to ashes in his mouth.

"I saw Maggie earlier. She said she and Miss Vaughan-Lloyd have taken in a teacher. Five children have been billeted at Plas Norton, too."

"Five? That will create a lot of extra work for Dolly, won't it, Mim?"

Miriam smiled. It was typical of Aneurin to consider others. While Emrys was ruled by principles, his son was guided by compassion.

"She would be within her rights to refuse the extra responsibilities," Emrys said.

Miriam shook her head. "Miss Fitznorton agreed to take them."

"Then let Miss Fitznorton do England's dirty work, not your sister."

In the silence that followed, Miriam took a sip of water. She found any discussion of politics uncomfortable, but especially at mealtimes. While she respected the fervour of her husband's views, and admired his determination to live by his beliefs, there were times when his uncompromising stance left him out of step with people around him.

"They're just children, Emrys. It isn't their fault they've been evacuated. It would be uncharitable of Miss Fitznorton and Dolly not to help them."

"If everyone refused to take them, they'd have to go back. If it comes to a war, do you really want Wales to be dragged into it?"

"Of course not. But..." She shook her head. There was no point in arguing.

Aneurin spoke up. "I'm still praying that Hitler will see the risks he's taking and pull his troops back out of Poland. He's already taken Czechoslovakia; God willing, he'll decide that's enough."

Emrys raised a dark eyebrow. "We're all praying for that, Aneurin. But Hitler is doing what imperialists do, is he not? They take what they want. They see it as their country's right. It matters nothing to them who they crush. It's what England has been doing for centuries. It astounds me, the hypocrisy of the English who are speaking up now for Poland, when they were willing to let Czechoslovakia fall. Did you see them rush to the defence of the people of Spain when the Fascists took over there? Did they help the people of Abyssinia against Italy? Of course not. They were too busy protecting their own interests, maintaining their grip on their own empire. Yet now, suddenly, we are all to believe that plucky little England is on the side of freedom and justice. How are we to put aside centuries of English oppression here in Wales, to offer them our aid now? Weren't enough Welsh lives sacrificed on the altar of British imperialism a generation ago? You're too young to remember, but believe me, those of us who went through it will never forget."

Emrys tossed his knife and fork down onto his plate, making Miriam flinch. Gravy splashed onto the white tablecloth.

"You haven't finished your dinner yet, *cariad*," she murmured.

"I've lost my appetite. Excuse me; I'm going to finish my sermon ready for the morning." He limped from the room, the lines on his face hewn deeper than usual.

In the awkward silence left by his departure, Miriam and Aneurin exchanged a rueful look.

"I wish he wouldn't pontificate at the dinner table," Aneurin said, dragging a hand through his hair and making it stick up in a way that made her want to comb it back down.

Miriam couldn't help defending her husband. She hated to see division between father and son. "It's the way he sees it, and you won't change him. It's because of love, you know. He loves his country, and worries for its future. He feels Wales deserves better than the treatment it's had over the years. And he doesn't want you, or any other young man, to go through the things he and his generation experienced."

"It's different this time, though. What happened at Gallipoli was pointless. To die fighting against Nazism would be seen by most people as a worthy sacrifice. A noble act, even." He took off his spectacles and polished them with his napkin, frowning. Frustration seeped from every pore on his young face. In his different way, he was as much an idealist as his father.

Miriam gathered up the plates. "It's time to wash up," she said, changing the subject. It wouldn't help for her to become embroiled in this discussion. Her own views might align with Aneurin's, but her loyalty was owed to her husband.

Subdued, Aneurin dried the dishes while she washed them.

"Forget about it now," she urged, taking the tea towel from him. "You haven't told me yet how youth club went yesterday evening. Were the children worrying about what's going on in the world? It will be strange for them, having so many evacuees arriving at school."

"I'm sure it will. But we made sure they had fun, to take their minds off it."

She knew he would have put a brave face on his concerns, and hopefully the gentle, pretty Hilda Hughes, who led the group with him, had given him a reason to smile. Miriam nursed hopes that Aneurin would fall for Hilda one day, and she strongly suspected that Hilda did, too. The girl had shown signs of carrying a torch for Aneurin ever since they were in school together, and had jumped at the chance to help him lead the young people's group when the previous leader went off to college. So far, they'd made a good team, but the lad had not yet given any indication that he returned Hilda's feelings.

"Was Hilda there last night?" she asked.

He rolled his green eyes. "Yeees. Hilda always comes to youth club. She's like part of the furniture."

She tutted at the flash of his mischievous grin, and put the last of the dishes and pans away. "That's not a very nice way to talk about a young lady, is it?" she pointed out as he left the room.

As Aneurin went upstairs, Emrys called from the hallway. "I'm going to look in on Mr Davies," he said, putting on his coat and hat. "I promised I'd pray with him this evening."

Closing the front door behind him, Miriam headed for her armchair in the parlour and picked up her knitting. This was always a pleasant hour, when the day's chores were done and she had the room to herself for reading or sewing or knitting, and never more so than on a wet night. There was a cosiness in being warm and dry while raindrops lashed at the windowpane. Hopefully the weather would improve by morning, when the men would cycle the four miles up the grassy slopes of the mountain, Moel Carnau, where Emrys grew up and where his mother and brother, Idwal, still farmed. Emrys preached to the isolated Welsh-speaking farmers who gathered in the tiny chapel there one Sunday each month, and stayed for a couple of nights.

Miriam sometimes went to the mountain chapel too, although she often felt out of her depth, understanding so little of the language in the sermon and prayers. On the Sundays she stayed at home, she would attend the service along the street where Emrys was the regular minister, and listen to the visiting preacher. Hopefully his replacement would be a good one this month. The previous one had been so boring, she'd fought to stay awake. As Emrys liked her to give a detailed account of the sermon, she had no choice but to give it her full attention.

As her needles clicked and the cardigan she was knitting gradually grew, she remembered the days when Emrys had been a charismatic visiting preacher to the chapel she'd attended since girlhood with her mam. She supposed she'd set her cap at him, making her parents worry for her future. In marrying the much older Emrys, she'd taken on a stepson only eight years younger than herself. Now, with the advantage of maturity, she could understand her parents' concerns. Aneurin was now the age she had been as a bride, and although she'd be delighted if he became engaged to Hilda, twenty-one did seem young to settle down.

Still, she had no regrets. She was proud of the home she'd created in the manse, and, although it hadn't always been easy, she enjoyed the role of dutiful, devoted minister's wife and caring stepmother. The only thing missing was a child of her own – but she wouldn't be thirty for a few months. They had time, and prayer, on their side.

She wouldn't give up. After all, it hadn't been in Emrys's mind to remarry, but she had made it happen through love, persistence, and sheer force of will. If she could move her unbending husband, perhaps the Almighty could be similarly swayed by proof of devotion.

TEN

Miriam

Soon after Emrys returned from visiting Mr Davies, the doorbell rang. Miriam set aside her knitting and went to answer it.

She recognised the man on the doorstep as an infrequent visitor to the chapel, the sort who only attended the Christmas carol service and occasional weddings or funerals. Sharing the shelter of his umbrella was a young woman, little more than a girl really: a pretty blonde, sagging under a coat too warm for the season. Ghastly pale, her lips looked bloodless, edged with a line of worn-away scarlet lipstick. She swayed on her feet as the man lifted his hat.

"Good evening, Mr Evans," Miriam said.

"Good evening, Mrs Powell. Reverend Powell," he acknowledged as Emrys joined her.

Behind them, a creak on the stairs told her Aneurin had also heard the bell.

Mr Evans rubbed one eye wearily with the back of his hand. "This young lady here is Mrs Finch. She's the last of our evacuees from London. She needs a billet, and frankly you're our last hope."

Sensing Emrys stiffening beside her, Miriam braced herself for an awkward discussion. She had been on the point of inviting the visitors in, but given their purpose, it would only cause friction. It wouldn't be kind to raise their hopes only to have them dashed by her husband's refusal to support anything connected with English war plans.

"I'm afraid you'll have to try somewhere else." Emrys's voice was firm.

Before Miriam could offer any polite excuses, the woman on the doorstep dropped her suitcases with a loud thud. Miriam let out a gasp as one burst its catches on impact, releasing its contents like a jack-in-the-box popping open.

The woman said nothing. She was toppling forwards, her knees buckling and her neck limp. Miriam and Emrys dived forwards at the same moment, just as Mr Evans made a lunge for the woman's armpits, and an undignified tussle ensued to prevent the poor creature from falling onto her face.

Mr Evans grunted, his cheeks turning scarlet. "I can't hold her," he yelped. "My back!"

To Miriam's surprise, Emrys bent and scooped the girl up into his arms. He staggered backwards up the step into the hallway, one arm under her knees and the other supporting her neck. Blonde curls cascaded in a shower of gold against the dull brown sleeve of his cardigan. The woman's head lolled as Emrys swung her towards the parlour with surprising strength and carried her across the room to lay her down on the sofa.

Miriam followed, Mr Evans at her heels. "Fetch the smelling salts from the first aid box," she told Aneurin, who had appeared behind them.

He stood stunned into inaction, his gaze seemingly magnetised by the girl on the sofa.

She lay insensible, as beautiful as a fallen angel with her hair spilling over a cushion and her parchment-pale throat exposed and vulnerable. Mindful of her dignity and Aneurin's rapt attention, Miriam darted to tug her skirt hem down over her knees.

Emrys sucked in a sharp breath and crossed to the fireplace, where he leaned an elbow on the mantel. He observed the scene, one hand over his mouth as if he didn't trust himself to speak. Miriam wondered briefly if he'd hurt himself when he picked the girl up. Worse, might he have taken pleasure in holding such an attractive young woman in his arms?

"Smelling salts," she urged Aneurin again, more sharply this time.

"Poor thing," Mr Evans said. "A nip of brandy might help, perhaps?"

Emrys glared at him as if he'd sprouted horns and a tail. "We don't have alcohol in this house."

The man muttered an apology, then set down the wooden box he'd been carrying and scurried out towards the hall, almost colliding with Aneurin on his way back with the bottle.

The smelling salts weren't needed: the girl was coming round, faint colour rising in her cheeks and long, mascara-painted lashes fluttering.

"It's alright – Mrs Finch, is it?" Miriam addressed the girl, bending to pat her hand. "I'm Mrs Powell. Miriam. You lie there for as long as you need. I'll go and fetch you a cup of sweet tea."

Violet-blue eyes smudged with shadows gazed up at her, confused at first, then melting with gratitude.

On her way to the kitchen, Miriam realised Aneurin had helped Mr Evans gather up the evacuee's belongings from the doorstep. The boy was blushing over a pair of French knickers in oyster-pink rayon and lace in one hand and an equally glamorous brassiere in the other. She snatched them from him, along with the other sundry items Mr Evans was holding: a couple of blouses, rolled-up stockings, more knickers, and a bundle of folded cloths she guessed must be the poor girl's sanitary rags.

"I'll take these," she muttered. "They'll need washing after lying out there in the rain. Put the rest of her things in the hall, would you?"

The tea in the pot was hours old: cold now, and stewed. She clattered about the kitchen to prepare another, unsettled by the sudden turn in events. An image of the girl in Emrys's arms kept replaying in her mind, like a film that had got stuck and kept repeating the same few seconds. The sensual richness of her hair on his sleeve; her slim, stocking-clad legs draped limply over his arm. He hadn't carried Miriam over the threshold of their home when they were first married, as tradition demanded: he'd said he was too old for such things, and he wouldn't care to spend their first days together with an injured back. She'd never been swept up in his embrace like that. But he'd dashed forward and saved this girl from a tumble that could have smashed her beautiful features on the unforgiving tiles of their doorstep. He'd done it without thinking. It was the stuff of romances. A resentful prickle lodged between Miriam's shoulder blades.

When she returned to the parlour, all three men were staring at the girl as if she were an exhibit in an art gallery. She was silent, slumping back against the cushions, wan with fatigue.

"She can't stay here," Emrys said. His mouth set in a hard line.

"But Dad—"

"You know my position, Aneurin."

Emrys had often spoken of the need for Welshmen to remain neutral and not do anything to support England's war, if Wales was to have any hope of independence. Miriam had sympathised. But that was before an exhausted English girl lay on their sofa, pathetic and alone.

Mr Evans straightened, as if stiffening his resolve. "Reverend, we've walked the streets of Pontybrenin for the past two hours and been turned away from every door."

"That's unfortunate, but evacuees from London are not my concern."

Miriam supported the girl to sit up, making sure she could remain upright unaided before passing her the cup and saucer. It gave her an opportunity to study the new arrival more closely. She wasn't reassured.

No wonder she'd been turned away. What wife or mother of a son would want such a tempting creature in their home? An evacuee child was one thing, but to share a kitchen and dining table with such a glamorous young woman, whether married or not... To have her sleeping and bathing just along the landing... Aneurin's moony expression was enough to prove that only trouble could result from allowing her to stay.

Mr Evans was persistent, even in the face of Emrys's implacable scowl. "She's exhausted, and no wonder: a woman in her condition shouldn't be tramping the streets. In the end, I thought to myself, who can I rely upon to treat a stranger with Christian charity? I couldn't take her to Reverend Appleton – he's already got an evacuee, a male teacher. It wouldn't be suitable, her staying at the vicarage with two single men. Naturally, my next thought was to bring her here to the manse. And especially with Mrs Powell's sister being a midwife."

Miriam's attention snapped to the woman's stomach. *A woman in her condition?* The girl's coat had fallen open when she sat up, revealing a loose-fitting dress. Her tummy did seem to bulge more than the fine contours of her cheekbones and jaw would suggest.

This changed things. If Miriam's prayers were answered this month, it would be a blessing to have another woman around who shared in the precious experience of pregnancy. They could help one another. And the girl looked so tired, so vulnerable. She and her unborn baby needed looking after. Miriam would enjoy helping her care for an infant.

Mr Evans still hadn't given up. "As much as I hate to bring this up, Reverend, it's my duty to remind you that potential hosts who refuse to accommodate evacuees can be subjected to substantial fines."

"Then if others have also turned her away, it seems the British government will soon be raking in funds to prosecute their ungodly war," Emrys growled.

Miriam knew that the threat of a fine wouldn't stop Emrys sticking to his principles. He was the sort of man who would gladly go to prison rather than conform to a rule that went against his beliefs. She laid a restraining hand on his arm before he could say anything more.

"Would you excuse us for a moment?" she said to Mr Evans.

He folded his arms and nodded.

Catching her husband's elbow, she pulled him out to the hallway.

He glared at her. "You're not thinking of—"

"Emrys!" she hissed, interrupting him.

Surprise at her disobedience registered in his eyes before his scowl returned, but she cut him off.

"Mrs Finch is not a political point to be made. She is not England, nor the War Ministry, nor foreign policy. She isn't responsible for the war. She's an expectant mother in need of sanctuary. And did the Lord not tell us: 'I was a stranger, and ye took me in'? We have a moral, even a *sacred* duty to offer her refuge. Will you ignore her plight, like the priest and the Levite in the parable, or will you be a Good Samaritan?"

He would hate it, her quoting Scripture against him, and especially with Mr Evans eavesdropping in the room behind them. Nevertheless, she held his gaze. A muscle flickered just below his eye as his mouth tightened.

She brushed her hands down the front of her skirt and stepped back into the parlour, where the young woman sat twisting the wedding ring on her left hand.

All eyes fixed upon Miriam, as if everyone in the room held their breath.

"Mrs Finch can stay," she declared.

ELEVEN

Norma

The quiet seemed unnatural. No voices; no traffic. The only sound Norma could hear from her single bed was birdsong trilling through the window. Barely moving, she lay on her back, palms spread out over the crisp, clean sheet covering the firmly sprung mattress. The blankets were tight over her breasts, as if someone had tucked her in. She couldn't remember anyone doing that for her before. Not even when she was small.

The walls were covered with flower-sprigged paper, and striped curtains stirred gently as fresh, pure air wafted in. She pushed against the blankets and sat upright, swinging her legs out. Her toes curled and dug in as they landed on the thick pile of a rug that reached almost to the edge of the room. No bare, draughty floorboards here. Across the room, her sewing machine sat in its case near the door. One of her suitcases lay on a chair with yesterday's clothes neatly folded on top of it. The other stood on the floor beside her handbag, between the chair and a heavy wardrobe. Looking down, she realised she was wearing her nightdress, and a vague recollection swam back into her mind of being helped to undress by the dark-haired woman who had spoken up for her the previous night.

In a flash of panic she fumbled amongst her clothes, until the rustle of paper reassured her that her money was still in her bra. She let out her breath in a rush and dragged her hands over her face, then crossed to the window and pulled open the curtains, squinting at the lavish expanse of green outside.

The room overlooked a long garden surrounded by hedges. Beyond, a grassy hillside rose steeply, scattered with grey rocks and rough tussocks, like pimples on an adolescent's face. High up, she glimpsed the sparkle of a stream. The rain had stopped, although the lichen-spotted flagstones of the garden path still glistened. At the end of the garden stood a tree laden with ripe red apples. She couldn't remember seeing them growing before, only stacked on a barrow or in a greengrocer's box.

A throb of discomfort sent her out onto the landing to find a bathroom, tiptoeing past the stairs in case she was seen in her thin nightdress. The bathroom was clean and bright, a world apart from the shared facilities at Mrs Bishop's boarding house, where the basin only had a cold tap and the chipped enamel had almost worn off the bath, stained with limescale by a persistent drip.

She'd only just made it back to her room when the stairs creaked, and the woman who'd helped her the night before appeared, carrying a cup and saucer.

"Ah, you're up. I hope you slept well, Mrs Finch. You were so exhausted last night, I had to help you to bed."

Norma blinked. Would she ever get used to her new name?

"I did sleep, thanks. Don't think I've ever been so comfy. But it feels funny, you calling me Mrs Finch. Call me Norma." She accepted the cup and perched on the edge of the bed.

"Norma it is, then." There was a slightly awkward pause. "I'm Miriam."

"Thanks for letting me stay, Miriam."

"You're welcome."

Norma wrinkled her nose. "I'm glad to hear that. I had the

impression me turning up went down like a bucket of cold sick with your husband."

She clamped her lips together, suddenly aware that she might have been too bold. *Best never to bite that hand that feeds.* There was no telling how long she'd need to make use of the Powells' hospitality, and she'd fallen on her feet with this room. It was like paradise compared with any other place she'd ever stayed.

Seeing how Miriam's face had frozen with embarrassment, Norma tried to backtrack. "Not to worry, eh? All's well that ends well. Thanks for speaking up for me. I don't think I could have walked another step around the streets with that Evans feller, people shutting the door in our faces every house we went to." She drained the last of the cup and handed it back. "Lovely cup of char, that."

"Please don't think badly of my husband. It isn't you personally as such, it's... Anyway. You're here for as long as you need." Miriam dropped her gaze. "Some of your clothes unfortunately fell out of your suitcase in the rain last night, but I've put them to soak and I'll wash them tomorrow."

"That's nice of you, but I don't mind doing my own laundry." She rose and pulled the bedclothes straight, to emphasise the point. She didn't expect special treatment. A bed and a bit of grub were enough.

"Do you have a warmer nightdress for the winter? You might find that one a bit... insubstantial."

Norma looked at Miriam's sensible buttoned-up blouse, skirt and cardigan, then down at herself. Her nipples were rosy peaks poking at the panel of lace on the bodice of her flimsy satin nightdress, which clung revealingly to her rounded abdomen.

"I s'pose I might need to make myself another one. I made this one for my wedding night," she said. Emotion gathered in her throat, and she let it show. It wasn't a lie, after all, and it wouldn't hurt for Miriam to think she'd had a blissful wedding and a doting husband.

"*You* made it?" Norma couldn't tell if she was shocked or impressed by the figure-hugging column of pink satin she'd created.

"My boss got me the fabric cheap. A bias cut's wasteful, if you're not careful how you place the pattern pieces, but I managed to make some undies with what was left. If there's a market in town with a draper's and haberdashery, I could make one for you, if you want. I've still got the pattern."

"Goodness. That's a generous offer, but I don't think it would be suitable for me." Miriam looked away. "Well, then. The rest of us have already had breakfast, but I can make you some toast or porridge. If there's something in particular you'd like, just say: I can add it to our order at the grocer's next week."

"If you show me where the kitchen is, I can make myself a bit of toast."

Her hostess continued as if she hadn't spoken, turning towards the door and pausing with a hand on the doorknob. "I'll speak to my sister Maggie about coming to check on you. She's a midwife."

"Oh, no. I ain't got no money for that," Norma protested. She would put off breaking into her twenty shillings until she absolutely had to.

"But it's important to make sure you and the baby are healthy."

"I've managed this long without any midwife interfering. I s'pose there'll come a point when I'll have to get one, but until then I'll be just fine."

"Nonsense. I'll be seeing her anyway, so I'll make sure there's no charge for a quick check. You don't want to take any risks, especially after you were so worn out last night." The finality in her tone, as well as her determined expression, gave Norma the sense that this unassuming woman might just have a core of steel. She left the room before Norma had time to argue.

Norma screwed up her face, then shrugged. As long as it wouldn't cost anything, she might as well go along with it. She put on yesterday's clothes and folded her nightdress before tucking it under her pillow. Using the small bathroom mirror, she applied rouge, powder and mascara, but didn't bother with her usual crimson lipstick. With her suitcases safely stowed under the bed and her handbag shoved into the bottom of the wardrobe, the room looked tidy enough to please the strictest landlady.

She wasn't sure yet what to make of Miriam, who looked much younger than her husband yet who was equally middle-aged in her manner and clothing. A bit of make-up and a haircut would do wonders, and Norma's fingers itched to make her some prettier, more stylish clothes. Still, it was none of her concern if the woman was content to look old before her time.

The lack of noise in the house when Norma descended the stairs was almost unnerving. A grandfather clock ticked a regular beat in the hall, at the far end of which came faint sounds from a room which she rightly guessed was the kitchen.

Miriam cut two slices of bread and slid them under the gas grill when Norma entered. A plate with a knife and spoon, a pot of jam, and a china butter dish lay on a clean cotton tablecloth.

Norma's stomach rumbled as she took her seat. "You've already eaten, then?" she asked, realising Miriam was tidying up, not cutting any more slices for herself.

"Yes, we were up early. My husband is preaching on the mountain today, in the chapel he attended as a boy. He'll stay with his family and then come back home on Tuesday evening. I'll go to our own chapel just along the road this afternoon and this evening. You're welcome to join me."

"I'll give it a miss, thanks. I'm not really one for all that religious malarkey, to be honest." She wasn't sorry that the stern-faced minister she'd met the previous night wouldn't be around for the next couple of days. Her few blurry memories of the evening's events included him standing at the fireplace with a horrible scowl and his deep voice venting something or other about the English. He'd made her feel about as welcome as a wild pig in a synagogue.

It seemed Miriam wasn't pleased with her answer. Her lips pursed, but to Norma's relief she didn't try to force the issue.

"There's to be an announcement by the prime minister shortly after eleven o'clock. I'll go and turn on the wireless in the parlour."

It was on the tip of Norma's tongue to joke that she wasn't interested in politics either, but she thought better of it. The woman meant well. Norma polished off the last couple of mouthfuls of her toast, licked the crumbs from her fingertips, and quickly washed up her plate and knife. She'd just dried her hands when the grandfather clock started to chime the hour.

In the parlour, Miriam stood at the window overlooking the street, her fingers drumming on the sill. Sunlight washed over her, bringing out deep honey shades in her dark brown hair.

Norma hugged her arms around herself, not sure whether to sit. Miriam had been more than hospitable, but it wasn't as if this was home. The room smelled of furniture polish overlaid with a faint, delectable scent from roses in a crystal vase on a bookcase full of well-worn volumes. There were few ornaments, and no mirror. A couple of religious texts in frames, an embroidered sampler, and a small, plain wooden cross were the only adornment on the walls.

On the wireless, the prime minister's voice sounded weary and full of strain. He explained that there had been no reply to Britain's request for German troops to withdraw from Poland. Then came the blow everyone had been dreading. "This country is at war with Germany," he announced.

The two women stood in silence for several moments, then Miriam turned the wireless off and leaned against the sideboard with her head bowed.

"Heavenly Father, let it be over quickly and without bloodshed," she said in a voice that was little more than a whisper.

"Amen," Norma said. She might not be religious, or prone to praying, but it didn't hurt to try. Perhaps if enough people joined their wishes for peace, the Almighty might intervene. No doubt people up and down the country were praying for peace, or for victory, which would amount to the same thing. It occurred to her that people in Germany were probably praying for the same. Would all those efforts from the two nations just cancel each other out?

A shuddering movement of Miriam's hunched shoulders made

Norma take a step closer. Sure enough, the other woman's face had crumpled and she was fishing in her pocket for a handkerchief. Warily, Norma laid her palm lightly on her sleeve and left it there until she had composed herself.

"I'm sorry," Miriam said, dabbing at red-rimmed eyes. "I'd held out hope that it wouldn't come to this."

Although Norma was born after the Great War ended, she'd seen plenty of disabled veterans begging on the streets of Stepney, and had heard women whisper to one another that their menfolk had come back from the trenches utterly changed. Perhaps Miriam's intensity of emotion was linked to that?

"Do you remember the last war?" Norma asked once Miriam had composed herself.

"I do, although I was only little when it began. My brother Len volunteered and died at the Somme. My brother Stanley was conscripted and blinded. My husband was in the Territorials, and went off willingly to fight. But he was injured at Gallipoli. It changed his view of war, and of Britain, forever. My sister Dolly's husband, Ivor, was gassed and still suffers from weak lungs."

"Crikey. No wonder you're upset."

"It's not just the past. It's the future that frightens me, and what might happen to my other brothers, Ted and Jack, and my nephew Alfred. Worse still, I fear what will happen if Aneurin is called up."

"A— what? Who?" Norma frowned. It wasn't a name she had ever heard before.

"Aneurin. My stepson."

"The boy from last night, d'you mean?"

"He isn't really a boy, although I still often think of him as one. He was twenty-one in April."

"A few months older than me, then."

"You're young to be married and expecting," Miriam remarked. "Though I suppose I believed myself more than old enough to be married at your age. It's only now I'm older that it seems terribly young. Of course, the government thinks twenty-one-year-olds are of an age to fight. Some of Aneurin's friends have already had to sign up. But if *he* enlists, his father will never forgive him." She released a heavy sigh. "There's scarcely a family in Pontybrenin that hasn't been blighted by the effects of the last war. And yet mankind doesn't seem willing to learn from the past."

TWELVE

Norma

First thing on Monday morning, Norma asked Miriam for directions into town and set off to explore. Given the town's small size, the directions hadn't been complicated. The Powells lived just along from the chapel where Miriam's husband was the minister. Their back garden sloped upwards onto the foot of a mountain called Moel Carnau, on the northern edge of town. Miriam had sketched a quick map on the back of an envelope, pointing out that her midwife sister lived on the western edge of town while her other sister, a housekeeper, lived in a big, fancy place a few miles to the south-west. Past the eastern limits of Pontybrenin was a coal mine. In the town centre was a library, a hotel, some shops, and the bank where Aneurin worked – although Norma felt like pointing out that she'd probably never have enough money to need a bank. More interestingly, Miriam mentioned a cinema and an Italian coffee shop. They could provide somewhere to while away a few hours, until she could find work. For now, Norma would explore the shops.

Unfortunately, it seemed it would be far easier to find a church or chapel than a decent shop. She walked the length of the high street, then frowned. There was so little to interest her. She had no reason to visit the stationer's, the chemist, or the establishments selling food. She wasn't much of a reader, so there was little point in going to the library, which stood on one of the side streets. The cinema would be nice for a date or with a friend, but not much fun on her own. There was no Woolworth's. No fish and chip shops or stalls selling jellied eels or whelks. Only one ladies' clothes shop, and a peek through the window left her convinced that Welsh women must all be old and staid, or else care little for current fashions. This impression was reinforced by the street's single hairdressing salon, which looked as if it still offered the same styles as twenty years ago. That only left a newsagent, a jeweller, and the market.

The market, at least, had a yarn stall brimming with skeins of wool in a variety of colours, and a draper, with a haberdashery attached which was well stocked with buttons, thread and trimmings. She fingered the fabrics in the draper's stall, lingering over a bolt of sky blue, printed cotton while queuing behind several housewives buying blackout material at a shilling a yard. Luckily, she didn't have to look at anything so plain: she loved the colours in shops like this, and picturing how the cloth would drape and fold over the body, how it would work for different styles of garment, and how to combine it with accessories.

Clothes were a way to express herself and to make a statement to the world: *I'm here, I'm worth looking at, deserving of your attention.* Making pretty things that showed her at her best was a way to make up for the years of poverty, when she'd had next to nothing and hardly anyone had shown any interest in her.

For now, she'd content herself with her second favourite thing: refashioning garments that had been cast off. She'd spotted a secondhand clothes stall, and spent a pleasant half hour picking out a couple of maternity dresses that could be adapted without too much trouble or expense to add individuality. With the dresses wrapped in a bundle along with ribbons and thread, it was time to take the weight off her feet.

There were a few pubs, but a woman couldn't go in by herself without inviting scorn. With luck she'd soon meet a good-looking young feller who'd be willing to overlook her condition and take her out for a bit of fun now and then. Meanwhile, the coffee shop would do.

Pushing open the door to Contadino's café, Norma inhaled appreciatively. It smelled like the café in London where Dickie used to treat her to a bit of cake when the mood took him: inviting, with the rich, slightly bitter aroma of good coffee. It was the only thing she'd found in Pontybrenin so far that could in any way compete with the capital.

She took a seat near the window. A latticework of sticky tape criss-crossed the glass to protect it. Across the street, a man wearing a striped apron was applying the same to the windows of the butcher's shop, a reminder that people here feared Nazi bombs just as Londoners did, even though this small town far from the east coast of England must be much safer than the city.

Only a few of the café's tables were occupied, and the murmur of talk seemed all about the war, as it had been in the draper's shop queue. A woman at a nearby table was grumbling loudly to her companion about the rough speech of the evacuee boy who'd been billeted with her. Norma didn't want to be reminded of the unwelcoming attitude of the housewives when Mr Evans had first tried to find her a billet. She kept her back to the woman and tried to focus her thoughts on other things.

Could she stick it out in Pontybrenin for however long the war might go on? The previous conflict had lasted four years. The way she felt this morning, she'd struggle to last here for four days. There was so little to do, and the people weren't nearly as friendly as the cheery shopkeepers on the Mile End Road. Even Miriam couldn't really be described as pally. She was too guarded for that; too polite.

The hills edging the town made Norma feel hemmed in, too. It was all so very small, and lacking in the colour and vitality she was used to in the city. Everyone looked alike: there was no variety in the languages spoken or the styles of dress or the colour of the faces. There were no men with ringlets and kippahs or wide-brimmed black hats. No West Indians or Lascars in sailors' uniforms. And, quite apart from the lack of things to do in her spare time, with so few shops it might not be easy for her to earn money. All she had was a few coins in her purse and the twenty shillings she'd hidden under a drawer liner back in her room at the manse. She couldn't live off that for long. She needed work.

At least the café offered some sophistication. Its marble-topped counter looked impressively luxurious. A coffee machine stood towards one end of it, bristling with levers and nozzles, polished to a mirror shine. With a brass eagle on its domed top, it was as magnificent as any coffee machine in the capital. A middle-aged man with a mouth that drooped at one side was operating it, deftly making coffee in two cups simultaneously.

A younger man, slim and lithe in his black waistcoat and trousers, carried the cups to a couple in the corner. She watched him, admiring the swift precision of his movements and the grace with which his hips moved, almost like a dancer. She was still enjoying the view when he turned towards her and the flash of interest in his eyes told her he'd caught her looking. A smile played at her lips while he approached. Conscious of her stomach, she pulled her handbag onto her lap to hide it.

"*Buongiorno, signorina,*" he greeted her in a pleasant voice, his lilting Italian accent bolstering his charms. Twinkling tawny eyes regarded her boldly. "You must be a new customer. If I'd served such a beautiful lady before, I would remember."

She tilted her head and looked up at him from under her lashes. "As it happens, you're right. I arrived in town yesterday."

"And what do you think of Pontybrenin?"

"I wasn't too keen at first. But all of a sudden, things seem to be looking up."

"Suddenly they're looking up for me, too. So, how can I tempt you, *signorina*?"

She caught her lower lip with her teeth. "You could tempt me with all sorts of things, I reckon. But a nice, strong black coffee will do to start with."

"It will be my pleasure."

While he fetched her coffee from the man on the other side of the counter, she noticed he glanced back at her several times. She took out her compact and powdered her nose, then refreshed her lipstick, ignoring the disapproving clucks of an elderly woman at the next table who presumably thought it unseemly for a woman to touch up her make-up in public. Norma didn't care. It gave her a charge of energy to know she'd made an impression on a good-looking young man. She flicked her hair off her shoulder as he returned with her coffee.

"I'm Johnny," he said, setting the cup and saucer in front of her.

"That don't sound very Italian."

He gave an expressive shrug. "People here find it easier to say than Giovanni."

"Well, I'm very pleased to meet you, Johnny. I'm Norma." She held out her hand, and laughed when he kissed it instead of shaking it.

"I'm pleased to meet you, too, Norma." The way he rolled his tongue around her name made it sound unexpectedly luscious.

The older man behind the counter beckoned, frowning as if he disapproved of Johnny lingering at her table.

"Who's that?" Norma asked. "I think he wants you."

"He's my uncle Vittorio. I'd better go. But I hope you will soon be back and sample some other things from our menu? We make our own pies, and the best *gelato* – ice cream – in Wales."

"I'll sample anything you're offering," she replied, loading the words with meaning and relishing the way his eyes gleamed in response.

Sauntering towards the counter, Johnny sent a quick wink back over his shoulder before continuing to serve the other customers.

She took her time over her coffee, then gathered up her gas

mask, parcel and handbag, carefully concealing her tummy while she headed to the counter to pay.

The coffee had given her energy, and her flirtation with the delectable Johnny Contadino had put even more of a spring in her step. As she retraced her steps back towards the manse, she turned her thoughts in a more hopeful direction. Getting her sewing machine out would be sure to lift her spirits further: she'd ask Miriam for permission to use the dining table at the manse, and start altering today's purchases. And while she was sewing, she'd put on her thinking cap and work out a way to earn a few quid.

THIRTEEN

Norma

Although the manse was comfortable, Norma couldn't feel at ease somewhere so quiet. It was hard to sleep without the sounds of voices or traffic on the road, and with no glow from streetlamps to light her room through the curtains. The silence felt unnatural.

On Tuesday, she went out for another walk to explore the local area a little further. Although she'd spotted a path heading onto the grassy slope of the mountain, edged with overgrown brambles and trees, she decided to put off a trip in that direction until she'd exhausted Pontybrenin's attractions. Unfortunately, there were disappointingly few to be found.

She couldn't afford to buy coffee every time she headed into town, so contented herself with peering in through the window of Contadino's café to see if Johnny was there. He was, but he didn't notice her, and embarrassment led her to move on after a few moments. People already looked at her funny, she assumed because her clothes and make-up were a bit smarter than they seemed to be used to. Well, she wasn't about to start wearing anything drab. People might be fed up about being at war, but going around looking dull and miserable wasn't likely to cheer anyone up.

On this visit she discovered a post office, but it saddened her to reflect that there was no one who might write to her. Would she find any new friends in Pontybrenin? Miriam was a polite hostess, and Aneurin had seemed pleasant enough when they ate their evening meal on Monday night, but both were shy, and it was hard to know what to talk to them about when they had so little in common. She had established that Aneurin worked in the bank in the centre of Pontybrenin, and hoped to work his way up to become a branch manager one day. He'd nodded when she said she'd worked as a seamstress, but sewing wasn't likely to interest a banker, and as she'd clammed up when Miriam asked about her husband, conversation had soon ground to a halt.

The manse was a good-looking house, Norma supposed as she returned from her walk. It was certainly the largest and most comfortable private house she'd ever had the good fortune to stay in. The kind of house a child might draw, with a central front door and a window either side. Three equally sized and equally spaced windows upstairs lent it an attractive symmetry, even if its grey stone and dark brown-painted window frames were too sober and colourless for her taste. Its small front garden had a flagstone path leading from the wrought iron gate to the front door, but she bypassed that and walked down the side alleyway to the back door which led into the kitchen. No one was in sight, and it was only when she reached the top of the stairs that she heard any sound other than her own footsteps and the relentless, gentle ticking of the grandfather clock.

A muffled exclamation came from the bathroom. Norma tapped the door softly with her knuckles. As it was ajar, she risked a peep.

"Everything alright in there?" she asked.

"Oh! Mrs Finch. I hadn't realised you were back from town." Miriam was balancing on the side of the bath, reaching up to the top of the window with a tape measure. As she wobbled precariously, Norma's eyes widened.

"What are you doing up there?"

"Measuring up for the blackout."

"Can't your husband do that? It don't look safe to me, you clambering about."

"I'm not expecting him back until this evening. There's a fellowship meeting on the mountain on the first Monday of each month, and he likes to stay for that, before visiting members of his flock or seeing to any repairs at the chapel the next day."

"At least let me give you a hand."

Miriam gasped. "You can't go climbing in your condition."

It was funny, having someone say that to her. Since she'd fallen pregnant, most people had been too busy disapproving of her to express any concern for her welfare. Perhaps this was the difference it would make, people believing she was married. Or perhaps Miriam was just unusually nice.

Norma tipped her head to one side and eyed Miriam's stockinged feet on the edge of the bathtub. "Alright. Perhaps I shouldn't climb, but if I stand here, I can at least give you something soft to land on."

Miriam grinned, quickly hiding it as if she didn't dare let go of her prim and proper facade. *Interesting.* So she did have a sense of humour. Perhaps life in the manse needn't be all doom, gloom and God-bothering, after all.

"Pass me your notebook and pencil, and tell me the measurements. I'll note them down so you can concentrate on not braining yourself if you go toppling off."

It felt good to be useful to someone. She'd loved her job in the Goldmans' tailor's shop, working mainly out the back with the other seamstress and a young apprentice tailor. Over the six years since she left school, she'd honed her skills and become one of their most versatile workers, making it all the more disappointing that they'd been so willing to let her go when she fell pregnant. She'd taken pride in her abilities: her hand sewing was neat, she was quick and accurate using a machine, and she had a creative flair for alterations that had earned the business repeat custom.

Although Mr Goldman was loath to allow any unnecessary talking while they worked, it had been fun chatting with the other seamstress and teasing the apprentice for his crush on his neighbour during their brief lunch breaks. They'd stand in the small yard out the back while the apprentice smoked a ciggie, and now and then she'd have a puff even though she didn't really like it, just to join in. She'd felt as if she'd almost found a friend, until she started going steady with Dickie, who didn't like her talking and laughing with other men.

The shop was where she'd met Dickie. He came to get his trousers altered when the Goldmans were out at the bank, and she was the only one free to measure him. She'd slipped the tape around his waist, acutely conscious of the heat of his body and his masculine smell. She looked up, amused to catch him staring down the neckline of her blouse, then held his gaze while she knelt to measure the length of his inside leg. The way he sucked in his breath and the flare of interest in his blue eyes had made her unable to hide a small smile of satisfaction, and she hadn't been surprised when she found him loitering outside the shop at the end of the day.

She gave herself a mental shake. It wouldn't do to dwell on Dickie. He was out of her life for good, and she had to make the best of things. Wanting Miriam to see her as capable and helpful, she noted the numbers down in her neatest handwriting and followed her into each room.

The bedrooms revealed some interesting insights into the Powell family. She hadn't expected that Miriam and her husband would sleep in separate beds, but somehow it made sense. It was impossible to imagine either of them ever enjoying the kind of fun she'd had with Dickie: the giggling, heady moments when he'd pushed her against a wall and tugged her knickers down, and she'd felt a certain pride in how his desire for her was so strong it made him cast all restraint aside. That was her power: to make him lose control and abandon himself to passion. Miriam and Emrys's bedroom, though, was as neat and ordered as their personal appearance. The idea that either of them might have a passionate thought was so ridiculous that it almost made Norma laugh aloud.

Entering Aneurin's room when he wasn't there felt like an intrusion, so she waited near the door while Miriam stood on a chair to measure the window. Like his father's study, his room was neat and tidy, and stacked with books on shelves. Striped pyjamas poked out from under his pillow, and a novel with a bookmark in it lay on his nightstand together with a notebook and a glass still half-full of water. It was odd to see a young man's most personal space when she barely knew him, and she couldn't help wondering what he'd think if he knew she'd been in there.

Soon all the windows had been measured.

"I wasn't sure how much cloth I'd need, so I bought twenty yards last week," Miriam said, leading the way to the kitchen and filling the kettle with water.

"*Twenty?* You could probably black out the whole street with that much. You could make most of Pontybrenin invisible." She let out a giggle, but stopped when she realised Miriam was being serious.

"I thought I can use whatever's left for the chapel. If the war continues into the winter, it'll be dark when we have the evening service, and it will be impossible to read our Bibles and hymn books without lighting. The organist won't be able to read his music, either. I'm going to have to cover the windows."

Norma had walked past the chapel a couple of times. Although it was smaller than the churches in London, the windows must still be eight feet tall. There were a few on each side, not to mention two at the front and the fanlight above the entrance. Miriam would have her hands full with all those blackout curtains to make.

"I'll give you a hand if you like," she said.

"I couldn't possibly expect you to..."

"You'll be doing me a favour. I'll be happier if I can make myself useful."

"Well... If you're sure, that would be very kind." Miriam still looked hesitant.

"Why don't we start cutting after lunch? If I set my machine up on the dining room table, we can get a little production line going."

The relief on Miriam's face was pleasing to see. Norma set up her sewing machine while Miriam made potted meat sandwiches. After calculating how much fabric she'd need for each curtain, with a channel for a wire or pole and a hem around three sides, Norma started measuring and cutting, taking care not to scratch the polished surface of the table with her sharp scissors.

Miriam stood with the list, looking anxious. "We'll need a curtain for the front door, too, and we must remember to turn off the hall light before we open it at night. A member of our congregation has signed up as the local Air Raid Precautions warden, and he said we mustn't allow even a chink of light to show, else we could be fined."

"I'd be more worried about a bomb landing on me bonce, but hopefully we won't be getting none of those here. If we do, I'll have come all this way for nothing," Norma remarked.

"No, I'm sure you're right. It's purely precautionary." But Miriam sighed and looked distracted as she laid the note down and went back to the kitchen to start preparing a steak and kidney pie for the family's dinner.

Norma had made all but one of the curtains for the upstairs rooms when she heard the clink of the front gate, then the front door being opened and the sound of heavy footsteps on the tiles in the hall.

"Miriam! Where are you?" It was Reverend Powell, sounding even fiercer than he had on the night Norma first met him.

Through the open doorway, Norma saw Miriam emerge from the kitchen with an apron around her waist.

"You're back earlier than I expected, *cariad*. Is there some kind of problem?"

His deep voice came out like the rasp of an engine. "It's worse than a problem, Miriam. It's a catastrophe."

FOURTEEN

Miriam

Before Miriam could establish what could be so wrong, Emrys strode into his study and pulled a pad of writing paper out of the drawer in his desk. His chair almost toppled as he wrenched it out. Sitting down, he seized the fountain pen from the blotter.

"Emrys, *cariad*. You haven't even taken your shoes off. What's so urgent? Is there something wrong with your mother?"

"There will be soon, if I can't stop what's happening."

"Stop what? What's upset you so much?"

She crossed the room and touched his arm. It was trembling, as was the hand holding his pen. He held it poised above the paper, then capped it, tossed it down, and buried his face in his hands.

"I don't know what to do, Miriam. I have to stop it, but I don't know how." His breaths were rapid and shallow, making her own stomach lurch. Twisting in his chair, he buried his face in her apron, holding her in a fierce grip.

She hushed him, stroking his hair as she might a child that had woken from a nightmare. "Whatever it is, there'll be a way forward. Take some deep breaths and tell me."

When his breathing had slowed, she dragged the other chair from the corner and sat beside him.

"It happened this morning. I'd stayed at the farm overnight, but went back to the chapel first thing to get ready for Mr Daniel's funeral. Outside, the schoolchildren were playing, then above their noise I heard a car. I was surprised, so I stopped what I was doing and went out to see."

Miriam nodded. It was rare for any motorised vehicle to attempt the steep lane as far as the tiny school. There was no village within a mile, only isolated farms dotted over the rugged slopes, which were ideal for grazing sheep and ponies, but not much good for growing crops except a little wheat on the southern edge, and in places a few acres of oats.

Moel Carnau wasn't a high, dramatic sort of mountain, but a rolling upland, golden in summer sunshine but bitter and bleak in winter. Life on its barely tamed slopes bred a tough sort of person. People up there knew the land and its seasonal moods as if it was family: they had to, to scratch a living from it. Everyone living there spoke Welsh; English was rarely heard, though the children learned it in school.

"It was a military car: painted khaki, and driven by a girl wearing a uniform, would you believe. When it drew up outside the school, a major got out. Without thinking, I greeted him in Welsh. He stared at me and asked me, speaking very slowly as if I was stupid, if I could speak English."

"Go on."

"He showed me a list of the farms on the mountain, and said he wanted to check whether the acreage listed for each one was correct. Every farm was on that list, up to a good fifteen miles' distance from the chapel out towards the west, and within around five miles towards the north. He tried reading the names out, but he was hopeless. I had to help him pronounce them. It might have been funny, if not for the reason he came."

Agitated, he loosed her hand and paced between his desk and the window. "They plan to take it, Miriam. All of it. Every acre.

Every farm. The chapel, and the Baptist chapel over on the western side. The school is within the boundary they've drawn, too. Even the tavern. They want it all for an artillery range. Everyone living there will be forced to leave."

Miriam's mouth gaped. It didn't seem possible that so many people could so easily be turned out of their homes.

"I told the major to wait, and got the teacher to send one of the children to fetch Mr Huws and Mr Siencyn, who were hedge cutting up at Beili Gwyn. He repeated it to them. They want every building empty within the next few months. Every human being, every sheep, horse, goose and turkey will have to go, he said. All so they can bring up their vile weapons and blast the place to pieces with shells."

"But where will the farmers go? There must be dozens of families living on the mountain."

His fists had clenched at his sides. "Do you imagine the English government cares about that? There were nearly forty farms on that list. Forty families will lose their homes, their livelihoods, and their way of life. More than that, they'll lose their culture and their community. Neighbours; friends from childhood; fellowships of believers. All of it torn apart at the whim of the War Ministry and the stroke of some administrator's pen, so the English can perfect their arts of killing on our ancestral land. The major didn't even realise that a few months from now we'll be coming towards the lambing season. He said he'll ask if an extension can be given. As if he was doing us a favour. I wanted to spit in his face."

"They'll have to allow people longer, surely? None of the farmers could move at lambing time."

"They shouldn't have to move at all!"

"No, of course not. But Emrys – if the War Ministry gives this order, and Britain is at war... It's hard to see how it can be stopped. Won't they have emergency powers...?"

He thumped a hand onto the windowsill, eyes blazing as if he hadn't heard her. "It's even more than the principle of it, Miriam – though that should be reason enough for them to put an end to the scheme. It's personal. My family's farm was on that list. Powells have lived and worked the land for generations, yet Mam and Idwal are to be forcibly evicted from the place where we were born."

The force of his words seemed to pummel her. She knew what the mountain meant to him and to his brother and mother, who still farmed there.

His voice was hoarse with the violence of his outrage. "It's no better than murder, Miriam, for if this happens it will surely kill my mother. It will rip the heart out of her and Idwal and everyone up there. And also out of me. As God is my witness, I'll find a way to stop it. I can't sit back and see a proud way of life destroyed."

FIFTEEN

Norma

It was years since Norma had been inside a church. The chapel where Emrys was the regular minister was nothing like the one where her gran's funeral had taken place. That one had had elaborate stained-glass windows. This one was spartan inside. No incense, no fancy tiled floor or golden eagle on the pulpit. Like the church in London, it had hard wooden pews, but this building also had a gallery of seats upstairs with a wooden handrail along its edge. Downstairs, organ pipes soared behind the pulpit, which was accessed by a short flight of steep steps on either side.

The wooden pews, gallery and pulpit were polished to a high shine, light bouncing off them from the sunshine flooding in. No wonder Miriam had been worried about blacking out the tall windows. It had taken them two days to make up the window coverings for the manse, with Norma sewing so fast her arm ached from turning the hand crank of her machine for hours at a stretch, and Miriam climbing a stepladder to screw hooks into each window frame for the stiff, black curtains. It was a nuisance putting them all up every evening before sundown. Norma had been tempted to leave her bedroom window covered all day, but it made the room feel claustrophobic. Even the endlessly wild green view from the window was better than being stuck permanently in the dark.

Both women gazed upwards at the chapel windows, which stretched far beyond the reach of the stepladder Miriam had been using at home.

"Blimey," Norma said. "You'll need a bleedin' fireman's ladder to get all the way up there."

Beside her, Miriam stiffened, as she always did when Norma said anything off colour. It wasn't even as if Norma swore all that badly. Certainly nowhere near as much as her gran had done, or her colleagues back home. She'd never used the F word, or the nasty C word Dickie and his pals used. She didn't even say "bloody", or at least not often. But the way the senior Powells looked at her sometimes, anyone would think she had a tongue like a fishwife. It was enough to make her want to say something properly outrageous, just for the fun of seeing stuffy old Emrys blowing a gasket.

She'd noticed that Miriam never said anything remotely resembling a curse or blasphemy. Every word she, the reverend and Aneurin spoke was measured and polite. Even when the rev came home the other day in a right old tizzy over the War Ministry wanting the mountain for an artillery range, he hadn't uttered a single swear word as far as Norma could tell. It amused her to wonder if his telephone conversations in Welsh contained any cursing. For all she knew, he could be peppering every sentence with filth. He'd been a soldier in his younger days, after all. But she doubted he could bring himself to do it.

Miriam's shoulders slumped wearily, and her bottom plopped down onto a pew. "I'm sure there must be long ladders here somewhere," she said. "We won't be able to put a curtain up that high every time we need to put the lights on, so I imagine we'll need to block the top of the windows off with card or something."

"You know what, Miriam? You look done in, and my arms are aching just looking at those windows. It's not as if the lights will be on tonight, so why don't we down tools and go and treat ourselves to a coffee in town? I reckon we deserve it, don't you?"

"Oh, but... Do you really think we should?"

"All work and no play makes Miriam a dull girl, you know. And we wouldn't want that, would we? You want to be nice and cheerful and bright when your husband finishes whatever he's doing in that study of his this evening. I can help you sort some grub when we get back; it's no bother. Let's take these headscarves off and doll ourselves up a bit, and then hit the town."

Ignoring the alarm registering on Miriam's face, Norma practically dragged her back to the manse. Miriam might be content to go out with her face bare, but there was no way Norma would be seen in Pontybrenin with her hair bundled up in a scarf and no make-up. Especially not by Johnny Contadino, whom she'd very much like to get to know better. She'd soon slicked on some lipstick and eye make-up, dabbed on some powder, and brushed her curls back into shape. Pleased to have restored her appearance, she skipped downstairs to find Miriam setting the telephone receiver down in its cradle in the hall.

"I've arranged for us to meet my sister Maggie at the café," Miriam said, looking pleased with herself. "It will give you a chance to get to know her, and she can tell you about the antenatal clinic and the maternity home."

"Gawd! A maternity home. You must think I'm made of money. I don't need no clinic, neither. I'm as fit as a butcher's dog. Come on, now – shake a leg. There's a piping hot cup of coffee with my name on it, and I ain't planning to let it go cold."

They marched briskly into town, the exercise and fresh air lending their cheeks a glow by the time they reached the café. Norma held her handbag across her tummy and walked behind Miriam, who waved towards a sensibly dressed woman already seated at a table near the window. She was unmistakably Miriam's sister: although the older one's hair was cut in a short, bobbed style, it was the same shade of dark brown as Miriam's, and they both had lively, intelligent green eyes.

Norma kept her back to the counter while Miriam introduced her to Maggie, who reached out to shake her hand.

"Pleased to meet you," Norma said, though she wouldn't be pleased at all if Maggie should try to make her shell out on completely unnecessary doctors. She leaned her folded arms on the table in front of her as Johnny approached to take their order, hoping he wouldn't notice her lack of a waistline or her wedding ring.

"*Buongiorno* to my favourite customers," he greeted them, making Norma giggle.

Maggie raised a stern eyebrow, but her eyes held a twinkle. "Now, Johnny. I'm sure you say that to everyone," she admonished him.

His answering grin made Norma's heart skip. He was the handsomest man she'd seen in ages, better looking even than Dickie, whose nose and teeth had been a bit crooked, now she came to think of it. If both men stood together, Dickie couldn't hold a candle to this charming Italian, whose effortless grace was much more attractive than Dickie's pugnacious, stocky arrogance. It would be like comparing a racing greyhound to a bulldog.

"Will you have coffee also, or have you decided to try our delicious ice cream today, Norma?" he asked after Maggie and Miriam had both placed their order.

"I was going to have a coffee, but I could let myself be tempted," she said, allowing her eyelashes to flutter in a way men always seemed to like. The intensity of his gaze suggested Johnny was no exception.

Miriam and Maggie exchanged a glance as he returned to the counter.

"What?" Norma asked.

"Nothing." Miriam examined her fingernails.

Maggie was less reticent. "We're not used to those kinds of London ways, Mrs Finch," she said. "Welsh married women don't flirt with men who aren't their husbands, unless they're careless of their reputation."

It was on the tip of Norma's tongue to protest that she didn't have a husband to worry about, but she could hardly do that. If a family as religious as the Powells found out the truth about her, they'd kick her out on her ear, and then what would she do? She fumed in silence while Miriam explained the circumstances of her arrival in Pontybrenin, making her fainting spell sound much more melodramatic than it had actually been.

"I was just tired and hungry, and came over a bit dizzy," Norma protested. "It weren't half as bad as you'd have people think."

"You were out cold for at least a minute, and your face was as pale as that marble counter," Miriam retorted. "You were lucky we caught you before you hit the ground. Emrys had to carry her inside and lay her down on the sofa, Maggie. Frightened us all half to death, she did."

They were interrupted by Johnny, brandishing his tray with a flourish.

"Coffees for Mrs Powell and Miss Cadwalader. And *gelato* for Norma – with an extra scoop on the house, but don't tell Zio Vittorio," he added with a conspiratorial wink.

"My lips are sealed," Norma promised, gratified when he dropped his gaze to her mouth before tearing himself away to attend to other customers.

"I'd be happy to examine you and check your blood pressure while I'm out on my rounds, Mrs Finch. Did it tend to be on the low side when you attended the maternity clinic in London? That could explain the dizziness."

"I ain't never been to no maternity clinic."

"Oh, dear. We must rectify that, mustn't we? Do you know when your baby is due?"

Maggie had spoken quietly, but Norma blushed fiercely and looked around to check no one had overheard their conversation. Johnny wouldn't look twice at her if he realised that she was in the family way.

"December some time," she muttered. "I ain't exactly sure."

"Hmm. Let's discuss it when I visit."

"We must make sure your baby is healthy," Miriam insisted. "And you, of course," she added as an afterthought.

Norma pursed her lips. Miriam's habit of going on about the baby was annoying. She kept asking when Norma was going to start knitting or sewing a layette, and whether she'd bought any nappies yet, but Norma didn't want to think about any of that. Given the chance, she would much prefer to forget all about her pregnancy and go on as normal. All the fuss about seeing a midwife and checking her blood pressure and not climbing ladders and not picking up anything heavy or stretching to reach things got on her nerves.

Scooping up a hefty dollop of ice cream, she stuffed it into her mouth. Miriam wouldn't expect her to talk with her mouth full. A shiver travelled through her as the ice cream melted over her tongue, deliciously smooth and refreshing. It rivalled anything she'd ever tasted in London, and she was silent until she'd scraped every drop of sweetness from the bowl. By then, Miriam had moved on to telling her sister about their efforts with the blackout blinds.

"I haven't had a minute to think about ours yet," Maggie grumbled. "I attended two births yesterday, and a tricky one the day before. The blackout has been the last thing on our minds, but I suppose we'll have to sort it out soon. The risk of being fined wouldn't worry Venetia, but she always feels she should set a good example."

"Who's Venetia?" Norma asked, curious.

"My landlady."

"Maggie's more like a friend than a tenant," Miriam said proudly. She leaned towards Norma, discreetly lowering her voice. "Venetia – Miss Vaughan-Lloyd – has a lame leg from polio when she was young, and she has spells of being bedridden from time to time. It's Maggie who sees to the day-to-day running of the house, even though she works long hours."

Norma thought quickly. "No wonder you're too busy to make

curtains, Maggie. But as it happens you're in luck. I could make them for you."

"Oh, I couldn't ask you to—"

"I'd be happy to. My rates are very reasonable. Sixpence an hour, and I'm a fast worker."

There was a stunned silence, as if she'd said something shocking. Miriam showed a sudden interest in a speck on the tablecloth. Surely they hadn't expected her to work for nothing?

Perhaps she should have asked Miriam for permission to use her dining room table first, but she'd only just had the idea. There hadn't been time to work out the finer points of her plan before seizing her opportunity. She'd been told to make herself at home, but maybe using her skills to earn a few pennies wasn't included in that. Her spirits sank. If she couldn't sew, how would she make a living?

Miriam cleared her throat. "I suppose you could suggest it to Miss Vaughan-Lloyd, Maggie. It's true that Norma works quickly, and her sewing is very neat. It would save you having to fret about it."

Maggie sent Norma an appraising look, as if weighing up whether she could be relied upon.

Norma shrugged. Her pulse had quickened at this unexpected possibility of earning a little money, but she didn't want to seem pushy.

"It's up to you. I was planning to speak to the draper in the market, and maybe advertise with a card in the post office. I'm sure I'll have plenty of interested customers once word gets around. Not every woman has the time or skills to make curtains, whereas I've served me apprenticeship as a seamstress, so they're a doddle for me. Don't get me wrong, I'd rather be making clothes, but a girl's got to earn an honest bob somehow."

"Alright." Maggie nodded. "I'll note the measurements when I get home, and if you can finish them to a high standard by Wednesday there might even be an extra shilling in it for you."

Norma beamed, promising she'd get it done. She'd head

straight to the draper's for the fabric as soon as she had the measurements. There was no time to waste: the Powells wouldn't approve of her working on Sunday, but she could make a start on Saturday, and still have Monday and Tuesday for sewing. She'd get the task done on time even if she had to work all through Tuesday night to finish off. Perhaps Miriam might even let her make a start straight away, using the leftover cloth she'd intended to use for the chapel, if Norma promised to replace it as soon as she was paid.

By the time her attention returned to the conversation the sisters had moved on to discussing the War Ministry's visit to the mountain. It wasn't a topic Norma found particularly interesting, and her bladder was full, so she squeezed past Miriam and headed towards the ladies' toilet.

She'd kept her handbag in front of her and was glad that Johnny was distracted, carrying bowls of soup. By the time she emerged with her lipstick freshly reapplied and her hair smoothed over, he was behind the counter making coffee.

Steam hissed from the shiny machine as he operated the levers.

"You're ever so clever using that thing. I wouldn't know where to start with all those handles and nozzles and spouts," she said, her tummy hidden behind the marble counter while she leaned her elbow on its cool surface. Men always liked a girl to look as if she was impressed, and it wasn't too much of a stretch: the machine did look complicated.

With a smug grin, he handed the cups to a waitress, who glared at Norma before delivering the coffees to a nearby table.

"It's not so hard when you know how. This machine is like a woman. You have to treat her firmly, but with respect. And you have to listen to her. When she starts to get noisy, it's time to reduce the pressure – or she might explode."

"And can you handle a woman as skilfully as you handle that machine?"

A flush of colour rose under the faint shadow of beard growth on his cheeks. "It's not good for a man to boast. But I have had no complaints."

"I bet you haven't," she said, giggling. It gave her a lift to flirt like this, and to see that frank appreciation in his eyes.

Behind her, Miriam and Maggie were still chatting. Norma propped her right hand under her chin, keeping her left hand out of sight. She made her blue eyes wide, fluttering her lashes the way men always seemed to like.

"When's your next day off, then, Johnny?"

"A day off? What's one of those?" He shrugged expressively. "We only get one day off from this place, Norma. That's Christmas Day."

"Gawd – that don't seem very fair. Not even Sundays?"

"No." He busied himself wiping down the surface of the counter.

"Well, what time d'you finish in the evenings?"

"Around ten or eleven. We open at six in the morning, and we close after the last bus arrives in town."

"Flamin' heck. I was wondering about going to the pictures or dancing or something. Not much chance of that, then."

Regret lent even more charm to his puppy-dog eyes. After glancing around as if to check his uncle and the sullen waitress weren't looking, he leaned across the counter. Their heads were so close, his breath fanned her ear.

"If we have no customers, we can sometimes close a little earlier. Monday is often quiet. Why don't you come in on Monday evening, and then, you and I can... you know. Talk."

She pushed out her lower lip. "Hmm. I'll have to see. I might be busy on Monday."

It wouldn't do to make it seem too easy, even though she'd already decided to come. There wasn't any other fun to be had in Pontybrenin, after all. A late night chatting across the counter with Johnny Contadino might be the best this dump of a town had to offer. He was the nicest-looking young man she'd seen since arriving nearly a week ago. The only nice-looking young man, really, unless she included Aneurin, and with his glasses and shy seriousness he couldn't hold a candle to Johnny's swarthy Mediterranean looks. Aneurin was probably as sober and boring as his miserable old dad. She couldn't imagine him flirting like this.

"If you come, I'll make it worth your while," Johnny said.

"Oh, yeah? How will you do that, then?"

"Coffee on the house. Or more ice cream."

"Your ices and coffee are very nice. But to tell the truth, they weren't what I had in mind."

With an arch look, she spun on her heel and sashayed back to Maggie and Miriam's table.

"You and Johnny seem very friendly, considering you've only just met," Miriam remarked, getting up to let her pass.

"I was just telling him his ice cream was nice. Thought I'd give you two a bit longer to chat on your own. You don't want me forever in your way, do you?"

SIXTEEN

Miriam

Emrys had written a dozen or more letters since his return from the mountain. It had fallen to Miriam to take them to the post box and to replenish their dwindling supply of writing paper, envelopes and postage stamps. He'd written to their Member of Parliament, to the district council, the parish council, and the War Ministry. He'd also written to the *Times*, and the *Western Mail*, to the National Farmers' Union, and of course to the local newspapers and his many contacts among the Welsh-speaking community. So far, the lack of any outrage voiced in the press over the potential impact on his family and parishioners had left him irritable.

For the four nights since returning from Moel Carnau he had barely slept, coming to bed late after spending hours in his study. She'd given up on waiting for him. Even if she could stay awake after all the housework and chapel affairs and helping Norma with the blackout curtains, he wouldn't be in the right frame of mind for talking or lovemaking.

Their only intimate encounter in the past week had been on the night Norma arrived. Passing Emrys's bed, Miriam had been startled when he caught her wrist and pulled her down to kiss him.

He'd shifted in the bed and kissed her stomach through her cotton nightgown, making her gasp when he caressed her hip. She'd been more than willing to be dragged under the sheets with him, as if slipping underwater to be carried away by the tide.

Afterwards, back in her own bed, she'd lain awake listening to his slow breathing. Could the evening's unusual events, when he'd carried the beautiful blonde in his arms like a hero in a romantic novel, have caused his unexpectedly ardent arousal? Staring into the darkness, she'd remembered the heat of his eager hands roving over her flesh, and his groan when he pushed into her. Pressing her thighs together, she pushed the heel of her hand against the bush of hair which was still sticky from the result of his sudden passion. Her eyes fluttered closed as she pressed there, silently replaying the rhythm of him moving and filling her, until a gentle wave of pleasure lapped over her body from the tips of her toes to the top of her head. While her breathing steadied, she asked herself: when he was in her, had his thoughts been on his wife, or on their pretty blonde guest?

It was pointless to dwell on such imaginings, however, and the events which had precipitated his early return from the mountain were enough to distract him from any lustful thoughts. He was fiercely intent on preventing the eviction of his family and their neighbours who formed his congregation in the chapel on Moel Carnau.

In an attempt to cheer him, Miriam had spent hours this evening cooking his favourite mutton *cawl* with dumplings and boiled potatoes, and a treacle tart with custard for pudding; but his interest barely flickered when she set them down on the table. Even as she ladled the richly aromatic stew onto his plate, he still couldn't bring himself to smile.

Aneurin, at least, was trying to be pleasant. He remarked upon the flavour of the *cawl*, then shared an amusing anecdote about one of his colleagues losing his lunchtime sandwich to a stray dog in the park.

"I suppose Saturday evenings in Pontybrenin must seem quite

dull to you, Norma," he remarked as the conversation faltered. "What would you be doing on a Saturday night if you were in London?"

Norma looked up from her plate and blinked, as if he were a stranger she'd never noticed before. "I'd be out, of course. Either at bingo, or dancing, or down the pub."

Emrys's hands stilled.

Norma laughed gaily, a tinkling sound. "Now and again, I used to sing a bit. In pubs, you know. You can't beat a good old ding-dong round the Joanna."

Miriam cringed at the look on Emrys's face. He laid his knife and fork down. A muscle twitched faintly near his eye.

Aneurin frowned, puzzled. "A *ding-dong*... Oh – you mean singing. A singsong around a piano?"

"Course! What else? My Dickie used to say I could make it to the big time one day, you know, up the West End. All I needed was a bit of luck, for one of them talent scouts to be in at the same time as me and offer to put me on the stage. Not much chance of that now, of course." The eager wistfulness in her voice fell flat.

Miriam pondered what she meant. The war, perhaps, which had brought her far from the opportunities she might have found in the city. Or impending motherhood, which would make it impossible to make a career as a singer, working in theatres at night. Perhaps she was just sad at being far away from the man she loved.

"You must miss Dickie," Miriam said, sending a sympathetic smile across the table. "I can't imagine what it must be like, being so far away from your husband. Will he be able to visit you soon? I haven't noticed any letters arriving... But then, I suppose it's only been a week."

Norma's blue eyes had turned surprisingly hard and cold. One eyebrow hitched, and her painted lips twisted before she skewered a piece of meat with her fork.

"Can't say I miss Dickie all that much, actually. He ain't a very nice man, as it turns out. So you'll be glad to know I don't plan on giving him your address. Believe me, you wouldn't want him turning up on your doorstep like a bad penny. Not that that's very likely, what with him being in prison." Anyone might think, from the way she shrugged and continued eating, that consorting with villains was an everyday occurrence.

Emrys had already been staring at her as if he'd allowed a demon into the house. Now, Miriam sensed his simmering temper rising towards the boil.

"Did you not consider informing us of your criminal associations when you first arrived at our door, Mrs Finch? Did it not occur to you that we should have a right to know what kind of person we're harbouring in our home?"

"Emrys..." Miriam laid a hand on his arm.

"The character of this household must be beyond reproach. Aneurin has a responsible position at the bank and as a youth leader in the fellowship, and I have my standing in the community. People look up to us. You should have considered that before accepting our offer of a billet, if your husband is serving a prison sentence."

Norma sat up straighter. Something sharpened in her face. Far from embarrassing her, his reproaches seemed to embolden her.

"Well, excuse me for not realising quite how la-di-da you all are," she said. "Scared I'll show you up, are you? It must really irk you having someone like me in your nice middle-class house. Don't you worry though, Emrys love. I won't go bringing any juicy scandal down on your head. I promise to keep my wicked, common London ways under wraps and not go shouting from the Pontybrenin rooftops about my *criminal associations*. Like I had any choice about those anyway." She tossed her napkin down on the table. "Lovely stew, Miriam, but if it's all the same to you I won't have no pudding. I find I've got no taste for it all of a sudden." She got to her feet.

Aneurin leaped up, reaching to help her with her chair; Emrys rose with obvious reluctance and glowered as she stalked from the room.

"I told you it was a mistake to take her in," Emrys growled, throwing down his own napkin. "Your kindness does you credit, Miriam, but it makes it too easy for people to take advantage of you. Now this is the result. What do you suppose he did, this husband of hers? He could be a thief, for all we know. She could have been planted among the evacuees to find a household to prey upon. She might send for him, and creep down in the night to let him in. He might be violent. As if we didn't already have enough to worry about, with my family threatened with eviction, now we discover this."

Miriam began clearing the table, scraping Norma's leftover stew onto Emrys's plate. Maintaining a merciful silence, Aneurin helped, gathering up the water glasses and pushing the door open for her to pass through to the kitchen with the stacked plates. She hated the strain of discord within the household. Her initial fear, that Emrys might be captivated by the loveliness of the blonde he'd held in his arms on that first night a week ago, now seemed ridiculous. He'd never be charmed by someone like Norma. It was more likely that he would send her back where she'd come from with a couple of pounds to ease his conscience, than that he'd ever desire an intimate knowledge of her.

Yet in spite of the evening's revelations, Miriam didn't want Norma to go back to London. She made life more interesting, for all her surprising – sometimes shocking – city ways. She brought a fresh vitality to the days, which Miriam found she enjoyed. Her bright chatter often made Miriam smile. And she had been helpful, nipping round with the duster and the carpet sweeper, and making the blackout curtains. On Sunday, she'd taken it upon herself to do all the mending in Miriam's sewing basket, while Miriam was in Chapel. She'd never dare tell Emrys that Norma had done such a thing on the Lord's Day, but she had appreciated the gesture.

Then there was the matter of Norma's baby. It was strange that a young woman who seemed to love sewing so much had shown no interest in making anything for her own child. When Miriam had asked if she'd started to prepare the baby's layette, Norma had avoided her eye and said there was plenty of time yet. She never talked about the child, never voiced excitement or affection. She'd never said the baby's father was looking forward to their child's arrival. On the one or two occasions Miriam had glimpsed her touching her stomach as if feeling the baby move, Norma's expression had suggested dread rather than delight. Perhaps she was worried about how she'd provide for it, with her husband locked up in prison.

If Miriam had been going to have a baby, she'd be spending every waking moment dreaming and planning and making things. She'd be one of those pregnant women everyone cooed over, relishing every moment and glowing with the radiant hope of that joyful moment when she could hold her child in her arms. She'd thrill in her body's fruitful power, and praise God every day for this most precious gift. But perhaps the Lord had a different path in mind for her. A different way to become a mother.

As she scrubbed the dishes and set them to drain, Miriam fought to subdue this new idea. Emrys would almost certainly never agree to it, and it was wrong even to consider pinning her own hopes onto another woman's unhappy circumstances. However reluctant she might be to face up to her impending motherhood, surely even a flighty girl like Norma would never be willing to hand over her child to someone else and then walk out of its life... Would she?

SEVENTEEN

Norma

"We'll be needing the table in half an hour, Norma, if you wouldn't mind...?" Miriam's voice trailed upwards and off, as if she'd been asking a question instead of issuing an instruction.

Norma nodded, eyeing how much was left to finish. She hated having to stop sewing halfway along a seam. Luckily, she'd have time to complete the yard or so left of this one and pack up ready to lay the table before dinner was served.

As Maggie and her landlady lived in a four-bedroomed house with a lot of large windows, and they'd wanted their blackout curtains lined with attractive fabric to complement their furnishings, this was a demanding but potentially lucrative job. Curtains were boring to make, though. Seemingly endless straight seams and hems made for a tedious few days at the sewing machine. As she raised the needle for the last time and secured the threads, she rolled her aching shoulders and pushed her hands against each side of her neck, easing out the crick.

She'd finished packing up and was setting out the knives and forks when Emrys entered the room. He faltered at the sight of her, his mouth buttoning up in a hard line.

"Evening, Emrys," she said, enjoying the reaction she could evoke with her deliberately cheery tone. No doubt he'd like her more if she wore drab, plain clothes and spoke in a modest murmur. Perhaps he'd like her to call him Reverend the way his congregation did, instead of speaking to him as if they were on a level.

"Good evening," he replied, taking his usual seat. His dark hair was rumpled and the buttons on his cardigan were done up askew.

"You look like you've been dragged through a hedge backwards. Busy day at your desk, was it?" She cocked her head to one side and eyed his cardigan.

He mumbled something and fumbled with his buttons, scowling. She had the sense that he hated being caught out appearing less than perfect.

Their evening meal of sausages and mash with runner beans from the garden was eaten in silence, the atmosphere soured by Emrys's obvious bad mood. Watching his dour expression, and the way Miriam fussed around serving him, sent a flare of irritation through Norma. Alright, so the man had his responsibilities, and she could understand why he was upset about the army taking over his mother's farm, but did he have to make everybody else tense and miserable, too? Even Aneurin wasn't trying to jolly him along tonight.

"I'll be off out in a bit, once the washing up is done," she announced as she polished off the last mouthful of mashed potato. She couldn't stick another evening of this atmosphere, not when Johnny Contadino had said Monday nights at the café were quiet.

Emrys eyed her balefully, dabbing at his mouth with his napkin. "The doors will be locked at ten o'clock," he said.

Norma couldn't help it: she laughed. It was ridiculous for him to treat a twenty-year-old woman like a child. "I'd better get my glad rags on now, then. There's not a minute to lose."

"Don't you want any rice pudding before you go?" Miriam asked as Norma got up.

"No thanks. Got to watch my figure, ain't I?" With her shoulders pushed back and chin lifted, she exaggerated the wiggle of her hips as she left the room. Let grumpy old Emrys get an eyeful of what Johnny might be getting his hands on later if he played his cards right.

The twilight was deepening by the time Norma reached Contadino's, and Johnny's uncle Vittorio was putting up the blackout against the last window. Conscious of her thickened figure, she checked the drape of her loose coat and held her handbag like a shield as she entered the café.

The air was warm and humid from the steaming coffee machine, and she reached up to pat her hair, worried it might start to frizz. The gleam of the ring on her finger when she moved her left hand still caught her by surprise, and she wiggled it off, tucking it into her purse ready to put it back on later. Johnny wouldn't be interested if he thought she was married.

As if he'd been waiting for her to arrive, Johnny caught her eye at once, beckoning her to the counter with a smile that lit up his face.

"*Buonasera*, Norma," he breathed in that delicious Italian accent that could make a nun swoon. "Coffee tonight, I think, not ice cream, to keep you awake. I hope you will stay for a while, so we can get to know each other?"

"I'm in no rush to go," she replied. Emrys's declaration that the doors to the manse would be locked at ten flitted through her mind, but she dismissed it. She didn't believe for a second that Miriam would permit her to be locked out.

Settling herself at a nearby table where she could watch the comings and goings with her lower half concealed, she sipped her coffee, making it last.

While Johnny attended to the customers, his uncle prepared hot drinks and passed orders through a hatch in the back wall. Every time he carried food or beverages past her table, Johnny sent her a cheeky smile. He wasn't the only one whose gaze was drawn in her direction, and it gave her the old heady feeling to know she was being openly admired. Another man kept sending her glances over the shoulder of his female companion, until curiosity got the better of her and she twisted around to send a resentful glare Norma's way.

Norma ignored her. She wasn't interested in poaching other women's men. What she needed was one who was free to offer her the security she longed for: a nice little house where she could continue her fledgling sewing business and feel like a queen bee. Ideally he'd be handsome, of course, and charming – like Johnny, in fact.

She could think of worse fates than becoming Mrs Contadino. That could be a pretty good life, as long as she didn't have to serve customers in the café and she could follow her own path with her sewing. Maybe one day he'd have his own café and then he could leave it to his staff to run things, so he wouldn't have to work such long hours anymore. She'd set up her sewing enterprise in a flat above the premises until she'd achieved enough success to set up a shop of her own, maybe next door. She'd have customers queuing round the block for a bit of her city-girl style, and maybe she'd even put *London – Paris – Milan* on the sign above the door, because having an Italian surname would make it seem quite convincing that she'd been to such fashionable locations. Johnny would be in awe of her talents and her glamour, and at the end of each working day he'd be so happy to see her that he'd swing her up into his strong arms and kiss her breath away. He'd bring a meal home that had been cooked in the café so she wouldn't need to do more than just warm up their plates, and then they'd wash up together before going into their bedroom, and it would be passionate and glorious and free, not a bit like the kind of drunken fumbling she'd had with Dickie in the alleyway next to the pub, that had been exciting and fun until it hurt and he wouldn't stop. But she wouldn't think about that now. Johnny was different, and Dickie was in the past.

She'd been drifting in her happy dream for a while, her coffee no more than a dark ring staining the bottom of her cup, when

Johnny approached with a fresh cup and bent to whisper in her ear.

"Zio Vittorio has gone out the back for a cigarette. After him, it will be my turn. When he comes back, pretend you're going home, and then nip round the corner. We can talk on our own, yes?" Keeping his back to the other few customers, he indicated which direction she should take, then gave her a wink before whisking her empty cup away. She hid a smile. It was obvious what he wanted: she could read him with her eyes closed.

Dickie had been equally transparent. She'd never been sure if he excited or repelled her. Most of the time she'd felt a mixture of both. She couldn't say she'd missed having a lover. She only missed being able to tell herself – *fool herself?* – that someone loved her. It's what she'd told herself whenever Dickie was rough, when he left bruises or didn't pause to ask if she still wanted it – that he couldn't help himself because his desire for her had overwhelmed him. That his love for her had made him get carried away. She'd almost believed it most times.

The idea of a secret assignation was exciting. What would it be like, being alone with Johnny? He moved so quickly and efficiently around the café. Would he be like that as a lover? Would his kisses taste sweet and warm, like coffee and cake?

Her excitement quickly dimmed when she stepped outside the café. It was so dark, darker than any evening had ever been when she lived in London surrounded by lights and streetlamps. Not even London would be lit up tonight, of course, given the threat of air raids. It took a couple of minutes for her eyes to adjust enough to make her way around the corner of the building into the back lane, groping along the cool windowpanes of the café and then the rough brick walls to keep herself steady.

It'll be alright. There's nothing to be scared of.

Around the corner, the orange glow of a cigarette end lit Johnny's face. She made her way towards him, taking short footsteps, feeling with her toes to make sure she didn't trip.

"Norma? Is that you?" His voice held a smile that made some of the tension in her shoulders seep away.

"Course it's me. Who else do you think would be daft enough to follow you round here?" She sniffed suspiciously, nose in the air. "Pooh! What's that horrible smell?"

"It's the bins. The dustmen aren't due to collect the rubbish until tomorrow morning, so they're full."

This wasn't shaping up to be the romantic moment she'd imagined.

The cigarette glow arced suddenly as Johnny flicked it away, and she heard him puff the smoke from his lungs before he reached for her. The sudden warmth of his hand grasping her wrist almost made her reel back, but she let him pull her close. One arm snaked around her, and she moved her hands to his chest to prevent her stomach from pressing against him. Her pulse quickened as his warm breath met her ear. It was good to be wanted, but her senses were sparking unpleasantly from the combination of horrid smells: not just the rotten odour of the bins, but also cigarette smoke and garlic on his breath as it wafted into her face. It reminded her of someone: a flash of unpleasant memory, nothing more, but enough to set her heart racing for the worst kinds of reasons.

"You're so beautiful, Norma. Don't pull away. I've been wanting to kiss you since I first saw you."

Her nervous giggle was smothered as he bent to kiss her, his wet tongue parting her lips in an eager invasion. It felt all wrong. She froze, letting it happen as if her body was someone else's and she was only observing the way one of his hands moved to squeeze her buttock, the other drawing her in still closer until she was pressed against the length of him. It must have only been seconds, but the time seemed to stretch. It would be alright, though. The urgency of his fumbling and his passionate, if clumsy, kisses, suggested if she just gave him what he wanted it would soon be over and done with. Then she could scurry back to the manse, where she felt out of place but safe.

Amid the fog enveloping her brain came the thread of a potential solution: perhaps if she used her hand on him, it would give him enough pleasure to satisfy him. That had been enough for Dickie, in the early days. She was on the point of reaching for the buttons on his trousers when he lifted his face, pausing as if he was thinking.

Maybe she should have been more encouraging. Perhaps if they tried again, somewhere away from the bins, it might not be so skin-crawlingly awful.

"Perhaps we could go somewhere else?" Her voice came out like a croak.

"No – I don't want to. I..." His right hand moved to trace the roundness of her belly.

Instinctively she stumbled backwards to put some distance between them. "Don't touch me there," she said.

"How did I not see? You are..." He seemed to shudder, and his shoes scraped on the path as he turned away. "You are going to have a baby. You're a bad girl, Norma. If I'd known, I would not have..."

"What do you mean, I'm a bad girl?" Her arms crossed defensively over her stomach.

"You have been with someone else. Lots of other men, perhaps."

"Hang on a minute. Don't you dare. Don't you dare tell me I'm a bad girl for letting a man have what he wants. I ain't done nothing that you wouldn't have been happy to do yourself, if I'd let you." She was shaking, fists curling and uncurling against the bite of his condemnation.

"It's different for men."

"No it ain't. Be honest, you'd have been up there like a rat up a drainpipe if you'd thought you was the first. And it ain't like you was planning to marry me, was it? You was just going to have your fun and hang the consequences. Well I made that mistake before, with *one* feller, I might add, and look where it's got me."

A stream of Italian words accompanied the sound of his

retreating footsteps. The back door of the café opened, spilling light onto the overflowing dustbins.

Norma stamped her foot. "Don't bother seeing me home, then!" she yelled as the door swung closed.

Darkness swallowed her. She dug her nails into her palms and fought to control her breathing. It probably wasn't ten o'clock yet, but it was late, and even if she had a wristwatch, she wouldn't be able to see it clearly enough to tell the time.

Just put one foot in front of the other and you'll get yourself back. They won't have locked you out; it was only that Emrys is full of bluster.

The evening air had turned chilly, and she tugged her coat around her as she walked. Though her eyes pricked, she wouldn't cry. Johnny Contadino didn't deserve her tears. No man did. They were all the same: selfish hypocrites who only wanted one thing. Well, except Emrys Powell perhaps. She couldn't imagine a Bible thumper like the reverend ever trying to get into a girl's knickers. He'd be quick to call her a bad girl, though. Those words had stung. Worse than that. They'd cut deep.

She'd never been a bad girl, not really. But she might as well be, for all the good it had done her to try to be nice and give men what they wanted.

A voice ripped through her thoughts, the memory unbidden but lurking in the back of her mind ever since she'd tasted the garlic and smoke on Johnny's breath. *Be a good girl for Uncle Des, now, and do what I say. Good girls do as they're told.* It stole her breath and left her gasping, her hand clutching her throat in the darkness. The muscles tensed in her limbs, as if her legs were about to break into a run, but under this star-studded night with only a sliver of moon, she could barely see where she was going.

She quickened her pace, holding in a whimper. Screwing up her eyes to make out the outline of the road, she held her panic in, and locked the memory of that voice away in the past, back where it belonged.

EIGHTEEN

Norma

Nothing looked the same without streetlights, even after Norma's eyes had adjusted. The balls of her feet stung: she shouldn't have worn her nice heels tonight. It wasn't as if Johnny Contadino's interest in her had depended on her choice of footwear. When a group of drunks tumbled out of the Bridge Inn, she thought for a nasty moment they might follow her, but the darkness turned out to be her friend, enabling her to tiptoe away unseen.

Now, though, with the hulking shape of the chapel up ahead, the night didn't feel so friendly. The idea of having to walk past the graveyard in the dark made the hairs lift on the back of her neck in a way they never would by daylight. She bolted past, arriving breathless at the garden gate. The windows of the manse glared at her, blank and unwelcoming.

It's just the blackout making them look like that. The Powells are all in there. They won't leave me out here all night.

As she headed past the side of the house towards the back door, a cobweb stuck to her face. She squealed, dashing her hands over her cheeks and her hair, checking the spider hadn't landed there.

Shuddering, she made it to the door, almost tripping on the edge of the step.

The door wouldn't open. That couldn't be right. But pressing the handle again still didn't work, even when she tried giving it a shove with her shoulder.

Her heart thumped, and she leaned her forehead against the glass pane. Now what was she going to do? Emrys had locked her out, just as he'd threatened to do.

She rapped gently on the glass. "Miriam?" she called, then called again a little louder, her voice a fearful squeak.

Minutes ticked by with no response. Norma hugged her arms around herself, tucking her hands under her armpits. A dizzy feeling swept over her, bringing her out into a cold sweat. She couldn't spend the whole night in the garden. There wasn't even a shed she could sleep in. But she had nowhere else to go.

A noise in the hedge made her jump. Something was snuffling. "It's just a hedgehog, or a mouse or something," she said aloud, her voice shaky in the darkness. Then she jumped again at a faint sound behind her, just as the door swung inwards.

Aneurin stood in the gloom of the kitchen, a finger held up against his lips as he peered around the edge of the door. She'd never been so pleased to see anyone. She flew up the step, wanting to throw her arms around him, but stopping short. Her limbs trembled with the force of her relief, and her handbag and gas mask dropped to the ground.

"Thank you, thank you," she murmured. Tears welled in her eyes, and she swallowed them back so hard they almost choked her. Unable to shake off the fear she'd felt out in the darkness, her breathing was still rapid and uneven.

"It's alright," he whispered into her panic. "You're safe. I wouldn't have left you out there in the dark."

She realised he'd taken one of her hands and was holding it as gently as if it were a fluttering bird. The thick-lashed green eyes regarding her through the lenses of his spectacles were kind. Undemanding. Still, her lungs couldn't seem to take in any air.

"Squeeze my hand," he said. "Go on, squeeze it hard. That's it. That's what's real. Keep squeezing, and I'll squeeze back. And look around you, now. Tell me what you see."

"What I—?" Still gasping, she screwed up her face, confused. "I see the kitchen."

"What do you see around you in the kitchen, right at this moment?" His voice was calm.

How could he be so calm?

"I see... Oh, this is silly. I see the table."

"Good. And what else?"

"Erm... The stove." Encouraged by his nod, she continued. "And the sink, with the dishcloth hanging on the tap. And the tea towel on the hook." Her gaze snapped back to his as she realised her thoughts had slowed down.

In the pause, the rise and fall of her chest steadied. Though she gripped his fingers a little longer, grateful for the contact, now that she had control of herself, she released the pressure. Blood rushed back into her fingers, making them tingle.

"Better?"

She nodded, hoping she hadn't hurt him by gripping so hard.

Pulling out a chair, he gestured for her to sit.

She sank down, still holding on to his hand, and he sat opposite her without attempting to pull it free.

His touch wasn't like anyone else's that she'd known. As a child, the only times she could recall being touched was when Mum or Gran gave her a slap or a pinch, or a teacher smacked her, or when Uncle Desmond's horrible, calloused fingers intruded where they shouldn't. As an adult, being touched by men like Dickie, she'd found their hands possessive, not gentle. This was so different. She shook her head, bewildered at herself and still shattered by the aftermath of her panic.

Inexplicably, Aneurin seemed content to sit and wait for her to collect her thoughts.

"How did you do that?" she asked. "I mean, how did you know it would help?"

"My mother had asthma. She used to get frightened when she couldn't breathe, and Dad would talk to her just like that. He'd sit her down and stroke her hand and tell her to look right at him, and he'd talk about little things. What the weather was like, or what a bird in the garden was doing, or he'd ask her what she had for breakfast yesterday. And it used to work. Almost every time, anyway."

His eyes were sad.

It was odd to think of Emrys as capable of such patience and kindness. He'd always struck her as hard and cold, like a slab of Welsh slate.

She realised Aneurin had been stroking his thumb in a circle in her palm the whole time he was talking. Round and round, with the back of her hand cradled warmly in his. But she could tell he wasn't doing it because he was after something, the way other men would be if they touched her. He didn't seem to expect anything from her at all. Not saucy banter; not a kiss; not to sit on his lap and give him a cuddle. When she shifted to pull her hand back, he let it go without comment, his expression unchanged.

"You can't have been very old when your mum was ill?" she asked, to refocus her thoughts.

"I was ten when she passed away. Old enough to remember her, for which I'm grateful."

"That's nice. I don't remember much about my mum."

"Were you very young when she passed away?"

It wasn't an unreasonable assumption, she supposed. She kicked off her shoes, glad of the cool tiled floor under her aching feet. Aneurin was being kind, but that didn't mean she could trust him with her secrets. She didn't like people knowing about the years before her gran took her in, and the various foster homes she'd lived in after she and Ronnie were taken away from their mother. If he knew about all that, he'd think even less of her than he probably already did. It seemed safest to make a joke of it, and to dodge the question with a half-truth.

"I started living with my gran when I was eight. I expect your dad lost his sense of humour at a similar age. Serious chap, ain't he?"

"It's true that he takes his responsibilities to his flock and to his family seriously."

"Well, I reckon his boss up there has a wicked sense of humour. He must look down on us humans and have a right old chuckle at our expense."

His silence suggested she'd shocked him. A religious family like his wouldn't be in the habit of making jokes about God.

"You look like you could do with a cup of Ovaltine," he said at last, surprising her.

"Don't go to any more trouble on my account. You have to be up early for work in the morning."

He smiled, already on his way to the larder for the milk and malt powder. "It always helps me sleep better."

"Most people I know use gin for that."

Only the slightest hitch of an eyebrow indicated he'd heard her. While he measured milk into a saucepan and set out two cups and saucers, she delved into her purse and slipped the wedding ring back onto her finger. Could he have noticed that she wasn't wearing it when she came home? It was an uncomfortable thought. What would he think of her? He wasn't to know that she wasn't actually married. Might he have thought she was going out to commit adultery?

She chewed the edge of a ragged cuticle, pondering. Wondering if Emrys had made Ovaltine for his late wife.

"Was she nice, your mum?" she asked, while he stirred the milk with a wooden spoon.

A faraway look crossed his face. "She was quiet. Gentle. Often ill, unfortunately, but she would let me sit on her bed while I read a book or a magazine. She liked to have me there beside her. When she was up to it, she'd read to me, or tell me stories."

It sounded lovely. A shame there hadn't been a happy ending.

"What sort of stories did she tell you?"

"Old ones. Bible stories, of course. And folk tales. *The Mabinogion*."

"The mabby what?"

He grinned. "*The Mabinogion*. It's a collection of ancient Welsh tales. Full of heroism, romance, and magic. You could look for an English version in the library, if you ever get tired of sewing."

He turned off the gas and poured the milk into the cups, then stirred them and handed one to her.

"Tell me about your mother," he said, sitting down. "And your gran."

She sent him a suspicious glance across the top of her cup. Usually when men showed an interest in things that mattered to her, it was an attempt to charm their way into her knickers. It followed on from telling her how pretty she was, or how lovely her singing was, or what a smashing smile or lovely pair of pins she had. But Aneurin seemed genuinely interested. For a daring moment she contemplated telling him about the day the social worker came; about the cockroaches, and the mouldy walls slippery with damp, and how the matron at the kids' home had said Norma was the dirtiest little girl she'd ever clapped eyes on. But the words wouldn't come. She'd never tell anyone about that if she could help it.

"Gran was strict," she said. "No one would ever dare cross her. Your dad's pretty strict, too, ain't he? I didn't think he meant it, about the door. It's not as if I'm a little kid to be told what time I have to be home."

He didn't seem to notice that she'd steered the conversation away from her past.

"My father is a man of his word. He's a good man, Norma. The best kind of man, really. But he's someone who likes the security of rules, whereas it seems to me that you're someone who likes to be free. You're a bird that longs for air, and to soar, not to be caged." He paused. "I guessed you probably wouldn't be back by ten, so after he'd gone to bed I waited in the parlour until I heard you at the door. I expect he knew I would. But we'll pretend I didn't, and in the morning, nothing will be said. You've both made your point, haven't you?" Draining his cup, he got to his feet. "Finished?"

She handed her cup and saucer over and gathered up her gas mask, shoes and handbag. Her limbs felt heavy. Perhaps Ovaltine wasn't such a bad way to make her sleepy, after all.

While he rinsed the cups, she chewed the inside of her lip. She wasn't used to having a conversation with a handsome, single man that wasn't loaded with double meanings. And he *was* handsome, she realised. She hadn't noticed before because he wasn't showy or flirtatious. He didn't brag and throw his weight around to impress her. He treated her like a person, instead of like a prize he wanted to win.

"I'll go up to bed," she said. "Thanks for waiting up to let me in. It was nice of you. Thoughtful, like."

"You're welcome." He had the sweetest, softest smile. It unlocked something inside her. It made her want to step right up to him, into his arms, and lay her head against his chest.

"Night, then," she said, turning for the door.

"*Nos da*, Norma."

It seemed to her a funny thing to say: North Star? Was that the one sailors used to guide them? But it didn't matter. She nodded, grateful for his kindness. As she crept upstairs to her room, she felt she had made a friend.

NINETEEN

Miriam

Miriam knew what she would find even before she reached the bathroom. She'd been hungry all the previous day, craving toast with generous spoonfuls of jam or honey, and biscuits with her tea. She'd gone to bed early, fighting off a headache. Her insides felt squishy and muddled, as if someone had put them through a mincer, and she'd woken as exhausted as when she went to bed, curled up and pressing her fists to her stomach against the pain.

Sure enough, there on the sheet of toilet paper was the scarlet smear she dreaded each month. Within an hour or two she knew it would be a flood. This was the mark of her body's failure; of her uselessness. Her body emptying itself, not just of blood, but of the life she'd prayed for. The death of her imagined baby, along with her faith that God would one day condescend to allow her to hold her own child in her arms.

Back in bed, she pulled the sheet around her ears. She should have gone downstairs to make a soothing warm drink and to prepare a hot water bottle, but she couldn't face the possibility of bumping into Norma or Emrys. Sobs racked her, muffled as she pressed her face against her pillow. Curled up with her limbs in a tight fold, a low, keening sound escaped her. It shocked her, how much she sounded like an animal. Pressing the back of one hand to her mouth to quieten the noise, she wept, hardly able to see for tears at the agony of it all.

Why was life so cruel? Miriam and Emrys could offer all the love, security, and solid moral character that any child could need. She'd prayed for a baby for so long. Years, now. When would her prayers be answered? Why should someone like Norma be blessed, when she was so lacking in any enthusiasm for motherhood; when she didn't even have a home of her own in which to bring up a child; and when her baby's father was a common criminal best left to rot in jail?

As if her unkind thought had conjured her, Norma's voice called Miriam's name. The doorknob moved and the bedroom door swung open.

Miriam cried out for shame at being caught weeping in bed. Swiping her hands over her wet cheeks, she swung her legs out from under the blanket and sat up with her back to the door, arms hugging her aching stomach.

"Are you alright?" Norma asked, sounding uncertain. Then: "Oh. Sorry, it looks as if that was a stupid question. You're obviously not. Is there something I can do?"

Miriam shook her head and tried to inject warmth into her hoarse voice. "I'm fine, thank you. I'll come down in a moment and make breakfast. Just give me... Give me five minutes."

Footsteps padded across the room, then the bed dipped as Norma perched beside her. "I brought you a cuppa. Thought it was unusual that you hadn't come down yet. I wondered if you might be a bit under the weather." She held out the cup and saucer.

Norma had made the tea stronger than Miriam liked it, but fresh tears blurred her eyes as she accepted it, her throat too full for speech. No one ever brought her tea in bed.

She took a sip and nodded, blinking. It burned as it went down, making her tongue sore, but it was good.

"Better?" Norma asked, hopefully.

Miriam risked a glance at her through swollen eyes, then quickly stared into her tea. A pregnant stomach was the last thing she wanted to see.

"Alright now?" the girl prompted, as if Miriam hadn't heard her the first time.

What answer could she give? Manners dictated that her answer should be yes, but it wouldn't be true. Only one thing could make her feel better, and it would be another long month before she'd know if it were possible. Any chance of things ever being alright felt more remote than ever. Her shoulders slumped and she gave a slight nod, hoping it would be enough to satisfy.

"Can I ask what's wrong? I mean, you don't have to tell me, obviously. I just thought, if you'd like to, I don't mind listening. Or... Maybe I could give your sister a tinkle on the blower, if you'd rather talk to her instead?"

"No, no. Don't telephone Maggie; she knows all about it anyway, and there's nothing she can do. Nothing anyone can do." She blew her nose, then sucked in a deep, ragged breath. "It's just one of those things. Just... life, I suppose."

"Shitty sometimes, ain't it?"

Caught by surprise, Miriam spluttered over her mouthful of tea. She wasn't used to women using profane language.

"I might not have expressed it quite like that," she replied, dabbing her lips dry. "But yes. Sometimes it can be." She sat up a little straighter. "Thank you, Norma. It was kind of you to look for me, and to bring me tea."

Norma regarded her steadily. Her lashes were already coated with mascara, even though she couldn't have been up long this morning. Even without her youthful fertility, the girl already had every physical advantage: a glowing complexion, glossy hair, violet eyes, and a prettily tilted nose. Why did she feel the need to gild the lily by adding cosmetics, even when she was at home?

"There's no need to thank me, Miriam. You've been good to

me, ain't you? You and Aneurin. I s'pose you know he let me in the other night when your Emrys locked me out."

Stated so baldly, the words made Miriam wince. Heat rose in her cheeks. "I'm sure he wouldn't have left you out all night. The door is *always* locked at ten – it wasn't anything personal against you. He did tell you, and after that he couldn't be expected to go back on his word."

"I ain't going to argue with you about that. You've got to side with him, seeing as he's your husband. You've been nice to me, though, ever since I arrived. It's no trouble for me to try to pay you back with a little bit of kindness, considering."

Norma put her palms on her thighs as if preparing to stand, but then gave an involuntary jerk and laid a hand on her swollen tummy. A strange expression crossed her face. It wasn't the kind of dreamy look Miriam might have expected from a woman who had just felt her baby move. If anything, she looked troubled. Fearful, even.

"Is it the baby?" Miriam asked, hoping the words sounded pleasantly casual, not laced with bitter envy.

"Yeah. It catches me by surprise now and then. Most of the time I can forget about it. But then it'll give me a nudge and it makes me feel a bit..." She grimaced. "Well, a bit peculiar, to tell the truth."

"I would love that feeling, if it were me," Miriam whispered. She knew her agony of longing must be etched in every line and pore of her face, but she couldn't hide it.

"Oh Gawd, really?" The blue eyes widened, making Norma's mascaraed lashes look spidery against her eyelids. "Is that why you're crying? Because you want a baby?"

Miriam couldn't speak. Her hands twisted in her lap. At last she nodded. There was no point trying to deny it when she'd made it so obvious.

Norma puffed out her painted lips and let out her breath in a rush. "Blimey."

"I'm sorry. I didn't mean to make you feel awkward."

"You didn't. But it's a bit ironic, really, ain't it? 'Cause I'd swap with you quick as *that*." She snapped her fingers.

For a split second, a dizzying, mad sense of hope sparked in Miriam's breast, almost enough to make her forget how her head and stomach were aching. Perhaps they *could* swap. Perhaps Norma coming here with an unwanted baby was God's answer to Miriam's prayers.

"D'you know what I reckon?" Norma said, her voice suddenly sharp and loud in the otherwise silent house. "I reckon that God of yours must have a warped sense of humour. I mean, how else do you explain that he's made me a mother and not you, when I won't have the foggiest clue what I'm doing and you'd be a natural at it? If you ask me, he must be having a right old belly laugh at us, when he ain't shaking his head at the state of the world with all the madness and people killing each other. Either he's entertaining himself at our expense or he just don't give a damn. It's got to be one or the other, don't you think?"

"You mustn't say things like that." Shocked, Miriam laid a restraining hand on Norma's sleeve, but the younger woman shook it off and got to her feet.

Norma snatched the empty cup from the nightstand before striding around the bed to the door. "I'll put the kettle on again," she muttered on her way out.

Under her breath, Miriam groaned. The pain in her stomach made her hunch over and direct her thoughts inward, instead of on the evacuee's flippant blasphemies, which had set her teeth on edge. She'd have to say some extra prayers for her later.

The tumultuous force of her sorrow had ebbed, like a storm passing over. But it would return. For all she knew, it would return every month for years to come, each time breaking her heart into more and more pieces.

TWENTY

Norma

Norma had been so busy sewing, she'd seen little of Emrys over the past fortnight, for which she was grateful as she still hadn't forgiven him for locking her out. She was sick of working with boring black fabric now, but the chance to earn a few shillings had been welcome. Miriam's sister Maggie had been so pleased with the speed and accuracy with which Norma had completed her commission, she'd recommended her work to some of her pregnant ladies, who were too busy with older children or too worn out to spend hours making curtains. Most people, though, had now completed their blackout arrangements for fear of falling foul of the air raid warden. To have any chance of being independent again, Norma needed another job, and the best chances of finding one would be in the centre of town.

Before setting out, she dressed carefully in her smartest navy blue two-piece with a jaunty little hat she'd re-trimmed with a new band and feather. She'd altered the blouse by adding a fresh white collar and a scarlet ribbon tie, and replaced the plain buttons on the front with red ones. It was surprising how much difference such small changes could make, and even though she missed her hour-glass figure, wearing patriotic red, white and blue made Norma feel cheerful as she strolled towards the high street, nodding at anyone she passed.

She turned her nose up in the air as she passed Contadino's, not wanting to be reminded of that embarrassing encounter in the back lane with Johnny. Even thinking about it made her skin feel as if bugs were crawling over her.

First, she popped into the market to leave her details at the draper's stall and the secondhand clothes stall. Both stallholders noted her name and the telephone number of the manse, but with such little enthusiasm that she wasn't convinced either of them would help her.

"I'll call in regularly and see if anyone needs any alterations or repairs," she said, making a purchase at each stall to encourage them to view her efforts kindly. "You can see the quality of my work from what I've done with this outfit. And I've had six years working for one of the best tailors in Stepney, so your customers can rest assured I know what I'm doing."

The dress shop in Pontybrenin seemed as good a place as any to try next. The outfits on the mannequins visible in the gaps between the tape on the window of Evelina's Modes hadn't changed in the previous fortnight. One wore a plain tweed two-piece, while the other wore a crepe dress in dark brown. Hardly inspiring compared with the shop fronts she'd seen in London.

A bell tinkled as she entered the shop. The sound seemed to startle the petite, ample-bosomed proprietor, making her wobble alarmingly at the top of the wooden stepladder she was using to reach a stack of boxes at the top of high shelves.

"I'll be with you in just a tick, dear," the woman said breathlessly over her shoulder, her arms full of cardboard boxes. One small foot felt in midair for the next step.

"Here, let me help you with those." Norma rushed to her side and reached out to take the boxes so that the woman could avoid any mishaps as she climbed down.

"Oh, that is good of you," the woman said as Norma carried the boxes over to the counter. "I'm Evelina Proudfoot."

"Norma Finch." Giving her assumed name still felt uncomfortable, but she'd have to learn to brazen it out.

As they shook hands, Miss Proudfoot's lively brown eyes slid over Norma's outfit, lingering for a moment on her stomach before returning to meet her gaze. Norma had a feeling she was the sort of woman who missed nothing.

"What can I do for you, dear?" Miss Proudfoot asked, patting her greying hair back into the control of its rigid set.

"Actually, I was hoping I can do something for you."

"Really? Well, you already did, didn't you? I could easily have taken a tumble carrying this lot, and you arrived just in time to save the day."

"I was glad to help. I don't like to see anybody struggle."

"Quite right. But that wasn't why you came in."

Norma offered her brightest smile. "Am I right in thinking this is the only boutique for ladies in Pontybrenin?"

A quirk of Miss Proudfoot's delicately pencilled eyebrow suggested she was amused by the question. "I suppose you could call it that. There's a secondhand clothes stall in the market. But Evelina's is the only shop selling new frocks."

"I thought so. I'm an experienced seamstress newly arrived in Pontybrenin, and I'm looking for work. I was wondering if you might have any jobs going. I can do alterations and repairs, but I can make garments from scratch, too. Bespoke, like. And I love fashion. So..." Her voice trailed off as the sympathetic look in Miss Proudfoot's eyes caught her off guard. She'd been anticipating resistance, not this pitying kindness that made it harder to shrug off her disappointment than an outright refusal.

"Why don't we have a chat about your idea over a nice cup of tea? I haven't had one since eight o'clock and I'm parched. D'you take milk and sugar? I'm sure I've got a packet of digestives here somewhere, too. Keep an eye on the counter for two ticks while I put the kettle on." Miss Proudfoot bustled to the back of the shop, wide hips swaying, and squeezed behind a curtain that obscured another stack of boxes.

While she waited, Norma gazed about her. Even though it was old-fashioned, the shop had a welcoming, cosy feel. Every inch of wall space was packed with items. Rails in the centre displayed frocks on wooden hangers. On shelves, hats balanced on their stands beside co-ordinating shoes and handbags. Labels on drawers with polished brass handles revealed that they contained belts, knitwear, hosiery, lingerie and nightwear. In one corner, where a narrow staircase climbed out of sight, a sign boasting *Furs, Corsetry and Fitting Room* pointed upwards.

She caressed the garments on the nearest rail, unable to resist the urge to check their quality with her fingers. It was decent stuff. Ready to wear, but not the cheapest sort. These items would be for the middling folk of Pontybrenin, Norma guessed. The poorest women like the miners' wives and factory workers would probably make their own clothes or buy secondhand from the market. The richest would either use mail order or go out of town and buy from a department store.

"I remember stocking a two-piece costume very similar to yours a couple of years ago," Miss Proudfoot said as she emerged from the rear of the shop with a tray. "The fabric had that same polka dot print, but the collar and buttons were different."

"Maybe it's the same one," Norma replied, accepting a china cup and saucer festooned with designs of roses. "I bought this one in the market and altered it."

"Ah, I did wonder. You made a good job of it. Take a biscuit. Two, if you like."

Norma permitted herself a glow of pride. "Thanks. I'm pleased you like my sewing. Back in London I worked for a tailor for six years, and since I got to Pontybrenin a few weeks ago, I've been making blackout curtains. But fashion's where my heart is, so I want to make clothes again. And I thought, if your customers ever order something special, or if they need alterations done... Maybe I could help?"

"My dear, I'm afraid I don't offer that kind of service. Most of my clientele would probably take up hems or adjust seams themselves, if they need it done. And if they want something special made up, they'll go on the train to one of the bigger towns."

Norma's face fell. She laid the biscuit in her saucer, half eaten. But something in her couldn't leave it at that. Hadn't she always had to struggle to get what she needed?

"How about a trial period? You could put a notice in the window offering one alteration with any item over, say, fifteen shillings? I'll do it for free for the first two weeks, and you can see if people like it."

"Mrs Finch, your enthusiasm is admirable, but it wouldn't be reasonable for you to work for nothing. What would you expect in return?"

"Only the chance to give them a proper fitting, upstairs in your fitting room. If they're particular enough to want a hem shortened, it'd give me a chance to offer things like shortening the sleeves or taking in the waist for a fee. And maybe you could let me put up a sign in the fitting room, offering other alterations and mending and that. It might encourage your customers to buy even if the garment isn't a perfect fit, if they know they can easily get it altered." The ideas rolled off her tongue before she had time to think.

"I'm not sure... I have to say, you don't look as if you'll be able to work for very long. What happens in a few months' time when your child is born and you're too busy caring for it to sew for my customers? I wouldn't want them to get used to having that kind of service, only to disappoint them."

Yet again, the baby was going to ruin everything she tried to work towards.

"Why don't we give it a try and see what happens, before we start worrying about that?" Although she tried to sound positive, she couldn't keep the desperation out of her voice.

Miss Proudfoot shook her head. "It's an interesting proposition, but I'm afraid I can't imagine it working. Still, tell me where you're staying, Mrs Finch, in case anyone does ask for alterations."

"I'm billeted with Reverend and Mrs Powell in the manse on Ebenezer Street." Norma allowed her shoulders to slump, then squared them again. There would be some other way. She'd find it. "Well, then. I won't keep you any longer. Thank you for your time, and for the cup of tea, Miss Proudfoot. It was a pleasure to meet you." Wearing her smile like a mask to disguise her disappointment, she reached out to shake Miss Proudfoot's hand.

"I hope our paths will cross again, young woman."

But as she left the shop, Norma felt depressingly sure they wouldn't. Perhaps coming to such a small, out-of-the-way town had been a mistake.

TWENTY-ONE

Norma

Three weeks into her stay, Norma was growing accustomed to the Powell family's routine. Each weekday, Aneurin left for his job at the bank before Norma got up, then worked in the garden after arriving home in the evenings, building an Anderson shelter in case of air raids. On Friday evenings, he went out to youth club, but was home by nine. His entire social life seemed to revolve around the chapel just along the road, where Emrys was the minister. Despite everything Norma had heard about preachers' children being the wildest, that was far from the case here. Aneurin was level-tempered, kind, and didn't appear to have a rebellious or difficult bone in his body. If anyone was likely to be a firebrand, it was his father.

Emrys spent most of his time either out at meetings, or shut away in his study, or making telephone calls in which he expounded some argument or other in Welsh, incomprehensible to Norma but important to him, judging by the way he'd jab his finger or shake his fist, passion infusing his deep voice. He struck her as an angry man, frustrated by a world in which people rarely lived up to his expectations. Although she couldn't imagine him ever being violent, and indeed he made it clear that he was fervently against the idea of war, she could well imagine him using words to cause wounds. He seemed to possess the knack of making others bend to his will by sheer force of character.

Gentle Miriam was fully occupied with housework and pastoral visits to the wives and mothers of Emrys's flock, most of whom lived in the neighbouring streets on the northern side of Pontybrenin. Now and then she met up with her sisters, or visited other members of her large family, but she didn't see them as often as Norma might have expected. Her busy life didn't leave much time for social calls. Luckily, she didn't seem to mind Norma using the dining room for her sewing. Her current lack of employment at least meant she had time to make things for herself.

On Sundays, the family's routine varied according to which week it was. Chapel twice, of course, which Norma had stubbornly refused to attend. She wasn't interested in all that God-bothering. The Almighty had never featured in her childhood, except as a harsh judge who spied on everyone and found them lacking, if the manipulative, dire warnings of the adults working at the children's home were to be believed. She'd had her fill of people looking down on her – the last thing she needed was more judgement and condemnation.

Norma didn't suppose God would care for the presence in his house of an unmarried pregnant girl who liked a bit of make-up and a gin now and then, and who had lied her way out of London. If she got to know the respectable ladies at the chapel, she'd have to maintain the pretence of being married. While she didn't regret the actions she'd taken in order to be evacuated, she didn't want to have to constantly tell lies to satisfy their curiosity and be accepted.

On the first Sunday of each month Emrys preached at the chapel on the mountain, Moel Carnau, where his mother lived on a farm with her other son, Idwal. On the Sundays in between, Emrys and Aneurin liked to walk or cycle up there to visit after the morning service. If the weather was fine, Miriam went too, taking a basket of provisions for her mother-in-law.

"Would you like to come up to the farm with us today?" Miriam asked. "We should make the most of the sunny afternoons before the weather turns cold, and you can see where Emrys and Aneurin were born."

"You don't want me tagging along when you're visiting your in-laws," Norma replied, watching as Miriam packed tinned peaches, a bag of flour and some soap flakes into her basket.

"If I didn't want you to join us, I wouldn't have invited you. Do come; I'd be pleased to have your company. I'm sure Aneurin would enjoy having another young person along, too. We're taking a picnic, and you might like seeing the ponies and the sheep. The fresh air and exercise will do you good. It's important for you to stay strong, for the sake of the baby." Perhaps she caught the glower Norma tried to hide at that last bit of advice, as she quickly added, "And for your own sake, too, of course."

At the sound of a footstep behind her, Norma looked around. Emrys stood in the doorway wearing his Sunday suit, one dark eyebrow raised.

"Leave her be if she doesn't want to come. She'd probably rather spend the Lord's day sewing or drinking coffee in town."

She bit her lip, knowing it infuriated him when she did any sewing on a Sunday. It was tempting to do some, just to annoy him, but she'd spent all of Saturday and almost all of Friday cutting and pinning. A change of scene might do her good. Sunbeams were lighting up a vase of dahlias Miriam had set on the windowsill. It *was* a lovely day, and with October only a week away, it was true that there might not be many more in the coming months. And she'd never been to a farm before. Even though she wasn't sure she'd enjoy the walk uphill, it would be nice to go somewhere different after exhausting Pontybrenin's attractions within the first week of her stay. Better still, it was a chance to annoy Emrys, who she guessed wouldn't want her joining them.

His gaze had already slid past her. "It's half past twelve. Are you ready to go, Miriam? Where's your hat?"

"My hat's on the hall stand. You go on ahead if you like. I'll be along in a minute," Miriam said, tucking a tea towel around the goods in the basket.

"I'll come, an' all," Norma said, noting smugly that he seemed taken aback.

Miriam's answering smile was gratifyingly wide. "Lovely! We'll head off as soon as we've changed our clothes."

Norma soon regretted not taking up Miriam's offer of some sturdier shoes. Her sensible low-heeled lace-ups had been fine for the streets of London and Pontybrenin, but on the rough path leading up the mountain slope she could feel every sharp pebble through the thin soles.

Emrys and Aneurin led the way with the heavy basket and a parcel wrapped in brown paper, chatting in Welsh while the women followed. Emrys was surprisingly strong for a man with a bad leg. He was the only one among them who flouted the government's recommendation to carry a gas mask: when Norma mentioned it to Miriam, her mouth looked pinched and she said that he would obey the law, but where he had a choice he preferred to avoid doing things that were in any way connected to the war.

Norma trudged uphill, uncomfortably aware of her damp armpits. Her cheeks bloomed scarlet and her forehead soon turned shiny with perspiration. She didn't enjoy the sensation of getting breathless, and the breeze up here would surely ruin her carefully curled and pinned hairstyle. Having committed herself to the walk, she had no choice but to get on with it, but now and then she muttered under what little breath she had, wincing at the rough ground and concentrating on trying to avoid the larger stones. With all her attention on her feet, her view fixed on the uneven path and the long grass on either side, it came as a surprise when Aneurin turned back to offer her his arm.

"I'm fine, thanks all the same," she mumbled. He must think her an ugly mess.

When he sent a confused look Miriam's way, she couldn't help feeling bad, but she didn't want to have to accept anyone's help. Let him think her rude, rather than realise how out of sorts she felt in this unfamiliar environment. She kept her head down, nursing all kinds of grumpy thoughts.

At last, the path levelled off ahead. Emrys and Miriam sat down on a tussock beside the track. Miriam pulled a Thermos flask out of Emrys's knapsack and was already pouring tea into a couple of small enamel mugs by the time Norma drew up alongside them, eyes on her feet to avoid tripping or treading in dung.

"Thank Gawd for that," Norma said, wishing she'd brought her handbag with her powder compact. "I was beginning to think we'd never bleedin' stop climbing. You never said it'd be so steep."

"Don't you think it was worth it?" Aneurin asked, half shocked, half amused.

"What, torturing my poor feet and getting in a hot, sweaty mess?" She frowned, her attention focused on the humps of grass as she looked for somewhere to sit that wasn't covered in black pellets of animal poop.

"You look lovely to me," he said in a low voice that only she could hear, laying his sweater on the grass and gesturing for her to sit on it.

His quiet compliment made her toss her curls and look at him properly. Seeing the shy admiration in his gaze gave her a little fizz inside, the one she'd always felt when men looked at her. But when she batted her lashes back at him, he glanced away to reach for a long stalk of grass, his ears turning pink. If he was flirting, he wasn't nearly as practised at it as Dickie or Johnny. Somehow, his bashful sincerity made it much more flattering.

"I'm afraid we'll have to share cups," Miriam said, topping hers up and passing it over to Norma, then pouring another for Aneurin.

"Well, what do you think?" Aneurin asked. He accepted the cup and sipped at his tea, peeping at Norma over the rim.

"Fine, yes," she responded, inspecting the grass in case she put her hands on an ants' nest or something dirty or stingy.

"Not the tea. The view out that way."

She huffed, plopping down onto his sweater and looking around to humour him.

Time slowed, her heart temporarily skittering to a halt as she opened her eyes wide to take it all in. It was extraordinary. Nothing she'd ever seen was so beautiful. Miles and miles of fields spread out below, lining the space between them and the more rugged peaks silhouetted on the distant horizon. Although the grass up here was coarse and pale, lower down in the valley were patches of vivid emerald, edged with darker lines of hedgerows. Here and there were knots of farm buildings, and to the south a larger cluster of houses and factory chimneys that must be Pontybrenin, with the high winding wheel of a coal mine peeping over them beyond. She felt like a giant, or a boy with a train set, gazing down on a world made tiny.

"Well, I never." She blinked, realising the Powells were all looking at her.

A smug smile played at Aneurin's mouth. Miriam looked pleased, as if Norma was a child who had said something clever. Even Emrys wasn't scowling, for once. He nodded, as if acknowledging the effect the landscape was having on her, then pulled a packet of sandwiches from his knapsack. Lowering his chin and closing his eyes before unwrapping them, he murmured a brief prayer of thanksgiving.

"Heavenly Father, we thank you for this place, for its beauty and peacefulness. We thank you for each other and for this food. Bless it, and the hands that prepared it, and all of us as we eat. In Jesus's name. Amen."

Automatically, Norma joined the others in murmuring "Amen". Had Emrys really meant it when he included her in his thanks? He didn't even like her.

Her throat felt full, making it hard to swallow the mouthful of cheese sandwich she'd bitten into. Inexplicably, she found herself having to blink away tears. *Stop taking on so*, she told herself. He was a minister. He'd have included anyone in that prayer who'd happened to be with him. It was his job. He'd probably pray for blessings on Hitler himself if he was sitting with him on this slope looking at that view.

"I wish I was a painter or a photographer," she said once she'd finally managed to swallow her sandwich. "It would be lovely to be able to capture that view and look at it any time I need reminding." She shook her head, unable to express her sense of pure and overwhelming contentment. Her limbs felt pleasantly heavy now that she was sitting down. Her feet and lungs had stopped hurting, and thanks to the tea her mouth no longer felt parched.

Beside her, Aneurin nodded, his green eyes as dreamy as she guessed her own must be as they gazed out at the view.

"Imagine if you could put this feeling in a bottle," Norma went on. "People would queue round the block to buy it, wouldn't they?"

Even Emrys's stern face twitched into a smile at that. "I'm glad you can see how special this place is. Pant Glas, the farm where I grew up, is a couple of miles farther along. The Powell family has farmed this mountain for generations, as their neighbours have done. This place, this earth, is in our blood. It's been beloved for centuries – millennia, even. Our Celtic forebears buried their king up here. There's a stone cairn up on the ridge, which people say marks his grave."

"Which king was that? He picked a corker of a place to end up."

"Legend has it that his name was Gwraldeg. His beautiful daughter, the Princess Morfydd, married a soldier called Teudfal who had travelled all the way from Greece. The ancestral line of the Kings of Brycheiniog descended from their union."

"It's a nice story, but the cairn predates any of those medieval legends," Aneurin pointed out, leaning back on his elbows. "It was more than likely constructed centuries earlier."

"Well, whenever it was, I'm not even going to try to remember any of those names," Norma replied, then flapped and ducked as an insect buzzed loudly next to her ear. "Oh!" she squealed, struggling to rise. "I didn't know there'd be wasps up here."

"It's alright," Aneurin said, offering his hand to help her up. "It's a honeybee, not a wasp. If you keep still, it won't hurt you."

"Looks a lot like a wasp to me. I bleedin' hate wasps. Nasty little sods."

"They're part of God's creation," Emrys said, reverting to the severe, disapproving tone she found so annoying.

"Yeah, well so are tapeworms, but I bet you wouldn't want to find one in your sandwich," she retorted, still reluctant to sit down while there was any chance of being stung.

Emrys looked away.

"Then there's fleas," she pointed out, warming to her subject. "And cockroaches. Or flies. They're all God's creatures, ain't they? Still can't say I'm keen to have one buzzing around right next to me lughole, though. And then there's rats. Bet you won't be inviting any of them to your picnics, will you?"

"She has a point, Dad," Aneurin said, his shoulders shaking with the effort not to laugh. Although he covered his mouth with his hand, it would be impossible for Emrys not to notice his mirth.

She held her breath, anticipating an answering blaze of disapproval.

To her surprise, a twinkle of amusement softened Emrys's face. "The Lord's ways are mysterious," he conceded, smiling along as Aneurin and Miriam chuckled openly, before his features settled back into their usual solemnity.

Norma hitched an eyebrow. *Wonders will never cease. Perhaps old Emrys has a sense of humour after all.* Tucking her dress under her bottom, she sat down again gingerly.

They lapsed into a companionable silence. Miriam had packed a Welsh cake for each of them, and Aneurin beamed when she passed them over.

Norma gazed at hers uncertainly. It looked a bit like a sultana scone that hadn't risen. Taking a cautious bite, she was pleasantly surprised by how buttery and sweet it was.

The scene spread out below them looked so peaceful. The only sound to be heard was the twittering of birds. Once again, she found herself trying to think of a way to capture the essence of it. The colours were vivid, like the embroidery silks in her sewing tin, and the shapes of the fields reminded her of patchwork. She couldn't paint, but she could sew. Perhaps she could create a picture with cloth – little scraps of it, in different colours. Some plain, some printed, with felted wool and embroidery to create texture and detail... She found her brain almost fizzing with the possibilities, the fingers of her right hand curling as she imagined holding her needle and thread.

"It's so beautiful up here," she said, trying to imprint the scene in her memory. "I can see why you'll miss coming up when the army takes it over. It's a real shame."

Emrys gave no reply, and an awkward silence descended. He dusted his palms on his trouser legs and struggled to his feet, taking a moment to steady himself on his good leg. It was only as he lifted his knapsack to continue walking that Norma realised tears were glistening on his cheeks.

TWENTY-TWO

Miriam

Miriam wished she could provoke something other than disappointment in her mother-in-law's eyes, even just once.

"Did you bring baking powder, like I asked you?" The old woman's thin hands, knotted with blue veins, swollen at the knuckles and roughened by a lifetime of hard work, sorted through the items in Miriam's basket. One at a time, she lifted them out and gave them a cursory examination before plonking them down on the scrubbed oilcloth covering the kitchen table. It didn't seem to occur to her to thank Miriam for the provisions.

"I'm sorry, Gwenllian. The grocer had run out this week."

Gwenllian tutted and began stacking the tins and packets on the shelves in the larder. "No doubt you've got plenty at home for yourself," she muttered.

Miriam's jaw clenched. Gwenllian had clearly intended for Miriam to overhear the comment; if she hadn't, she would have spoken in Welsh.

Emrys and Aneurin had lingered outside the whitewashed farmhouse to speak to Idwal. No doubt the three men were sharing news of Emrys's crusade to save the mountain from the military.

Soon, though, they traipsed into the house, wiping their boots on the mat in the hallway.

A heavy black kettle hung on a cast iron arm beside the fireplace. Gwenllian reached to swing it over the fire. Although she batted away Aneurin's peck on her wrinkled cheek, the change in her demeanour was immediate, her dark eyes taking on a glow of pride. Gwenllian's grandson was the light of her life, Emrys had told Miriam before they were married. Perhaps if Miriam had given her mother-in-law more grandchildren, she too might have been rewarded with a share of affection. As it was, she feared she could never live up to the saintly qualities of Sioned, her stepson's late mother.

Miriam's resentment of her husband's first wife only made her feel more inadequate. What kind of woman could be so unchristian as to envy someone who'd spent much of her adult life bedridden, and who hadn't lived to see her only child grow up?

Idwal breezed past them to reach into the larder for butter and a battered tin Miriam knew would contain a fruited tea loaf. As always, except in the harshest depths of winter, his shirt sleeves were rolled up, revealing wiry, sun-tanned arms. Nut-brown eyes shone merrily from his craggy, weather-beaten cheeks.

Norma's eyes were everywhere, taking in the surroundings with a stunned expression, as if she'd suddenly stepped out of a time machine into a bygone age.

"It's a pleasure to meet you, Mrs Finch. I trust you're enjoying your stay in Wales?" Idwal beamed at Norma. While he spoke, he cut slabs of the fruity bara brith with a generosity that made his mother's eyebrows fly up.

"I'll do that, Idwal. You can warm the teapot once the kettle boils," Gwenllian said, nudging him out of the way with her elbow. She spread a scraping of butter onto each slice and cut them in half before doling them out.

Norma sat down on the nearest chair and smoothed her dress over her stomach. "Call me Norma, not Mrs Finch. Wales seems very nice, thanks." She offered Idwal a smile before biting into the cake.

"It's a bit quieter than you're used to, I suppose?"

"Not half. I can't imagine living somewhere like this. Back home, there are people everywhere. Blocks of flats full of families living in each other's pockets. It's never quiet. At night, you can always hear voices, and cars or lorries passing on the street outside. It's never completely dark, neither, with the streetlamps lit. But on our way up here, we didn't see another building within sight of this farm. However do you cope living up here all by yourselves? It would drive me dotty."

Idwal shrugged good-naturedly. "It would drive *me* dotty – *benwan*, we would say – to be somewhere so busy as London. Most of the time I find animals easier to deal with than people. Life here is good, Norma. Our air is healthy; our spring water is pure. We have as much fresh produce as we could ever want. And we have lots of opportunities to be sociable. On Sundays we gather in the chapel, of course, and exchange news. Next Sunday we'll celebrate our Harvest Festival. In the spring we'll have our Eisteddfod, when we come together for poetry and music performances, and our Cymanfa Ganu, when we sing hymns. The children go to school and to Sunday school, so they all know each other. Although you can't see our neighbours from here, there must be forty farms on Moel Carnau, and we know every one of the families living in them. We could call upon any of them if we need help, and they in turn will call upon us. For slaughtering, say, or shearing; or fixing a roof, or the harvest."

Norma looked doubtful. "I can see how that would work for jobs like those, that you can plan in advance, but with no one nearby, and with no phone boxes or electricity up here, what do you do for medicine if one of you is ill? How do you even get letters and the daily papers, without proper roads? It's more like 1839 up here than 1939."

"The postman rides by on a pony, and the doctor will come the same way if we send for him. If we need help, we put out a white sheet, and someone will come. There's a sense of fellowship, you know. A warmth that binds people together who need each other. You might not have seen any of our neighbours, but believe me when I say we are always there for each other. In Welsh, we call it *cymdogaeth*."

Emrys nodded. "There's no English word capable of expressing what *cymdogaeth* means," he said. "You might say neighbourhood, or community. But those words don't explain the bond – the collaborative, spiritual, united relationship between the people and this place. Just as the people of the north pole have many words for snow, so Welsh has many words for what you might think of as community, or society."

Idwal's eyes twinkled. "That's not to say it's easy, mind. We always pull together, but it doesn't mean we always get along."

Emrys's brother could always be relied upon to be friendly, but his mother's coolly appraising stare made Miriam feel obliged to defend Norma.

"We have to remember that life here is very different from what Norma's used to," she said. "You can't blame her for being curious. Even Pontybrenin seems quiet for someone who's only ever known a busy city before."

Norma nodded, colour rising in her cheeks as if she'd realised she might have been tactless. "Well, if anyone can make living in the middle of nowhere sound like it might be nice, it's you, Idwal. And if this fruit cake is anything to go by, you've convinced me that the food is scrummy. I bet you're dreading having to move off your farm when the army takes it over. It's a crying shame."

Gwenllian sniffed. "So you've heard that rumour, then. I can tell you, it won't happen. The army poked around up here in the last war, and nothing came of it. Besides, my Emrys knows a lot of important people. They will make the government see sense. And we have God on our side. He tells us, if we put our trust in Him and do good, so we shall dwell in the land and be fed. Doesn't the Scripture also tell us, if God be for us, who can be against us?"

Idwal murmured "Amen", then carried the butter and bara brith back to the larder.

Emrys's face had taken on a grim, solemn expression, as if he felt the weight of his mother's expectations like a burden. Nothing had happened since the army officer's visit three weeks ago, so there was a chance that Gwenllian would be proved right. Perhaps there was no need for him to campaign so anxiously about the fate of the community on the mountain.

Casting about for a way to change the subject, Miriam's gaze fell on the basket of mending beside Gwenllian's fireside chair. "Norma has a talent for sewing," she said. "Since she arrived, she's been making blackout curtains for us, and for my sister and her friends, and she's clever at making and altering clothes, too. She worked for a tailor in London – didn't you, Norma?"

"It must be nice to be able to sew," Gwenllian replied, with a bitter twist to her mouth. "I can't see well enough to thread a needle these days, even if I could hold it. Not with my hands like this." She held them up, and Norma's forehead creased in a frown.

"My gran's fingers were all knotty with arthur-itis like yours," Norma remarked. "Always complaining about them, she was. And her knees. Never stopped her catching me and tanning my backside if I didn't do as I was told, mind you. And of course it gave her a good excuse to leave off the sewing and get me to do it for her instead, which left her more time to go down the pub or the bingo hall of an evening. There was nothing she liked better than a pint of stout or a drop of gin with her pals."

The girl's pretty blue eyes were wide and apparently guileless, but Miriam had a feeling she must have known exactly how her words would land with Emrys and his mother.

Luckily, Idwal laughed, lightening the disapproving atmosphere.

"Perhaps if I'd been blessed with a granddaughter, she'd offer to help me with my sewing and mending," Gwenllian remarked, her mouth wrinkled up as if she was sucking on a lemon.

Norma sat back. "My rates are very reasonable," she said.

Deliberately, she examined her red-painted fingernails before sending a level look across the table as if to show the old woman she wasn't in the slightest intimidated.

Miriam shifted in her seat, running her tongue around suddenly dry lips. Idwal pushed a cup of tea towards her, and she accepted it gratefully.

"How are the preparations for the harvest festival coming along, Mam-gu?" Aneurin asked his grandmother, his gentle voice relieving the awkward silence. "Which songs will the ladies' choir be singing this year?"

Dear, kind-hearted Aneurin – always the peacemaker. He invariably seemed to know just what to say to mollify his grandmother's abrasive manner. Gwenllian was soon chatting away with him in Welsh.

A passing glance towards Norma nearly made Miriam choke on her tea, as the evacuee sent an unmistakable wink in her direction. Swallowing hard, she hid the urge to grin back, ducking her face behind her cup and saucer.

In all the years she'd been visiting her mother-in-law, she'd never before had an ally.

After a couple of hours at the farm, it was time to make their way back down the mountain ready for Emrys to prepare for his evening sermon. It was obvious to Miriam that Emrys's leg was paining him. His gait was more awkward on the downward slope, exaggerating his limp, and with each step his face set harder. Knowing him, he was endeavouring not to show how much his old wound still hurt. He hated showing any kind of weakness, and particularly this one, which reminded him of how much his life had changed after the brutal carnage at Gallipoli.

The young people kept up a brisk pace, but Miriam slowed her steps and threaded her arm through her husband's elbow. If only he would lean on her, she would gladly help him. Gradually they fell behind Aneurin and Norma.

"I'm not sure I like the idea of them being alone together," Emrys said. "You don't think Aneurin would be... susceptible... do you?"

"They're hardly going to get up to anything walking down the mountain together, with us a few yards behind."

"But he's young, and she's pretty – if you like your women painted and artificial. If there's ever any risk that she could exert that kind of influence over him, she'll have to go."

"Where else would she go? She has no one."

"I neither know nor care. If she sets her cap at my son, or encourages him to have any hopes in that direction, she can find another billet to taint with her rebelliousness and vulgarity. She'll land on her feet; her sort always does."

"She's a married woman, Emrys, and she's expecting. Even if he did like her that way, he wouldn't do anything about it. And I'm sure she wouldn't, either. Neither of them could have any thoughts in that direction."

"I hope you're right. I won't stand for adultery under my roof. Perhaps I should speak to him. Remind him that whosoever looketh on a woman to lust after her hath committed adultery with her already in his heart."

Miriam pushed away the suspicion that insinuated its way into her mind. Was it possible that Emrys had had such thoughts about Norma himself? But no – he'd made it clear she was the last kind of woman he'd find appealing.

A feeling of solidarity with Norma made her want to defend her again. The girl wasn't some brazen hussy intent upon seduction or corruption. She was just a bit more outspoken than they were used to.

"I know you find her a little challenging at times, but in some ways, I can't help admiring her. Norma is such an open book. I've never met anyone else who's so unafraid to be themselves. I envy her that unashamed, bold way she has."

"A little more shame could only improve her, in my view."

Miriam sighed. "She can be a little brash, and she's prone to being tactless, I suppose. But she got on well with Idwal today, didn't she? He could see she meant no harm."

"My brother is one of those people who sees the good in everyone. Our father was the same."

"And Aneurin."

He nodded, then exclaimed in pain as he stumbled on a rut in the rough track.

Miriam supported his arm as he righted himself. It seemed an opportune moment to divert his thoughts. The last thing he'd want would be for her to refer to his physical weakness.

"Let's not rush back down the hill. There's plenty of time yet. We can amble along and enjoy the views." She hoped her smile looked relaxed, so he could join in the pretence without any blow to his pride.

"Hmph. We had better make the most of them while we still can, I suppose. Until the army turns us all off the land."

TWENTY-THREE

Norma

Norma wasn't sorry to leave Pant Glas farm behind and head back towards town. Emrys's brother Idwal was jolly, but his mother was a bit of a sourpuss, constantly making remarks that seemed calculated to make her daughter-in-law feel bad. Miriam didn't deserve to be treated so unkindly. She deserved a medal for putting up with her grumpy husband and the incessant demands of his flock, who were constantly calling at the manse asking for something or other. Miriam seemed to spend her life ferrying pots of tea and plates of biscuits to Emrys's study, visiting sick members of his congregation, and cleaning or arranging flowers in the chapel. She did it all patiently, and without complaint. If the evictions went ahead and her mother-in-law ended up moving in with them, she'd need that patience in bucketloads. Norma had better find a means of supporting herself by then, so she could move out and not be forced to share her accommodation with the old woman.

Lost in her thoughts, she barely noticed when Aneurin asked her what she thought of the farm.

She caught her lip in her teeth, pondering how to answer. Aneurin had been nice to her. She wouldn't want to upset him.

Pant Glas was obviously a place he dearly loved, and somewhere he felt at home. But to her it felt as remote as living on the moon.

"It's a very pretty place," she said, choosing her words more carefully than usual.

"It is," he agreed. "I'm glad you liked it."

"It is a bit bleak, though. Barren, even. I was expecting there to be more trees."

"It isn't barren. Did you see how red the earth is? It's fertile. On the farms on these southern slopes the farmers grow wheat, barley and oats. And it's good pasture for grazing."

She nodded. "Alright. Not barren, then. I still wouldn't want to live there, though. Nice as it is, it wouldn't be my cup of tea. Not even a teeny bit." She hoped he hadn't taken offence.

"No, I don't suppose it would appeal to city folk. It's a good life, but not an easy one."

"Especially if you don't even speak the lingo. What is it you call your gran? Mam-something?"

"*Mam-gu.*"

"Funny word, that. Mam-ghee. Ain't never heard of it before." She squinted up at his face, noticing again how nice it was. "Maybe you could teach me some bits of Welsh? Then I could surprise your dad. Might even put a smile on his face." She nudged his arm and winked to take the sting out of her words, and he sent her a wry smile back.

He shifted Miriam's basket to his other arm. It must have been heavy still, given that the tins and packets had been replaced by a loaf of bread, a wedge of cheese, eggs, and butter from the farm.

"What would you like to be able to say?" he asked.

"How about starting with please and thank you? My gran always said, in this life good manners will carry you further than good looks."

"Wise words indeed. Alright. To say please, you'd say *os gwelwch yn dda*."

Norma's eyes goggled. "You what?"

"*Os gwelwch yn dda*," he repeated.

"Bleedin' heck. I wish I hadn't asked now. What a mouthful – I'll never manage all that."

Their shoulders bumped together companionably as he broke the word up into its syllables and got her to repeat them. At last, she was able to say the whole thing.

"I'll be saying that all the time now," she said, grinning with delight, then put on the sort of posh voice her gran used to put on when the social worker called round. "Could you please pass the salt, *os gwelwch yn dda*. Another biscuit would be delightful, *os gwelwch yn dda*."

"Exactly right. Good girl."

Her steps faltered as a cold shudder passed through her. "Don't call me that," she said, all jollity gone. Folding her arms across her chest, she picked up her pace, sending loose stones skittering across the path.

"What...? A good girl? But why?"

"I don't like it."

She was expecting him to laugh in her face or tell her she was being stupid, but he didn't. His brow furrowed in concern.

"I'm sorry. I didn't realise it would... Might I at least ask why it upsets you?"

She twisted her mouth, then set off again down the slope with him keeping step beside her. To give him a full explanation would be impossible. She didn't have the words to describe those memories of Uncle Desmond saying *Good girls do as they're told*, and anyway she didn't want to open up the box in her mind where she kept them locked away. But she'd have to tell him something, or it would be even more awkward. She tossed her curls and sent a quick glance behind to check that his parents were still too far off to hear their conversation. They must be walking much more slowly, as they were nowhere in sight.

"Look, I ain't a bad girl, as such. But being good don't get me nowhere. I'd rather be bold, or exciting, or clever, or brave, than be good. Goodness ain't for me."

Aneurin was watching her keenly. He had such intelligent, thoughtful eyes under those glasses.

"I believe you *are* good, Norma. You're also all those other things, and more." The words took her by surprise.

"That's very nice of you I'm sure, but I don't see how you can say that."

"It took courage to come here, didn't it? To leave the only place you'd ever known when you didn't know where you'd end up."

"Seems to me that running away don't need much courage."

"Is that what you were doing?"

Oh, but he was too clever by half. His gentleness made a reckless part of her want to tell him everything, but she resisted. Nothing positive could come of him knowing she was the sort of girl who let a rotter like Dickie Tucker have his way with her and land her in trouble.

"What were you running from, Norma?" Persistent as well as clever, it seemed.

"People's judgement," she said bitterly. "And a murderer, of course."

His nostrils flared. "Then you have the kind of courage that doesn't falter in the face of doing the difficult but necessary thing to protect yourself and your child."

She stopped abruptly, staring at him.

He turned back, the late afternoon sun weaving caramel lights in his hair.

"I dunno where you got those specs of yours from, but I wish I had a pair," she said, then smiled as he reached up and removed his glasses.

His eyes widened as he turned his gaze from her to his spectacles. He polished them on his neatly pressed handkerchief before putting them back on and sending her a quizzical look.

"My specs? Why... are you short-sighted, too?"

"No. But I don't see myself the way you do, and you make me wish I did. I figured maybe it's the glasses." She sent him another wink before setting off again.

"I don't need special lenses to see what a remarkable person you are," he replied.

She wasn't used to people saying nice things to her. She certainly wasn't used to praise. His good opinion made her tummy feel funny, like winning a dare or finding a silver sixpence in the street. Excited; joyous. If only more people saw things the way he did, specs or no specs, her life might have been very different.

"I wish everyone saw me like that. I want to be someone, you know. Someone like my old boss, Mrs Goldman. Smart and successful, and employing lots of girls to make lovely things, with a name for quality. I want to be known as the best seamstress in town, and make clothes that make women feel beautiful, the way I feel inside when I wear something lovely, as if I... Well, anyway. Let's just say it changes how people see you if you dress well. If I could be successful like Mrs Goldman, people would look at me and think 'I want to be like her.'"

So I'll never be hungry or dirty again. And no one else will ever look down their nose at me. She kept the last part to herself. She didn't want him knowing about those aspects of her past. It would be a shame to spoil his good opinion of her.

"You'll do it, Norma. You have it in you. The drive. The determination. You've already proved that. And if the clothes you wear are anything to go by, you have the skill. One day you'll be every bit as successful as you hope to be now."

"D'you really believe that?"

"I wouldn't say it if I didn't."

She continued walking, hugging the words to her. Her feet had started hurting again. She'd be glad to get back to the manse and kick off her shoes, flop onto her bed and put her feet up. She glanced up at Aneurin to make a joke of it, but her breath caught in her throat.

From behind them, the low setting sun had thrown his face into shadow, but his hair was lit by a halo of copper and rose. Without thinking, she reached for his arm and stepped closer, pointing at her discovery.

"Look at that!" she exclaimed as he followed her gaze. "I never knew the sky could hold so many colours. But then, until today I don't think I've ever seen so much of it all at once." Her eyes drank it all in: the indigo of the few clouds hovering over the dark silhouette of the sweeping mountain ridge; the shades of pink blurring with scarlet and vermilion, like a sweep of rouge across a peachy young cheek.

Aneurin's face, she realised belatedly, was angled towards hers, gazing in wonder as if she was even more beautiful and awesome than the crimson-daubed heavens. Men had desired her before – she'd seen it written in their eyes. But she'd never seen a man look at her with such exquisite tender joy, as if just being with her in this moment was enough. As if to look at her and drink her in, the way her own eyes had devoured the view, could be enough to satisfy. As if he wanted, not to possess her body, but to feel everything she was feeling, to know her heart and her thoughts.

It stirred something deep and unfamiliar inside her. A yearning that tugged at her, like an insistent buzzing low down within. Instinctively, she stepped closer, and in the same instant he did the same, as if their bodies were magnetised, moving as one. Her lips parted as she took in the longing in his soft, dark eyes.

His hand crept to her cheek. His thumb brushed along her cheekbone, soft and warm as a sigh. Her eyelids fluttered as her gaze fell upon the sensual curve of his lower lip. As his head bent towards hers, desire slammed through her chest. But in the same moment, Miriam's voice called from behind them.

"Aneurin! Come quickly! Your father's hurt his ankle."

Norma almost teetered forwards as his hand dropped.

Aneurin stumbled back with a grimace like pain crossing his gentle face. After a brief squeeze of her shoulder, as if to tell her he'd felt it too, he trotted back along the track the way they'd come.

She stood alone in the middle of the path, almost winded by the force of what she'd so unexpectedly felt. Tipping her chin towards the sky, she gulped in a lungful of the purest air she'd ever breathed, the breeze cooling her cheek where Aneurin's warm palm had cupped it. Her insides knotted in confusion, the deep pooling desire left without an outlet. A soft moan escaped her, carried by the wind towards the clouds.

Not a word had been spoken since she'd pointed out the sunset. Nothing had happened, not really. But she knew that in their shared moment on the mountainside, everything had changed. She'd never see Aneurin as dull and unremarkable again.

TWENTY-FOUR

Norma

Over the couple of days following the visit to Pant Glas farm, Norma had the sense that Aneurin had been avoiding her. They hadn't been alone, and there had been no opportunity to discuss the moment when they'd come so close to kissing.

She supposed it was probably a good thing that they hadn't had a chance to repeat the experience. There couldn't be any future for her with Aneurin. His father would never permit it. Even if the Powells knew she wasn't married, Emrys would still stand in their way, and Aneurin wouldn't want to attach himself to a girl who'd got herself pregnant outside of wedlock. The very idea of it would probably send him running into the arms of the girl at youth club Miriam was always going on to him about.

Knowing that didn't stop her thinking about him. She'd gone from barely being aware of him at all to constantly looking for him and wondering what he was doing. Noticing and liking every little thing about him – the way his smile started as little more than a twitch of soft, full lips, before bursting into bloom like a flower. His habit of polishing his glasses with a handkerchief whenever he was thinking deeply about something. The way he stroked a finger along his top lip when he sat reading in the parlour in the evening. The way he leaped to help her or Miriam without a moment's hesitation. Most of all, the way the atmosphere lightened when he was in the room.

From the window above the kitchen sink, she watched him shovelling earth over the top of the corrugated metal Anderson shelter he'd sunk into a pit in the ground. He'd slogged over it every evening after work, and on weekends, with no help from his father, who didn't appreciate such a visual reminder of the war in their back garden. He looked more like a labourer or tradesman than a bank clerk, with broad shoulders under his grubby shirt, and a light tan on forearms that were surprisingly sinewy after all his hours of physical work. It suited him. Looking at him made her tummy turn over, making her think of their almost-kiss. She shouldn't allow herself to feast her eyes on him like this – not when he believed she was married. Not when she was carrying another man's kid. It would be cruel to them both to get carried away.

After setting the last of the clean dishes on the draining board, Norma ran some cold water into a glass and carried it outside. Aneurin had earned a break, and they couldn't avoid each other indefinitely.

"*Diolch,*" he thanked her shyly, wiping his hands down his muddy trouser legs before accepting the glass. Leaning on his spade, he gulped the water down without pausing, then dragged a forearm across his forehead, leaving behind a muddy smear that made her grin.

Shading her eyes from the low evening sun, she inspected the shelter. The trench in which it stood was deeper than she'd realised. "Blimey, you've been working hard. It must be almost finished now, surely?"

"There's not much left to do on the outside, now that it's pretty much covered in earth and sunk into the ground. But I still need to put duck boards on the floor, and make some seats or bunks. Some sandbags and a door to shield the entrance, too."

"It's a shame you didn't build it a few weeks ago. I could have slept in there when your dad locked me out."

He shook his head wryly at her mischievous wink.

"D'you really think we'll need a shelter, though? The Germans aren't likely to send bombers out this far, are they?"

"I hope not. But the factory is less than a mile away. And there's the coal mine on the other side of town. As much as we'd all like to believe it won't happen, Pontybrenin could be a target. I'd rather regret wasting my time on this than regret having no shelter if the need arises."

She stooped to peer inside the dark, earthy interior. Even in this period of relatively dry weather, it smelled damp and uninviting, like metal and mushrooms. "I hope I never have to go in there. It gives me the willies just thinking about it. I'd rather just take my chances."

"Promise me you will use it, if the time comes. You have to keep yourself safe."

"Pfft. It ain't like anyone would miss me if old Hitler dropped a bomb on me nut, is it?" Although she'd made a joke of it, it was sobering to acknowledge her lack of family and friends. She was still rearranging her features, trying to look cheerful, when he took hold of her shoulders.

"I would miss you," he said, swivelling her gently around to face him.

In the V at his throat where his shirt collar was open, his pulse throbbed. Her gaze skimmed upwards and caught his.

She swallowed, temporarily speechless.

"Mim would miss you, too," he added, dropping his hands and stuffing them into his trouser pockets.

Her shoulders missed the warmth of his hands. Had she imagined an undercurrent of emotion beneath his frown?

He was probably just being polite. Out of habit, she opened her mouth to make light of it, but the concern in his eyes stopped her.

He really meant it.

It warmed her inside to think she might matter to someone, even just a little bit, and to know Aneurin would worry about her being in danger. To her gran, she'd been an obligation, even a nuisance, and her so-called friends at the Goldmans' had dropped her as soon as she was no longer respectable.

She watched him with a lump in her throat as he hefted his spade and carried it to the shed. Only weeks ago, he and Miriam had been strangers. Now, they both seemed to see her as a friend.

The following afternoon, Norma was in the dining room when Aneurin popped his head around the door, looking for something. He paused at the sight of her with a bottle of oil and a narrow pipette in her hands, her sewing machine before her on a sheet of newspaper.

"Sorry to disturb you," he said, frozen in the doorway. "I didn't realise you were still in here. Usually I can hear you humming while you sew."

"No need to apologise. It's your house, after all – you can come in here any time you like," she said. "I'm just servicing my machine."

"Really? *You* are?"

"Course. How else will it keep going?"

Getting back to work, she dripped more oil into the series of lubrication holes along the top of her machine, wiping the black surface over carefully with a rag she kept for the purpose. Next, she dripped a tiny amount into the moving parts on the top, working them up and down to make it spread. Picking up her screwdriver, she unfastened the shiny silver face plate, before brushing out the cavity with a soft paintbrush. Deep in concentration, she didn't realise at first that Aneurin had come to stand beside her. His rapt attention made her falter.

"I'm impressed," he said. "Although you're right to point out that I should have expected it. You have so many skills and talents."

She straightened, wondering if he was being sarcastic, but his praise seemed genuine.

"It ain't that clever, really."

"Perhaps not to you. But I've never seen a woman using a screwdriver or maintaining a machine before. There's no reason why they shouldn't, of course. Mim's sister Maggie worked in a munitions factory during the last war. I daresay she used machinery too."

"It shouldn't really be so surprising. I wouldn't get much work done if I couldn't keep me own machine going. If it ain't cleaned and oiled regularly it'll wear out, and I can't afford to buy another one. Besides, when you think about it, sewing is engineering."

His brows drew together. "I'm not sure I understand..."

"Course it is!" She picked up the tablecloth, which she had folded and hung on the back of a chair to keep clean while she oiled the machine. "Sewing is making something flat and square, like this, fit perfectly against something with curves."

Holding the fabric against her chest to illustrate the point, she quickly folded the shape of a dart at her side bust. When she looked up to see if he'd understood, she realised his cheeks had flushed scarlet. As he raised his eyes from her bosom to meet her gaze, he rubbed his jaw. A flare of mischievous pleasure ignited inside her, and she took a step closer, tilting her head to the side as she lifted the tablecloth up to his shoulder and held it there with one hand. With the other, she smoothed it down over his chest and under his arm.

"Even a man's body is curved, see? So the fabric has to be fitted and shaped. And then you have to allow for movement. We call that ease. The human body isn't still, is it? It needs to be able to bend and turn."

His chest and arm were surprisingly wiry for someone who spent most of his life at a desk. All that digging for the Powell family's vegetable patch and Anderson shelter had paid off. She stroked the cloth over his bicep.

"Muscles have to be able to flex. People talk about garments fitting like a second skin, but cloth can't stretch the way skin does, so it all has to be calculated to make just the right shapes to accommodate the body, in just the right size, constructed in just the right way to make the fabric fit perfectly. Even if you think you're the same size as someone else, everyone's body is unique. The breadth of the shoulders. The circumference of the chest. The waist..." She had allowed her hand to drift down his breast towards his stomach, but the way the rise and fall of his chest quickened and his breath turned shallow told her going further would be madness.

She stilled, her gaze shifting to his mouth, their proximity turning her thoughts to their almost-kiss. Did he, like her, lie awake at night imagining what it would have been like if they hadn't been interrupted? She must have pictured it a dozen times, and each time it was wonderful – sometimes passionate, sometimes tender, caught up in his arms in a moment of desire that would make the rest of the world disappear.

"I'd better let you get on," he mumbled, his voice sounding strangled as he took a hasty step backwards. The moment over, he wrenched the door open to vanish somewhere along the hallway, leaving her alone to fold the tablecloth back up and marvel at how warm the room suddenly felt.

TWENTY-FIVE

Norma

Still without work since her visits to Evelina's Modes and the market had proved fruitless, Norma was mainly filling her time by helping Miriam with housework and by sewing for pleasure. She'd found some scraps of blue, green and brown fabric in Miriam's sewing basket, and had cut them into tiny pieces before arranging and stitching them onto a background of calico, nine inches square. Bit by bit, she was layering them into a picture. In her mind's eye, she could imagine how embroidery in threads of different shades could be used to create texture. If she could just find some more scraps in shades of pink and coral, she might be able to capture the essence of the walk down the mountain: the sunset sky, the sweeping slopes and rolling valley below. Creating the picture was helping her remember those moments when the beauty of the place had been so extreme her soul had felt as light and free as a dandelion seed on the wind.

Already she had ideas for another scene, with the white-painted farmhouse of Pant Glas against a backdrop of golden-green, and tiny frayed patches of ecru and palest grey to represent the sheep grazing the sward. It could be a gift to the Powells to thank them for their hospitality. Even though Norma did her best to help around the house, she sensed that her presence was still a bone of contention between Miriam and her husband. It wouldn't hurt to keep them sweet.

Emrys had been even grumpier than usual after twisting his ankle and jarring his back on their way back down the mountain. Aneurin and Miriam had helped him hobble home to the manse, his face white and drawn. And if his physical pain wasn't enough to frustrate him, today he was in a temper after seeing Miriam writing out the registration form for each member of the household. Norma remained at the kitchen table, sipping her cup of tea, trying to shrink into the background.

Emrys glanced up and scowled at her, then jerked his head to indicate that Miriam should follow as he limped out to the hallway, leaning heavily on his stick. Although Miriam closed the door discreetly, Norma couldn't help overhearing their conversation.

"You're indirectly supporting this war again," Emrys said, his deep voice clipped as if he was having to rein in his bad temper.

"It's the law, Emrys," Miriam replied, not unreasonably. "The enumerator is just doing their job. Making it awkward for them won't stop the war."

"What do you think they'll use all that information for? Why do they need our ages and occupations, do you think?" He ploughed on without waiting for her answer. "It will be so that they can force people into jobs in their war machine. The sort of job your sister did in the munitions factory last time, until the accident that could have killed her. Is that what you want? To be sent to work in a factory for twelve hours a day, making weapons that will be used to murder and maim? For your skin to turn yellow and for your lungs to be filled with poison?"

"I'm sure it won't come to that. Maggie was an unmarried girl who needed a job. I'm a housewife, so fully occupied."

"And what about Aneurin? You've put his name on the form. They're already calling up boys his age. They'll see that he's a twenty-one-year-old bank clerk, and send his conscription letter in the next post." He muttered something, his voice fading. Norma guessed they'd taken the conversation to his study. A door slammed.

Norma shuddered, suddenly cold. It wasn't just the thought of Aneurin being called up, bad though that was, and especially since she'd come to like him so much.

It was the registration form. She'd broken out into a sweat earlier when she spotted it on the kitchen table and Miriam had asked if she had a middle name. There were probably all sorts of awful consequences for giving false information to the government. The gut-clenching, sick feeling was only slightly reduced by recollecting that it was Miriam who had completed the form. Maybe, if Norma's lie should ever be found out, they'd make some allowance for the fact that she hadn't claimed to be Mrs Norma Finch in her own handwriting. But that wouldn't work if the enumerator asked her to confirm her details during their visit, before writing out her new identification card.

Perhaps she should just come clean, admit that she'd lied about her name and being married? Then Aneurin would be free to kiss her if he still wanted to, and she wouldn't have to fear the consequences of her deception catching up with her. But how could she tell the truth, given the way people had viewed her in London? People in Pontybrenin were traditional, devout, and not likely to be forgiving. Miriam, perhaps, might find it in her heart to let it pass and accept an unwed pregnant woman in her home, but Norma was sure Emrys never would. So she was stuck with her lie. And once she was given an identity card later tonight, that lie might even make her a criminal.

Thoughts of prison ambushed her mind. Could she be put away for giving a false name? Abandoning her cup so quickly the last few dregs slopped into her saucer, she dashed to the garden, sucking in air.

She hadn't felt so frightened since the night she'd been locked out. Aneurin's advice that evening came back now. His calm, melodious voice urging: *Look around you, now. Tell me what you see.*

Norma blinked and turned her thoughts outwards. There was the hedge, noisy with chattering birds. The path. The Anderson shelter, heaped with earth. The apple tree, its leaves turning golden. And behind them, the mountain.

Since she'd been up there, it no longer seemed to loom forbiddingly over her. Now, it was a reassuring presence. A guardian. A familiar, even friendly face. The mountain didn't judge her. It wouldn't care what name was written on her identity card, or whether she enjoyed going out on a Saturday night, or whether she was married or not. Its colours might shift with the seasons, or the time of day, or the weather, but it was still essentially the same. Whatever madness infected the world, it would always be there, constant in its solidity. It would still stand when all the fighting was over.

Her breathing slowed. The way forward had become clear. She'd claim a headache – that, at least, wasn't a lie – and take to her bed early. Then, when the enumerator wrote out her identity card, she wouldn't have misled him. If anyone should ever challenge her, she could claim it was all a misunderstanding.

TWENTY-SIX

Norma

Norma was so engrossed in the task of unpicking the delicate side seams of a powder blue silk dress that she barely noticed Aneurin's soft knock on the dining room door. Distracted by the movement as it swung open, she almost dropped her embroidery scissors.

"Hello," she said, eyes widening in surprise. Aneurin hadn't sought her out since she smoothed the tablecloth over his chest.

"I'm sorry – am I disturbing you?" He rubbed his ear, shuffling in the doorway as if he wasn't sure of his welcome.

Her sewing could wait if there was a chance to talk to Aneurin. Something about his polite earnestness made her melt a little inside.

"It's alright," she said. "Come on in."

His shy smile as he closed the door made her heart rate dance.

He crossed the room to pull out a chair. Leaning forward in his seat, his fingers plucking self-consciously at his cuff, he darted a glance at her face before turning his attention back to the fabric spread out on the table in front of her.

"Mim told me Evelina Proudfoot from the dress shop has sent some work your way," he said. "You must be pleased."

She glowed, glad to share her excitement. "Not half. Working on a wedding dress instead of boring old curtains – I'm like a dog with two tails! One of Miss Proudfoot's customers has brought the date of her wedding forward because her feller's joining up. There isn't time to get a new dress from Cardiff, so she's wearing her sister's from last year. Something borrowed and something blue all in one go, ain't it? Luckily, she's a bit slimmer than her sister, so I can adjust the fit without too much bother. Although I have to go carefully, 'cause silk's the very devil to work with. Her mother's got a nice new dress from Evelina's Modes, peach crepe with a pleated skirt and pintucks down the bodice..." She stopped, realising he wasn't likely to be interested in the finer details of Miss Proudfoot's customers' attire. "Anyway, that's by the by. It's nice to see you, but you don't usually come looking for me. I've had the impression you've been avoiding me lately."

He cleared his throat. "I need to talk to someone. And I thought of you."

"Me? Not Miriam, or your father? Or that girl from the church that Miriam's always going on about?"

"Don't you start on about Hilda," he replied, suppressing a groan. "It's bad enough that Mim keeps trying to throw us together."

"Is that what you want to talk about? Hilda?"

"Golly, no. I do like her, but not like that." His cheeks turned pink.

Norma nodded and lined up her sewing tools as if it was vital for them to be in a specific order on the tabletop. Hearing that Aneurin wasn't interested in the girl his family were keen on had given her a kick of pleasure that she probably shouldn't be feeling.

"I actually need to talk to someone about the war."

"I'm not sure I'll be much help, but I'm happy to listen."

He exhaled nervously. "Winston Churchill said on the wireless yesterday that the government is preparing for the war to last at last three years. Which means pretty soon I'll either have to go and fight or register as a conscientious objector. If I fight, I could end up killing people. People I don't personally have any quarrel with. Which isn't exactly an appealing prospect. But if I don't fight, I might face prison. That's what Dad thinks I should do, of course." He rubbed a hand over his jaw. "Either way, I'm a bit stuck, to put it mildly. I have to choose between my duty to God and to my father, or my duty to the struggle against Nazism. My duty to Wales, versus my duty to Britain."

Norma had given up pretending to look at her scissors and threads. Her heart constricted as she watched the emotions crossing Aneurin's serious, gentle face.

He took off his glasses and rubbed his eyes. "I couldn't talk to Hilda about this. She'd just tell me what she thought she *should* tell me. Whereas you'll speak common sense. You're not afraid to say what you really think."

"Gawd knows where you get the idea that there's anything sensible about me. When I speak my mind, more often than not I put my foot in it."

"I would value your opinion. What would you do if you were in my place? I know I can rely on you to be honest."

It was a painfully bitter irony that the first person to see her as someone they could respect didn't realise she'd been lying to him since the first time they met about who she really was. If only she could be as honest as he believed her to be. Living a lie made her feel sick inside, but she couldn't afford for the Powells to find out she wasn't really married. It would be a disaster.

Voicing her real opinion about his situation might stir up a whole lot of trouble. But if she held back and told him what she thought he wanted to hear, that would make her like Hilda.

She sucked in a sharp breath. "Alright, if you're sure you want me to be honest... I think you have a duty to yourself before anything or anyone else. You need to do what *you* think is right, even if that goes against what some old book says, or what your dad thinks. You're the one who'll have to live with the consequences of whatever you do, so you should be the one who gets to choose without him pushing you. But that's easy for me to say, because if I upset him and he kicks me out I can just find another billet, whereas you've got more to lose, ain't you?"

His chin dipped. "You think I'm weak. I can understand why."

"That ain't what I said. It ain't weak to want to make your dad proud of you, and it ain't weak to want to do what's right. All I meant is, there's times when you can't please everyone, no matter what you do. So you might as well please yourself."

There was a pause. She hated seeing him so dejected. A kind heart like his shouldn't have to be torn between such powerful demands. She wasn't sure Emrys deserved the kind of devotion that might send a man to prison, but after growing up without a father, and with a mother who disappeared for days at a time leaving hardly any food in the house, how could she be expected to understand filial loyalty?

"I suppose I'm jealous, in a way," she confessed, her voice snagging.

He looked up, as if she'd surprised him.

"I've never loved anyone so much that I'd live my life to please them. No one ever loved me enough to make me want to." She tried to plaster on her bright, defiant smile, but neither of them was fooled.

His face flooded with a compassion that could easily break her if she wasn't careful. She twisted her hands in her lap, already regretting showing him a glimpse into a part of her past that she never shared.

As if he knew she could go no further along that path, he changed tack. "I know you don't much like my father, but believe me – he's a good man."

"Maybe so. But the trouble with good people is they're always telling others how to live. And sometimes they don't know half as much as they think they do. They think life is simple, and I dare say it is if it don't cost you nothing to be good. When you won't starve if you don't steal. When you won't get hurt if you say no to the fella who's pushing you to do something you know ain't right.

When you won't land up in prison if you won't do what the government says you should."

"What makes you say these things, Norma? What have you been through?"

He reached across the table and threaded his fingers through hers. Their warmth, and the caress in his voice, made her chest feel brim-full with gratitude and hope, along with something much more complicated and more dangerous.

Touching him was madness. It awoke too many feelings and sent her off into silly daydreams that could only lead to hurt. She squeezed his hand reassuringly before pulling hers away. She had better steer their conversation back towards his decision.

"Don't go worrying about me," she said, trying to convince herself as much as him. "I'm made of stern stuff, and you've got enough to think about with your own problems. So... Come on. What's your heart telling you?"

"My heart?" His voice dropped. Low, and deep, it sent a delicious shiver over her skin that intensified at the emotion in his expressive eyes. "Norma, my heart is telling me things I can't say out loud to anyone. Especially not to you, as much as I long to."

The air between them seemed charged, so full of feeling it was hard to breathe. She flinched as Emrys's distinctive limping footsteps tapped along the tiled floor of the hallway and paused at the door.

"Aneurin?"

Aneurin was already out of his seat by the time the door opened, crimson staining his cheekbones as he brushed past his father. "I was just checking on the blackout and asking Norma if she wants some Ovaltine," he said. "Do you want some, Dad?"

Norma had no interest in lingering when she could lie on her bed and ponder what Aneurin had meant. What more might he have said if he'd had the chance? Under the weight of Emrys's critical gaze, she feigned a yawn and stretched out her arms.

"I think I'll turn in," she said, sauntering towards the doorway where Emrys blocked her path. "I've done all I can for today. Don't want my peepers to get all red and sore." Deliberately, she fluttered her eyelashes at him, making him take a startled step backwards.

She couldn't help a wry smile as she climbed the stairs. Men like Emrys, when faced with a pretty woman, were like kids left alone in a room with a chocolate cake: they knew they mustn't touch, but the urge to poke their finger in and taste was hard to resist. Even though she knew it could only reinforce his dislike of her, it was perversely satisfying to see how easily she could disconcert him by holding up a mirror to his own weakness. He deserved a bit of discomfort for making his son feel so guilty about wanting to do the right thing.

TWENTY-SEVEN

Miriam

Miriam wished the weather would break. Thick black clouds loomed over Moel Carnau, making the air oppressive and threatening rain. It seemed everyone was irritable, and none more so than Emrys. Norma's habit of humming or singing while she sat at her sewing machine in the dining room didn't help, reminding him of her presence in the house. It riled him that her songs were secular, sometimes verging on vulgar, and filled with music hall innuendo... And if only the girl wasn't so thoroughly *English*.

Emrys's nerves were frayed to breaking point with waiting for news from the War Ministry about the future of the farms on the mountain. They'd heard nothing over the past few weeks, convincing most of the farmers that it must have been a false alarm. Emrys, though, was less trusting. He was sure trouble was coming, like the thunderstorm currently brewing over their heads.

Aneurin seemed quiet. He'd volunteered to help Miriam expand their small vegetable patch, and spent the short hour of daylight after work each evening in the garden with his shirt sleeves rolled up, digging, planting, and hoeing weeds.

The nights were drawing in, bringing a chill to the evenings and early mornings. Soon, Norma might find it too cold to sew in the dining room after dark. They would all end up gathering in the kitchen or parlour as the two warmest rooms. Miriam hoped being forced to spend more time together wouldn't cause friction between Norma and Emrys.

Emrys's fears about Aneurin being susceptible to Norma's charms had made Miriam keep a lookout for any sign that he might have developed inappropriate feelings. Not a word or gesture had passed between them under her watchful eye, but once or twice she'd spied what might have been a wistful gaze when he thought no one was looking. Provided it remained at that, they'd be safe. With Norma's belly growing larger by the week, it was hard to imagine that any boyish infatuation on Aneurin's part could last. Besides, today's developments meant the boy had more serious things to worry about.

That morning, Miriam had found Emrys standing beside the doormat in the hall, a bundle of letters in his hands. The colour had leached from his face, leaving it parchment white. Harsh lines slanting downwards to the bridge of his nose made him look suddenly much older in the faint light through the glass in the front door.

"Emrys? What is it?" Her stomach clenched.

His grip on the letters was so fierce, she had to tug on them to make him loose them. The first, in an official envelope marked *On His Majesty's Service*, was addressed to Mr A. E. Powell.

"Oh, my."

She bit her lip, clutching the letter, wanting to hide it in her apron pocket. She saw the same thought in her husband's eyes, but shook her head. It wasn't for them to hide it. It was for Aneurin to decide what to do.

With her mouth dry, she carried the letter to the dining room and laid it beside the boy's plate, as carefully as if it might explode.

His knife stilled an inch above his toast for two or three beats before he laid it down. Worry crossed his angular features fleetingly before he picked up the letter and tore it open.

A muscle flickered in his cheek as he scanned the words. At last, he looked up and faced them across the table.

Miriam groped for Emrys's hand.

"I'm expected to report on the twenty-first," Aneurin said.

Emrys's eyes were glowing coals. "What will you do?" he asked. A simple enough question, but it was loaded with expectation.

"I don't know yet."

"Thou shalt not kill, Aneurin. Scripture could not be clearer."

"I know, Dad. You don't have to tell me."

"Don't I? Then why are you unsure how to respond to their demand?"

Aneurin's mouth twisted. "Because it's not so simple. If there were Nazis marching through Pontybrenin today, rounding people up or murdering people we know, could I turn the other cheek? If they came to Pant Glas, could you stand aside? Could you let them take Mam-gu away without fighting back? Would you let them take Miriam?"

"Until that day comes, it isn't your fight."

"I'm not so sure that leaving the people of Poland and Czechoslovakia to their fate is the right thing to do. What happens if Hitler decides he wants more, and turns his ambitions towards his other neighbours? Wouldn't we want other nations to help us if our freedom was threatened? It's easy for those of us who live with the luxury of liberty to look the other way, but that liberty would be lost in a moment if the Nazis invade Britain."

Emrys's back straightened as if he was a young recruit on the parade ground again. "Spoken like a boy who's never spilled his blood on foreign soil in a pointless and protracted war. It isn't the kind of noble struggle you might imagine, Aneurin. It makes desperate beasts of men, then grinds them into nameless, faceless meat, blood and bone. It leaves human beings as nothing more than fertiliser for foreign fields. Believe me, son, evil perpetrated for a just cause is still evil. Killing is a sin, for whatever reason it's done."

Aneurin nodded, then got to his feet, leaving his toast

untouched. "I know, Dad. My fear is that doing nothing might be an even greater sin. But I promise I will pray about it. I have a couple of weeks to decide. Now... I have to go to work." He paused at his father's side on his way out of the room, as if to say more, but Emrys turned his face away.

Their exchange had made Miriam's heart sink.

Aneurin's voice had been gentle, as if he hated to argue; yet it seemed he might not bow to his father's warnings, even though he must have an inkling of the bitter experience from whence they came. That moment of soft-spoken, quiet rebellion was a reminder that he was a man now. She must learn to stop thinking of him as a boy. He was twenty-one, legally of age to do whatever he liked, without his father's permission. He'd been working at the bank for several years already. And his country deemed him plenty old enough to travel overseas and fight in a foreign land, to risk being maimed and traumatised like his father, or worse, to spill his life blood into soil many hundreds of miles from the beloved mountain where he was born.

The door closed softly behind him.

Emrys's head bowed.

"Don't let this come between you and your son, *cariad*," she whispered as he covered his face with his hands.

"What more does England want from us, Miriam? It's already taken my health and my peace by sending me to Gallipoli. It's threatening to take my family's home and heritage. And now... Now it wants to imperil my son, his body and his soul. It's too much."

Wrapping his arms around her, he buried his face in her hair, clasping her so tightly to him that her neck ached.

She fought for words, but none came. In the end, there was nothing she could say. Nothing she could do but hold him.

TWENTY-EIGHT

Norma

Though it felt good to have money in her purse, seeing the young bride's tears of joy when she tried on the dress Norma had altered was even better. It fitted her perfectly, and Norma's changes had made it look fresh, no longer like her sister's hand-me-down. Miss Proudfoot had promised to recommend Norma to any future customers who needed similar alterations.

The coins she'd earned made her purse satisfyingly heavy. Needing more colours for her cloth picture of the mountain, she called in at the market to visit the draper and secondhand stall. Both stallholders recognised her, and she beamed when each man pulled out items he'd set aside to show her. She told both about her work for Miss Proudfoot's young bride, careful to phrase it as a passing remark, rather than a boast. In a small town like this, word might get around quickly, and she wanted to gain a reputation as a skilled seamstress, not as a gossip. While chatting over her purchases, she managed to haggle down the prices with a bit of flattery and a smile. Thanks to her regular visits, she sensed that both men were starting to see her as a loyal customer.

"Remember to pass on my name if anyone needs any sewing

done," she said to each as she left, more hopeful this time that they might do so.

The clock above the town hall showed it was almost time for the bank on the high street to close. She'd taken to lingering until this time whenever she was in town, hoping to "happen" to catch Aneurin as he left work. She'd managed to do so several times in the past fortnight. Walking home together, he always offered to carry her packages, and she enjoyed the time in his company.

Neither of them mentioned the tense atmosphere between Aneurin and his father. Norma sensed he would prefer not to think about it, and that her light-hearted chatter helped steer his thoughts away from the topic of the war and enlistment.

It seemed she'd timed her walk to perfection again. Delaying starting out, she fidgeted with her shoelaces under the porch of the Station Hotel for a couple of minutes, so she could pretend meeting Aneurin was a coincidence. Hidden from view behind one of the pillars of the hotel entrance, she watched as he emerged onto the street. The bank staff took longer over their goodbyes than usual, each one shaking Aneurin's hand. One or two patted his shoulder. This, of course, was his last day at the bank. By next Monday, he'd have either enlisted or registered as a conscientious objector.

While his colleagues walked away, he stood as if oblivious to the rain, then at last shook himself and put up his umbrella. Norma hid a smile at the way he craned his neck to look up and down the road before his shoulders slumped. Could he be disappointed that she wasn't there? It was a delicious thought.

"Nye!" she called out as he turned towards home, delighting to see the way he immediately spun on his heel at the sound of the pet name she'd started using for him on their walks. Had her own face lit up like his? He seemed to grow an inch taller as he spotted her waving. Barely glancing to check for traffic, he loped across the street, feet splashing in the puddles on the road, and joined her under the shelter of the porch.

"Fancy meeting you here again," she said with a pert smile.

"Why, yes. Anyone might think I've had a regular routine that led me to be in this spot at the same time each day. Although... not anymore."

His solemn expression made her arms ache to hug him. But she could hardly embrace him in the street. Instead, she bent to pick up her shopping bag.

He reached for it at the same moment, and their foreheads bashed together painfully, making them both lurch back.

"Ouch!" She rubbed her head wryly, laughing as he also rubbed his.

"Are you alright?" He stepped closer, sweeping a gentle hand across her brow and down to her cheek, holding it there for several heartbeats as he frowned, searching for any sign of injury.

Her eyes widened at the longing awoken by the sensation of his tender fingers on her skin. It made her want to lean into him. To turn her cheek into his palm and kiss it. The dizziness she was feeling had nothing to do with the bump on the head.

"I'm fine. Are you?" she whispered.

Blinking, he seemed to drag himself out of his reverie with an effort. He removed his hand to rub it across his mouth, then cleared his throat.

"Yes, yes. Don't worry about me." The tormented glance he sent towards the sky belied his words.

Perhaps he was thinking about the bank, regretting having to leave.

"Have you made your decision yet, about whether to enlist?" she asked, almost timidly.

His shoulders lifted in a small shrug. "I want Dad to be proud of me. But above all else, I want to do the right thing. In the future, I want to be able to look back and feel that I've played my part in making the world a better place. But I don't relish the thought of getting hurt, and I'd be lying if I said I'm not scared of being killed."

The thought of any harm coming to him made her shudder.

"I'm also afraid of being the sort of man who doesn't have the courage to stand by his beliefs. It would be easier to allow myself to be swept up into the war machine, even if it swallows me whole, than to go against it and risk seeing contempt in people's eyes on the street."

Reaching out, she squeezed his hand. She wanted to say that nothing invited contempt like having a bare ring finger and a pregnant belly, but she couldn't do that without inviting unwelcome questions.

They couldn't stand here all evening, with so much between them that couldn't be spoken aloud.

"Perhaps a night out would cheer you up," she said to lighten the mood, nodding towards a notice announcing a dance scheduled for the weekend. "Hilda would probably be happy to go with you."

"Don't." He flashed a raised eyebrow her way before pulling her shopping bag from her hand and offering his elbow. With his other hand, he held the umbrella over both their heads as they set off along the pavement.

Tucking herself close to his side, she squashed the inner voice that said she was pleased he didn't want to go dancing with Hilda, given how much she wished she could go dancing with him herself. She was enjoying being close to him far more than she should. He was only being gentlemanly in letting her snuggle up to his side. If he suspected his family's "married" evacuee felt anything more than gratitude for the shelter of his umbrella, he'd be mortified.

"I don't know why you're not keen to go out. Personally, I'd love the chance to go dancing again like I used to, but no one wants to see a pregnant woman the size of a barrage balloon doing the foxtrot."

"Hush. You're hardly the size of a barrage balloon."

"I will be before long though, won't I? I feel like a bleedin' elephant already."

Beside her, he snorted with amusement.

"You can laugh, but I do. A great big galumphing elephant. And elephants ain't much cop at dancing."

It made her feel she sparkled, seeing how she could make him laugh in spite of his sadness a few moments ago. Despite an edge of excitement at being with him as they chatted and walked along, in a funny sort of way she still felt at ease. With him, she wasn't an unwelcome outsider or an object of envy or disgust. With him, she could say she felt at home.

"Do you miss your life in London a lot?"

She sighed. "Truth is, I do. More than I ever thought I would."

"What do you miss most?"

"Feeling like I'm part of things. I liked my job, and the people I worked with. Most of all, fun. Going out to the flicks or the pub. Laughing. There ain't much laughter in the manse when you're not there, Nye."

The rain intensified, drumming at a manic rate on the umbrella as they turned off the high street towards their shortcut through the park. The clouds were an ominous black, sending the temperature dropping. Norma shivered. They had just reached the park gates when the rain turned to hail, pinging fiercely onto their feet and coating the path with ice. Norma squealed as a crack of thunder boomed overhead.

"Let's head to the bandstand to wait it out," Aneurin shouted over the hammering of the hail on their umbrella. He guided her safely across the slippery ground as they stumbled, half-running, for the shelter of the wrought iron bandstand.

Aneurin took off his hat, leaving his dark hair endearingly tousled, then removed his rain-spattered glasses and shook himself like a dog, sending water droplets and tiny hailstones flying like a cloud of glitter.

"Are you alright?" he asked. Without his spectacles his eyes looked larger as he peered at her, anxious and intent. "Running might not have been wise, in your condition."

"Pfft. I ain't lost the use of me legs, have I? I can still run a few yards. And I'm not a needle – I won't rust."

The freezing hail and the brief burst of running, together with the crack of lightning that flashed across a sky now dark as twilight, made her buzz with a rush of energy. Heaven was bringing down its might upon them, but far from making her afraid, she felt ablaze with light. Being alive, being with him – alone with him – was enough. She'd never felt so weightless before, not caring what she looked like or what anyone thought of her. Although she must resemble a drowned rat, she could trust him not to look down on her for being a soggy mess.

"How would you say 'it's hailing' in your language?" she asked. It fascinated her, the way he could think and speak in both English and Welsh. She couldn't imagine having such an ability with words.

"*Mae'n bwrw cesair.*"

She grinned. "I like the sound of it – the way you roll it around your mouth like an old man chewing on a Mint Imperial. Tell me something else in Welsh."

Laughing softly under his breath, he dragged a hand over his face as if he was thinking. "*Rwy'n dwlu ar dy wên hardd di*," he said at last.

Something in his expression thrilled her even more than the rich rolling sound of the words.

"What does that mean, then?"

One hand went up, as if to ward her off. Awkwardly, he studied his feet. "Maybe one day you'll work it out for yourself."

"Ooh, that's mean! Well, whatever it is, I can't get over the way you roll your Rs. How on earth do you do it? I can't, however hard I try."

He shook his head as she pursed her lips to copy him.

"That's because you're trying to do it with your lips. You have to use your tongue." He did it again, rolling an elongated rrrrrrrr like a cat's purr. It made her stomach flip.

"It must be quite something to have such a clever tongue," she said, unable to help a mischievous smile lighting her face.

Even in the dim remaining daylight, the ferocity of the blush spreading from his neck to his forehead was apparent. Could he be any sweeter?

Laughing, she reached out beyond the shelter of the bandstand to catch some of the hail. She couldn't resist licking the icy pellets from her palm, tasting their mixture of freshness and soot as they melted instantly on her tongue. The storm was easing now; soon it would stop. On an impulse, she leaned out again to gather a last handful in her chilly palm, then popped a pinch of ice into his mouth.

The contact of his lips against her fingers seemed to give them a will of their own. Instead of dropping them back to her side, she allowed them to splay out across his cheek, the warmth of his skin irresistible. Her thumb rubbed against the prickle of his faint, dark stubble as she registered the hitch of his breathing. Hers matched it, equally irregular. Her pulse thudded.

His eyes widened, the pupils deep and black.

Something hot and insistent uncurled inside her. It took only the slightest movement of her hand into his hair to pull his head down towards her waiting lips.

He was so unlike Dickie. So unlike anyone she'd kissed before. Hesitant. Soft. It was like falling into each other. The exquisite tenderness in the way he hardly moved, just yielding as if he couldn't help himself melting deeper towards her.

Low down in his throat, he made the tiniest of noises. It almost made her knees buckle with desire.

She threaded her other hand into his hair. Nothing mattered outside the moment. He tasted perfect. He kissed her like a man who wanted to give, not to take. She could spend her whole life in his arms and be content.

But without warning he pulled away, his face etched with anguish. The look in his eyes made her breath snag like a fraying thread.

"This is wrong," he said.

The words left her reeling. As she opened her mouth to tell him he needn't worry, the sound of running footsteps approaching along the gravel path slammed her back to reality.

A child burst through the bandstand's open side, panting.

"Sorry," the girl said. "I didn't mean to..." She shrugged shoulders that looked skinny even through her threadbare coat, and backed away, eyes downcast. Her voice had struck a chord: it wasn't the sing-song lilt of one of the local children, but marked her out as a Londoner like herself. Tendrils of hair hung like hanks of wet string about her cheeks.

With her senses still blurry from the kiss, Norma gathered herself.

"It's fine. Don't worry... Are you alright, darlin'? You look soaked through."

The girl nodded, eyes flicking back out towards the wet shrubbery as if she might take to her heels again.

"It's alright." Norma stooped and reached a hand towards her, as if she was a frightened animal. "We ain't cross, are we, Nye?"

Aneurin had been standing with his head bowed and his arms wrapped around himself, looking out at the rain. Now, he rubbed his glasses with his handkerchief and slid them back onto his nose. "No. Not at all." It seemed he had to force the words out.

"I'm Norma, and this is Nye. What's your name, then, eh?" Dropping to a crouch, Norma gazed searchingly into the little girl's grubby, rain-streaked face.

"I'm Audrey." The child frowned, her chattering teeth thick with a layer of yellow plaque. Her clothes were grubby and, Norma noted, ill-fitting. Bony wrists jutted out below the cuffs of her coat, and the hem of her skirt didn't even reach her grazed knees, revealing a pair of scrawny bowed legs with grey socks limp around her ankles. "Are you from London, missus? You got any food in that bag?"

It was as if she'd decided Norma's familiar accent meant she could be trusted. Norma's heart crumpled as she shook her head. If only she'd called in at the grocer's on her way back to the manse.

"Shouldn't you be in your billet, where it's warm and dry?" Aneurin asked gently.

Audrey's eyes widened. "Don't think it's time to go back yet. I have to stay out till teatime."

Norma saw her own shock registered in Aneurin's expression.

"They can't expect you to stay out in weather like this, Audrey darlin'. You'll catch a chill."

Audrey's mouth twisted and she gazed at her feet, shuffling them in her rain-drenched canvas plimsolls. "Don't think they care," she muttered.

The ache in her knees forced Norma to stagger upright. In her anger, she barely noticed Aneurin appearing at her elbow to support her. "They'll bleedin' well have to start caring, 'cause I ain't having that," she declared. "You should be having your tea in front of a nice cosy fire, not hanging round the park in this weather."

"Where's your billet, Audrey?" Aneurin asked.

"On Alexandra Avenue. But I'm telling you, they won't want me turning up at this time. The shops only just shut, and the pubs ain't open yet. I usually wait until then before I start walking back."

"Don't worry, we'll make sure they don't give you no bother." Norma struggled to keep the anger out of her voice. Perhaps they should take the child back to the manse, instead of to her billet? Miriam wouldn't turn her away. But Audrey's hosts needed to be made to face up to their responsibilities. They would be receiving an allowance for her keep – the least they could do was to keep her dry and fed.

She nodded to Aneurin, who picked up her bag once again. Although the hail had stopped, the rain had barely let up, and Norma noticed the anxious way Audrey looked out into the park.

"We'll let you share our brolly. Won't we, Nye?"

Wordlessly, he handed it to her, and she put it up over the child's head, taking hold of her small, sticky hand. Audrey's fingernails were black around the edges, and again Norma had to bite back angry words. The poor kid must have been outside ever since the end of the school day.

"Lead the way, darlin'," she said, forcing a cheerful note into her voice as if the worst thing they were about to face was a bit of damp weather.

TWENTY-NINE

Norma

It wasn't far to Audrey's billet – a large, detached house in Alexandra Avenue, one of the poshest streets in Pontybrenin. Most were like the one Audrey led them to, bay-fronted with a gable decorated with mock-Tudor beams, and stained-glass windows that had probably looked smart lit up in the days before the blackout. These houses had driveways in their long, neatly trimmed and bordered front gardens, and some even had cars parked outside. One house a couple of doors away was in a very different modern style, with sleek white curves and a balcony, more like an ocean liner than any house Norma had seen before. But she paid it no attention. The architecture wasn't what they'd come for.

At Aneurin's side, Norma seethed as the smartly dressed middle-aged woman who answered the door claimed the little girl had got it all wrong.

"Of course she's allowed to come home. What a naughty thing to tell people, Audrey! You'll have people believing all sorts of nonsense."

As Audrey stepped inside and whispered goodbye, her brown eyes round and solemn, Norma knew the woman was lying. Still, hopefully she'd change her ways now that she'd been caught out. People like her cared too much about what others thought to risk any damage to their reputation.

"Do you think Audrey will be alright?" Norma asked as they closed the gate behind them at the end of the driveway. She looked up at the house with a sense of foreboding.

"Mrs Arthur assured us she would. We'll have to take her at her word."

Aneurin was pensive as they trudged along together under his umbrella. The rain had eased, and by the time the chapel and the manse came into view, he'd given the brolly a shake and folded it.

If she didn't say something now, the opportunity would be lost.

"Are *you* alright, Nye? You've hardly said a word since... Since the park."

He squeezed his eyes shut and tilted his face towards the heavens. "How can I possibly be alright when I'm in love with another man's wife?" He sounded as if the words were torn from him. Pulling her under the comparative privacy of a tree, he took hold of both her arms, then promptly let go and clapped a hand over his mouth, as if he didn't dare release the words he longed to say.

"Aneurin. Nye..." She reached for him, longing to reassure him, but he took a step away and held up a hand.

"I wish you were free, Norma. Seeing you is what I look forward to most every day, but it's destroying me. I don't want to be the kind of man who covets his neighbour's wife. But when I see the way you pull yourself up every time life knocks you down and somehow summon the determination not to be cowed, how can I help loving you? I need some of your strength of will to help me resist what every muscle and sinew strains to do – to stop myself taking you in my arms and throwing everything I know to be right and true to the wind. I've never understood passion before – but I see now why people sometimes commit terrible sins for love. For you, I'm frightened I'd do anything – even damn my own soul. But how can I, when I'd damn yours along with it?"

"You won't. I promise you won't." Again, she laid a hand on his coat sleeve, but he pulled away, shaking his head as if to clear his thoughts.

"I can't do this. I won't be that man." Stumbling away, he almost ran up the path to the front door and let himself in, leaving it ajar for her.

Norma stood forlornly on the pavement, fighting the desperate urge to tell him he had nothing to fear for his soul. There was no marriage certificate or commandment to stand between them. But how could she risk telling him the truth? It wasn't just the thought of what Emrys would say. If he found out she'd lied, he'd probably throw her out on the street, and she had nowhere else to go. More than that, she couldn't jeopardise her friendship with Miriam, who had looked after her more than her own family had ever done. For the first time, she had people in her life who seemed to really care about her. Most importantly of all, would Nye still feel all those wonderful, beautiful things about her if he knew what she really was?

Someone passing on a bicycle sent her a curious look. She'd have to go inside, or invite comment from the neighbours. Emrys was precious about his household's reputation – it wouldn't do to be the cause of gossip.

Squaring her shoulders, she assumed her customary breezy mask with an effort and went inside to find Miriam.

THIRTY

Miriam

Miriam brooded as she arranged the dinner plates and tureen in their usual positions on the dresser. Norma had been talkative since yesterday when she and Aneurin arrived home together. Apparently they'd met a young evacuee while crossing the park on their way home and had returned her to her billet close to Maggie's lodgings in Alexandra Avenue. While the child's hosts sounded ungenerous, Miriam had to acknowledge that not everyone would enjoy having a child billeted on them. For all anyone knew, the girl's behaviour might be troublesome. But when she'd tried to point this out in a reasonable sort of way, Norma blew up as if she'd hit a nerve.

"She has to stay out of the house in all weathers, right until the evening. And then, when they finally let her in, they don't let her go upstairs until bedtime, in case she wears out the stair carpet by going up and down too much! It's disgusting, that's what it is. A flippin' disgrace. They shouldn't take a kid in if they ain't prepared to look after it." Slamming the last saucepan down on the draining board, she'd stomped off to her room looking as if she was on the verge of tears.

Miriam sighed and went back to the kitchen, her thoughts turning to Aneurin. He, by contrast, had barely said a word over their evening meal, his appetite unusually slight. No doubt he'd been conscious of his father's watchful gaze, as if Emrys was trying either to read his thoughts or to somehow convince him using telepathy to follow his conscience instead of the government's order to enlist. She knew how heavy the weight of that steady look could be. How it could bear down on the shoulders and the top of the head. Hopefully it had made Aneurin reflect on the right path to take. He wouldn't want to hurt his father, or to go against the Commandments. Even if the cost of doing the Christian thing might be prison.

The boy had still been quiet when he went off to youth club, but Miriam hoped a couple of hours with the children and with Hilda Hughes would brighten his mood.

Without warning, the kitchen door banged open, making her jump and spill tea leaves over the rim of the teapot onto the table. Emrys stood in the doorway, his face like the wrath of God.

"Where is she?" he demanded. "That viper we took to our bosoms. That scheming, adulterous whore."

Miriam felt the colour drain from her face. "What's happened?" she asked, the tea leaves forgotten.

"Go and fetch her. Bring her to the chapel. They need to explain themselves."

He stormed out as abruptly as he had entered, flinging open the front door.

Miriam's fingers trembled as she untied her apron and hung it up. Her knees quaked just as badly while she climbed the stairs, and she took a moment to steady herself before knocking on Norma's bedroom door.

"Come in!"

The younger woman had been lying on the bed with a fashion magazine, but she sat up as Miriam entered the room and sent a charming smile. It quickly faded.

"Is something wrong, Miriam?"

"Something's happened. I don't know what. You'd better put your shoes and coat on, and come with me."

"Where?"

"Over to the chapel."

"But... Won't the youth club be on? Nye went over there earlier, didn't he?"

Miriam put her hands behind her back to stop them twisting. Norma's use of such an informal name for Aneurin couldn't mean anything... Could it?

"Youth club will have finished about ten minutes ago. The children will have gone by the time we arrive. We'd better hurry – Emrys is waiting."

Hilda had just stepped out of the door to the chapel schoolroom when they arrived. Her face downcast, she paused when Miriam greeted her, then drew back as Norma caught up with them. Hilda said nothing, merely looked Norma up and down with a disgusted twist to her lips before running to the gate where her father was waiting to walk her home.

"That's her, is it? The girl you had your eye on for Nye." One of Norma's eyebrows lifted in a high arch. "I can see why he ain't keen."

The words came as a blow. Miriam hadn't realised Aneurin had discussed Hilda with Norma. She brooded on it as they went inside the building, wondering what other thoughts and feelings the two had shared, and what could have made Emrys so angry.

Aneurin sat on the front pew, bent forwards with his face in his hands. He looked up with a tortured expression when they entered.

"Here she is. The adulteress." Emrys's voice rang out as he descended the pulpit steps to face them.

At Miriam's side, Norma blanched.

"Don't blame her, Dad. It was my fault."

"You are both to blame. But *she* is the one who has broken her vows."

"What's all this about?" Norma's voice squeaked nervously and she inched closer to Miriam's side.

It was a good question, one Miriam also wanted answered.

"You were seen in the park. Embracing." Emrys's cheeks were mottled with high colour as he advanced towards Norma, the fury in his face making her shrink.

Aneurin jerked to his feet and moved to stand between them, facing his father.

"Leave her alone—" he began, but to Miriam's surprise Norma pushed past him and poked a finger at Emrys's chest.

"I don't know what you've been told, but I ain't surprised you've been so quick to think the worst of me. You've been itching to find a reason to have a go ever since I got here, ain't you?" She turned towards Miriam and Aneurin, blue eyes ablaze. "You can't deny he's always hated me, can you? He hated the idea of me before he met me, and then when he saw what I was he hated me more. I'm not a person to him, I'm just a common, godless tart, and an English tart at that."

"Can you deny it?" Emrys demanded. "Did you kiss my son?"

There was a moment when Miriam still believed it might all be a mistake. That it could blow over and be forgiven. But that was before Norma tossed her head and fired back her reply, equally baldly.

"Yes. As a matter of fact, Emrys, I did. And I ain't sorry, neither."

Emrys nodded, as if she had confirmed every belief he'd ever held about her. "Then I have nothing more to say to you, except that you can go back to the house now and pack your bags. I want every trace of you gone within an hour."

"Emrys! You can't expect a pregnant woman to find somewhere to stay at this time on a Friday night, and in this weather."

He paid no attention to Miriam's plea. "I would expect nothing better of her," he said before turning his gaze upon his son. "But *you*, Aneurin. You!"

Never had so much disappointment been held in one word. Miriam felt it like a wound on Aneurin's behalf. It was as if all the air left the room.

"I know it was wrong. I've fought it, believe me I have. But I love her, Dad."

"*Love?*" Emrys repeated the word as if the very idea was inconceivable. "She's a married woman! It isn't your place to love her. The moment you had any inkling that you'd started an – an infatuation – for this creature, you should have come to me. We would have sent her away, and prayed for you. We could have put a stop to it before it went so far. Before you put yourself in this position. To think that you allowed yourself to be compromised like this." He raked a hand through his hair, and Miriam saw that it shook as badly as her own.

"I know it's wrong, Dad, but the heart follows its own path. That's why I've made my decision about tomorrow. I know you'll be even more disappointed in me, but I'm not going to register as a conscientious objector. I'm going to enlist. If I join the forces and go away, it will save both Norma and me from any further temptation, and when I'm on the other side of the world perhaps we'll eventually forget about each other. It was my fault we kissed, not hers. I'm the one who coveted another man's wife, so the sin is mine. Norma, I can't bear the thought that I might lead you into adultery." He sent her a look that made Miriam's heart ache for him.

"Nye..." Norma reached for him, only for Emrys to knock her hand down.

"Get away from my son!" he roared, lifting his hand again as if he meant to strike her face.

"Emrys!" Miriam exclaimed again. "We are in God's house."

Aneurin had moved to shield the girl, his nostrils flaring as if he wouldn't hesitate to hit his father back. The two men squared up to each other, snarling like dogs with their hackles raised.

"*She* is the one who has led you into temptation. Before she came here, you would never have dreamed of looking upon a married woman, and you wouldn't have contemplated compounding your sin by enlisting. Thou shalt not kill, Aneurin. And whoso committeth adultery with a woman lacketh understanding: he that doeth it destroyeth his own soul. A wound and dishonour shall he get; and his reproach shall not be wiped away." Emrys recited the Scriptures in a voice that resonated with all the power he had gained in his years of ministry.

"Stop it!" Norma shrieked, her hands over her face as if she couldn't bear it any longer. When she dropped them, Miriam saw that her cheeks glistened with tears. "It weren't adultery! Stop saying that, will you? Stop accusing him," she pleaded, on a sob. "It weren't no sin, alright? He didn't do nothing wrong, 'cause he's free to love me. Nye, you don't need to join up for my sake, 'cause I ain't married. I never 'ave been."

THIRTY-ONE

Norma

A rush of bile filled Norma's throat, and she pressed her fist against her mouth to fight it. This was unbearable. Her confession hung in the air around them, impossible to retract. Her legs buckled, sending her lurching for the front pew. Sinking onto it, she clutched her head to try to stop it pounding, and closed her eyes.

Miriam had moved to Emrys's side. She clung to his arm.

Aneurin was the first to speak, his voice cracking. "What do you mean, you're not married?"

"I'm not. I was s'posed to be, but he jilted me. I had a lucky escape, although I didn't know it at the time. He's in prison. He's probably been hanged by now, or will be before long." It occurred to her, belatedly, that perhaps she could have claimed to be a widow soon, which might have been better than this. Because when she opened her eyes, she could see what they thought of her.

Liar. It was written all over their faces. She'd expect nothing less from Emrys. But seeing it in Miriam's gentle face... In Aneurin's shock and distress... It crushed her heart to dust.

"I'm so sorry I lied to you," Norma said quietly, hoping Aneurin would see the truth in her face. "I never wanted to. When

I left London, it felt like the only way I could have a chance to start again."

Now that he knew his son was blameless, Emrys's expression had changed. At least she'd managed to spare Aneurin from his father's wrath, even if it meant taking it upon herself.

"Not an adulteress, then, but still a whore. A lying, deceitful whore with a bastard in her belly." The words fell upon her head like a stoning.

Deliberately, she straightened her back and lifted her chin. "You're not the first person who'd take pleasure in seeing me broken by the weight of their contempt, Emrys Powell. Well, maybe I deserve it. I've been stupid, after all. Stupid enough to think a lie could save me. Stupid enough to trust in a man's promise to look after me. But my baby don't deserve it. None of it is the kiddie's fault."

"God's word is clear. The sins of the fathers—"

She cut him off impatiently. "Yeah, well it's clear about something else an' all. Something you seem to conveniently forget. Judge not, lest ye be judged. See? Turns out I did learn something from those soddin' nuns in the end."

"Get out! I won't have you swearing in this place."

Enough was enough. She got to her feet, reaching for the back of the pew to hold her steady as the ground seemed to sway away from her. "You know what, Emrys? You can stick your rules up your bleedin' arse, along with your sneering and your judgement. I've had a gutful of it."

Somehow, she managed to walk past them. Let Emrys bluster as much as he wanted. It was all over anyway. She'd been found out, and it was clear from Aneurin's face as she passed him that any love he'd believed he felt for her had been shattered. As she opened the gate at the end of the path, she heard him call out to her, then rapid footsteps.

"Norma, look at me. *Look at me!*" He grabbed her arm and swung her around, not roughly like Dickie, but still with a fierceness she hadn't known was in him. "Why didn't you tell me the truth? I've been praying to not love you. Fighting it every time I saw you. Every time my thoughts turned to you. Every day. And now you say you were lying all along?"

Knowing the hurt she'd caused him was somehow even worse than her own pain.

"Are you going to call me a lying whore, an' all?"

"I don't believe you're a whore. But—" His voice broke as his chest heaved.

"But..." she repeated. He didn't need to say any more. She understood, but it didn't make it any less agonising. "I'd better go," she whispered, her eyes awash with tears.

"Are you *anything* you said you were? Or was it all lies?"

She paused, not wanting to say the words aloud. But she'd already made such a mess of things. Telling the final truth wouldn't make any difference now.

"I'm not really called Norma Finch. My real name is Norma Sparrow. But everything else was true."

A shadow crossed his face. "I thought I knew you. But it was all built on sand."

He trudged back up the path, looking beaten. More than anything, she wanted to run to him, to fall on her knees and beg his forgiveness. No one had ever felt what he'd felt for her, or made her feel the way he'd made her feel. And now, just when she'd found the kind of love she'd never even dared to hope for, she'd lost it. She'd made the best, the kindest and sweetest man she'd ever known, despise her. There could be no coming back from this. She'd lost him, along with her friendship with Miriam and the safety of the manse, for good.

THIRTY-TWO

Miriam

Miriam found Norma in the dining room, folding fabric and stacking it on a large square of brown paper. Her sewing machine waited beside the door in its case. There was a wild, uncontrolled air about her that Miriam hadn't seen before.

"Don't worry, I'll soon be out of your way," Norma said, not looking at her. Her voice was hoarse.

Miriam folded her arms. "I don't expect you to leave tonight."

"P'raps you don't, but *he* does."

"If you mean my husband, I've persuaded him that we can't expect you to leave until the morning."

The girl flicked a glance towards her, revealing cheeks streaked with black mascara. She snorted under her breath. "Generous of him, not to put me out on the street right away," she said, then started wrapping the paper around the parcel and tying it up with string. Her fingers fumbled with the bow, and she had to re-do it.

"It's not for your sake, but for the child's," Miriam said. It was important to be clear. "I won't compound your wrongdoing by allowing your baby to be put in danger. But if you feel any kind of gratitude to us at all for the hospitality we've provided over the past seven weeks, I would ask you to leave Aneurin alone from now on."

She watched as Norma's shoulders rose and fell with a shuddering breath.

"You won't need to worry about that now, anyway. He's made it clear he wants nothing more to do with me."

"Can you blame him?"

"No." It was little more than a whisper. Norma sniffed and wiped her face on her sleeve. "I ain't had much choice over what's happened to me in the past six months or so, but I did choose to lie. Even if my reasons weren't as bad as you think, I still have to take the blame." With the parcel wrapped up, she held it to her chest. "I never meant to cause any hurt, Miriam. I hope you know that. Especially not to Nye."

Perhaps the truly Christian thing to do would be to open her arms and tell her all was forgiven, but too much damage had been done.

"He didn't deserve to be lied to. None of us did."

"I know. I was never proud of it."

There was a pause. If she wanted sympathy, it was too late for that. Miriam turned towards the doorway, but Norma hadn't finished.

"Is he alright? Aneurin, I mean."

"He's in the chapel with his father. They were talking when I left. He's still planning to enlist tomorrow. Tonight's events have made him want to get away." She let the words hit home. "You can imagine, I hope, how much distress that has caused."

Norma's cheeks had drained of colour. "He won't have made his decision lightly. Emrys will have to accept that he can't dictate everything his son does."

As she moved to push past, a flash of anger made Miriam block the doorway with her arm.

"That's not fair! How dare you find fault with Emrys for wanting the best for his son?"

"Ask yourself this, Miriam: what's the use of having so much godliness, if it makes you lose your humanity?"

"I never met anyone so ungrateful. After everything Emrys has done for you!"

"Leave it out. We both know Emrys wouldn't have given me so much as the skin off his custard if you hadn't forced him to. Now, I'll go upstairs if you don't mind. I need to finish packing ready for the morning."

Stung, Miriam stepped aside. "I'll expect you and all your things to be gone by half past nine," she said.

Whether or not she had meant to, Norma had caused untold damage. Miriam had been a fool to insist that Emrys take her in.

She couldn't watch the girl stomp off upstairs. It was too great a torment to see that swollen belly, full with a child that should never have been conceived. It was too unfair that she had been blessed with something she had no right to claim, when Miriam and Emrys had been denied the chance to love their own child, born within the proper bounds of marriage. How could God be so unjust?

Whatever secret hopes she'd harboured that Norma might choose her to adopt her unwanted child were smashed. Emrys wouldn't agree to them adopting an illegitimate baby, and especially not Norma's. He'd believe that the sins of the parents would be visited on the child. He'd always be watching it, waiting for some wicked trait of its parents to show.

Her hopes that Aneurin and Hilda might have a future together had been wrecked, too. Aneurin felt forced to volunteer for a path of unspeakable danger that might ultimately cost him his life. And poor Emrys, crushed by disappointment and sorrow that his son was choosing violence instead of resistance.

So much grief, and all of it caused by Norma – her beauty and her lies. In just a few weeks, Norma and the war had torn Miriam's family apart.

THIRTY-THREE

Norma

Norma left the manse laden with her possessions, dreading the twenty-minute walk into Pontybrenin almost as much as the humiliating prospect of trying to convince someone to take her in. Her two suitcases bulged with the extra maternity clothes she'd made over the past few weeks, and with those in one hand, her sewing machine weighing down her other hand, a parcel of fabrics and trimmings in a shoulder bag, and her handbag and gas mask also slung round her neck, her hands and back were aching even before she'd reached the end of Ebenezer Street.

As she'd expected, no one had offered to help her. Miriam had stayed out of the way, and she hadn't heard Emrys and Aneurin return during her night of fitful sleep. Maybe they'd stayed in the chapel all night to pray, calling curses down upon her head, for all she knew.

Up at half past five, no longer able to fight her whirling thoughts, she'd packed and tidied and dusted and swept under the bed, making sure to leave her room as neat as it had been on the night she was taken in. She'd left only one thing behind: the patchwork picture she'd made of the mountain. There was nothing to be gained by taking it with her, as it would only remind her of what she couldn't have. Perhaps one day, when things calmed down, and when Aneurin – please God – survived the war, Miriam might be able to look at it and remember the happy picnic on Moel Carnau, instead of Norma's deceit. By then, of course, Aneurin might have settled down with a nice girl like Hilda who met with his family's approval, but she turned her thoughts away from that. They hurt too much.

As she struggled towards the town centre, the circulation in her hands almost cut off by the weight of the items she had to carry and her spine threatening to snap, she couldn't stop thinking about Aneurin. Had he already gone to enlist? Would he hate being a soldier? Did he now despise her as much as Emrys did? He'd been so different from anyone else she'd known. He'd made her feel different inside.

With Aneurin, she'd felt like the best and bravest version of herself. He didn't see her the way other men did – as something to be fought over and claimed. In his eyes, she was something to be fought for and shielded. He was the first man she'd kissed who'd resisted the urge to act upon his desires. The first who believed in something more important than himself. Who'd treated her like something precious, not something to be used.

Although she told herself she'd always landed on her feet before, this time felt different. This time, she felt hollow. Adrift. Like a dirty old crumpled-up sweet wrapper or ciggy packet dropped in the gutter to be carried off down the storm drain.

Life had always been a swirling, polluted current. But before, she'd known how to ride it. Now, in her exhaustion, she seemed to have forgotten every survival tactic she'd ever learned. The past few weeks, when Aneurin had seen her as clean, had deceived her into seeing herself that way. It had made the contempt in the Powells' faces come as an unwelcome shock, reminding her of what she'd have to face now that she'd revealed the truth.

She'd made such a hash of things. She'd lost a friend in Miriam and the best kind of man in Nye, as well as a place to lay her head.

But as her gran used to say, *When one door closes, another one will open*. She paused in the middle of the street, closing her eyes to grope for the faint hope that the next door to open wouldn't be any worse than the one she'd just left behind.

The only place she could think of where she might be welcomed was Evelina's Modes. She arrived before the shop opened, and saw the shock register on Miss Proudfoot's face when she lifted the blind on the door to find her standing outside.

"This is a surprise, Mrs Finch..." Miss Proudfoot's eyes widened as she took in the sight of Norma's bags and sewing machine on the pavement.

"Yeah. Thing is, I'm not really Mrs Finch. I'm Miss Sparrow. And when I told the Powells they kicked me out. This was the only place I thought I might be welcome..." A lump rose in her throat as the expression on the shopkeeper's face showed she'd presumed wrongly.

Miss Proudfoot sent a swift glance up and down the road. "Come in off the street for a minute." She picked up one of the bags and almost threw it inside the shop, hustling Norma into the tiny back kitchen as if she was an embarrassment. "What were you thinking of, coming to me?"

"I dunno. I'm sorry. It's just, you've been nice to me before. And you know I'm a good worker. I thought maybe you might be able to help. I've got nowhere to stay tonight."

"My dear, please don't think me unsympathetic, but I don't have room for you here. You'll need to look for another billet if you want to stay in Pontybrenin. Perhaps the billeting officer will help you. But we must be realistic. If you're not married, I doubt many people would be prepared to take you in. Given your condition."

The bell on the shop's door tinkled, sending Miss Proudfoot into a flutter.

"I have a customer. You understand, Miss..." She frowned, as if she couldn't remember what name to use. "You can leave your bags here and come back for them later, if it makes it easier for you. But for now..."

Lugging her stuff around the town could only slow her down and wear her out, so Norma left her bags and sewing machine and nodded to the pretty customer as she passed through the shop.

"Ah, Miss Fitznorton. What a pleasure to see you. The stockings arrived yesterday; let me wrap them up for you." Behind her, Miss Proudfoot's voice sounded artificially bright as Norma stepped out onto the high street in the chill of the October morning. Her hands still burned, with red lines across her palms from the weight of her belongings; looking at them, the sight of the gold ring on her left hand unleashed a wave of nausea. She tugged it off, stumbling along the pavement towards Pontybrenin's only jeweller's shop. It was time to be rid of this reminder of her lies.

Afterwards, once she'd found a new billet, she'd go and sort out her identity card. Although admitting her real identity had probably damaged her relationship with Miss Proudfoot, in a way it had been a relief to drop the pretence. From now on, there would be no more deception. No more Mrs Finch. Norma Sparrow was back, come what may.

Try as she might, she couldn't persuade the stern-faced jeweller to offer her more than fifteen shillings for the wedding ring.

"But it cost me thirty!" she protested.

"That's London prices for you." The man pushed the ring back across the counter. "Fifteen, take it or leave it. It's up to you."

She took the fifteen shillings, as he must have known she would. No doubt it would soon be in the window on sale for twenty-five, but she might as well cut her losses.

Across the street, Contadino's café promised warmth and the comfort of coffee. Her spirits sank when she glimpsed Johnny behind the marble counter. She hadn't seen him since that awful, excruciating evening when he'd been horrified to realise she was pregnant. Her steps faltered, then a customer came out, releasing an enticing aroma of fresh coffee. Taking a deep breath, she went in.

Johnny's eyes widened at the sight of her. No doubt he was

shocked to see her with her belly even bigger and no make-up, her hair a mess and, if he cared to look hard, no wedding ring. But she'd had enough of people disapproving of her, and her money was as good as anyone's. She marched up to the counter and looked him in the eye.

"Morning, Johnny. I'll have a coffee if it ain't too much trouble. Just a small one." She didn't want to spend any more of her precious cash than she had to, when she'd be needing it for rent or a rail ticket back to London.

"Take a seat, if you can find one," he muttered, fussing with cups and saucers. "I'll bring it over."

There were no empty tables. A few patrons looked curiously towards her before resuming their conversations, but most were disinterested. For once, she was glad to be invisible.

An old man at a nearby table gestured towards an empty chair. "You can sit by here if you like, beaut. There's plenty of space at my table."

She swallowed, uncomfortable at the prospect of sitting with a stranger, but her need for a seat and a hot coffee with plenty of sugar was greater than any awkwardness. With his shock of white curls and snowy beard he looked old enough to be her grandfather, so she shouldn't have to worry about him getting frisky.

"I couldn't help overhearing just now," he said when she sank gratefully into the chair opposite his. "Is that a London accent? Are you one of them evacuees?"

She nodded, then looked up as Johnny brought her coffee. Despite her earlier decision to brazen it out, she tucked her left hand under the tabletop before addressing him.

"Johnny, can I ask you something? Do you know of anywhere I might be able to stay for a few nights? Things haven't worked out with my billet, so I'm looking for a new one. I just wondered if any of your customers might have mentioned having some space. I wouldn't give 'em no trouble."

Johnny frowned and shook his head. "I think all the billets in town have been taken. You could try asking at the post office, maybe." He picked up the old man's empty cup.

"I'll get this young lady's coffee, Johnny," the man said. "And bring another one over for me. We'll have two toasted teacakes as well, when you're ready. My shout," he added to Norma as Johnny headed towards the kitchen.

"I don't expect you to—"

"You'd be doing me a favour," he said, cutting off her protests. "I'm glad of some sensible grown-up company, to be honest. I'm living with my son and daughter-in-law and my two grandsons these days. They could talk a dead man to sleep, those two boys. So I like to escape here for an hour or so every Saturday morning." His blue-green eyes twinkled, making some of the tension in her shoulders ebb away.

"Thanks, then. It's very kind of you." She stirred three teaspoons of sugar into her cup, needing the energy after the sleepless night and the burdensome walk. Perhaps it would give her a bit of pep for finding a new billet.

"Your name wouldn't be Norma, would it?" the man asked, unexpectedly.

Her eyes widened across her cup, and she lowered it back to its saucer.

"How would you know that?"

"My daughter Miriam told me about her pregnant evacuee from London. Said she was young and pretty as a rose, and blonde with big blue eyes. There can't be all that many girls fitting that description in Pontybrenin, can there?"

Wordlessly, Norma nodded. Then she shook her head. Her thoughts were so jumbled, she couldn't think how to respond.

"Nice to meet you at last, Norma, after hearing so much about you. I'm Joe."

He'd reached across the table and held out his hand, so she shook it briefly. "Nice to meet you, too, Joe."

"If you don't mind me saying, Norma, I'm surprised to hear you need a new billet. Mim led me to believe she rather liked you.

Said you had some funny city ways, but that you were kind-hearted, and you'd been helpful round the house. Said you put old Gwenllian in her place, too, when you went up to the farm. Mim appreciated that, you know."

She caught her lip with her teeth. It was nice that Miriam had spoken generously about her to her father, but not so pleasant to have to explain her predicament.

One of his bushy eyebrows lifted as he eyed her speculatively. "It wouldn't be that husband of hers, would it? He can be a bit of a funny one, can Emrys. I know he wasn't too keen on having you to stay at first."

"Things just got a bit tricky, that's all."

"How's that, then?"

Their teacakes arrived, and she busied herself spreading butter on hers, hoping he'd forget the subject by the time she'd finished. But when he laid down his knife, he prompted her again.

"I might be able to help you find a new billet, see – but it would be easier if I know what went wrong."

She wiped her hand on her napkin and heaved a sigh. "Look, I kissed his son, alright? And we was seen. Someone told Emrys, and he went off like a balloon that had been pricked. Anyone would have thought we'd been doing the dirty in the middle of Pontybrenin High Street, the way he kicked off."

"Oh, aye?" He watched her as he sipped his coffee, apparently curious but not at all shocked by this revelation.

"Thing is, they all thought I was married. I mean, I'd told them I was. So he was worried about Nye's soul – you know what Emrys is like – and in the end, to stop him banging on about adultery and that... Well, I had to admit that I'd – maybe – misled them a bit." She poked at a stray raisin on her plate, unable to meet his gaze.

"Misled them a bit?"

"I lied." She looked up, expecting to see disgust, but meeting only interest. Strangely, the mildness of his reaction made her eyes prickle more than if she'd had to defend herself. "I came here for a fresh start. In London, no one wanted to employ a girl who'd got herself into this kind of mess, and I had nowhere to go. It would have been the same here if I hadn't pretended to be married, so I told everyone my name was Mrs Finch. And it would've been fine. No one would've been any the wiser, if…"

"If Aneurin Powell didn't have such good taste in women? To tell you the truth, I'm impressed. I'd never have thought the lad had it in him. It's good to know he's finally crawled out from under his father's thumb." He chuckled softly at the way she spluttered into her coffee.

Whatever she'd thought he'd say, it wasn't that.

"Well, he don't like me anymore. Not now he knows I deceived him." Coffee sloshed over the rim of the cup as she put it down. Memories of the previous evening's events made her stomach churn. "People round here will soon find out what's happened, and then all they'll see when they look at me is a girl who's no better than she ought to be, and a liar to boot. I should probably go back to London. They won't approve of me there, either, but at least it's home. As much as anywhere is. There'll be places that take in girls like me, I expect. It's not like it's going to be like this forever, is it? Just until…" Her fists had been balled in her lap, but now she gestured to her belly and looked up at the ceiling to blink away the sudden burning in her eyes. Her chest heaved as her mind struggled against the realities she faced.

He waited until she'd finished blowing her nose into her handkerchief, as if he understood that she needed to gather herself.

"Whether you decide to go back is up to you, of course. But there's no rush to go dashing back to London straight away. Leave it with me for a bit, flower. Let me go and have a word with a couple of people, and then meet you back here later." He took out an old-fashioned pocket watch from his waistcoat and frowned at it before tucking it away again. "Shall we say three o'clock? I'm not as nimble as I used to be, but I should be able to get back here by then, hopefully with some good news for you."

"I dunno… It's kind of you to offer, but there's no reason why you should go to all that trouble. You've never even met me before."

"No, but when you came to Pontybrenin my family said they'd look after you, and you haven't told me anything that makes me think we shouldn't stick by that."

Three o'clock was hours away. If he couldn't find her somewhere to stay, she'd have to fetch her things and get a ticket back to London, a journey of several hours. The prospect of crossing the city and trying to find an institution to take her in late on a Saturday night wasn't pleasant. If she was going back, she'd be better off not to wait, but to set off straight away.

On the other hand, Joe seemed confident, and his gentle smile looked genuine. He clearly meant well. Perhaps she should give him a chance. If the worst came to the worst, she'd just have to spend some of her money on the cheapest room the Station Hotel could offer, then catch a train in the morning. It was a gamble, but perhaps one worth taking.

"Alright, Joe. I'll see you back here at three o'clock. And thanks. I appreciate the help."

He nodded, picked up his cap and delved into his trouser pocket for a small leather coin purse before laying a couple of shillings on the table. "Should be enough for a bite of lunch there, as well as the coffee and teacakes, as long as you don't go mad. Thanks for your company, Norma. I'll see you this afternoon."

THIRTY-FOUR

Miriam

The silence in the manse that morning was like a malevolent presence breathing in Miriam's ear, an unwelcome reminder that Aneurin and Norma were both gone and Emrys had not yet returned from the chapel, where he had vowed to spend the day in prayer and fasting for his son. She'd stayed in her bedroom until she heard the front door close, watching through the net curtain as Norma tottered down the front path, adjusting her grip on her heavy bags as she went, as if they were already hurting her hands. Her shoulders were held back and her blonde head tipped up at a proud angle as she passed out of sight.

Watching her had evoked a mixture of emotions. There was relief at knowing the girl could cause no further turmoil. Oddly, there was also a flat sense of disappointment; of losing a friend. Norma didn't look back even once. Didn't the girl also feel that same loss?

Scrubbing the bathroom was a welcome distraction, directing Miriam's pent-up energy into action. Afterwards, with hands red and itching from the scouring powder, she wandered through the other rooms with a duster, running it swiftly along the picture rails and polished surfaces before stooping to sweep it along the skirting boards. Although she was used to being alone in the house, today it felt so empty she half expected her footsteps to echo.

Reluctant to confront whatever state Norma might have left her bedroom in, and wondering if the girl might have stolen from them or left a mess to wreak revenge for being thrown out, she left her room until last. As she pushed open the door, she held her breath.

However reprehensible her morals had proved to be, Norma had at least left her room spotlessly clean and tidy. Thankfully, nothing appeared to be missing. In fact, something had been left behind on the pillow: a piece of fabric, smoothed out on top of the bedspread. Puzzled, Miriam picked it up. It was a patchwork square, about the size of a cushion cover, but the pieced-together patches of fabric weren't of a regular shape or size, like patchwork Miriam had seen before. As understanding dawned, she plumped down onto the bed and spread the panel over her lap.

It was a picture, with scraps of colour making up a countryside scene. Shades of coral, pink and indigo made a sunset sky streaked with cloud, while an assortment of greens and yellows below were clearly intended to depict a landscape. Areas of padding and embroidery added depth, with the shapes of wheeling birds in dark thread, and clusters of creamy knots as if to represent grazing sheep. She recognised stem stitch, French and bullion knots, lazy daisy stitch, and a variety of unfamiliar stitches making a foreground of wild grass and flowers. It was beautiful. Exquisite, in fact. A tiny, delicately worked bee in the corner brought a flash of memory: their picnic on Moel Carnau, nearly four weeks earlier, when they'd laughed together with the sun on their faces and shared cheese sandwiches and a flask of tea.

As her fingers traced the silk embroidery threads and the textures of the fabrics, she couldn't help but wonder what had made Norma create something so evocative of that day, and why she hadn't taken it with her. After everything that had been said, why would she leave any kind of parting gift? The way it had been laid so carefully on the pillow, spread out and perfectly straight, suggested it hadn't been left behind by mistake. She'd meant for Miriam to find it and keep it.

Should she show it to Emrys? He might feel more kindly disposed towards Norma if he saw the artistry she'd used to create a picture of the view from his beloved mountain. But the wound caused by Aneurin's decision to enlist after Norma's betrayal was still raw. Emrys might tear the embroidered scene up or throw it away. Miriam didn't want to take that chance. Nothing so lovely deserved to be destroyed. It would be better to put off showing him, at least until his emotions were less overwrought.

In her own room, she folded the panel and tucked it under the paper lining in the drawer where she kept her nightdresses. She'd only just finished tidying them when the doorbell rang, making her jump and turn pale. What if Norma had come back? What would she say to her?

Downstairs, a familiar, white-bearded figure wearing a flat cap peered through the stained-glass panel in the front door.

"I thought I'd call in to see my little girl," her father said when she let him in.

She stepped gratefully into his arms, glad of the comfort of being held against his whiskery cheek.

"Oh, Dad – I'm pleased that you did. Lots has happened since I last saw you."

"Best you put the kettle on and tell me all about it, then."

She lit the gas under the kettle while he hung his coat and cap on the hall stand.

He grunted under his breath as he eased himself down at the kitchen table. His back had given him trouble for years, but lately he seemed to be struggling more, and she'd noticed him limping. The colder weather probably didn't help.

"Aneurin's gone to enlist," she said, setting a plate of biscuits on the table while the tea leaves steeped in the pot.

"It'll be the making of him," her father said.

"Will it, though? When I think about our Len... And Stanley, near enough blinded..."

His face clouded. "There's always a cost to doing the right thing. All you can do is pray, Mim. As a minister's wife, you'd know all about that."

She put a cup and saucer in front of him, along with a small jug of milk, then poured tea through a strainer before sinking into the chair opposite.

"Emrys hasn't taken it well."

"Wanted him to be a conchie, did he?" He picked up a digestive biscuit and dunked it in his tea before taking a bite.

She nodded, unsure what to say.

"Hitler's a sight worse than the Kaiser ever was. Emrys must realise that, surely? We have to throw everything we've got at him, try and make a quick job of it so it doesn't drag on like the last time. You should both be proud of the lad for being willing to play his part."

He reached to pat her hand, and she squeezed his in return, noticing how gnarled it was compared to hers. The liver spots and the lumpy veins and knuckles made him seem suddenly more fragile. Fear of loss snagged at her again – it must be all this awful war talk. It made her think of her remaining brothers, Ted and Jack, who'd been too young for the Great War but might get sucked into this one if it didn't end as quickly as Dad hoped.

What would it do to her father if he lost another son? Seventy years old, arthritic and not always in the best of health, it would hit him even harder than it had done in 1916. It was easy to picture the impact of such a shockwave of grief blasting into her family.

"You still look troubled, Mim. What else is on your mind? Whatever it is, you can tell your old dad." His eyes twinkled over his cup.

"We've had a little bit of bother just lately. Partly Aneurin's decision to enlist, but not only that." Keeping details to a minimum, she explained that he'd developed an inappropriate relationship with their evacuee, who'd been revealed as deceitful and immoral and thus asked to leave. The scandalous nature of the story made her cheeks feel hot as she relayed it to her father; she put her palms against them to cool them.

He raised an eyebrow. "Where's the girl now?"

Miriam huffed out her breath. "That's no longer our concern, is it? She's made her bed; she'll have to lie in it. We can't have a girl like that in this house."

"Some might say it's exactly the right house to open its doors to a girl who was so scared of people's condemnation that she felt she had to live a lie."

Her mouth felt dry, even though she'd only just swallowed the last of her tea.

"I suppose you'd be too young to remember much about our Len," he said after a pause.

"I remember when he died in the war." It was exactly why Aneurin shouldn't have disobeyed his father. "Such a waste of a young life," she added bitterly.

Sadness flickered in his face, making his mouth turn down. "I hope he didn't think so. He volunteered to go, believing it was the right thing to do."

She closed her eyes briefly, smoothing the woollen fabric of her skirt over her thighs. Whatever her brother had believed, he'd paid the highest possible price for his willingness to serve.

"He got a girl pregnant, you know, before he went. Jenny, her name was. A skinny little *dwt* of a thing. Her mam threw her out, so your mam and Maggie took her in. I was proud of them for doing right by her. For being more concerned about being charitable than being righteous."

"I didn't know about any of that. What happened?"

"She lost the babe. Probably for the best. After Len died, she married someone else – a coal miner who didn't have to go off to war – and had a whole clutch of kiddies. But the point is, your evacuee didn't do anything that a million other youngsters haven't done before her... Myself included."

Miriam's eyes goggled. "You're not telling me that you and

Mam..." She attempted a rapid calculation, unsure how long would have passed between her parents' wedding and Len's birth.

"Not your mam. She was too scared of the consequences, so she made me wait until we were legal and above board. But not all the girls I knew were so careful..."

He picked up another biscuit, snapping it in two and staring at it as if to avoid her shocked expression. A flush had swept up his neck and under his white beard.

"Sometimes a girl will want that sort of company when they're lonely or in need of affection. There was one... Oh, it was a long time ago now, and you don't need to know the details. Maybe it was wrong, and I should have given her love in other ways. But it didn't feel wrong at the time. Let's face it, Mim – most of us men don't have the restraint your Emrys and Aneurin have, especially when we're young. For some lads, and for some girls too it must be said, their physical desires shout louder than their fear for their souls."

She pushed back her chair and moved to the sink, turning her back towards him to avoid her feelings showing in her face. Her skin crawled with mortification at hearing about her father's immoral behaviour. Even if it had happened when he was young, before he met her mam, it was still wrong. And she was sure her mother would have been horrified if she'd known. Although perhaps she had. Hadn't Dolly mentioned something of the sort when lending her the Marie Stopes book?

"I don't know why you told me all this. It's embarrassing."

He huffed impatiently. "Anyone who could be hurt by you knowing is long dead. I told you because I hoped you'd see it's not right to kick this girl out onto the streets. If you don't want her living under your roof... Well, I suppose that's understandable if Aneurin's carrying a torch and Emrys isn't keen, although the lad's old enough to make his own decision about who he wants, as well as whether to fight. But at the very least, Mim, you should find her somewhere else to go."

"Even if I agreed with you, Dad, who else would want her?

And if I did find somewhere, I've no way of telling her now. I don't know where she's gone."

"So you've washed your hands of her? A pregnant girl with no family round here, and barely any money. Does she have friends she can go to?"

"I expect so. She's been here for seven weeks." But a rush of hot shame swept over her. It wasn't really true. There was Miss Proudfoot, but Norma's only real friends had been Aneurin and herself.

Joe's chair legs screeched on the kitchen floor as he levered himself up from the table with both hands, frowning. "On a cold day like today she'll be taking shelter in Contadino's," he said. "But if you're too set on clinging to your high horse to help the girl, I'll sort it. She can have my room at Ted and Ceinwen's, and I'll bunk down with their two little rascals until she can get herself settled somewhere else. Still – think on what I've said, my beaut."

Miriam crossed her arms defensively and didn't kiss him back when he dropped a bristly peck on her cheek before leaving.

How she wished he'd understood her position. It was an uncomfortable feeling, knowing that she'd disappointed her father, especially as his arguments had sent doubt insinuating its way into her mind, where previously she'd felt certain.

THIRTY-FIVE

Norma

Joe pushed open the grey-painted front door. It wasn't locked, so either the neighbours were trustworthy in this part of town, with its narrow terraced houses opening straight onto the road, or the Cadwaladers had nothing worth stealing.

"Go on in, my lovely. Mind the step," he said.

Norma stepped inside the dark, narrow hallway, only to stagger backwards into Joe's burly chest as a small boy dressed in a cowboy hat and brandishing a gun launched himself from the foot of the stairs.

"Stick 'em up!" the boy yelled.

From behind him, a small white dog skidded into the hall and yapped at her with equal ferocity.

Joe bellowed over Norma's shoulder. "Stop that barking, Patch. And as for you, Lenny Cadwalader. What in God's name d'you think you're doing, you little devil?"

The boy stared, eyes and mouth round.

Patch sniffed at Norma's ankles, then lost interest. His stump of a tail wagged briefly at Joe, before he ran off along the hall as if there was something more important to investigate.

"Sorry, Gransha. We thought it was just you coming home." A taller boy with a mop of brown curls hopped down the last couple of stairs, his boots clattering on the linoleum.

"And it's alright to give an old man a heart attack, is it?"

"I was being Billy the Kid," the younger one said, waving his toy gun around to demonstrate. "Sorry, missus," he mumbled to Norma after a nudge from his brother.

"Get outside to play in the gully before I tan both your backsides," Joe growled. The twinkle in his eyes when Norma stepped aside to let him pass belied his tone. "You alright, flower? Sorry about that. Little live wires, the pair of them. And you mustn't mind Patch. He's a yappy little thing but unless you're a rabbit or a fox he won't do you any harm."

Norma followed him towards the kitchen. Although Joe hung his coat, cap and gas mask on the hall stand, she didn't like to take off any of her things just yet. Not until she was sure she'd be welcome to stay. She hesitated in the kitchen doorway. This place was small, not more than half the size of the manse, and although it looked clean, the paintwork was chipped and the sparse furnishings plain and well worn.

"I don't want to put your family to no trouble," she said.

"Don't be daft." The lines at the corners of Joe's merry green eyes fanned out, carving rows of wrinkles down his cheeks. His was such an open, friendly face. "Don't stand there in the doorway, beaut. You'll make the place look untidy. Come on in. The privy's out the back, through that door, if you need it. The paving's a bit loose, so don't trip when you're out there in the dark. It's one of those jobs we keep meaning to do, but we all know it's there so..." He shrugged. "Ceinwen – that's my Ted's wife – Ceinwen will be home in a bit. She went out to a jumble sale earlier, and I expect she'll have stopped to talk to a dozen or more of her friends before it occurs to her to come home."

She nodded again, wishing she had the energy and clarity of thought to think of a suitably pleasant reply. Everything hurt. Her palms were almost blistered, her fingers rough and sore. The muscles in her back and legs burned. Her neck was so stiff she could hardly turn her head. Even her groin ached, the baby seeming to weigh her down more heavily today.

"Are you alright, my lovely? You look a bit peaky." Joe reached to take her arm, but she shook her head, shrinking away.

She didn't want to seem rude or ungrateful, but finding herself in this poky kitchen belonging to a stranger, dependent on an unknown family for help, made everything seem too much. Her thoughts were as crowded and muddled as this house would be if she joined the five people who must already feel cramped. Her chin dipped to her chest and she closed her eyes against the throbbing in her forehead, wanting to shut everything out, even Joe's well-meant concern. She needed space. To be away from other people, their kindness and curiosity and occasional cruelty. To regroup. She needed a plan, but her numb brain couldn't seem to form any coherent ideas.

"I'll be alright if I can just lie down for a bit," she mumbled.

"I haven't moved my stuff into the boys' room yet, or stripped the bed, but I can do it now if you can hang on while I do it?"

"I don't mind. I just..." She swayed on her feet, and he relented.

Within minutes she was upstairs in Joe's tiny bedroom, curled up on his narrow, lumpy bed. As she laid her thumping head on the pillow, her nostrils filled with the smell of hair tonic. The pillowcase was coarser against her cheek and the woollen blanket rougher than the ones at the manse, but she closed her eyes, grateful for a chance to breathe.

The baby had been quiet today, as if it knew the trouble it had caused and had decided not to draw attention to itself. She'd felt not a single flutter or kick since yesterday, not even when she'd had coffee. Perhaps... Perhaps it was dead.

An icy prickle sliced down her spine. Would she be glad? It would save her the bother of getting it adopted. With a raw, red palm she caressed the solid mound of her belly.

A tickle against the side of her nose made her reach up to

scratch it; in a daze, she realised her finger had come away wet. How was it possible to weep without even realising? Her eyes were leaking tears, beyond her control. Too exhausted to fight them, she curled up a little smaller, hugging her belly. Only when she felt a prod under the weight of her resting hand did she permit herself the indulgence of a silent sob, her face contorting painfully as the muscles in her throat tightened.

I'm glad you're alive. Although I'll have to give you up, right now you're all I've got.

Would it know these thoughts? Could she communicate them through her caressing hand and the flesh and fluid between her and the child? Suddenly it mattered that it knew she didn't hate it. That even though she'd felt all along that it was unwelcome, they were still bound up together.

She used to feel as if the baby was a pirate. Not the cheery, swashbuckling sort like Errol Flynn in the pictures, but the wicked sort that used cunning to steal on board a vessel to seize control of it at sword point. She'd embarked on this voyage unknowingly, back in the spring. During those moments with Dickie she'd been swept along with little choice in where she went. She still didn't know where she'd end up.

She wanted to be free of it all, and for the child to be free too. To be back in charge of her own destiny and to shake off the condemnation that weighed her down. But regaining her freedom would come at a terrible price. The price of knowing she'd failed as a woman. Of forever having to live with the knowledge that she was an even greater failure as a mother than her own mum had been. Because Mum might not have cared for her much, but at least she hadn't given her away willingly.

The numbing shock of the previous night's events had ebbed while she was waiting for Joe to return to Contadino's café, conscious of curious glances from other patrons and suspicious looks from Johnny. He had seemed determined to avoid speaking to her.

What was it about men? They all ditched her once they'd got

to know her a bit. But none had left an aching chasm inside her the way Aneurin had when he cut her loose. She was drifting now, a ship that had lost its mooring and been carried on the tide out of the safety of the dock and into dangerous waters.

Her heart constricted as she remembered the way Nye used to wish her goodnight. After a while she'd learned that it was *nos da*, not "North Star" as she'd first thought. But North Star suited the way she thought of him. In a remarkably short time he'd become not only her favourite person, but a point of light by which she could navigate the darkness of the circumstances in which she'd found herself.

Now he was gone. No one truly cared about her. No one respected her or trusted her. Joe had been charitable today, but it was out of a sense of obligation because his daughter had kicked her out. If she was to disappear, no one would be sad. They probably wouldn't even notice. Or if they did, they'd be like Emrys and Miriam – relieved to be rid of her. Despite all her efforts, she'd made a mess of everything.

At least it was a comfort to know that Aneurin wouldn't have to feel guilty about loving a married woman anymore. Even though telling him the truth had ruined her life, she'd been able to set him free. She wouldn't have wanted him to reproach himself for his feelings, as he would have done when he'd believed himself to be sinning. Now he knew he was in the clear. She was the only one guilty of sin. Even though it was breaking her, she was glad to have released him from that kind of crisis of the soul.

Resting seemed to have roused the baby to wakefulness. It jabbed and prodded at her insides, each nudge a reminder of how badly she'd failed. Why couldn't she be allowed to have the chance to start over? To have the love of someone good and kind, someone who'd be faithful and tender, who might even put her first now and then, and who'd calm her fears and make her smile and hold her up to make sure she didn't fall. She'd never fooled herself that she was worthy of someone like Nye, but the light in his eyes, like a sky full of stars when he looked at her, had swept her up in imaginings.

Stupid girl, the poke against her bladder seemed to say. *Stupid, stupid, stupid. He'd have realised you were no good sooner or later. Better for it to end now than further ahead, when your heart really would have shattered into a million pieces.*

It was impossible to think of the future. Her racing brain couldn't reach for it. Too much had changed too quickly. If she'd had choices, she'd be with Aneurin now. He'd be looking at her with that adoring, trusting, giving expression, as if he'd move heaven and earth if she asked him to. There'd be no lies; no shame. He'd be so relieved she was free to be his, the past wouldn't matter. But that was a pointless fantasy. Nye was part of her past now, along with Dickie. So were her brother, Ronnie, and Gran, and Mum, the only people apart from Nye who'd ever cared about her... The jolt of pain in her chest when she thought of all she'd lost made her gasp.

Remembering the past wouldn't help her. She couldn't unpick those stitches and rework them. Safest not to think forward or back. She'd have to just wait and see what would come.

THIRTY-SIX

Norma

Norma sat up, rubbing her eyes, and swung her legs off Joe's bed. A high Welsh voice, which must belong to Ceinwen, drifted up the stairs.

"I'm back! What a rumpus that was. I practically had to fight my way through to the kiddies' clothes stall. I saw your Miriam coming out of the church hall as I arrived, Joe. She said you're planning to invite her evacuee to stay here. Have you heard what the girl has done, though...?" The voice faded towards the kitchen.

Norma's heart sank. She couldn't skulk up here forever. Joe needed a chance to move his things, and she'd have to collect her bags from Evelina's Modes. And now she'd missed any chance of meeting her new hostess without her bad reputation preceding her.

Retrieving her handbag, she delved inside it for her powder compact, then flinched at the sight of her ravaged face in the mirror. A bit of powder covered the worst, then she refreshed her slick of scarlet lipstick and pressed her lips together to seal it before tidying her hair. She needed her armour on before going downstairs.

The wooden stair creaked under her stockinged feet, bringing the dog skidding around the corner. His vigorous wags suggested he'd accepted her presence in the house, and it was impossible not to smile at his cheerful little face with its nut-brown patches over each eye and its lolling pink tongue. He greeted her on his hind legs, as if eager to be patted, and she sat down on the bottom stair to avoid her stockings being laddered by his claws.

"I ain't got nothing for you, little feller," she murmured, displaying her empty palms, which he promptly licked enthusiastically. For a minute or so she made a fuss of him, putting off the moment when she'd have to face Ceinwen. When she got up, brushed the loose white fur off her dress, and straightened her shoulders, Patch raced ahead of her to spin in a joyful circle in the kitchen doorway.

"You seem to have won over the dog and my father-in-law, I'll say that much for you." Although the words sounded grudging, Ceinwen's tone was amused. Her small dark eyes, like currants in a soft round bun, held a knowing gleam as she looked Norma up and down with the air of someone forming a judgement.

Norma was spared any need to respond as Joe came in through the back door, wiping his boots on the mat.

"Ah, there she is. Are you feeling better since your nap, flower?"

"Yes, thanks."

An awkward silence ensued as they both looked to Ceinwen, who seemed in no hurry to pronounce her verdict. Her work-roughened hands were in constant movement, peeling and quartering potatoes, then dropping the pieces into a saucepan of water.

Norma folded her arms over her chest. She wasn't going to await her fate like a mouse under a cat's paw.

"I heard from upstairs that you've been told some gossip about me. So if you've already decided that I'm some kind of trollop, tell me now and I'll get on my way. You won't be the first to think it, and I daresay you won't be the last, neither. But let's not waste time, 'cause if I've got to hop it, I'd rather go before it gets dark."

One of Ceinwen's brown eyebrows lifted. "I like to make up

my own mind about people, as it happens, so climb down off your high horse. I have been talking to Miriam, so it won't come as a surprise to you that she hasn't exactly given you a glowing reference. But according to her you weren't out to rob anybody. Seeing as my sons are too young for you to seduce, my Ted is a one-man woman, and Joe here is past all that, I don't see any reason to send you packing just yet."

"I could take offence at being called past it," Joe remarked, eyes twinkling. "But no, I'm not looking for another wife. I had one for forty-three years. That's plenty for one lifetime."

Grateful though she was for his attempt to inject humour into the situation, Norma couldn't smile. Having to depend on charity made her twitchy.

"If this house isn't good enough for you after the manse, that's fair enough. No one's forcing you to stay. The front door's behind you; make sure you close it on your way out. But if you're staying, there's a bowl of runner beans here that need stringing."

Ceinwen's blunt talking was easier to cope with than pleasantries. At least it was straightforward; there were no hidden undercurrents to navigate.

"Pass me a knife, then," Norma said.

The two women nodded at each other across the small, square table. Ceinwen slid a bone-handled knife towards Norma. It was so old, the blade was worn to two-thirds of its original width.

"Now then, Norma. Miriam said you can cook, but in this house the kitchen's my domain. If you want something to eat, check with me first that I'm not planning to use it for that night's tea. If you make yourself a cuppa, ask the rest of us if we want one while you're at it. If you dirty something, wash it up. And if you use the last of something, tell me so I can replace it. As long as we stick to those rules while you're here, we should be fine."

"Understood." Norma fingered the knife. Rules were fair enough, but she was already wondering how long it would be before she and Ceinwen found themselves at odds. "Got anything sharper?" she asked. "You could ride bare-arsed to Margate on this, it's so blunt."

Behind her, Joe smothered a chuckle. "I'll go and move my bits and bobs into the boys' room, and leave you girls to it."

Ceinwen sniffed. The way her spine straightened suggested Norma had succeeded in needling her. "When the blade gets dull, we sharpen it on the edge of the back step. It worked perfectly well for me, but feel free to have a go if you think you can improve it."

"Nah, it's fine. I expect I can make do." Happier now she'd shown she was no pushover, Norma lowered herself onto the stool and started running the blade along the edge of each bean, noting the size of Ceinwen's slices before cutting her own and tossing them into the bowl.

"When's it due, then?" Ceinwen asked after several minutes had passed in silent work.

"Christmas or New Year." Norma didn't elaborate. It wasn't as if her child's birth would be a happy event in her life.

"That'll be a nice Christmas present for you."

Norma's knife stilled for a couple of heartbeats. The remark was well-meant, but there was nothing she could say in response that wouldn't make her look bad. With heat rushing into her cheeks, she concentrated on the beans.

"I was lucky with my boys, especially having Ted and Mim's sister Maggie looking after me. Has she been keeping an eye on things for you?"

"She checked me over once. Everything was fine."

"We'll have to tell her you're staying here. That's if Miriam hasn't told her already, of course. I used to be a nurse until I married Ted, so I'm sure between us we can keep you ticking over. Is it true Aneurin wanted to marry you?"

"I..." She swallowed hard, taken aback by the sudden turn in the conversation. "If he did, he never said. I think he believed he loved me for a while. But it's over now."

"Mim said he did, when I saw her at the jumble sale earlier."

Pretending her voice wasn't threatening to crack, Norma said the first thing she could think of to distract Ceinwen from the subject of her lost love. "Did you get anything nice at the jumble sale?"

It worked: Ceinwen's grin made her cheeks look like rosy apples. "I did, although I wish I'd got there earlier. They had some smashing winter clothes for the boys. They're forever ripping their shorts and snagging their jumpers, and I've got no interest in sewing or knitting, so I was glad to get a couple of things."

"I could help with the mending while I'm here, if you like. I'll have to get my sewing tin from Miss Proudfoot's, but it wouldn't be no bother. I've got to collect my things from her shop anyway."

"Oh! Would you? That would be helpful. There's some darning to be done, too, and a couple of missing buttons to sort out, if you're sure you don't mind. You can use my sewing tin until you're ready to fetch your things..." Ceinwen's tone was noticeably warmer and more cheerful. "Perhaps you and I will get on, after all. Just as long as you remember my Ted is already taken, we should be fine."

THIRTY-SEVEN

Miriam

At least one good thing had come out of all the mess Norma had caused, Miriam reflected, more than a week after the evacuee had left the manse, and a day after Aneurin left to begin his basic training in Brecon. Emrys was so bitter at his failure to convince Aneurin to register as a conscientious objector, he'd turned to his wife for comfort.

The night his son enlisted, Emrys had laid his head on her breast and wept, clinging to her for reassurance. The following night he went further, joining her in her bed. She sensed he longed to bury his pain in her, to blot out his unspoken feelings of failure in a physical solace she was more than willing to give. But all week, her dad's words had preyed on her mind.

"Do you think we did the right thing when we asked her to leave?" Miriam asked Emrys when he finished his nightly prayers on his knees beside his bed. Out of respect for his feelings, she still avoided mentioning Norma's name.

"How can you doubt it? She might have cost me my son. I doubt he would have enlisted if not for her." He got up, his leg troubling him as it always did, then slipped under his blankets.

"But Aneurin's away now, so she couldn't carry on pursuing him if she was here. And she had no friends or family to help her find a place to stay."

"She'll fall on her feet. Her sort always does."

"I've been wondering if we should have let her stay. If the Christian thing to do would be to show forgiveness and invite her back."

His black brows drew together. "Forgiveness is one thing. Trusting her, or inviting temptation in, is another. Would you lead Aneurin into sin so readily? And her, too? Leave things as they are. I want him to be able to come home without being drawn back into her clutches."

She fidgeted with the elasticated cuffs on her nightdress. "Apparently she's staying with Ted."

"Hmph. If your family was so keen to help her, it would have been more sensible to billet her with Stanley. It's not as if he can be led into temptation by a pretty face these days."

Not for the first time, Miriam felt a prick of jealousy. Did Emrys think a man would have to be blind to resist Norma's charms?

"You think she's pretty, then?"

Now she had his full attention. "You surely don't imagine *I* could be attracted to a painted Jezebel like her?"

"Most people would probably think her beautiful. Even without her make-up, she has those lovely blue eyes and that soft blonde hair, and that way of smiling. And of course there's the way she walks, holding herself like a starlet in a film. And she always looks stylish, doesn't she? She's the only woman I ever saw who doesn't look frumpy in a maternity frock. Whenever we went out in Pontybrenin, I noticed men looking at her. And I can't blame them for... Well, for desiring her."

Emrys turned away onto his side and reached for the switch on the lamp. In the darkness, she heard him thump his pillow into shape. Then, silence.

She bit her lip, remembering the book Dolly had lent her, and what it said about married love.

"What about me, Emrys? Do you feel any desire for me? I feel it for you. I hope you know that. I worry sometimes that you don't look at me that way. Because I'm not stylish, and not especially pretty either. But I still need to know that you feel something when you see me."

His voice sounded confused, and perhaps a little exasperated. "Why would you want to be looked at the way men look at her? The feelings I have for you go deeper than lust. You're my wife. More precious than rubies. Don't cheapen yourself with this kind of talk."

"Is it cheap to want my husband to want me?" On an impulse, she sat upright, fumbling with the buttons at the neckline of her nightdress, before tugging it over her head and dropping it on the floor. Her hair felt silken on her bare shoulders.

Emrys's mattress creaked as he shifted in his bed. "What are you doing?"

"If you turn on the lamp, you'll see."

He shielded his eyes from the glare as the bulb lit up. When he turned back towards her, they widened.

"Miriam—"

"Don't say anything. Please. Just look at me." Her heart pounded as she waited, eyes closed as she resisted the instinct to cover herself. The clock ticked a regular rhythm into the silence, six or seven times before she heard him move. Her eyelids snapped open as he clicked the lamp off and plunged them back into darkness.

"I don't know what's brought this on," he muttered.

Before she could change her mind, she reached across the distance to his bed and lifted the covers to slip beneath them. She pressed her naked body against him, running her hands upwards to touch his face. Through his cotton pyjamas, she could feel the solid warmth of him. The way he flinched from her. His breathing was shallow and rapid, as if he wanted her too, but wouldn't let himself show it.

"There's no one in the house but us. Please, let me touch you. I'd like you to touch me. To kiss my breasts." When she'd read that enticing suggestion in the Marie Stopes book, a longing had swirled deep in her groin. Naked beside him, it reawakened, fiercer than ever.

His breath hissed inwards. She stopped it with a kiss, then slid a hand under the waistband of his pyjamas, reaching lower to cup the curve of his buttock.

"Miriam—" he said again, but less fervently this time, as if she'd robbed him of the will to fight.

Emboldened, she traced a line of kisses from his mouth down the roughness of his chin and along his throat, where his pulse throbbed at the neckline of his pyjamas. A low groan rumbled as she took hold of one of his hands and placed it on her bottom. He squeezed, caressing the plump softness of her flesh.

Delighted, she flicked his buttons open, moving lower and lower as the cloth parted, following the line of his chest with her lips. As she arched up onto her knees to kiss the fuzz of black hair on his belly, the bedclothes slipped and she shrugged them off, exposing her nakedness to cool air.

Goosepimples rose on her limbs. She tipped forward to push her breasts against his chin, not minding the roughness of his night stubble but relishing its drag on her skin. She gasped as the hot moistness of his mouth found the peak of her nipple.

"Oh, Emrys..." It had never been like this. They'd had moments of closeness, physical intimacy, even, but they had never been passionate. She'd never been able to let go, knowing he, too, had lost his own rigid self-control. Her throat arched, head tipping back in wonder at the flood of sensations washing over her body where his hands grasped and his tongue blazed across her breasts.

Aching for him, she helped him jerk his pyjama trousers down, rushing to be free of the barrier. His erection prodded against her hip, and she sensed him unravelling when she dared to stroke it, curling her hand around it and tugging in a way he'd never allowed or encouraged before. By the time he flipped her onto her back and pushed his fingers between her thighs she was more than ready. She clamped her legs around him and dragged him in, reeling him into her like a mermaid luring a ship onto rocks. Farther and farther in, wave on wave, until her mind shattered and pricks of light filled her eyes where they squeezed shut.

All that mattered was this feeling. This moment. She was full of him. She'd claimed her power as a woman, as his wife, and she'd never felt so alive.

THIRTY-EIGHT

Miriam

The next morning, Miriam awoke in Emrys's bed, her shoulder aching from their awkward sleeping position. He was curled against her back, one heavy arm thrown across her. To her surprise, a fresh erection pressed against her buttock although she'd done nothing to provoke it. Smiling, she permitted herself a sly wriggle against his nakedness before rolling over within his embrace.

"*Bore da,*" she murmured against his neck, wishing him a good morning. Never had she said it so triumphantly.

Black lashes fluttered and she infused her gaze with love as his eyes blinked and focused. A couple of heartbeats passed, then he shifted to create a gap between them.

"It must be time to get up," he mumbled, extricating his arm and rolling over, almost toppling off the narrow bed in his haste. Scooping his pyjama bottoms off the floor, he bunched them in front of him and yanked open the door without another word or glance in her direction.

Miriam's smile died. The sound of running water from the bathroom sent a clear message that the night's intimacies were over. She might as well get dressed and face the day.

By the time he joined her in the dining room, it was already close to nine o'clock and she was halfway through breakfast. He remained silent while she poured a cup of tea and pushed the toast rack across the tablecloth towards him.

"I've been thinking," she said, ignoring the way his hand faltered before he recommenced buttering two triangles of toast. "If it's alright with you, I'd like us to try sleeping in a double bed, like my parents did. Twin beds are more modern, I know, and I'll admit it's easier to change the linen and to clean under them, but... It was nice being able to sleep beside you last night. A wider bed would be more comfortable."

His frown came as no surprise. For all his traditionalism in religion, he despised old-fashioned, Victorian things like double beds, spurning them as firmly as he rejected an English Prince of Wales and unquestioning obedience to Britain's Empire. But the sound of the doorbell left no time to debate the point.

Quickly, Miriam untied her apron and made her way along the hallway to the front door.

"Idwal! This is a surprise. Do come in," she said. It was rare to see her brother-in-law anywhere but on the farm. He'd have been up for hours already, dealing with the livestock. What could have brought him down from the mountain so early in the day, with his weather-beaten face lacking its usual easy smile?

"Is Gwenllian alright?" she asked, taking his coat and cap.

"Not really," he said. "Is Emrys in his study?"

"He's in the dining room, finishing his breakfast. I can make you some toast, too, if you'd like."

He'd already disappeared into the dining room, as if he couldn't delay even for a moment. Her stomach knotting, she hung up his things.

At the table, the brothers were conversing in rapid Welsh. She recognised the word for postman just as Idwal retrieved a piece of paper from his jacket pocket. Emrys scanned the page, colour draining from his cheeks until they matched the paper in his hands.

"The first of January?" The thump of Emrys's fist descending onto the tabletop made the cutlery bounce and his cup rattle in its saucer.

Idwal dragged a hand through his thinning thatch of hair. Miriam had never seen him like this. Dejected. Defeated, even.

"I'll fetch more tea," she murmured, not quite knowing what to do.

Neither man acknowledged her when she returned. All their attention was on the letter. Could there be something wrong with Gwenllian? Or was it something about the farm, perhaps?

"What's happened, Idwal?" she asked.

"Read the letter to her, Emrys. I must have read it a dozen times, but I still can't take it in."

Emrys rubbed a hand over his mouth. "See for yourself," he said, pushing the paper across the tabletop.

She smoothed it out, scanning the words. It was from a land agent in Chester, more than a hundred miles away in England's north-west.

Dear Sir/Madam,

Pontybrenin Artillery Range
Pant Glas

In connection with the provision of this range, it is necessary to requisition all/part of the above-mentioned property, which I understand you own/occupy.

This letter is sent in order to give you as much notice as possible that VACANT POSSESSION of the whole property, including house and buildings (if any), will be required on 1st January next, so that you can immediately start making arrangements for any necessary alternative accommodation and disposal of livestock.

She pushed it away. No wonder both men looked so shaken and angry.

"Only landowners will be compensated. Tenant farmers get nothing," Idwal said.

Her eyes widened. Without financial compensation, how would he start again?

"We'll sell what produce we can at the November fair," he continued. "It's lucky the ewes haven't been tupped yet – I was intending to put the ram in with them this week. But I've just sowed my wheat on the lower fields. How will I harvest it next year, if...?" He scratched his head in bewilderment. "And if everyone has to sell their stock at the same time, how will we all get a fair price?"

"You're talking as if this is decided. We can still fight it," Emrys urged, leaning forward.

Miriam stared. Had he not understood the letter?

It seemed Idwal, at least, understood. "It *is* decided, Emrys. The country is at war, and if this is the price we must pay to stop Hitler, then I suppose it will be a sacrifice worth making. When it's over, hopefully the government will return the land to us."

"But who knows how long that will take, or where you will be by then? With nigh on forty families all selling their livestock and finding new homes at the same time, how many will want to return, or even be able to, by the time the authorities decide they may? And if there's another war in the future – rather, *when* there's another war, for there's sure to be, over and over until the end of days, for nation shall rise against nation, and kingdom against kingdom – then how many times will you let them take your home from you? Idwal, if you don't fight this, you'll be left with nothing, and so will all the other families. You deserve better than this. It's not right." Desperation lent roughness to Emrys's rich voice.

"And if I do fight it, I'll still be left with nothing, but I'll have wasted precious time when I could have been making plans."

A gloomy silence fell. Emrys bowed his head and buried his face in his hands.

Miriam's heart ached for them.

Idwal cleared his throat. "Will you look after Mam here, until I can find us somewhere? I'll try to get a farm nearby, if there are any, but with others looking too, we need to be realistic. I might have to move away."

"There's always a place here for her, and for you, should you need it. You don't even need to ask." Emrys crossed the room to squeeze his brother's shoulder.

Miriam blinked rapidly. Her stomach had plummeted with Idwal's request, and Emrys's immediate acquiescence had sent it down further. He was right, of course. They couldn't refuse her mother-in-law accommodation. Even if Emrys had paused to consult her about such a significant change to their domestic arrangements, she would have felt obliged to agree. But the thought of living with Gwenllian, hearing that sharp tongue voicing her strong opinions daily about everything from Miriam's cooking and cleaning to her childless state, made her feel as if the walls were closing in. How on earth would she cope?

THIRTY-NINE

Norma

Three weeks under Ted and Ceinwen's roof had made Norma grow more restless with each passing day. Although she appreciated their generosity in letting her stay, she didn't fit in. Ceinwen's territorial attitude to her kitchen made it awkward to set foot in there. She was so much in control of her household, with her own ways of doing things, that Norma felt she was in the way. She and Miriam had rubbed along well enough, and her assistance in Miriam's household had been gratefully accepted. But Ceinwen seemed to think any offers of help were a criticism of her housekeeping.

Ted was nice enough: a man of few words, he'd come home from work in time for his tea, ruffle his sons' hair and silently devour his evening meal as if he hadn't eaten a bite all day. He and Ceinwen were fond parents, often laughing at their boys' antics. They chucked them indulgently under the chin or hugged them far more often than they boxed their ears or sent them to bed early for being naughty. It made Norma wish she'd known such affection when she was small.

Young Joey and Lenny would always have someone to turn to.

Without Aneurin to talk to, Norma felt lonely, even in the busy hubbub of the Cadwaladers' household.

She still felt guilty about taking Joe's room. Her arrival meant the two boys now shared a single bed, with Joe sleeping in their bedroom. Although he'd never voiced any complaint, he must find it difficult. The boys went to bed earlier than him, and had a habit of playing pranks like putting itching powder on his pillow or folding the sheets so he couldn't get his legs all the way in. He must be longing to have his own bed back, lumpy and narrow though it was.

Her melancholy was made worse by feeling ugly and unwieldy, in a way she'd never felt before. Her belly was now huge and marked with scarlet lines that would forever reveal her past to anyone who might one day see beneath her underwear. If she should ever be lucky enough to find another man she could care for, there'd be no escaping her shame, unless she could contrive to always undress in the dark.

Not that she was likely to ever find anyone who could measure up to Aneurin. The brash, arrogant fellows she had found attractive in the past no longer appealed. Now, she wanted someone gentle, who might see beneath the surface and yet still, somehow, love her. If she couldn't have Nye, she could only be content with someone exactly like him.

When she wasn't kept awake by thoughts of what she'd lost or fears for her future, the baby's frequent kicking and prodding prevented her from sleeping comfortably. Could it sense that their time together was limited? Every flutter, poke and kick was a reminder that soon she'd have to give birth to it – and then give it up. She'd be free then to find a job and somewhere else to live. But she couldn't seem to visualise that part of her future. Her imaginings kept getting stuck at the painful part, playing the handover to the social worker over and over in her head.

Once, she'd dreamed of making a success of herself. The Norma of a year ago had looked up to Alma Goldman and fancied owning her own sewing business one day. She'd pictured herself employing apprentices, managing them firmly but fairly, and running her workshop with a reputation for making top quality clothing at a reasonable price. No longer doing basic repairs, she'd pick and choose her work, making wedding gowns with elaborate beading, embroidery and lace. Inspired by the gorgeous dresses she saw at the flicks, worn by stars like Ginger Rogers, they'd be works of art, conveying beauty and glamour on the women wearing them. And Norma would be as smart as Katharine Hepburn, wearing the best her workshop could produce. People would look up to her, as she'd always wanted them to.

These days, she couldn't seem to conjure those imaginings. The day when she might be respected for her skill and business acumen was too far off. It felt like a pipe dream. An indulgence. There were too many obstacles in the way, too much grief in her heart, and too much pain looming on the horizon for her to ever imagine being happy.

She couldn't even forget her fears by focusing on her sewing. There was no space in the Cadwaladers' terraced house to use her sewing machine or to spread out fabric to cut out a pattern. Her sewing things were still at Evelina's Modes, stored upstairs behind a folding screen in a corner. Without space, she couldn't work, and without work, she couldn't afford to move anywhere with more space. It was enough to make her want to scream.

"Let me do more to help you," she suggested to Miss Proudfoot on one of her daily visits to the shop. "I could do with getting out of Ceinwen's way, and there's only so many films I can watch at the Rialto. You know I'd happily sew for you, and I could serve your customers too, give you a chance to take the weight off your feet."

"Oh, my dear. You know I can't have you on display. My clientele wouldn't like it." The regret in Miss Proudfoot's voice sounded genuine, so Norma pressed on, desperation making her stumble over her words.

"I could clean for you, maybe, or press the new stock. Out the back, of course, so none of your customers would see me. Or... or I could help you with your displays, change them every week perhaps, after closing time, to keep your customers interested..." The words tailed off, lodged against the lump in her throat.

"I'm sorry, dear. Word is out about your regrettable circumstances." Miss Proudfoot looked down, smoothing out the sheets of tissue paper on the counter. "I can't afford to lose any custom. Times are hard. They've been hard for years. I'm not one to judge – your things wouldn't be upstairs now if I was. But others do, as we both know."

"You'd think people would have bigger things on their minds to worry about, what with a war on. People dying around the world, and yet some folk have nothing better to do than look down their noses at girls like me." She swept an imaginary speck off her sleeve, hiding the resentment on her face. There was no point in ruining her chances with Miss Proudfoot by venting her anger. Even the strongest fighter had to recognise when they were beaten.

"If I get any requests for alterations, you'll be the first person I'll come to. Not that you'll be able to work for much longer. Your – erm... happy event can't be far off."

Happy event? What was happy about going through nine months of shame, only to experience hours of agony and then go against every instinct to hand her own flesh and blood over to someone else, knowing she'd never see it again? Never see her own kid grow. Never hold it in her arms or kiss it. Never hear its voice calling out for her. Never have it climb into her lap and ask for a cuddle.

All the pretty things she'd make in the future, and not one item would be for her own child. She still hadn't been able to bring herself to sew anything for its layette. She kept pushing thoughts of the baby out of her mind, but every day it grew harder to escape the inevitable prospect of pain.

"I'll go and get a few of my things. Move them out of your way. I don't want to impose," she mumbled, turning for the narrow stair. With her eyes blurring, she almost stumbled, but grabbed for the handrail and pulled herself up doggedly, needing to be on her own to regain her composure.

Keep your eyes peeled for that silver lining. It'll be over the horizon somewhere. Her gran's words came back to her as she climbed the stairs, but they only made her feel worse. Somehow, she pulled herself up straight and swallowed the swell of emotions down.

"Ah, well. There's always some poor bugger worse off," she muttered aloud, repeating another of Gran's sayings. It was hard to imagine anyone worse off than she was just now. She quashed a bubble of hysteria by pressing her hand against her mouth.

Her sewing things were neatly stacked behind a folding screen. How she yearned to use her machine, to lose herself in the pleasure of creating something new – but that would have to wait until she'd found somewhere else to live. Even if there were households with spare rooms left after the influx of evacuee kids, there couldn't be many as generous as the Cadwaladers, who were prepared to overlook what many would see as her dubious moral character.

She'd keep on trying to make the best of things. But using Ceinwen's sewing tools to help with the household mending had felt odd: she wanted her own familiar tin with the sharp scissors she'd had for years, and her pincushion filled with emery powder, with its matching fabric case that she'd made for her needles when she was still at school.

Underneath the tin was her package of neatly folded fabric, together with a bag of scraps. It brought to mind the patchwork panel she'd left for the Powells. Small enough to carry in her bag, and a useful distraction from reality. Perhaps she could make another. She wouldn't need her machine, and she could work on it in her room. She remembered the idea she'd had weeks ago, of capturing the farm on the mountain – its low, whitewashed buildings nestling in its shallow valley, with hedgerows of darker green and the line of the hillside in the background below the sky. As Aneurin's birthplace, it held a significance that went beyond the memory of her visit. It also recalled the moment he'd come close to kissing her for the first time.

He wouldn't have wanted to kiss her, of course, if he'd known the truth about her then. Still, she treasured the memory of his tenderness and the golden sunset in his rich brown hair. If he should ever return to her – an impossible dream, but one that persisted in spite of everything – then she could make him a gift of the picture, and he would know he'd been in her heart all the while. It would show him that she'd held on to what he meant to her.

She packed her shopping bag with enough fabric and thread to get started and descended the stairs with a new sense of purpose.

Her steps felt lighter as she walked along Pontybrenin High Street, her chin tucked downwards against the drizzle, not looking at the bank where Nye had worked, or the Station Hotel porch where she'd teased him about Hilda Hughes. Where was Nye now? Was he thinking of her? Had his dislike and disappointment ebbed at all? She hoped so. Hoped that one day her memories of him would be a solace, not a fresh wound.

On an impulse, she paused between the impressive columns outside the library, then pushed open the heavy door. If she couldn't work right now, she'd have to find other ways to better herself. Maybe she'd find some pearls of wisdom here.

The building's interior made her feel overawed. The windows were tall, high up on the dull-green-painted walls. No one was talking. A few patrons browsed the oak bookshelves, as if they knew exactly what they were looking for and where to find it.

Wandering farther in, her heeled shoes sounding over-loud on the linoleum, she came to a desk beside rows of small wooden drawers, all labelled. As she halted, uncertain, a young woman looked up with a smile that revealed perfect teeth, and Norma recognised her as one of Miss Proudfoot's customers.

"May I help you?" the woman asked in a low, well-spoken voice. She wore a smart dress of bottle green wool with mother-of-pearl buttons down the bodice. Ruffles at the collar and cuffs made it feminine rather than severe. Her long chestnut hair was pinned back into neat rolls, and her make-up was subtle.

Norma cleared her throat. "I want to know how to set up in

business. Sewing, and that. I already sew for people – alterations and mending and stuff. But I want to expand, make clothes and home furnishings and things, once I'm..." She waved a hand over her belly, momentarily speechless. She could hardly use the word *free*. "Once I'm able to get back to work," she added after a moment's thought.

"I'm sure we have some books that will help you," the woman said. "Let me direct you to the relevant sections."

"I ain't been in a library since I was at school," Norma confessed in a whisper, following her past the tall, imposing racks. It felt like a temple in here, somehow. A place where she should tiptoe.

The librarian beamed as if she enjoyed nothing more than introducing people to books. "Well, then, you're in for a treat," she said. "If you don't mind me asking, are you from London? You sound just like the evacuee children who are staying with me."

"I am. I arrived at the start of September. The weather was nice then."

"Not quite so pleasant in mid-November, unfortunately. Now, you might need to look in a few places to find what you want. The sewing section is here at 646. Needlework is a little further on. I suspect you'll be most likely to find what you're looking for somewhere on this shelf. But if there isn't anything, try along the back wall there, under Business."

It was like sifting through a treasure trove. Who knew that so many books had been written about sewing? There must be a dozen about dressmaking, tailoring, and making costumes; more about sewing for the home, crafts and embroidery. With so many topics to inspire her, Norma felt a buzz of excitement for the first time in ages.

Her first selection was a volume called *Sewing for Profit*. After flicking through the pages for a minute or two to confirm it offered the kind of information she needed, she carried it almost reverently to the desk.

Her brighter mood dimmed a little when the librarian asked for her details to give her a reader's ticket. The last time Norma had dealt with paperwork was to get her identification card amended, and she'd had to turn on the waterworks to avoid serious consequences.

The official then had glared at her. "Sparrow... Finch... You know, you could end up as a very different kind of bird for giving the wrong details to the authorities. A jailbird, I mean. You do realise it's a criminal offence to—"

She'd opened her mouth to lie her way out of it, but she couldn't keep depending on lies to get along. Look where they had got her. She'd settled for a version of the truth that she hoped would keep everyone out of trouble.

"It was a genuine mistake on Mrs Powell's part when she wrote my information down. She didn't realise I'd changed my name to get away from the man who did this to me. He's in prison, waiting to hang, and I couldn't risk him finding me." She let her eyes fill with tears – it wasn't difficult. The thought of prison had made her tremble. Luckily, there'd been a man dealing with her case. They were usually easier to soften up than women.

Norma wondered if the librarian would still be this friendly once she knew her new patron wasn't married.

"Norma Sparrow. Miss," she said, blushing as she handed over her new identification card. She swallowed and looked the woman warily in the eye, hardly able to believe it when there was no discernible reaction. No curl of the lip; no arch of the brow; no raking glance over her stomach. The young woman merely wrote out her name on two cards.

"And your address, Miss Sparrow?"

"I'm billeted with Mr and Mrs Cadwalader in Railway Terrace. Number twelve."

"With the Cadwaladers? I know some of them very well. Have you met Maggie? She was my nurse when I was an infant, but she's a midwife now."

"She's checked on me. Said I'm fit as a flea."

"Then I'm sure she's right. You're in good hands with her."

Tucking a card from inside the book into one of the two new reader's tickets she'd written out, the librarian filed it in a tray filled with hundreds of other cards, divided into sections, then pressed a freshly inked stamp onto the piece of paper pasted onto the front page of the book. "You'll need to return the book within two weeks. I hope it proves useful, Miss Sparrow, and if there's anything else I can assist you with, do pop in again."

Norma gazed at the book for a moment before slipping it into her shopping bag on top of her sewing tin. "Thank you," she said.

Relief brought a smile to her lips, almost as bright as her carefree former self might have worn before she met Dickie. It was uplifting, somehow, to be accepted. To be viewed as a would-be businesswoman who was entitled to borrow books like anyone else, and not just as some cheap little tart with a bastard in her belly who had a cheek showing her face in public.

This book could just be the beginning. There was so much here she could learn from. And if she could learn, she could improve herself. A better future might, after all, be within her grasp.

FORTY

Norma

With her shopping bag on her arm and her homemade waterproof gas mask case slung over her shoulder, Norma set off from the library with a spring in her step as she skirted the worst of the puddles. The quickest way back to Railway Terrace was through the churchyard. On this gloomy day, she suppressed a shudder at the sight of the graves. *It's the living what can hurt yer, not the dead*, her gran used to say, with her usual harsh wisdom. She'd cling to that as she passed, and not think about the corpses below her feet.

On the lych gate, the names of the town's war dead were engraved on a brass plaque. One of them made her pause. *Cadwalader, L.J., PTE*. Joe's son Leonard; Ted, Miriam and Maggie's older brother. Norma had come with the family to the Remembrance Day parade last Sunday, though she had hung back, having nothing black to wear. The Cadwaladers stood proudly to attention as a bugler sounded his mournful tune and a man with a bushy moustache and military uniform stepped forward to lay a wreath and give a salute. She remembered an awkward moment when she spotted Miriam and Emrys in the crowd, wearing the white poppies of pacifists in their lapels.

Afterwards, Joe had been furious. "It's disrespectful," he insisted. "Our Miriam used to be proud to wear her red poppy in memory of Len. I blame that ruddy Emrys. I wish he'd just let her be."

Norma closed the gate behind her, trying not to think about Aneurin and the chance that his name might also one day be inscribed on the war memorial. The thought was frightening enough to make her send up a quick prayer for his safety, though she wasn't one for praying as a rule.

The clock on the church tower showed it was half past four. Within an hour it would be dark. The soles of her shoes crunched on the gravel path as she passed the church and the elaborate memorial to the Fitznorton family, who, she'd been told, lived in a big house a few miles outside town. Joe's other daughter, Dolly, worked for them, and Joe had, too, in his younger days. Possessing these snippets of local knowledge made Norma feel a little less like an outsider.

At the back of the churchyard, beside the low, lichen-covered perimeter wall, was a massive tree with drooping branches. When she'd walked home from town one afternoon with Aneurin, he'd told her it was a yew tree. He'd had to explain how to spell it, as she'd never heard of such a thing before. Her ignorance had amused him, and it had been yet another thing he'd had to teach her about, but he hadn't made her feel stupid.

The memory of Nye's kindness brought back the familiar ache. It was remarkable how quickly he'd become her favourite person. A wobbly smile came to her lips as she remembered him showing her the split in the yew's thick trunk. It had been nearly big enough to stand up in. As they'd leaned in together to peer into its cobwebby, earthy interior, she'd felt a thrill of excitement at being so close to him. Nothing had happened, but something in his eyes, and the way he stepped back as if to gather his thoughts, had suggested he felt the same way.

As she passed the tree, her footsteps faltered. A child's voice was coming from inside the cavity in the trunk, singing a song from the radio which Norma recognised as 'We Are the Ovaltineys'. Why would a child be playing in a spooky place like the graveyard, and especially on such a wet day?

"Hello?" Norma called, approaching the tree.

The singing stopped.

"Are you alright in there? It's not very nice weather to be out playing."

The split in the trunk came into view, and Norma's eyes widened as she recognised the face peeping out.

"Audrey? Is that you?"

The girl she'd met in the bandstand sidled out, hugging herself. "Hello, miss."

"What are you doing out in the rain again, darlin'? This ain't the weather for hanging around in churchyards." Her face darkened. "Have they been making you stay out again?"

Audrey nodded glumly, tucking her hands up her coat sleeves and scuffing her toes in the earth as if she was embarrassed at being caught out.

"You must be freezing, darlin'."

"I'm alright. It's dry inside the tree. I'll go back a bit closer to teatime."

Norma swallowed the fury rising in her chest at the idea that Audrey's hosts were still making her stay out after school. The nights were drawing in, and the late autumn weather was bad most days. Next week the clocks would go back an hour, and it would be dark by this time of day.

The girl didn't even have a gas mask with her. What were her hosts thinking of, letting her go out without one? Norma had assumed they would mend their ways after she and Aneurin delivered Audrey back to them. That time, Aneurin had been polite as the old bitch insisted the girl must have misunderstood. "You have to give Mrs Arthur the benefit of the doubt," he'd reasoned afterwards. But Norma had had a bad feeling. She'd ignored it then, her thoughts still caught up in the afterglow of their kiss and his passionate declaration. Clearly, she should have gone back to check on Audrey instead of trusting the old couple to do the right thing by her.

"D'you fancy a cup of cocoa? It might help warm you up a bit. You never know, Contadino's might have a bit of cake left, too. I could fancy some, if you come with me. I don't like eating cake on my own," she added, as if Audrey would be doing her a good turn.

A slow smile dawned on Audrey's thin face. "Yes, please, miss," she said, slipping a grubby hand into Norma's.

"That's the spirit. Cake tastes better when you eat it in company, don't it? And you can call me Norma, remember. You don't have to call me miss, as if I was a mean old teacher."

Norma made herself chat brightly on the way to Contadino's, even though she was simmering inside. If she let on how angry she was, it might make Audrey clam up, and she wanted the girl to feel comfortable enough to talk. In the café, she ordered two cups of cocoa and the last two slices of fruit cake, pretending not to notice how Johnny Contadino's soulful gaze kept returning to her belly. She hadn't been in since the day she'd met Joe, for fear of meeting Miriam or her sisters. But there was no chance of encountering Miriam there at this time of day, when she would be cooking Emrys's tea.

Blinking away the vivid mental picture of Miriam in the homely kitchen at the manse, Norma turned on her most charming smile and focused her attention on Audrey.

"Now, then, darlin'. It's a few weeks since I last saw you. I want to hear all about how you've been getting along. How's school going?"

"It's alright, I s'pose," Audrey said, without enthusiasm. "One of our teachers has gone back to London, but Mr Winter is still here. I wish I could go back to London. Do you miss it, too?"

"Sometimes," Norma admitted, cutting her slice of fruit cake into smaller pieces. "I miss my old job, and the friends I worked with." She wasn't sure "friends" was an accurate description, considering she hadn't kept in touch with any of them. She'd shoved her past life in a box to be forgotten when she arrived in Pontybrenin, for fear of betraying her unmarried status.

"I miss me mum and dad. I tried to write to them, but Mrs Arthur took the letter and ripped it up. She said I was a tell-tale and I was selfish to make them worry about me."

"Mrs Arthur sounds like a right old cow."

Audrey giggled, looking around to check no one else was listening. "Mr Arthur's worse. It's his fault she won't let me in until teatime."

"Oh, yes?" There were so many things Norma wanted to ask about Mr Arthur. But Audrey was already looking worried, as if she feared she'd revealed more than she should. "What do you like to do, then? If the mean old so-and-so didn't make you stay out, what would you want to do indoors?"

"I like playing board games, but there's no one else to play them with here. When we was evacuated, my sister, Carol, had to get off the train before I did, so I can't play with her no more. Mum sent me a letter and said Carol is staying somewhere near Bristol." She paused to take a slurp of cocoa.

"It's hard being split up from your brothers or sisters, ain't it? I had a little brother, Ronnie, but we couldn't stay together. It'll be different for you, Audrey. Soon as the war is over, you and Carol can go back to your mum and dad, and then you'll be able to play as many board games as you like."

A lump rose in Norma's throat. How she hoped that would be true for Audrey and Carol. If it wasn't for her old photograph, she wouldn't even be able to remember what Ronnie looked like.

"Carol had all our marbles in her bag when we got on the train, so I ain't got those to play with, neither."

"What do you do to keep yourself busy when you're outside, then? I know you sing songs, 'cause I heard you. I like singing, too."

"I'm not allowed to sing back at the Arthurs'. He'd blow his top if I made that much noise."

The child's expression seemed to close down. She took a bite of cake, her face carefully blank.

Norma's breathing had turned shallow, as if something was pressing down on her chest.

"What happens when he blows his top?" she asked.

Audrey started crumbling the rest of her fruit cake, picking out the raisins one by one. "He shouts," she whispered. "And a couple of times he's chased me up the stairs with his shoe in his hand."

"Did he hit you with it?" On an impulse, Norma reached across the table and squeezed the girl's hand. "You can tell me if he did, Audrey. I won't be cross with you. You can tell me the truth about what the Arthurs are really like, and I promise to believe you." She knew only too well the fear of telling a grown-up what another adult had been doing, and of not being believed. Grown-ups stuck together.

The girl nodded, tears filling her brown eyes. "He hit me round the head with it. And then he put me over his knee and held me down. He pulled my knickers down to hit my backside with his hand. He... My ear was already hurting where he whacked it, and then he hurt my bum as well."

The first time she went to Contadino's, Johnny had told Norma about the coffee machine, and how it was liable to explode if he didn't release the build-up of steam pressure. Audrey's words made Norma feel much the same need for release. Her pulse throbbed in her ears, her vision blurring with the effort to remain calm in front of the child.

Be a good girl, now... She started, looking around. The words sounded so clearly, it was as if Uncle Des was sitting next to her. Under the table, she clenched her fists so hard it was almost enough to make her cry out. Somehow, she managed to focus on her hands long enough to regain control.

"Mr Arthur doesn't sound like a very nice man," she managed to say, hoping Audrey hadn't noticed how deeply she was affected by her story. "I don't like to think of you going back there tonight. Would you rather stay somewhere else, my darlin'? Somewhere they don't make you stay out in the rain, and where you're allowed to walk on the stair carpet and sing songs and not get a whack every time you step out of line?"

"Really? Can I come and live with you, Norma?"

"Oh, darlin'... There's not enough room in my billet. But I'll find you somewhere. You won't have to spend another night there, I promise. I'll come with you to fetch your stuff, and one way or another I'll make sure you have somewhere safe to stay tonight. You don't deserve to be treated the way the Arthurs have treated you. Nobody does. So we're going to put a stop to it, once and for all."

Leaving the money for the cake and cocoa on the tabletop, she helped Audrey shrug her sleeves into her wet coat before putting on her own. Whatever happened, she'd make sure Audrey didn't spend another minute alone with Mr Arthur. Even if she had to give up her bed at the Cadwaladers' and sleep on a park bench, she couldn't let the girl go back there.

FORTY-ONE

Norma

Norma didn't need Audrey's directions this time to get to Alexandra Avenue. She remembered the way, alright – and the big, posh houses. Last time, she'd let Aneurin do the talking. This time, she wouldn't be giving those horrible people a chance to sweet-talk her with lies. She had no intention of letting Audrey take another step over that threshold. She'd do whatever it took to make sure the girl was safe somewhere else before the night was out.

"You won't say I told tales, will you?" Audrey asked in a trembling voice, her hand in Norma's as they approached the Arthurs' grandiose villa.

"Audrey, you must promise me you won't worry. You're not in any trouble. The only reason we've come back is to make the Arthurs give me your things so we can find you somewhere nice to sleep tonight. You can wait here if you like, so you won't have to speak to them. I'll take care of it for you."

The child's relief was palpable as she hung back at the end of the driveway, where two brick pillars marked the boundary of the property. Leaving her there, Norma marched up the gravel path, noting with a raised eyebrow a gathering of garishly painted garden gnomes arranged in a rockery. Apparently having the money to buy a house like this didn't mean the owners possessed fine taste.

On reaching the front door, its glass pane blanked out from behind by brown paper, she rapped the heavy brass knocker. The sound of it echoed in the hallway, and she had to knock again before the door swung open.

Mrs Arthur folded her arms across her ample bosom at the sight of Norma on her doorstep. "You again! What do you want this time?" she asked, looking down her nose, noticeably less welcoming than she'd been when Aneurin had been at Norma's side.

"I want you to fetch Audrey's things. Pack them in her bag and bring them out to me. She won't be spending another night in this house. I'm taking her somewhere safe, where she won't be left out all hours in the pouring rain. Somewhere she won't be beaten. And once I've done that, I'll be reporting you and that feller of yours to the billeting officer, to make sure he don't send you no more evacuees."

"Just who do you think you are, young woman? You can't come here barking orders and accusations at me—"

"Save your breath for cooling your porridge, you old witch. Go and get the kid's stuff this minute, if you don't want me kicking up a stink on your doorstep. I've dealt with bigger and harder people than you before, and I ain't afraid to come in there and pack her bag meself if I have to."

As the woman's jaw fell open, her husband appeared in his cardigan and slippers, a pipe in his hand. A tall, heavyset man, he loomed menacingly in the doorway.

"What on earth is going on here?" he demanded.

"You must be Mr Arthur, I suppose. Well, I can tell you exactly what's going on. Your missus is just on her way upstairs to fetch Audrey's things, and to hell with the wear on your precious stair carpet. And then once I've got Audrey's bag, I'm going to take her somewhere safe. If you try and stop me, I'll tell the police what a filthy, nasty pervert you are."

"I beg your pard—"

"Get a move on, or I'll start shouting and then all your neighbours will know what you've been up to, you disgusting, horrible man."

Mrs Arthur had already started up the stairs, her round face scarlet, but her husband, it seemed, was less easily intimidated. Stepping outside, he stuck his beaky nose so close to Norma's face that she could smell the tobacco on his breath.

She stood her ground, fists clenching, even though the smell made bile fill her mouth.

"Get off my property this instant, and don't think for a minute that anyone will believe your disgraceful lies. I don't know what the child has been saying, but I assure you I won't stand for this. If you dare to utter another word against me or my wife, I'll sue you for slander, you little trollop."

Norma's voice rose. "You can call me what you like, but it don't change what you are. I ain't scared of you. You're despicable. Think it's fun to interfere with little girls, do you? Think it's alright to neglect them and beat them?"

"This is an outrage. You'll get nothing from us." Without warning, he seized Norma's upper arm in a steely grip and shook her so violently her teeth clattered together. As he wrenched her arm towards her back, he gave her a push and propelled her down the driveway quickly enough to make her stumble. "I told you – get off my property – and I meant it."

"Or what? Will you pull *my* knickers down and give me a thrashing, an' all? Let go of me, you bastard!"

The pain in her arm as she tried to twist out of his grasp made her voice come out as something close to a shriek. On reaching the gateposts, he gave her a shove that sent her sprawling on all fours on the road. The momentum of her fall pitched her forwards onto her face and stomach.

A sharp stinging in her palms and knees made her cry out even before the pain in her cheek and the blow to her belly registered. For a moment she couldn't get up. Her empty lungs had forgotten how to fill with air. By the time she'd struggled back to her feet, she felt as if every sinew in her belly and back had been stretched to breaking point. Everything hurt. At the edge of her awareness, she heard sobbing; but all her attention was on Mr Arthur's retreating back.

He'd reached his front door and stood silhouetted in the light. His eyes widened as he saw that she was no more than ten yards behind him.

"Call the police," he said to his wife, who had appeared beside him with a battered suitcase.

Mrs Arthur tossed the case onto the gravel, then screamed as Norma stooped beside the rockery and picked up a garden gnome.

As Norma lifted her wrist to wipe away a stream of blood that had trickled into her eye, the gnome's bearded face leered at her. Despite its cheerful blue hat, it looked sinister. Horrible little thing. Nasty, like the people in the house.

"Get inside, you stupid woman!" Mr Arthur bellowed, tugging his wife into the hallway and pulling the front door closed behind them.

Fury made Norma's aim wild. Hardly aware of what she was doing, she lobbed the gnome towards the door. Dazed, she recoiled as it smashed through the glass pane, leaving a hole in the blackout paper behind it.

High-pitched screams streamed through the gap.

"Bugger it," Norma muttered, dizzy with pain and the release of emotion. She'd only meant to smash the gnome, not the glass. Now she really was in a pickle. And her stomach hurt. Had he harmed her baby? Would it be alright?

With a groan, she reached for the suitcase, almost doubling over in pain. One of the catches had burst open as it landed, but for some reason her hand seemed to be shaking too much to refasten it.

On legs that had turned to jelly, she staggered back towards the gate, where Audrey was sobbing hysterically. A stranger had appeared beside her, and as Norma joined them, murmuring reassurances to Audrey that she'd be alright in a minute or two after a little sit down, several others also arrived. Their lips moved, but Norma couldn't hear anything over the strange ringing noise in her ears. Blinking to clear her dimming vision, she realised one of the faces was familiar.

"Hello," she said, aware that her voice sounded strange, like someone who'd been drinking. "It's a bit of luck to see you here. I think... I think I might be hurt."

The last thing she knew as her vision turned black was the sensation of hands taking the suitcase from her and grasping her under her armpits. She tried to call out for Audrey, but pinpricks of light were rushing past, and as hard as she tried, she couldn't stop them dragging her down into oblivion.

FORTY-TWO

Miriam

After a day at Pant Glas Farm and the subsequent hour-long walk back to the manse through a thick, misty drizzle that seeped through every layer of clothing, Miriam longed for nothing more than a cup of cocoa, preferably in the bath, followed by bed in her cosiest brushed cotton nightgown.

It had been an emotionally trying day. Gwenllian alternated between anger and tears at the prospect of having to leave the home where she'd lived for almost fifty years, since she was a young bride. Pant Glas was where she'd birthed and reared her sons, nursed her husband through his final illness, and where he'd died, like his parents before him, in the bedroom upstairs with the window ajar to release his spirit back to God and the mountain.

On their way home, Miriam and Emrys had talked about what was to come. He was no less anguished at the imminent loss of his family's home than he had been when Idwal first showed him the letter. They'd visited the farm every day since then, doing their best to help in practical ways while Idwal wrote letters to his landlord and the Farmers' Union and any connections he could think of who might know of a farm in need of a new tenant. Gwenllian couldn't manage the farm alone, so as soon as the livestock was sold, she would need to come to live at the manse, at least until Idwal was settled. Her situation beyond then was still unclear. Privately, Miriam clung to the hope that Idwal would find a new home that could accommodate his mother. But with forty other families also looking for somewhere to go, their options would be limited.

"Shall I make some supper?" she offered when they arrived home and shut the door against the frigid twilight.

Emrys shrugged. He drew the curtains before flicking on the light, and in its harsh glare she read the exhaustion in his face. Like his brother, he seemed to have aged years in a few days. Making the daily trek up and down the mountain would be draining for anyone, but with his old injury and his fragile emotional state he was worn out.

"You must eat more, to keep your strength up," she urged him. "Idwal and your mother need you. If you deny your body nourishment, you'll make yourself ill."

He sighed, rubbing his face where a muscle twitched under his eye. "I know you're right. I'll be in my study if you don't mind bringing something to me there?"

Miriam was making sandwiches when the telephone rang in the hall. The food would have to wait.

"I'm glad I've caught you." Maggie's voice sounded strained. "There's a tricky situation here, and as much as I hate to ask, I need your help."

"You know I'm always willing to help in any way I can."

"Yes, well... You might change your mind once you know what it is."

Miriam couldn't imagine any scenario in which she would refuse to help her eldest sister. "I hope it isn't anything too awful, in that case. It's been a difficult day. We've only just got back from the farm, and poor Gwenllian is beside herself – as you'd expect, given that they'll be evicted just after Christmas. It's such a cruel predicament for her and Idwal. And Emrys is wearing himself out..."

"They'll get the farm back once the war is over, I'm sure. Gwenllian will get through it with her family's support. Not everyone is fortunate enough to have that."

It seemed an uncharacteristically unsympathetic response. Miriam paused, frowning. Perhaps she shouldn't have offloaded her own problem before allowing her sister to explain hers. "Why don't you tell me about your tricky situation?" she said.

She heard Maggie release a huff of breath into the receiver, as if she was trying to decide how best to broach a difficult subject.

"There was an altercation in the avenue earlier—"

"An altercation? In *your* street?"

"One of the neighbours, Mr Arthur, was being very unpleasant. He'll be the talk of Pontybrenin by morning, I shouldn't wonder. He and his wife had a child billeted with them, and it seems they've been quite cruel to her. She was found in the graveyard, sheltering under a tree, and apparently she's frequently turned out of doors to fend for herself. It seems Mr Arthur has been abusive towards her. Violent, and possibly in even more unsavoury respects, too."

"The poor child!" Something about this story was familiar, but Miriam couldn't put her finger on it.

"You needn't fear for her. Venetia and I have taken her in. We've had a spare room since Miss Summerill went back to London, so we were glad to offer her the bed. Venetia's upstairs tucking her in now."

"An ideal solution. And very good of you and Miss Vaughan-Lloyd to offer her the billet. I don't understand the problem, though, if the girl is safe with you? How can I help?"

"It was Norma who found the girl."

"Oh." Miriam felt a chill in the pit of her stomach.

"She was kind enough to take her to Contadino's to warm her up. Then, when she found out what the poor child had been subjected to, she was naturally furious and determined not to allow her to stay in that billet any longer. She quite rightly demanded that the Arthurs hand over Audrey's things."

Miriam said nothing. It did sound as if Norma had behaved responsibly on this occasion, but it couldn't change her previous actions.

"Mr Arthur turned nasty. Verbally and, I'm sorry to say, worse. He twisted Norma's arm behind her and shoved her onto her face in the road, as if it was some kind of pub brawl. How a man can treat a pregnant woman like that is beyond me – it's appalling! But even though she was injured, she didn't let it stop her going back for Audrey's things. Whatever you think of her, Mim, that girl has the courage of a lioness. She stood up for what was right, even though she'd been badly hurt. Unfortunately, she did take things a little bit too far, but it's understandable really in the circumstances."

"What do you mean, she took things too far?"

Maggie cleared her throat. "She threw a garden gnome through one of their windows. Reckless, I know, but she was under extreme provocation. Mr Arthur has stopped threatening to press charges since we pointed out that we could tell the police he's not only assaulted a pregnant woman but also been cruel to a child in his care."

Miriam couldn't imagine what any of this had to do with her. If Norma had been injured, unpleasant though it was, it sounded as if she'd brought it upon herself.

"The trouble is, although she succeeded in getting Audrey and her things to safety, the cost to Norma has been quite serious. Her blood pressure is sky-high, Mim. She's bruised and grazed, and in so much pain she can hardly move. Not to mention the after-effect of shock on a woman in her condition. After a fall like that, there's a risk of a concealed haemorrhage, or her waters breaking and sending her into premature labour. She needs regular monitoring, peace and quiet, and strict bed rest."

"She's been living at Ted's, hasn't she? I'm sure Ceinwen can look after her."

"She won't get any peace there, with their two little tearaways. And it hasn't really been working, her living there. Dad isn't getting a wink of sleep. The obvious solution is for her to come back to stay with you."

"Absolutely not! You're asking too much after everything that's happened."

"Miriam, I knew you'd say that at first, but I also know you to be generous and fair. I wouldn't ask if it wasn't the only way."

"It isn't the only way. She can go to hospital if she's as ill as all that. Or you could take her, instead of the little girl."

"That won't work. Norma can't afford the hospital, and I couldn't monitor her here properly when I'm always either out at work or helping Venetia. You're free to keep a close eye on her. Audrey won't need nearly as much care as Norma, as she'll be out at school most of the time."

"I don't have enough room. Gwenllian will be coming to stay with us soon."

"You have *two* spare bedrooms. It's only while she's ill. Once she's well enough, I'm sure she'll be only too glad to move on."

"Emrys will never agree."

"Miriam! Perhaps I haven't explained this clearly enough. With her blood pressure this high, Norma is at risk of toxaemia. She's already fainted out in the street. Without regular monitoring to check for internal bleeding, and rest to bring down her blood pressure, she could die. Her baby could die. Do you really want their deaths on your conscience when you have it in your gift to show Christian charity and take her in, in their hour of greatest need? Whatever happened between you, I can't believe you'd wish her dead, or want her baby to suffer."

Feeling backed into a corner, Miriam suppressed a growl of frustration.

"What would Mam say if she was here now?" her sister went on, adding to the pressure as if mentioning the baby hadn't been enough to make her feel guilty. "Don't you think Mam would tell you to take her in? To be charitable?"

"Alright! You win, Maggie. Don't keep on. But don't think for a second that I'm happy about it. And I'll have to speak to Emrys first."

"Well, don't let him stop you doing the right thing. It *is* the right thing, I promise. Dad will be proud of you, and Mam would be too if she was still with us. Now, I must go. I need to finish cleaning up the wounds on Norma's face. I'll see you later. One of our neighbours will bring us to the manse in his car in an hour or so. Oh, and Mim… Thank you. I knew you wouldn't let me down."

Miriam hung up the receiver, fighting the urge to scream. Balling her fists, she tipped her head back to catch her breath. At a noise behind her, she turned, eyes widening as she saw her husband standing with his arms folded in the doorway to his study. His eyes glittered.

"What was all that about?" he asked.

FORTY-THREE

Miriam

Emrys's face was cold and hard. "I don't understand you. Do you want that woman here in your house, after everything that's happened?"

"No. But I—"

"Then why are you letting your sister push you into it? Don't we have enough to deal with already? There's my family, the farm, my flock..."

"I know, but I gave my word."

"I've lost my son because of that woman, in case you've forgotten."

Miriam lifted her gaze to his, frowning. "Now, that's not true. You haven't lost him. He writes to us. He'll come back here as soon as he gets leave."

"He's turned his back on everything I ever taught him. Everything I stand for. What else would you call it?"

She opened her mouth, but he didn't give her time to form an argument. Her thoughts were in a spin.

"You can't deny that she's to blame." He turned away, rubbing the back of his neck as if it ached.

Was he right, though? Was it really all Norma's fault that Aneurin joined up? Might he have stayed, if his father hadn't been so determined to tell him how to live? Emrys had put his principles before his family. Was it so surprising that Aneurin, in his way, had done the same? Perhaps the price Emrys was paying for his unwillingness to bend had been inevitable? It was impossible to put her swirling questions into words to challenge him openly about Aneurin. That battle would have to wait for another day.

"I don't know how you can even think of agreeing, let alone asking *me* to take her back in, the woman whose deceitful ways caused us so much trouble."

"You know I wouldn't in normal circumstances. But Emrys, she's dangerously ill, and all because she put herself in danger to protect a child. She needs complete rest, and we can't deny her that act of charity. Aneurin loved her, or at least he imagined he did. If we turn her away now, and she dies, which Maggie says is possible... And if Aneurin finds out we could have prevented it by putting our own righteous anger aside for a short time... Well, then perhaps we really will lose him. But if we do the charitable thing, then there's a chance he'll be grateful. I really believe we must. If we can't show Christian love and compassion for her, we can surely show mercy for the sake of her innocent child?"

He had sunk into his chair and leaned his elbows on the desk, his face in his hands. "You don't know what you're asking of me."

"I do. I don't like it any more than you do. I'll make sure you don't have to see her. I'll nurse her myself. And I won't give her the room she had before, overlooking the mountain. Your mother can still have that one. Norma can have the smaller one at the front. As soon as she's well enough, she can go back to my brother's or find somewhere else to go. I don't want her under our roof any longer than necessary."

Emrys pushed back his chair with a jerk, then limped to the fireplace and back. Miriam sensed he was wrestling with his conscience.

She waited, alert for the sound of an approaching motor car, conscious with every tick of the clock that Maggie and Norma could arrive at any moment.

When at last he spoke, it was as if the words were dragged from him unwillingly. "She has to go before Aneurin comes home. We can't risk them seeing each other again. By the time he gets leave, he'll have got over her. We can't have the sight of her reopening the wound."

Miriam let out a long breath, then crossed the room to lay her head against his shoulder. He stood, motionless, and she let it rest there for a minute until the ringing of the doorbell made her stiffen. They exchanged a glance, then he sat at his desk and shuffled his papers.

The message was clear: having Norma back was her choice, and though he wouldn't stop her keeping her word, neither would he help. Smoothing her skirt, she shut the study door behind her and trudged to the front door.

"Thank you," Maggie said, embracing her. "I know it can't be easy. Can you help me get her upstairs and into bed? We managed to get through to her eventually that the police wouldn't be coming to lock her up and that Audrey will be safe with us. She only agreed to leave her when we promised to inform the billeting officer of Audrey's whereabouts first thing in the morning."

"I haven't had a chance to air the room," Miriam said. "The bed isn't made." Cold dread lay in the pit of her stomach at the prospect of seeing Norma again, let alone having her in the house.

Maggie's gaze sharpened as if she'd guessed her time had been taken up in persuading Emrys to agree to Norma's return. "Nip up and do it now then, there's a love? We need to get her tucked up in bed as quickly as possible. And I don't want to keep our neighbour out any longer than necessary on a cold night. He gets anxious driving in the blackout."

The bedroom was above the parlour, where the fire hadn't been lit all day. It was cold. Miriam grabbed a bundle of sheets and blankets from the linen cupboard and made the bed, then laid a fire in the tiny grate and lit it. After washing her hands, she descended the stairs and gave her sister a nod.

Her first glimpse of Norma came as a shock. The young woman's usually immaculate blonde hair hung about her face like rats' tails, and one eye was almost closed over with an angry bruise and a graze that swept from her swollen cheek to her forehead. The scarlet and purple were vivid against the ghastly pallor of her face. Norma swung her legs out of the back seat of the car, and Miriam noticed both knees were grazed and her stockings torn. As she heaved herself upright with Maggie's help, then took weary steps towards the house, Norma leaned heavily on Maggie's arm, wincing as if every movement was agony.

Had Miriam imagined the flicker of despair in her features as their eyes met, before Norma's face once again clouded with pain? It hadn't occurred to her until now that returning here must be as difficult for Norma as it was for herself and Emrys. The girl would know how reluctant they were to take her in a second time.

Trailing up the stairs with leaden steps, Miriam felt as if there was a weight on her chest. She'd anticipated a wave of dislike on seeing Norma again, not compassion. But the girl's silent suffering was plain to see. She'd gone out of her way to save a child and now might lose her own.

In the small, plain spare bedroom, Norma sat submissively on the bed as Maggie unfastened her dress and pulled it over her head, manoeuvring it carefully past the cuts and bruises on the girl's face. Norma's shoulders and arms hung limply, thinner than they'd been a few weeks ago if Miriam wasn't mistaken. Hadn't she been eating properly?

Maggie kept up a calm commentary as she worked, unlacing and removing Norma's shoes, then rolling down her stockings. Miriam felt a pang as the fibres had to be unstuck from the grazes on Norma's knees.

"Could you fetch a bowl of hot water, lint, and some antiseptic, please?" Maggie asked. "I've already cleaned the wounds on her face and hands, but not these. And if you have a spare nightdress...?"

Miriam nodded, then faltered as Maggie lifted Norma's slip, revealing a large bruise blooming obscenely on her swollen abdomen. The sight of it made Miriam feel sick. No wonder Maggie was worried.

She left the room, closing the door quietly, and descended to the kitchen with an increasing sense of unreality. The sandwich she'd been making when the telephone rang was still on the bread board, the bread starting to curl at the edges. If Emrys still wanted it, he'd have to come and fetch it himself. Her priority now was to help Maggie save Norma's unborn child.

With Norma tucked firmly into bed, her grazes tended and her clothes in the laundry basket, Maggie picked up her bag and gestured towards the door. Miriam followed her onto the landing, remaining silent until her sister had closed the door behind them.

"Her blood pressure is still high, but so far there's no sign of bleeding. You'll need to keep an eye on her, though, and keep her in bed for the next few days. I'll pop in as often as I can, but if you notice anything unusual – if the uninjured side of her face starts to look puffy, or if she starts vomiting or complains of additional pains or tightening in her stomach, for instance – then don't hesitate to telephone me."

Miriam was surprised when Maggie paused halfway down the stairs. Peeping over her sister's shoulder, she saw that Emrys was passing on the way to his study, holding the plate with his sandwich.

"Good evening, Emrys," Maggie said in the brisk tone she always used when speaking to him, as if he were an acquaintance rather than her brother by marriage. "Thank you for allowing Norma to stay while she's unwell."

"Hmph," he muttered, turning away. "It wasn't as if I was offered any choice."

FORTY-FOUR

Norma

Despite three days of strictly enforced bed rest, Norma's body still hurt, even in places she didn't know it was possible to ache. Her mind, though, had started to recover from the fear and shock of the events a few evenings ago. She no longer dreamed of Mr Arthur's cruel, angry face, or of Audrey's terrified screams, or of her baby being born maimed by some terrible injury. She'd stopped fearing the police would call to arrest her for vandalism or whatever crime chucking a garden gnome through a window might be.

Now and then she'd wondered why she'd been put in the smaller spare bedroom. She hadn't heard any voices she didn't recognise, so it seemed there was no one else staying in Norma's former bedroom. Perhaps this was a way to take her down a peg, reminding her she didn't deserve the comforts she'd had before. Who could blame the Powells if that was the case?

Being back in the manse, even in a different room, her thoughts turned continually to Aneurin. Was the army already turning him into a hardened soldier? She couldn't imagine him ever killing anyone. Not even to save himself. To save someone else, perhaps.

That she could believe of him. But a man so gentle would rather die than kill.

Did he know she was here? She'd bet her last penny that he didn't. Not that he'd be able to come dashing back to her bedside even if he wanted to, which seemed hardly likely after their last encounter. That wounded look of his would be seared on her mind until her dying day.

Maybe one day there'd be a world in which a woman like her could love a man like him and it wouldn't matter what she'd done or what people thought, only that they brought out the best in each other and felt right together. But happy endings were for stories, not for a woman like her, who'd slid up to her knees into a pit of other people's disapproval and then sunk deeper with every attempt to drag herself out, until she was drowning in it. She'd get out, though, eventually. *Nothing lasts forever*, as Gran used to say – *not the good things and not the bad ones neither*. Just as soon as she was well enough, she'd start sewing again – and find a place to live where no one knew her. She'd start again.

Being helpless like this was no good at all. It was too easy for her thoughts to turn to the baby, as well as to Nye. Both directions held an abyss of pain she wasn't ready to face. She'd do better to get moving. The sooner she was up and about, the sooner she could leave. No doubt Miriam would be relieved to see the back of her. The woman looked worn out.

"I'm just going for a Jimmy Riddle," Norma said when the creak of the landing floorboard as she limped to the bathroom brought Miriam dashing upstairs.

"But you heard what Maggie said about complete bed rest. I can fetch the chamber pot again."

"I'll go back to bed straight away, I promise."

Norma leaned against the bathroom door jamb, trying not to sway in front of Miriam. The light-headed feeling would soon pass. It was only because she'd spent so much time lying down.

"Go and take the weight off your feet for a minute, Miriam.

You look like a bit of limp lettuce." Talking had made the graze on her face hurt, so she stopped, trying not to grimace as her jarred back and grazed knees protested against her feeble shuffle towards the toilet.

She gazed longingly at the bath, wishing she could soak her aching muscles in some nice warm water. But with Miriam so concerned about her going to the lav by herself, she wasn't likely to let her wallow in the tub.

The sight of her face in the mirror above the basin when she washed her hands made her eyes prick with tears, but she blinked them away and made herself lean in for a closer examination. It was only a graze and a bit of bruising. Nothing that wouldn't heal in a week or two.

That face will either be the making of you or your undoing – only time will tell which it'll be. Her gran's words floated back to her. This time, though, it had been her temper rather than her face that had got her into trouble.

She sighed and skimmed her sore palms over her belly. While she couldn't regret helping Audrey to get away from those awful people, she couldn't help wishing she hadn't put her baby at risk so recklessly. Through her dazed confusion the other evening, she'd been aware of Maggie explaining to someone in a hushed, urgent tone that the fall might have broken some of the unborn child's bones. A wave of nausea engulfed her at the memory. She gripped the edge of the basin. Not even born yet, and she'd let the poor little mite down umpteen times already.

Miriam's voice sounded at the door. "Are you done in there, Norma? You should be resting."

"Yes. I'm done," she said, and allowed Miriam to help her back to bed.

"I need to write some letters and run some errands. Do you need anything before I go out? Ted dropped your things round yesterday; I can unpack them for you if you like." Although the words were helpful, Norma sensed reluctance.

"No thanks. I won't be staying here long enough to need to unpack, will I?"

"Well, if you're sure. I'll leave you to rest, then." Miriam turned towards the door. Norma noted she hadn't bothered pretending she could stay as long as she liked.

"Actually, there is one thing. I took out a library book the other day. I'd like to read it. It was in my shopping bag with my sewing tin. I hate lying here with nothing to do."

With a nod, Miriam fetched the shopping bag, and Norma reached for it gratefully, glad to see the scraps of fabric in the bottom. The sight of the cloth and her tin made her fingers itch to get stitching again, although she wasn't sure if she'd manage it with her hands still scabby and sore from her undignified landing on the road outside the Arthurs' driveway.

"Don't overdo it, or we'll both have to answer to my sister."

"Thanks, Miriam. I appreciate everything you've done for me."

It was on the tip of Norma's tongue to promise to be good, but she wouldn't do that ever again. Not for anyone. She fixed her attention on the book, turning almost reverently to the first page, prepared to stumble over the text but eager to learn all she could.

The sound of a heavy sigh made her look up before she'd even passed the page of contents.

"Everything alright?" she asked.

Miriam had paused with her hand on the doorknob, her shoulders slumping as if in defeat or despair. "I still don't understand why you lied to me the way you did."

"Oh." They were back to that, were they? Norma closed the book and laid it on the bed beside her. "Well... How could I not? You and Emrys would never have taken me in if I'd told the truth. No one would. I'd have ended up in one of those awful institutions."

"But to go on lying, even after you got to know me. How did you live with yourself?"

Norma tipped her head back against the pillow. "Easy for you to say. Have you ever been looked at the way I have? Like you don't deserve to exist, just because you gave a man what he could easily take?"

Miriam frowned and took a step closer. For the first time since the argument in the chapel, her expression suggested she might doubt the assumptions she'd made.

"Are you saying you were... That its father forced you?"

"Not exactly. Look, it's complicated. I don't expect you to understand." She couldn't hope to explain it to Miriam, who had probably never had a sinful thought or desire in her life. Miriam would never have let things go so far with a man that there was no way to avoid letting him have what he wanted.

Miriam nodded, as if reassured that she hadn't misjudged her after all.

"It needn't have come to this if you'd kept yourself pure. You wouldn't have caused so much hurt to yourself, or to Aneurin and the rest of us."

Norma gave a hollow laugh. "Pure? I ain't been what *you'd* call pure since I was a kid. I don't even remember what pure is. Was I pure when I was seven or eight and Uncle Desmond used to give me chocolate and tell me I was a good girl for lying nice and still while he rubbed his—" The words jammed in her throat. With a strangled sound she bunched her knees up, making the book slide to the floor, forgotten. Tears stung her grazed face as they tracked down her cheeks.

"What was I supposed to do, eh? How could I ever have told you? Aneurin never looked at me the way other men had always done. Not even when I told him the truth and he was angry. Disappointed in me, yes. Hurt, yes, of course he was. But even then, there was no contempt. Other men saw me as a bit of meat. Something to use, not much more than a ruddy handkerchief when all's said and done. But not Nye. He saw me as something lovely. How could I not love him for being able to see me like that?"

"But what he saw was a fantasy. And you encouraged it."

Miriam had folded her arms across her chest, her face contorted with emotion.

"And there we have it. Thanks for reminding me what a dirty little tart I am. I'll do my best to bear it in mind. But if you've said your piece, I'd like to rest now. All this upset won't be doing my blood pressure no good."

FORTY-FIVE

Miriam

Miriam wrote the words *Dear Aneurin* at the top of the sheet of notepaper, then paused, her mind blank. What could she say about life at home? She could hardly tell him that Norma had been back at the manse for nearly a week, her blood pressure still high enough to make Maggie frown. Nor could she describe the circumstances that had forced them to take her in, which might turn his thoughts of Norma from disappointed hurt to concern for her welfare.

Nor could she burden him by confiding that the unremitting tension between herself and Emrys was beginning to wear her down. After the strain of the past few weeks, she was constantly exhausted. So tired by bedtime, her neck could hardly hold her head up. Her thoughts were slow, her movements lacklustre, as if her limbs begrudged the energy even the smallest gesture sapped from her. More than anything, she wanted to be able to lie down, to not have to think. To focus on nothing more than breathing and sleeping. Some mornings, the effort it took to fill the kettle and set it to boil was all she could manage before sagging down at the kitchen table and laying her cheek on the tablecloth.

She needed to buck up. Especially today, with Gwenllian due to arrive within hours. With a sigh, she began to write.

You'll be glad to hear that we are well. Your father is still doing all he can to prevent the evictions from Moel Carnau, but I'm afraid he now has little hope that right will prevail over might. Uncle Idwal has been selling off the livestock and looking for another farm, but he hasn't found anywhere local yet. With so many other families also moving, he seems to have resigned himself to the likelihood of having to look farther away. Your mam-gu *will be moving in with us today, bringing what personal effects she can. I've aired the bedroom at the back, so she'll have a view of the mountain.*

Although we don't have much room for extra furniture, your father is keen to bring the old grandfather clock here from Pant Glas. It's a shame we can't fit the dresser in our kitchen. I'm sure Mam-gu will miss it. She's bound to find it hard adjusting to life in town, where almost everyone speaks English, after a lifetime on farms where everyone speaks Welsh. But we will do our best to help her settle in.

She closed her eyes, filled with dread at the prospect of her mother-in-law coming to live with them. There was so much she couldn't say to Aneurin. Having recently lost the girl he believed he loved, and after making the momentous decision to enlist, he had enough worries of his own, without being troubled by problems at home. His letters to her and Emrys were brief, making her wonder if he felt constrained by his father's sensibilities as much as by military regulations. It must be difficult for him, knowing how bitterly his father resented his decision to join up. Heaving a sigh, she pressed on, struggling for anything fresh to say, then brightened at the thought that he would be happy to know Audrey was safe.

Do you remember the little girl you found in the park one afternoon? I'm sure you'll be glad to learn she has a new billet with my sister Maggie and Miss Vaughan-Lloyd. The Arthurs weren't taking suffi-

cient care of her. She will be well looked after now, and Miss Vaughan-Lloyd is pleased to have a new evacuee after the teacher who was billeted with them returned to London.

She tapped the end of her pen against her lip, thinking.

How are you finding army life? Is the training hard after working in the bank? It must be very different, doing so much strenuous activity and living so closely with men of all classes. You must be good at marching and polishing boots and buttons by now. We pray for you every day, and hope for the end of the war to come before you must be sent away.

Miriam had only intended to be out of the house for half an hour, long enough to go to the post office to buy some stamps and post the letter to Aneurin. But on her way back she was waylaid by a notoriously talkative member of the congregation keen to share details of her bunions and corns. The woman jawed on for ages, barely giving Miriam a moment to get a word in. When she finally managed to blurt out that she needed to get home for her mother-in-law, the other woman looked affronted.

"Well, why didn't you say? Don't let me keep you."

It was enough to make her want to scream. Anxiety gave her the impetus to dash back to the manse, but it was too late.

"Where have you been?" Emrys snapped as she stumbled over the front step, her face red with exertion. "I would have thought you'd be here to greet my mother, considering what she's going through."

"I'm sorry. I meant to be back in time. Let me make a cup of tea."

"Too late for that. We've already done it. Perhaps you could show Mam to her room, if that isn't asking too much?"

His tone stung, and she bit back a sharp retort, forcing a smile onto her face before greeting Gwenllian and inviting her to follow her upstairs.

"We thought you would like this room, with the view of the mountain," she said, before faltering at the expression on Gwenllian's wrinkled face.

"So I can gaze upon what I've lost, I suppose? Very thoughtful."

"This was our evacuee's room for a while, but she's in the smaller one at the front now. This one will be more comfortable for you."

The old woman pushed down upon the bed, as if testing the mattress. "Is it clean?" she asked, her nose wrinkling.

"Of course it is. I checked the room and stripped and remade the bed myself. Norma may not have been fastidious in her morals, but she was clean in her habits."

"I suppose I can try it, then. See if it suits." She sniffed and looked around, as if unconvinced.

Miriam was too tired to argue. "I'll help you unpack your things if you like. Help you get settled in."

"She's back, then. That evacuee you brought to Pant Glas."

"She is." Miriam paused, wondering how much Emrys had told his mother. Not for the first time, she felt a wave of annoyance that Norma had twice been foisted upon them on the brink of collapse. Why couldn't the girl do a better job of taking care of herself? It was as if she courted trouble. She'd been offered every kindness; Miriam and the Cadwalader family had given her more than anyone might expect.

"Norma's recuperating after an... An accident. She fell and injured herself. And her blood pressure has been dangerously high. So, naturally, we did the Christian thing and offered her somewhere to recover."

"I'll look in on her. See how she's getting on." Before Miriam could advise against it, Gwenllian hobbled out onto the landing.

Norma was sitting up in bed, wearing one of Miriam's bed jackets. As Miriam and Gwenllian entered the room, she set her sewing aside and covered it with a book. Fleetingly, Miriam wondered what she was making, and whether it hurt to sew with the grazes on her palms not yet fully healed.

"Two visitors today? All we need is a cake and we could call it a party," Norma remarked drily.

Gwenllian frowned, approaching the bed to peer at the girl's face. "What happened to you?" she asked. "You look like you've fought a couple of rounds with one of those bare-knuckle boxers from the colliery."

"If you think I look bad, you should see the other feller," Norma said, with a glimmer of a smile that made her wince and recompose her features.

"Doing a bit of sewing for the baby, are you?"

"Not exactly."

"No? I suppose you've made the layette by now."

"No..."

There was an uncomfortable pause. Norma looked at her hands.

"I see." Gwenllian's shrewd eyes narrowed. She looked at Miriam, who raised her eyebrows and shrugged.

It did seem strange that a girl so keen on dressmaking hadn't even started making clothes for her own baby, when it was due to be born in a matter of weeks. But then, Norma had always appeared unenthusiastic about the prospect of motherhood.

"Well, I'm here now," Gwenllian said, having apparently decided to take charge. "I may not be able to hold a needle like I used to, but I can still knit, if I don't do it for too long at a time, and I've got some nice soft white yarn. I'll come and sit with you for a couple of hours each afternoon, and you'll be surprised how soon we'll have a full set of matinée jackets, bootees and so forth. We've a saying in Welsh, Norma: *Deuparth gwaith yw ei ddechrau.* Two-thirds of the work is getting started."

"Oh. Well, thank you." Norma sounded surprised, and more than a little unsure, for which Miriam could hardly blame her. The idea of spending a couple of hours each day confined in a small room with Gwenllian sounded awful.

"So they've put you in this room now, then," Gwenllian went on, looking around as if inspecting the corners for dust.

"That's right. I used to be in the nice one, but it don't matter. I won't be here for long."

"I hope you haven't left any bed bugs in the other room. I've read that you city folk often have them."

Miriam caught her breath, waiting for fireworks.

"Funny, that," Norma replied, blue eyes cool but her voice even. "I've read that country folk catch all sorts from their animals. Ringworm and scabies and that. Fleas, too. Not spotted any on you yet, though."

Gwenllian nodded. Her mouth reminded Miriam of a cat's bottom.

"I'll come back tomorrow with my knitting," the old woman said, limping back to her own room.

"I'll look forward to it," the girl muttered as Miriam closed the door behind them.

FORTY-SIX

Norma

Norma had almost come to enjoy Gwenllian's afternoon visits. Something about the old woman's bluntness reminded her of her gran. It was obvious that Gwenllian's presence made life more difficult for Miriam, who seemed to be forever having to button her lip in the face of her mother-in-law's jibes. Norma felt guilty for adding to Miriam's workload, but with Maggie insisting that she do nothing more strenuous than visiting the bathroom, it seemed unavoidable. The cold late November weather didn't help as Miriam had to keep the fire going in Norma's room as well as the ones downstairs. She must be spending a fortune on coal.

The embroidered scene for Aneurin was coming along nicely, although her hands were still not quite fully healed, frustrating her efforts. The sky of corals, pinks and orange was almost complete, with a circle of rich egg-yolk yellow to suggest the sunset. Once the scraps of earthy brown, purple and green were in place to represent the fields and hillsides of the valley, she'd add the off-white rectangles for the farm buildings, then begin adding detail with her embroidery silks. However, she kept it hidden from Gwenllian by tucking it under her blankets and getting out one of the items she was planning to give away for Christmas. The picture of Pant Glas was a secret between herself and Aneurin – her gift to him, which she would hide somewhere in his room before she moved on. Although she'd never see his face when he found it, perhaps that was a good thing. If he still nursed anger towards her, she wouldn't have to see him throw it in the fire. She could stay in blissful ignorance and picture him smiling and maybe even holding it to his heart.

Straight after lunch, Gwenllian eased herself into the chair beside Norma's bed and set her knitting bag on her lap. She was huddled into what looked like a dozen layers of woollen clothing to avoid the draught from the window. A sofa would have less upholstery.

"What's that you're sewing today, then?" Gwenllian asked.

"Just a little felt rabbit. I thought Audrey might like it. I'm making him an embroidered waistcoat."

"He's a handsome fellow. Who's Audrey?"

Norma wasn't sure how much Gwenllian had been told about her return to the manse. "A little girl from London," she said cautiously. "Nye and I met her in the park once. Now she's living with one of Miriam's sisters."

To her relief, Gwenllian didn't press for further details. So far, Norma had been able to avoid mentioning the events that had led to her leaving the manse more than a month ago.

Gwenllian pulled out the matinée jacket she was making, and the knitting book she had borrowed from Miriam. The tiny coat must be almost done. Norma dreaded her finishing it. She'd have to coo and ahh over it, as if she was looking forward to the baby coming.

Within moments Gwenllian's long knitting needles were tucked under her arms and clicking away as she continued her rows of ribbing.

"So, Norma... Tell me why you haven't started yet. It's all very well making things for other people's children, but what about your own child? You've a sewing machine downstairs – Miriam's brother brought it round for you yesterday. When you're allowed out of bed, you could use that, couldn't you?"

Norma's stomach sank. She'd been hoping to avoid this subject. "There's plenty of time yet," she said.

"Tsk! The only time I ever knew a woman put it off as long as you, she'd lost a baby and couldn't believe she'd ever get to hold her little one in her arms. But her neighbours helped. Everyone on Moel Carnau rallied round and gave her their old baby things. Meant a lot to her, that did." She sucked in her cheeks, eyes moistening, then blinked and sent Norma a frank stare. "Is that what's stopping you? Have you lost one before?"

"No, thank Gawd. I just don't like thinking about being in such a pickle, that's all"

"You aren't the first, are you? And I doubt you'll be the last. It's a pickle is it, the way you see your situation? Ah, well. *Ni cheir y melys heb y chwerw.* There's no sweet without bitter."

"You're like my gran, you are," Norma grumbled. "She had a saying for everything, an' all."

"Hmph."

In the pause that followed, Norma hoped Gwenllian would move on to another subject. She was to be disappointed.

"What will you dress your child in, then, apart from this jacket I'm making? Fresh air? A clever girl like you could make a hundred lovely outfits."

"It won't be me dressing it, will it?" As the thin thread holding back Norma's despair threatened to snap, her voice dropped to little more than a whisper. "Clothing it will be someone else's problem."

The clicking needles stilled. "You're planning to give it up?"

Norma nodded. Drawing up her knees in the bed, she rubbed her thighs through the blankets and blinked rapidly. She hadn't yet let go of the hope that Miriam might adopt the child. Maybe if she just left the baby with her one day and went back to London, Mim would be too soft-hearted to let it go to some horrible children's home or foster parents. Miriam longed for a baby, after all. If one landed in her lap like that, surely she wouldn't be able to resist her maternal nature, whatever Emrys's thoughts on the matter?

"You don't have any family to help you look after it?"

"If I did, I wouldn't be here, would I? Stuck in the middle of nowhere, depending on the kindness of strangers who don't even like me."

"I see." Gwenllian sniffed. "It isn't easy having to live with others. Hard enough when they're your own family. *Gwell fy mwthyn fy hun na phalas arall.*"

"What's that mean, then?"

"Better my own cottage than someone else's palace."

"I ain't never had my own place, but I expect it's true. You'll be feeling it, won't you? Having to come and live here."

Gwenllian stared silently at her knitting for a few moments, pursing her mouth. At last, she cast a speculative glance towards Norma and diverted the conversation back towards the baby.

"Strikes me that if you can look after a sewing machine, you should be more than capable of looking after a baby. They only need to be fed and kept clean, and kept out of danger. You can keep your machine working, can't you? Easier with a baby in lots of ways. Not so many moving parts."

"Gwenllian, I know you mean well, but you're not helping. I'm only here because I'm stuck in this sodding bed, and I ruddy well hate it. Just as soon as I can, I'll be out looking for work, but right now I can't even work to feed myself, never mind feed anyone else. When your son decides I'm well enough to leave here, or even before that if he gets sick of Miriam climbing the stairs a dozen times a day to look after me, that machine will be the only thing keeping me from starving. So please – *please* don't talk as if things were simple, 'cause they ain't."

Without thinking, she rubbed her palms over her eyes, then winced at the pain in the grazes on her face and hands. How had it come to this? This time last year she'd been the kind of pretty girl who turned heads, happy in her job and doing reasonably well, thank you very much. Now she'd turn heads for all the wrong reasons. Knowing it was her own fault didn't make it any easier, and neither did Gwenllian trying to jolly her along.

"I think I liked it better when you were being mean," she grumbled wearily. "I could cope with that."

"Well, if that's the case, let's be frank with each other. *Mae'n rhy hwyr codi pais ar ôl pisio*. If you can't change what's been done, or what must be done, then you'll have to get on with it, won't you? A spirited girl like you, you'll come out the other side a little wiser, a little less free with your affections hopefully."

Norma sent her a glare and wiped her eyes more carefully this time. But it seemed Gwenllian hadn't finished.

"There. That's this jacket all done. I'll leave it to you to sew it together." With her bent arthritic fingers she gathered up the pieces and tossed them onto the bed beside Norma, then heaved herself back to a standing position. "When you've done that, young woman, you might want to think about at least making one outfit to make sure your child doesn't perish from cold before it can find a home. It'll be here and in your arms before you know it."

Behind her back, Norma poked out her tongue and crossed her eyes, rearranging her features into a more polite expression as the old woman paused in the doorway.

"I know how it feels to be unable to imagine the future," Gwenllian said. "When I picture mine, all I see is darkness. I must put my trust in the Lord to bring me through. You, my girl, are too young for despair. That woman I told you about... She had two fine sons in the end. And there'll be better times ahead for you too, one of these days, you'll see. Have faith."

Kindness was definitely harder to hear than harshness. Norma's chin trembled and she hugged herself to keep her emotions in check as the door closed. If only it was true that she was too young for despair. A while ago she would have believed it. But now, she wasn't so sure.

FORTY-SEVEN

Miriam

Miriam had always enjoyed making her Christmas pudding on Stir Up Sunday, even though Emrys disapproved of the Cadwalader family tradition of asking every member of the family to make a wish while stirring the mixture. This year, thanks to the war, it didn't feel the same. It was partly the food situation, with shortages of sugar in the shops and rumours about how food rationing would soon be inevitable. She'd been tempted to stock up on staple items but had refrained for fear of accusations of hoarding. Mostly, her despondency was due to the changes in her household since last Christmas. Who would have thought less than twelve months ago that Gwenllian would now be living at the manse, that Aneurin would be away training with the military, that Emrys and Idwal would be at their wits' end over the impending fate of their beloved Moel Carnau, and that a pregnant unmarried girl from the roughest parts of London would be convalescing in their spare bedroom after splitting their family apart?

With dried fruit and cherries glistening like jewels in the stoneware bowl, she added the final ingredients and wiped her sticky hands. The tradition was for the youngest family member to stir the pudding first, which for the past eight years had been Aneurin. If only she had a child. What a joy it would be to help them stir the heavy mixture and make a wish. Fleetingly, she considered asking Norma as the youngest in the household – but the girl wasn't family. Next in age after herself would be Emrys.

Before fetching him, she gripped the wooden spoon. There were so many things she *could* wish for, but which would she choose? An end to the war and Aneurin's return might count as two wishes. Norma's swift recovery would make a useful one, as it would reduce some of the tension in the household as well as making Miriam's hectic life easier. A change in the military's plans for Moel Carnau would be a good thing to hope for, too, as then Gwenllian could go back to Pant Glas and Emrys would be happy. No one could blame her for wanting any of those things. But as important as they were, they weren't her dearest wish – the one she had wished for on every Stir Up Sunday since she was married.

She squeezed her eyes closed and dragged the spoon through the pudding mixture. *I wish I could have a baby of my own.*

Steeling herself for the inevitable chilly response, she called Emrys and Gwenllian to the kitchen.

"Haven't you given up this vain superstition?" Emrys growled when he realised what she wanted.

"Humour me. It's not really a superstition – just a bit of harmless festive fun."

Grumbling, he made a token show of stirring the mixture before stomping back to his study without making a wish.

Her mother-in-law rolled her eyes but stepped forward to take his place. The weight of the mixture made her grimace, her swollen fingers struggling with the spoon.

"Thank you. *Diolch.*" Miriam smiled at her and began tipping the mixture into the basin she had prepared.

"Are those peas steeping ready for dinner?" Gwenllian asked, poking around the kitchen.

The tension ratcheted up between Miriam's shoulders.

"Yes. They've been soaking overnight."

"You didn't put the bicarb tablet in, I hope?"

"I always do."

Gwenllian shook her head and tutted. "It kills all the goodness. I would have thought you'd know that."

As she so often did, Miriam held back the defensive retort she'd very much like to give. Her mother-in-law seemed to take delight in criticising every aspect of Miriam's housekeeping. Who could have known there was a right way to hang damp laundry on the airer, or a correct order in which to dust, or a specific way to iron Emrys's shirts? Yet Gwenllian insisted on sharing her opinions on all of these and more. Considering Miriam had learned housekeeping at her own mother's knee and had eight years' experience of keeping her own home without any previous complaints about her methods, she found it a bit rich to have to face such comments.

"I'll bear your suggestion in mind next time I cook them," she said as sweetly as she could, ignoring the urge to grind her teeth. By the time she had covered the basin and set it on the hob to steam, all the pleasure she'd gained from making the pudding had been well and truly quashed.

FORTY-EIGHT

Miriam

When Miriam joined Emrys and Gwenllian at the dining room table and laid her napkin in her lap, she couldn't help noticing the way Gwenllian's eye kept being drawn towards Norma's sewing machine in the corner of the room.

"Norma will be glad to have that thing back," Gwenllian said. "It's about time your sister allowed her to get up and about a bit. All this time lying in bed won't do her any good, you know. And she needs to earn some money, doesn't she, to have a chance of moving out? Surely with all your contacts in the town, not to mention that big family of yours, Miriam, you could ask around and find her some work she could do for a couple of hours a day? It might buck her up a bit. Too much time alone with her own thoughts isn't healthy."

"I could ask, I suppose..." Miriam murmured, with a wary glance towards her husband. He hated it when anyone brought up the topic of their unwelcome house guest.

"I think you should. And while we're on the subject... I have a feeling there are things about Norma that you haven't told me." Gwenllian looked pointedly at Miriam and Emrys in turn.

"What has she been saying?" Emrys demanded.

"Not much, except that she intends to give her child away."

It made sense. Norma had no means of providing for a child, and even if she did, what woman could bear the shame of so visible a reminder of her past sins? Yet it gave Miriam a pang to think of anyone having to give their baby up. Certainly, she could never do such a thing.

Emrys stabbed one of his roast potatoes with his fork. "The best thing for it, I should think. It will have a chance of a better life, away from its mother's pernicious influence."

"What happened when she lived here before to make her leave?"

Miriam dabbed at her mouth with her napkin. Her mouthful of food seemed suddenly hard to chew, as if it was full of gristle. She swallowed, watching Emrys to see how he would respond to his mother's question. They had succeeded in avoiding this subject up to now.

"She told us a pack of lies," he said.

"What about?"

"She came into this house under false pretences, letting us believe she was a respectable married woman. She only told the truth when it was forced out of her. In the circumstances, we had no choice but to tell her to go."

"Well, well." Gwenllian frowned. For now, she seemed content.

Miriam relaxed and pushed some cabbage onto her fork. It was halfway to her mouth when Gwenllian spoke up again.

"What was it that forced her to confess her shame? She must have known you'd be shocked by her lies, and her immoral past. Didn't she realise you'd ask her to leave?"

Emrys stopped eating. "There was an argument."

"About Aneurin," Miriam added, sensing that his mother's curiosity hadn't yet been satisfied. Gwenllian adored her only grandson: once she knew he had been hurt, she'd understand why they hadn't let Norma stay.

"Aneurin?" Gwenllian's eyes widened. It put Miriam in mind of a blackbird that had just heard a worm burrowing under the grass.

"He loved her," Miriam replied. "He wanted to marry her."

"He *believed* he loved her," Emrys said, scowling. "He was distressed, and understandably so, because he believed his inclinations were adulterous."

Gwenllian picked up the salt and shook it over her food.

Miriam looked down into her own plate to hide her irritation. According to her mother-in-law, her cooking was always either too salty or not salty enough.

"So she admitted lying and carrying a bastard to spare Aneurin's conscience?"

Emrys cleared his throat. "She thought that telling him she was unmarried would mean they could be together. Her aims were selfish, Mam. She must have had her sights set on him from the start. That's why he went to enlist. To get away from her. If it wasn't for her, he might have—"

"Just a minute, Emrys. Is that the way you see it, Miriam? As a woman, you might take a different view."

Miriam took a sip of water. She didn't want to contradict her husband's account, but Norma's intentions might not have been quite as bad as Emrys had made them sound. As much as she should be obedient, she couldn't knowingly be unjust.

"I believe Norma would never have chosen to tell us. She came here to start a new life—"

"By hiding her true nature. A wolf in sheep's clothing," Emrys cut in.

"I saw her face that night when things came to a head. I believe she wanted to spare Aneurin, more than she sought any personal gain. I don't know how long she'd been hoping to be with him, but I don't think that's why she confessed."

Although he said nothing, Emrys had put his knife and fork down. The flickering of the muscle under his eye, and the way his mouth had compressed into a hard line, made it obvious he was fuming.

Gwenllian tucked into her roast beef as if she hadn't noticed the tension in the air.

"Well, well," she said again. "Imagine concealing such a terrible, shameful secret for months, and then feeling compelled to reveal it to the very people who had most reason to despise her for it. The people who had the power to sling her out onto the street... Terrible." She shook her head dolefully.

Miriam wiped her moist palms on the napkin in her lap, thankful that the subject seemed to have finally closed.

Emrys nodded and resumed eating, as if he, too, had relaxed.

Gwenllian's next remark fell into the silence like a shell blast.

"It seems to me that young Norma must be very brave. And to make such a sacrifice, she must have loved our boy very much. Very much indeed."

FORTY-NINE

Miriam

Miriam entered the dining room carrying a tray with a cup of tea and some plain biscuits. Norma was seated at the table with her sewing machine, a pile of assorted garments behind it and her tin of tools open at her side.

"It's good to be up and using my machine again," Norma said almost shyly.

"I expect it is. Don't go overdoing it though, or Maggie will have you confined to bed again, and I won't hear the last of it for not looking after you properly."

"Thank her again for me, won't you? Honestly, when you told me she'd recommended me to Dolly and got me this bit of work, I could have jumped out of bed and turned cartwheels."

"That would definitely not put you in her good books." Despite her reluctance to encourage Norma by being too friendly, Miriam couldn't help but smile. Ever since Dolly had sent a trunk of old clothes from the attics at Plas Norton with a request for them to be made into children's outfits for a Christmas party, Norma had been like a different person. Although she was only allowed to sit downstairs for a couple of hours each day, as it made her blood pressure rise again, that short time at her machine seemed a better tonic than any amount of quiet bed rest.

Miriam bent to poke the embers in the grate, trying to generate a little more warmth.

"What do you think of this? Do you think the little girl will like it?" Norma asked, holding up a pretty dress of candy-pink striped satin.

Rising, Miriam pressed a hand against the small of her back. It seemed to ache constantly these days, with caring for Norma and waiting on Gwenllian's whims on top of her usual tasks for the household and chapel.

"I should think any little girl would love it. Especially with that lace collar. It's lovely."

Norma beamed. It was touching to see the pride she took in her work, and her obvious pleasure at making things people would enjoy wearing.

Norma consulted the list Dolly had provided. "This dress is for... Shirley. And they want a bigger one from the same cloth for a girl called Barbara. D'you suppose they're sisters? That would be nice, wouldn't it? For them to match. But I won't make them exactly the same. I'll use these buttons instead for the bigger girl, and make a Peter Pan collar in pink. We all like our clothes to have a bit of flair and individuality, don't we?"

She paused and eyed Miriam's plain blouse and skirt, a faint flush rising to her cheeks. Clearing her throat, she bent back over her sewing, as if to cover up embarrassment.

Miriam brushed her hands down her clothes and left the room. It was silly to allow an innocent remark to sting. She knew the way she dressed couldn't be described as stylish by even the most generous-hearted person. She didn't aspire to be fashionable. But it bothered her that her clothes might be seen as dull. In a couple of months she would be thirty, the flower of her youth already gone. It was a depressing thought, and with a lump in her throat she headed upstairs to the bathroom to compose herself. Her emotions had been all over the place recently, with so many extra responsibilities and Emrys wrapped up in his own problems.

When she emerged, Gwenllian was waiting on the landing.

"Norma's downstairs sewing for the children again, I take it? It seems to have lifted her spirits."

Miriam nodded.

"Still no sign of her making anything for the baby, though?"

"Not yet." Lowering her voice to avoid any risk of being overheard, Miriam tugged at Gwenllian's arm and led the way into her own room.

"It's not natural, is it? Taking pleasure in making clothes for the little evacuees; putting herself at risk for that girl Audrey. All that trouble for other people's children, yet she won't lift a finger for her own. And all the while contemplating giving it away."

Gwenllian frowned.

"I don't know how she can bear it," Miriam went on, glad to have someone she could discuss the subject with, even if it was only Gwenllian. She couldn't talk to Emrys about Norma. "How can she stand to give her baby up? If I should ever be blessed, I could no more do that than I could put out my own eyes. I'd rather die than give up a child of mine."

"You can afford to say that. She can't. Giving it up is a greater act of love than keeping a child she can't look after."

"I know that's what people say in this sort of situation, but I still couldn't. It goes against every instinct. Even an animal will care for its young, won't it?"

"How would Norma feed a child? Clothing it would be easier for her than for some, I'll grant you, but the cloth and the thread will still have to be paid for, and she'll need to launder the clothes and the nappies. It will need a safe, secure home. She can't provide any of those things."

Miriam gestured towards the stairs. "She can work. Look at her now, earning money by her sewing."

Gwenllian shook her head and tutted as if Miriam was being foolish. "And what happens if she gets ill, or if her customers let her down? She has no husband to fall back on. No pension such as you would get if you ever had to bring up a child without Emrys. Who would help her if her child falls sick? Looking after a baby and a home would take all her time unless she had help. You mention animals, but you know, some of them will murder their babies and eat them, rather than see them suffer. You have to be realistic, Miriam. Giving her baby to someone else who has the means to raise it – that's a kindness, not cruelty. Don't look down on her for it. Never look down on any girl who's struggling in the mire, unless it's to lift her up out of it and hold her clear." She pointed a swollen, crooked finger towards heaven. "*He* knows what's in her heart, and the price she'll pay for trying to do her best for the child. She needs understanding from you, not condemnation."

A growing sense of outrage at this pious speech made Miriam splutter. "I don't know how you can say such things, when you are always condemning *me*, your own daughter-in-law. I've never made the kinds of mistakes she's made, and yet what support do I get to lift me from the mire when I'm struggling? Don't I deserve some understanding when I'm up and down the stairs all day, cooking your meals and... and... washing your laundry, and cleaning your room?"

It was enough to make her want to stamp her foot. In her fury, she put her hands on her hips.

"It's so unfair! You look down on everything I do, even though I've welcomed you into my home and bent over backwards to show you kindness. You spend hours knitting and chatting cosily in that girl's room while I work my fingers to the bone, and then stand there and defend her to me, even though her problems are all of her own making. How dare you!"

She was too angry to feel guilty for speaking so disrespectfully. Gwenllian's misplaced sympathy for Norma had ignited a flame inside her. Yet it seemed Gwenllian wasn't even upset. The old woman had straightened, dark eyes gleaming up at Miriam as if she was enjoying this sudden confrontation.

"I do dare. I'm not afraid to say what I think, unlike you, Miriam Powell. Do you imagine I don't know what's going on behind your polite phrases and the calm, smiling face you show me? When really, all the while you resent the very air I breathe. Go on – admit it. You'd happily drown me in that lumpy gravy you make, wouldn't you? Every cup of tea you pour for me, you're wishing you could put rat poison in it instead of sugar. Aren't you?"

A flush of heat rushed from Miriam's breastbone to her forehead. She hated conflict. It made her pulse race to hear that her feelings had been so transparent. She brought a hand to her brow, then dropped it to disguise the way it shook.

"How can you say such things?" she said.

"Because if they're not true, they ought to be. And if you can't understand why I like spending time with young Norma, then I'll tell you. It's because that girl has guts. She has the courage to stand up for herself. I've never once seen you do that before this moment. Not even when I've deliberately criticised you. Not even when I've occasionally been – yes, perhaps even a little bit mean. You've calmly rolled over and taken all the provocation I could throw at you. But Norma wouldn't. She'd never let anyone speak to her the way you let people speak to you."

"You're my mother-in-law! It's my duty to show you respect."

"Phooey to that. I put my mother-in-law in her place from the start. The first time she tried to interfere between me and my husband, I made it very clear she was to mind her own business. If you want my respect, Miriam, you first need to have some for yourself." To Miriam's surprise, Gwenllian gave an approving nod. "At least you've made a start today, my girl. Better late than never."

FIFTY

Norma

It was strange to be entirely alone in the manse, and especially on Christmas Eve. No doubt Emrys hadn't liked the idea of leaving her without supervision, but Norma supposed he'd had little choice. It was natural for his wife, mother and brother to go with him for the last ever Christmas service in the little chapel on the mountain. And surely even he had realised by now that if she was planning to rob them, she'd have done it long ago.

Norma had been confused at first when Miriam explained about the special Christmas Day service. She'd never heard of a Plygain before.

"A plug what?" she asked, pulling a face. "What's a plug got to do with Christmas?"

"It has nothing to do with a plug," Miriam said, sounding out the word again.

"*Plug-ine?*" Norma repeated. "Nope. I still ain't never heard of one."

"It's a tradition. There's no set order of service or programme. The congregation take it in turns to sing songs and carols they've prepared, and anyone who wishes to can take part. It happens every year, at dawn on Christmas Day. I don't understand many of the words, of course, as it's all in Welsh, but I still enjoy it. Although this year, I expect it will be rather sad."

No doubt it would be, as the last chance for the farmers to celebrate Christmas together.

"Are you sure you'll be alright?" Miriam asked again. "I don't like to leave you alone overnight, but we'll need to stay at the farm to attend the chapel at dawn."

"You go and enjoy yourself. I can make myself useful doing the veggies this afternoon, once you're gone, and if you sort the giblets and the stuffing and whatnot before you go, I'll pop the turkey in the oven when I get up in the morning. The last thing you'll feel like doing when you get back is cooking, and I'm quite capable of putting an overgrown bird and some spuds in the oven."

"But you're supposed to be resting," Miriam had protested, a hand on her brow as if even thinking about managing everything had brought on a headache.

"I'll sit down while I peel the veg. If my ankles start swelling again, I'll go straight back to bed, I swear."

It wasn't entirely true that she intended to rest, however. This was her first chance of any freedom in ages, and there were things she wanted to do. As soon as Miriam and Emrys had gone, she headed to the kitchen to peel and cut up potatoes, carrots and parsnips, then tackled the Brussels sprouts. For some reason, her fingers were less nimble than usual. They seemed a bit swollen, but she'd heard that was normal in pregnancy. It wouldn't be anything to worry about.

Once the veggies were sitting in fresh water in saucepans on the stove, she devoured a corned beef sandwich, then remembered seeing an unopened jar of pickled onions on the top shelf of the larder. Glad no one was around to tell her off, she clambered onto a stool, holding to the edge of the shelf to keep herself steady, and reached for the jar, but almost toppled as something beside it fell sideways with a thud.

Lifting the item down, she realised it was a book. Not a recipe book, though. It had an odd title: *Married Love*. Norma frowned. Why would a story about marriage be hidden away in such a dark corner on the top shelf of the larder? She clambered down awkwardly and took it into the kitchen along with the jar.

It must be Miriam's book. Neither Emrys nor Aneurin would choose the larder as a hiding place. But why had it been hidden? Curious, she flicked through it, crunching on a pickled onion so sharp she sucked in her cheeks and shuddered.

As she skimmed the pages, Norma's eyes widened. It wasn't a story at all. The book was about sex. About women feeling physical yearnings, like a hunger, and about every heart's desire for union with another. She scanned the pages, marvelling at the opinions expressed within, then clapped the book shut.

Colour rose in her cheeks. If the author was to be believed, things might have been very different for Norma if Dickie had been gentler. Perhaps with a more patient man, one who was more considerate and tender, Norma might experience the kind of delightful sensations described in the book. She drew in a deep breath, trying to keep her thoughts from turning to Nye. Longing for what might have been could only make her bitter. Carefully, she climbed back onto the stool and slid the book back into its dark corner on the top shelf. It wouldn't do for Miriam to realise anyone else had seen it. She'd have had her reasons for keeping it hidden.

The chiming of the hallway clock reminded her that almost an hour had passed since she'd been left alone. *Shake a leg, girl. It'll be dark in a few hours.*

Hurriedly, she wrapped the gifts she'd made over the past few weeks with brown paper and string. She'd made a beautiful camisole in satin and lace for Miriam. Imagining Emrys's face at the sight of his wife wearing it brought a mischievous smile to her lips. Perhaps it might help to provoke the sort of passion Miriam had been reading about in her sexy book.

Out of a sense of obligation, she'd monogrammed a white cotton handkerchief for Emrys. She'd embroidered another for Idwal, and others for Joe and Ted Cadwalader, whose kindness she wouldn't forget in a hurry. Gwenllian had a pair of soft slippers, and she'd sewn lace edging and some delicate white embroidery onto some dainty white handkerchiefs for Evelina Proudfoot, Ceinwen and Maggie.

She knelt to lay the gifts for the Powells under the small Christmas tree in the parlour. Unable to resist peeking at the other presents, she realised the largest had her name written on it in Miriam's neat handwriting. She picked it up and rocked back on her heels, surprised she was being given anything at all. Who would have thought when Maggie brought her back here that she'd still be stuck at the manse at Christmas, let alone getting a present? The package felt squishy inside the paper. Something to wear, perhaps, or some new fabric?

The felt rabbit for Audrey had already been passed on to Maggie, along with the gifts for the other Cadwaladers, but Norma hadn't felt able to ask anyone to deliver Miss Proudfoot's present. They were all so busy, Maggie and Miriam especially, and she was conscious of being a burden. Her ankles weren't all that puffy really. And it would be lovely to see Miss Proudfoot again, after weeks of being stuck indoors. It worried her that after such a long interval she might have been forgotten and lose out on any chance of being offered work for Evelina's Modes. *Out of sight, out of mind*, as Gran used to say.

She'd wrap up warmly and be back before dark, with Miriam and Maggie none the wiser. For all Maggie's constant talk about blood pressure, she felt fine. A bit achy, and frequently in need of the lav, but that was to be expected now that she was the size of a barrage balloon.

Not since her ill-fated visit to Contadino's in September had an outing to Pontybrenin seemed so exciting. Huddled into her coat, which barely fastened over her belly these days, and with a woollen scarf borrowed from the hall stand adding an extra layer of warmth around her throat, she slipped out of the back door, hiding the key under a flowerpot. Her steps weren't as nimble as they used to be, and she felt embarrassed at the way her size now affected her gait. No saucy wiggles for her these days: the best she could manage was a waddle.

There was a childish pleasure in being outside again, seeing how the season had changed in the five weeks since she'd first been cooped up inside. The cold was harsh, reddening her nose and making her eyes stream. It was a good job she hadn't bothered with mascara today. She'd paused only long enough to apply a quick slick of lipstick, the scarlet almost garish against her pallid complexion. She couldn't bring herself to face the outside world without any make-up at all. It would be like going out without stockings or shoes.

At the end of the road she stopped to catch her breath, frustrated by her own weakness. After a few moments she forced herself to carry on, but more slowly, allowing herself no more than a longing glance at a low garden wall that would make a perfect resting place. She'd been resting for a month and look how she'd ended up – feeble as a new kitten. If she wasn't careful, Miss Proudfoot would forget all about her, and some other girl would take any sewing jobs on offer. She needed to get stronger or be doomed to life as a helpless invalid, forever dependent on charity. The thought was awful enough to set her moving again – tottering a little, and breathless. By the time she reached the park, her shoes chafed in a way they hadn't used to.

One brief glance at the bandstand was all she allowed herself. The memory of kissing Aneurin there spurred her forwards, distracting her from the discomfort in her feet and back, and from the pressure of the baby on her bladder. Thoughts of the embroidered picture she'd created for him brought dimples to her chilled cheeks. It was finished now, wrapped up with special care in tissue paper, and hidden in a drawer in his room underneath his bundled socks. Next time he came home he'd be sure to find it there, but in the meantime, it should be safe from discovery.

The picture of the mountain view that she'd left for Miriam had never been mentioned. She'd sometimes wondered what had happened to it after she left the manse in the wake of that momentous quarrel with Emrys and Aneurin. Although she'd been disappointed when she'd finally been allowed downstairs to realise it wasn't on display in any of the rooms, she hadn't been surprised. Had it been thrown away? She wouldn't put it past Emrys to want to destroy anything connected to her.

A bench stood at the other side of the park, and she kept her gaze on it, willing herself to reach it. Something seemed to be not quite right with her vision, and even though she screwed up her eyes, it didn't stop it blurring. She shook her head to clear it, but that only made her feel dizzy. When she neared the bench, she sank down gratefully. Her feet and hands were throbbing so badly, if she didn't know better, she could almost believe her shoes and gloves had shrunk since she left the house.

Focusing on taking in what was around her, the way Nye had taught her, seemed to help her breathing settle back into a more regular pattern. Gradually she readied herself to tackle the rest of the journey. She'd come this far – the effort would have been wasted if she turned round now and went back without going all the way to Evelina's Modes. How could a twenty-minute walk be this hard?

The clock above the town hall chimed three o'clock. If she didn't get up now it would be dark before she got back to the manse.

You're almost at the high street now. Just another few hundred yards.

One last push.

A yard at a time, pausing at intervals to lean against shop windows and take some weight off her painful feet, she somehow made it to the window of Evelina's Modes. It was dark inside. Peering in, squinting against the blurring of her vision, there seemed to be no signs of movement behind the pair of mannequins attired in staid buttoned-up dresses.

She only saw the notice written neatly on a piece of cardboard when she reached for the door handle. Her eyes widened in dismay as she read it.

Evelina's Modes will be closed until Wednesday 3rd January.

The proprietor would like to wish all her customers a joyful Christmas and a peaceful New Year.

"You've got to be bleedin' well kidding me," Norma muttered.

The prospect of walking back made her want to groan. She brightened momentarily, remembering that Miss Proudfoot might still be at home, even if she had closed the shop. She might be upstairs in her cosy flat right now, listening to the wireless with her feet up on a footstool... But several attempts at knocking roused no response, and eventually she had no choice but to post the little wrapped gift through the letterbox and trudge painfully back in the direction from which she had come.

As she adjusted her focus, trying to stop everything seeming so strange, a thought reared up in her mind. Was this blurriness what Maggie had kept warning her about? Was she ill, and going to die here alone in this small Welsh town where no one cared about her? Her heart slowed with her steps. She hadn't had time to make anything of herself yet.

Would Aneurin be sad when they told him she'd kicked the bucket, or glad she was finally gone for good? Emrys would probably be smug – wasn't he always saying the wages of sin were death? How she'd hate to give him that satisfaction.

Contadino's was open, its windows bright in the dullness of the grey December afternoon. She hadn't had a coffee in ages, and it would be heavenly to sit down for ten minutes, especially if there was a chance she might soon shuffle off this mortal coil. The smell of freshly ground coffee beans and the low murmur of conversation as someone stepped outside and held the door for her made her decision to go inside inevitable.

Pretending not to notice the way Johnny's head flew round in shock at her altered appearance, she struggled out of her coat, dropped her gas mask box and scarf onto the table nearest the door, and flopped into a seat. Somehow, she forced herself to remain upright when every instinct was to lay her head down on the cool tabletop. Thank goodness she'd thought to pop her purse in her coat pocket when she set out. Johnny wouldn't be likely to offer her anything on the house these days.

"Norma," Johnny said, frowning as he approached her table. "You look... different."

"Merry Christmas to you, too, Johnny. I'll have a coffee please. Make it a strong one if you don't mind. I've got a killer headache coming on."

While he busied himself with the eagle-topped coffee machine, she tugged off her woollen gloves and pressed her fingertips against her throbbing temples. No more thinking about death. The hot drink would soon perk her up. When it arrived, she summoned a smile.

"You'll be getting that day off you've been looking forward to tomorrow, I s'pose, Johnny?"

The side of his mouth lifted. "Nice of you to remember. I hope you're alright? You don't look—"

"I know. You already said so." No doubt he meant well, but the last thing she needed was to be reminded that her looks, the one advantage she'd ever had in life, were ruined.

She took a sip of coffee, relishing the comforting feeling of cradling the cup in both hands and the hot, bitter liquid in her throat.

"Let me know if you want anything else," Johnny said.

"Ta, but the things I need ain't on a coffee shop's menu."

A job. A future. My looks and my confidence back the way they used to be. Aneurin. A home. A fairy godmother to magic me back to the manse in a glittering carriage made from a pumpkin.

Any of those things would be wonderful, but right now they all seemed equally unrealistic.

FIFTY-ONE

Miriam

They were trying to hide it, but Miriam knew the Powells' hearts were all breaking. At lunchtime on Christmas Eve, after Emrys had finished preaching in Pontybrenin, they'd accepted the offer of a lift from a member of his flock as far as the school at the end of the bumpy track on Moel Carnau. It saved Gwenllian the strain of walking all four miles to Pant Glas. Each of them had ridden in silence, before watching the car crawl away out of sight, grateful and sad to know it would return tomorrow morning to collect them after their final Christmas service in the chapel.

As one, they faced the school. The building was closed, of course. Its small yard stood silent, the cobbled surface glistening with a hard frost unmarred by footprints. It would never again buzz with children's happy voices. Inside, the walls would never again be covered with pictures or poems. The last lessons had been held and the last songs had been sung in its classroom a few days earlier. Several of the children had already moved away with their families, and Idwal told them he'd heard that the remainder had been distressed at the dwindling of their group, their misery magnified still more when the handbell was rung to mark the end of the school day for the final time.

Lingering there was pointless. They trudged across the silvered heathland towards Pant Glas, each step poignant with memories of happier journeys. Miriam remembered the first time she'd visited, fascinated to see the place where Emrys was born and grew up. She'd been in awe of him then, hardly able to credit her good fortune that a man like him had responded to her shy interest. He was still just as impressive, more than eight years on, in the way he stood by his principles and sought to make the world a better, more Christian place; but now that she was wiser, she knew he had feet of clay like any other man.

The struggle to block the military takeover of the mountain had brought out both the best and the worst in him. He'd worn himself to the limits of his stamina in supporting his community. He'd used every contact he could think of; dedicated hours to mustering arguments; spent every penny they could spare to send letters; and visited anyone who might be able to defend Moel Carnau from destruction. He'd been irascible. He'd come close to alienating his only child. Although he'd fulfilled his duty to his mother and brother, Miriam couldn't help feeling that he'd fallen short as a husband.

The farm buildings had a desolate air. Miriam shivered as she looked around. Gwenllian stumbled across the threshold, and as Miriam reached to support her arm, she realised the old woman's eyes were spilling over with tears.

"Oh, Gwenllian." Instinctively, she wrapped her arms around the old woman and held her.

Gwenllian's thin shoulders heaved under her heavy coat. A harsh, keening sound tore from her throat as if she was in agony. Miriam patted her back and crooned soothing noises. Usually so acerbic, Gwenllian had never seemed vulnerable before. For the first time, Miriam found she could sympathise with her mother-in-law.

Emrys and Idwal stood back, their own faces reflecting their torment. Emrys gazed at the expanse of iron-grey sky above the farmyard.

"*Fy nghartref.* My home," Gwenllian said after her rush of emotion had ebbed. Wiping tears from her eyes, she gestured around the hallway where few of the family's possessions now remained. "This is where I came when I was married. Where my husband and sons and grandson were born. Where Powells have lived for three generations. In the room above this one, my husband died in my arms. We carried him from this front door to the chapel to be buried, with all our neighbours paying their respects. How can I live anywhere else? How can I worship in another fellowship, and leave the man I love behind?"

Miriam took her hand and squeezed it.

"How can they do it to us?" Gwenllian went on, shaking her head in bewilderment. "They think they're just taking a mountain to tear it up with their guns, but it's much more than a mountain: it's the beating heart of everyone who's grown up on its slopes. Its air is in our blood. Its earth is in our bones. They're cutting us off from the very language we speak. It's not just the end of a few dozen farms. It's the end of the world."

"Mam." Idwal stepped forward, strain marking his kindly, weathered features. "Today, this is still home. We'll sit together and reminisce, and then give thanks for everything this place has been to us. For all that it's given us. Come inside, now. We'll light a fire in the kitchen and eat the last of the oatcakes and cheese for supper."

Later, they sat around the old kitchen table, its scrubbed surface pitted and scored from decades of use. Most of the parlour furnishings had already gone. They lit candles, the meaty smell of tallow mingling with the smoke from the peat burning in the fireplace. Miriam sat quietly and let them talk, boiling the kettle periodically to brew tea with the fresh spring water Idwal had brought in from the well. Often, they slipped into Welsh as naturally as they breathed, forgetting that she only understood a few words here and there.

The ending of a way of life seemed as painful as the demise of a loved one. It reminded her of the time after her mam died, when Mary had been laid out in her coffin and the Cadwalader family had gathered to mourn and share their memories of the woman who had not merely borne but also moulded them. A time of tears, but also of smiles, when the bonds of love and grief made any petty squabbles irrelevant. As Miriam and her father and siblings had done, Gwenllian and her sons had a cornucopia of memories upon which to draw.

The old grandfather clock had already been moved to replace the less valuable one in the manse, but the tinkling chime of Emrys's pocket watch told them it was ten o'clock. While Gwenllian prepared herself for her last night in her old bed, Miriam and Emrys wrapped themselves in their coats and went outside. He had brought a lantern to light their way to the privy, but they scarcely needed it: the moon had lifted its face above the hill and shone brightly through the scudding clouds.

"It's a sacrilege, you know. An act of violence against our nation – and they keep on doing it. Flooding our valleys; attacking our hills. They send our young men to die underground in their mines; to break their bodies in wars on foreign shores. And what do we get in exchange for our sacrifice? They bring their weapons to the very navel of our good Welsh earth to rape it with their wicked bombs. Every shell they drop here will be an insult to this land and the priceless heritage of its people. How will we bear it? The pain of such a wound. Such a loss... It's too much."

She laid her cheek against his sleeve. There was nothing she could say.

"I know it's wrong to hate, but when I think about what they're doing I can hardly help it. They're tearing the heart and soul out of this community. Its life, its stories, its songs, and its poetry will scatter to the four winds. Dividing forty or more families... It's like a rock being ground into sand. It can never be one entity again."

"Don't hate, Emrys. Whatever happens, don't do that. If you do, then they really will have won. You must hold on to your memories and pray that when the war is over, the mountain will be returned to those who love it."

The breeze sent chill fingers to lift her hair across her face. She tucked the wayward strands behind her ear, sending up a silent prayer for him to bear what must come.

Above them, an explosion of stars glimmered, their glory outshone by the almost full moon.

"More than anything, I shall miss this sky," Emrys murmured, his deep voice cracking on the words.

Without speaking, she reached for his hand.

FIFTY-TWO

Miriam

Miriam and Emrys rose from their cosy cupboard bed at five, roused by the ringing of the portable alarm clock he'd brought with them. As he lit the lantern, the glow highlighted dark smudges under his puffy eyes. Had he slept at all? Surprisingly, she had been exhausted enough to plunge easily into sleep, relishing the closeness of their narrow, straw-filled mattress as she curled against his back.

They stumbled over the cold flagstone floor into their clothes, chilled fingers fumbling with buttons. Miriam cracked a thin layer of ice on top of the basin of water she'd left out the night before. By the time she'd splashed her face and tidied her hair, her teeth were chattering. But there was no chance of a warming breakfast. It was time to go.

"*Nadolig Llawen.* Happy Christmas," she whispered when they reached the edge of the farmyard, where the danger of boots skidding on the icy cobbles had passed.

She supposed he might find the words ironic. This Christmas must be one of the least happy in his life, with his son away and his family about to be evicted. The responsibility for leading the final Plygain service in the chapel must weigh heavily on his shoulders.

He squeezed her hand through their mittens and kept hold of it to guide her across the frozen mountainside, his lantern lighting their way. In places it was hard to see the path, but he trod surely, as familiar with this place as he was with their parlour at home. Although she was aware that parts of the mountain were boggy and treacherous, his confidence reassured her. Here and there they zigzagged, following tracks between hidden pools and meandering along the banks of brooks to cross at simple wooden bridges, until after half a mile or so they reached the top of the lane by the schoolhouse and strode past it to the whitewashed chapel.

The girl who would usually have lit the stove before the morning service had already moved with her family to live with cousins in Carmarthen, so the task had fallen to the minister and his wife. Miriam guessed Emrys was glad of this opportunity to pray in silence before his flock arrived. She held the lantern while he unlocked the door with its heavy iron key, then lifted it again so that he could light the temperamental stove. Soon it was radiating a modicum of warmth into the musty chill.

"Two centuries, this chapel has stood here," Emrys said, gazing around the single room. "Built on faith. Built on the love of this community for the Lord and for each other. It's stood strong through winter storms and summer heat, and it's watched as generations fall away like wheat at the harvest. Never would I have dreamed that it all would come to an end under my ministry. I can only pray that God and my flock will forgive me for failing them."

It must have cost him to admit such a deep sense of failure. He'd lived his whole life by his ideals, holding himself and others to the highest of standards. She seized his arms, hoping to convey her love by the strength of her grip and the sincerity infused in her voice.

"Emrys, *cariad*, you haven't failed anyone. Doesn't the Word tell us that all things have their season? It's the nature of things to pass away. We all know how hard you've worked. Now, perhaps, it's time for acceptance, and to have faith that all things will work out for the good in the end."

He nodded, trembling with suppressed emotion. When she loosed his arms, he cradled her face in his hands and kissed her forehead. "Bless you, Miriam. Without you, I sometimes think..." He heaved a sigh, then murmured something in Welsh, as if the feeling was too heavy for him to express in anything but his own tongue. Although the words were unfamiliar, his meaning was clear enough.

Grateful, Miriam left him to pray in the wooden pew at the front. He needed the time to prepare himself. If this were a regular Sunday service, she would put up the board with the hymn numbers and prepare the pieces of bread and tiny glasses of red grape juice ready for Communion. But they wouldn't be needed for the Plygain. Emrys would only need to deliver a short reading and lead the prayers, with the rest of the worship conducted by the gathered congregation. He bowed his head, oblivious to her, murmuring prayers with the dim glow of the stove and their single lantern sending shadows over his face and magnifying his silhouette on the plain white wall beyond.

Still wrapped in her coat and scarf, she moved to one of the tall, arched windows. Outside, the sky was still charcoal black, softening to deepest blue in the east. But as she wiped the fog of her breath from the frigid glass, her heart skipped. Had she imagined it?

No – there it was again – a shining point of warm yellow bobbing across the faint glow on the eastern horizon. And another, to the west. Like fireflies, they seemed to float across the mountain, their numbers gradually multiplying, and growing larger as they drew nearer. Lanterns. The people of Moel Carnau: some walking, others perhaps travelling on ponies, gathering in their dozens to welcome the dawning Christmas Day.

"They're coming," Miriam said, excitement lending urgency to her voice.

Emrys lifted his head. "I'm ready," he said.

As the families entered with their lanterns, the glowing light in the high-ceilinged space grew brighter. Young and old, they came first to shake hands with Emrys and Miriam, then with each other, bonded in a fellowship forged over many years. He knew them all by name. She didn't need an understanding of the language to see the respect in which he was held by the farmers, the oldest of whom must have known him since he was a baby in Gwenllian's arms. Her breast swelled with pride as she watched. Here was the confident, authoritative man she had fallen in love with all those years ago.

All at once his expression changed. It lit with a moment's pure joy, then uncertainty, before settling into a stern mask. His shoulders had stiffened, and he reached to pick up a Bible, riffling through the pages as if to gain a moment to compose himself.

Curious, Miriam looked towards the door, rising to her tiptoes to see who or what could have caused such a dramatic change. There, standing a little awkwardly between Gwenllian and Idwal, was a young man in khaki uniform, holding his cap against his chest.

Aneurin.

Beaming, she threaded her way through the throng to throw her arms around him. Seeing his dear face again so unexpectedly, and on this occasion above any other, felt like nothing less than a Christmas miracle, and she told him so.

"Nothing could have stopped me coming back for this," he said as he hugged her back. Already his shoulders seemed broader, his arms stronger. He carried himself proudly, smiling and murmuring greetings to the people he knew. Although one or two looked askance at his uniform, most smiled and reached to touch his arm or to nod.

Gwenllian clung to his side, bursting with pleasure and pride to have her beloved grandson with her again. But there wasn't time for further conversation. Emrys had climbed into the pulpit and stood waiting expectantly. The people took their cue, settling into the pews, and the buzz of chatter quietened. The service was beginning. Realising there was no time to bridge the division between father and son, Miriam took her seat in the front pew with the rest of the family.

Although she wouldn't understand any of the words, she knew it wouldn't mar her experience of the occasion. There was a feeling in the air: a sense of togetherness. Of community. Despite everything this group of people faced, with the war and the imminent loss of so much that they loved, there was still the quiet joy of celebrating the advent of Christmas.

After the initial prayer, and a reading by one of the chapel elders, the whole congregation sang unaccompanied by any music. Miriam stumbled over the words in the hymn book Idwal held up for her, although the tune was familiar as the English carol 'O Come, All Ye Faithful'.

Rapt silence met Emrys's short speech – it could hardly be described as a sermon. Heads nodded, and a few dabbed at their eyes with handkerchiefs. Miriam gazed around her as the service proceeded. Silent messages passed as groups and individuals got up in turn, walked to the front and sang, some in solos, others in duets and trios. Some songs were sung only by the women, including Gwenllian, standing shoulder to shoulder with the farmers' wives and daughters she'd lived alongside for years. Some of the songs were jolly, raising a smile even though Miriam understood so few of the words. Some of the harmonies made the hairs lift along her arms.

Many of the songs were poignant, invested with such deep emotion that they made tears prick at Miriam's eyes. Although the chill of the cold building seeped into her back and her legs, and the hard pew made her shift often in her seat, she felt she could have remained there all day taking in the beauty of the sound and the golden light thrown by the lanterns onto the singers' faces. As dawn broke, pale winter sunshine flooded over the gathered congregation, and a joyful carol was followed by a final, heartfelt blessing from the pulpit. Miriam sat with her head bowed, filled with a sense of gratitude and calm. Amongst so much sadness, her heart was full of joy. She sent a silent prayer of thanks to the heavens for her many blessings. Today, she was more conscious of them than ever.

The congregation dispersed, most of them towards the tavern for a final shared breakfast. Emrys bid each one farewell. When only the Powells remained, he turned to face his son.

Aneurin stood in silence, hope warring with anxiety in his face. He turned his cap over in his hands.

Emrys asked him something in Welsh.

"Speak English, Dad, so Mim can understand." Aneurin glanced towards her to offer a translation. "He said, 'Could you not have worn something else?'"

A bolt of disappointment hit Miriam. The lad deserved a warmer welcome from his father. She moved nearer to Aneurin, threading her hand through the crook of his arm. Gwenllian stepped close to his other side.

"I'm sorry, Dad. It must be hard to see me wearing the same uniform you used to wear. They don't have enough new ones for all the recruits yet, so they've had to give us these old ones, and I don't have my civvies anymore. If I hadn't worn this, I couldn't have come, and it was important to me to be here to support you all." He squared his shoulders and took in a deep breath.

Emrys's shoulders had been held rigid, but now they seemed to slump a little. He lowered his gaze and nodded. It wasn't much of a softening, but it was something.

"You look very handsome," Gwenllian said, patting Aneurin's arm and gazing fondly up at him. "Norma is bound to think so, too," she added, almost slyly.

Emrys's eyes widened in horror. "Mam—"

"Norma?" Aneurin frowned, then sent an enquiring look towards his father.

Gwenllian smiled, widening her eyes as if in innocence, although Miriam realised with a sick feeling that the old woman knew exactly what kind of trouble she'd be stirring up. "She's been back living at the manse for weeks. Surely your parents mentioned it in their letters?"

"What...? She's at the manse now? Nobody's said a thing." He shook Miriam's hand off his arm and sent her an accusing look that pierced her through.

"She's cooking our Christmas dinner, so Miriam won't have to rush to put the turkey in the oven when we get back," Gwenllian said, ignoring her younger son's ferocious glare.

"Then I need to go now. I have to see her, ask her to forgive me. To tell her..." By the time his voice trailed off, he'd already reached the door.

"Aneurin!" Emrys called after him, limping to catch up, but the boy had gone, his boots kicking up gravel as he sprinted out to the lane and away down the mountain. Bitterly cold air poured in through the open doorway.

"What were you thinking, Mam?"

Gwenllian shrugged. Miriam could almost fancy there was a gleam in her eyes.

"He was going to find out when we got there, wasn't he?"

Emrys paced, a hand dragging through his thick hair. "If only the girl had gone before now. It's your fault, Miriam. You should never have let her stay so long. I should have insisted..."

Miriam threw up her hands. "She's been ill, Emrys! Her blood pressure rises whenever she does anything more demanding than sitting up for a few hours. And she has nowhere else to go. Even disliking her as you do, I can't believe you would deliberately endanger her life, or that of her baby."

"But if she'd gone, he wouldn't have known. He could have been free of her."

"We weren't to know he'd get leave to come home for the Plygain, were we?"

Emrys reached for his hat. On his way out, he lurched against the doorframe, pausing to lean on it as if the strength had left him.

"I can't lose him. Not my only son..." he said hoarsely. His eyes welled with tears as he sent back a despairing glance.

Miriam covered her mouth, fumbling for words. Before she could think of a way to offer comfort or hope, Gwenllian hobbled over and laid a gnarled hand on his coat sleeve.

"Don't you see the Lord's hand at work, son? Haven't I always told you that with God there's no such thing as coincidence? Trust in Him, and lean not on your own understanding."

"But... Do you really think God would mean for Aneurin to be with someone like that? A girl so steeped in sin?" For the first time, he sounded uncertain.

She held up a finger and wagged it at him. "If you're wise, son, you'll stop speaking of her like that. Because if I'm not mistaken, that girl may end up as your daughter-in-law. And in the midst of everything happening here, I for one am glad that at least Aneurin might have a chance of some happiness."

FIFTY-THREE

Norma

Norma had slept in snatches, racked with pains in her back that came and went, and a headache that hadn't eased since she'd arrived back at the manse the previous afternoon and headed straight to bed. As dawn broke on Christmas Day, she heaved her aching body out from the warmth of her blankets and shoved her feet into her slippers. Beneath her woollen bed socks, her limbs were so swollen from her knees down to her toes that the slippers barely fitted. That wasn't good. Usually her ankles went back to more or less their usual size after a night's rest.

Gingerly, she waddled to the bathroom, more like a frail old woman than a girl who'd only recently turned twenty-one. In the mirror above the washbasin, her face looked odd, somehow. Feeling ugly, she dropped her gaze and focused on washing her hands. They, too, were puffy, her fingers like sausages.

The turkey had been sitting on the cold slab in the larder since yesterday, plucked and dressed, ready for the oven with a thick slice of bacon draped across its breast. Its neck bulged where Miriam had packed it with a moist bread stuffing seasoned with chopped sage and onion.

Norma knelt to light the oven with a match, then hauled herself upright by holding on to a chair. Was carrying a baby always this painful? It was a wonder anyone ever had more than one. Who in their right mind would want to go through pregnancy again after experiencing it once?

The turkey was heavy. Lifting it and turning around in the confined space in the larder was awkward. Somehow, in spite of an awful, dragging pain in her belly, she managed to manoeuvre it to the oven. But as she closed the oven door, a strange sensation made her gasp.

Had she wet herself? Thin fluid had gushed down her legs, soaking her socks and slippers. As she leaned on the edge of the kitchen table, more fluid trickled down her inner thigh, and her abdomen was seized by a pain stronger than any she'd felt up to now. It was fierce enough to take her breath away.

Panic rose in her chest as she remembered gossip she'd once heard in a bus queue.

Her waters broke on the tram, you know. Made an awful mess. Course, her mum knew nothing about the baby, so she went to the nearest conveniences instead of going home. Poor little mite was born on the lav and drowned in the pan. Who knows if she did it on purpose? Police came for her, at any rate...

"Bleedin' hell's bells!" Norma swore as soon as the pain eased a little, despite an automatic nudge of guilt for swearing in the manse. Emrys and Miriam wouldn't like it. But then, they probably wouldn't like her leaking all over their kitchen floor either. She'd clear it up in a minute... But first, she had to get Maggie. If this was a sign that the baby was coming, she couldn't be on her own. She wouldn't know what to do, or how to keep it alive.

A frightened sob escaped her throat as she reached the telephone in the hallway, sore feet squelching in her slippers. Her hand trembled as she lifted the receiver to give the midwife's number to the girl at the telephone exchange.

An imperious voice answered the call just as another pain came on like a steam train rushing towards a tunnel.

"Is Nurse Cadwalader there, please?" she managed to gasp before it engulfed her.

"I'll fetch her for you. May I ask who's calling?"

"It's Norma. Norma Sparrow." Her knuckles had whitened on the receiver, and she rocked to and fro, her mind overtaken by pain. Dimly, she registered Maggie's reassuring voice at the end of the line.

If Maggie was coming, it would be alright...

Keeping her eyes closed and groaning with pain, Norma submitted unquestioningly to whatever Maggie needed to do. Fear had made her withdraw into herself, the way she'd often done as a child when facing something too big and awful to cope with. Now and then, Maggie's calm questions pierced the bubble she'd vanished into, and she slurred out answers as best she could between the tidal waves of agony sweeping over her.

"Been in pain for hours... Didn't realise... Need to mop the floor before the others get back... Can't have this baby – I'm not ready... Can't you stop this awful pain? I can't bear it."

"You need to stay calm, Norma. All this crying isn't good for your blood pressure, or for your baby. The pain will soon be over, and you'll forget all about it when you hold the baby in your arms."

"I won't! I won't hold it. I can't."

"Yes, you can. You'll start pushing soon."

"No! No, I won't."

Sobs racked her chest. How could she do this? All that lay ahead now was pain, terrible pain, and then her baby would forever be gone from her. She'd be forced to make that gut-wrenching, heartbreaking choice that wasn't really a choice at all, and then she'd have nothing. Nothing but memories of a baby whose face she'd never see; a child that would never be her son or daughter, but always someone else's. Once it was out, it would stop being hers.

"Calm down, Norma."

Maggie's tone was sharp, forceful like a teacher's. Norma half expected a thwack across the knuckles to accompany it. But then she heard another voice, a deep one, and an urgent pounding at the bedroom door.

"Norma? Norma, it's me!"

"Aneurin!"

Maggie had crossed the short gap between the bed and the door in the time it took Norma to scream out his name.

"You can't come in here," Maggie said as the door burst open and Aneurin rushed in.

With his arms around her, Norma's harsh sobs eased. She clung while he murmured reassurances into her ear. Could it really be him? She didn't know how or why he was here, and it didn't matter. Just being in his arms gave her comfort. She wasn't alone.

"I'm so sorry for everything," she whispered against his woollen greatcoat. "Can you forgive me?"

"Norma, *cariad*. I'm the one in need of forgiveness. I should have listened to you. I should have understood, instead of judging. I love you, Norma. *Rwy'n dy garu di.*"

She nodded, wanting to say she loved him, too. But a new torture was coming over her, making her feet pedal in the bed. A guttural, animalistic groan rose in her throat.

"Off you go now, Aneurin," Maggie said in her brisk voice. "This isn't the place for a man. Make yourself useful and put the kettle on, there's a good lad." She peered under the blanket that covered Norma's knees. "This is it, Norma dear. Not long to go, and then, before you know it, all the pain will stop."

FIFTY-FOUR

Miriam

By the time the car came to collect Miriam and the others from the chapel, Emrys was at a fever pitch of anxiety. He had locked the building for the last time and with the freezing wind nipping at their cheeks, they paid a final visit to Gwenllian's husband's grave.

Gwenllian, thankfully, was calm. As they set off, she craned her neck to look back at what would be her last view of the mountain for months, if not years, to come. Miriam was moved to hold her hand and was surprised when the old woman squeezed back. Squashed into the back seat between her husband and mother-in-law, there was little conversation to be had. The tense, gloomy atmosphere soon made the driver give up his attempts to chat.

Emrys gnawed at his fingernails most of the way back to the manse, rigid at Miriam's side. As soon as the car stopped, he hurried, limping, through the gate and into the house.

Miriam helped Gwenllian out of the car and took a few moments to thank the driver, promising to visit his elderly mother before New Year.

"Merry Christmas!" he called through the open window as he drove away.

Miriam couldn't help an ironic hitch of an eyebrow.

With Gwenllian gripping her arm for support, their progress up the short path into the manse was slow. Miriam frowned at the sight of her sister Maggie's bicycle leaning against the wall beside the front door.

On the threshold, both women froze. A plaintive, squalling cry came from upstairs.

"Is that...?" Gwenllian exclaimed.

Maggie's hat was hanging on the hall stand.

"I think it must be," Miriam replied. She could hardly believe it. A baby! And on this Christmas Day, of all days.

She dithered. The air in the hallway was rich with the aroma of roasting turkey. Perhaps she should check if it needed to be basted.

Emrys and Aneurin's deep voices floated from the study, raised in anger, with Idwal's quieter tone interjecting in an attempt to placate them.

Curiosity to see the new baby won out. As she hurried upstairs, she reasoned that Norma and Maggie's need was greatest. Let the men sort things out between themselves, and if the turkey was burned, so be it.

"I'm glad you're back," Maggie said in a low voice, her brow furrowed with concern. "We'll need to get some bottles and some milk. She's refusing even to look at the baby, never mind feed it."

"What? How could she...?" It was beyond Miriam's comprehension for a mother to behave in such a way.

"She's been dangerously ill, Mim. By the time I arrived she should have been in hospital, but it was clear she was close to delivering the baby. Thank God she didn't develop seizures. If she had, we'd have lost her, and probably the baby too."

Behind her, Miriam heard Gwenllian gasp. She must have followed her upstairs.

"I had no idea she was so unwell. If I'd realised, I wouldn't have left her yesterday." Miriam covered her mouth with her hand, shocked to think how narrowly a tragedy had been averted.

"She'll be alright now though, won't she?" Gwenllian asked.

"Hopefully, but she's not out of the woods yet. Toxaemia doesn't always go when the baby comes. If she starts to seem confused, or if she gets dizzy or sees spots, you must call the doctor straight away."

"How is the baby?" Miriam's mouth was dry.

"Small, but she has a good pair of lungs. She needs milk, though. I can fetch some, if you're willing to sit with them?"

"A little girl!" She blinked away tears. "Of course I'll sit with them. I'll watch them carefully, I promise."

"Thank you. Now, I've put her into one of your clean nightdresses and left the soiled bedding to soak in the bath, but I couldn't find any nappies or baby clothes. Norma's been too upset to talk to me."

"We wrapped some baby things up to give to Norma for Christmas, and put them under the Christmas tree," Gwenllian said. "I'll get them, then finish off sorting out the dinner."

Letting Gwenllian and Maggie go downstairs, Miriam tiptoed into the bedroom.

A drawer had been emptied of its contents and turned into a little nest with clean towels. Not quite a manger, but still her heart threatened to melt at the sight of the tiny Christmas baby wrapped up like a bundle. She pulled out her handkerchief and dabbed at her eyes, then crept over to the bed and perched on the edge of the mattress, laying a hand on Norma's shoulder.

As if she wanted to hide from the world, the new mother was curled up in a tight ball, knees drawn up near her chest and the blankets pulled up past her chin. Her blonde hair looked dull and had been scraped back from her blotchy face.

"I've just seen your beautiful little daughter," Miriam murmured. "She's a dear little thing."

Norma's eyes opened, the violet-blue startling against her red, puffy eyelids.

"Not my daughter," she said in a whisper so faint Miriam had to lean closer to hear. "She can be yours, though." Unfurling her limbs under the blankets, she reached for Miriam's hand and gripped it with surprising strength. "Will you take her, Mim? She deserves a mother who'll love her. When I think how different my life could have been if I'd had that..." Tears spilled onto her cheeks, but she made no move to wipe them away. Her eyes had fixed on Miriam as if her life depended on her reply.

Miriam's heart pounded as she thought of the baby tucked up in her little bundle of towels. Not so long ago, she'd hardly dared to hope that Norma might ask her this very question. It had been little more than a daydream, really, spun from eight years of longing for a daughter or son of her own. But a child's future couldn't hang on dreams. Real life wasn't so simple.

She lowered her gaze, staring at the plain woollen blanket as if it might be able to tell her what to do. It hurt to imagine what Norma's request must be costing her. The very thought of giving up a baby... Of being so desperate as to offer up a newborn child to someone who hadn't always been as kind as she might have been... Only weeks ago, Miriam would have clutched at such extraordinary generosity. Norma's sacrifice would have been the answer to all Miriam's prayers.

"Norma, I can't take her."

"But... you and Emrys could adopt her as your own. You'll be able to talk him round. You'd be good parents, and she'd have a smashing life with you."

Threading her fingers through Norma's, Miriam shook her head. She would have to let the girl down, but how could she bear to do it?

"I know you're both still upset with me for lying to you, but it ain't the baby's fault. If you bring her up, she'll be like you, not like me. Look at Nye – there's no one better, is there?"

Miriam swallowed and forced herself to meet Norma's gaze. She had to refuse, however distressing it was for them both.

"Norma, it isn't because of anything you've done, and it isn't because of Emrys. If you'd asked me a couple of months ago, I admit I would probably have said yes. But you must believe me – it isn't that I *won't* take her. I really can't."

Norma's voice rose as she clung to Miriam's hand. "I swear, you can bring her up however you like. I'll be gone – I won't interfere or get in the way. I'll go back to London just as soon as I can, and I'll never trouble you again. I'll promise never to see Nye again, if that's what it takes to make Emrys agree. There's no one in the world I'd trust more than you to care for her, Mim. You always do the right thing."

Miriam winced. Admittedly she'd tried, but had she really done right by Norma?

"Please," Norma went on. "I'll do anything. Whatever you want, just tell me."

Pulling her hand away, Miriam groaned inwardly at the prospect of adding to the torture Norma was already experiencing. She hadn't wanted to share her secret with anyone yet. But how else could she make her understand?

"I promise, it isn't because I doubt your intentions. You don't need to do anything to convince me. It's because of something else. Something that's a secret. So if I share it with you now, I must ask you not to tell anybody. I hadn't planned to tell anyone before I speak to Emrys."

Looking confused, Norma nodded.

"In that case... I'm so sorry, Norma. I can't take your little girl, because I'm expecting a baby of my own."

FIFTY-FIVE

Norma

All Norma's hopes lay in ruins. The agony of knowing how terribly she'd let her daughter down was an even greater torment than the physical pain she'd experienced during her delivery. What had been the point of running away and trying to make something of herself? She had still failed every bit as badly her own mother had done.

Miriam would make a wonderful mother, but not to Norma's baby as she'd hoped. There was no alternative now but to ask Maggie to call in a social worker who would take the child away to stay with foster parents until adoptive parents could be found. Maybe those new parents would be kind, or maybe they'd be like the Arthurs, and her little girl would grow up never being loved; being mistreated and neglected. Norma understood only too well the impact of such a fate upon a young child. She hid her face in her pillow and let her pain flood out until the corners of her mouth had cracked from crying and her eyes felt like bees had stung them.

One by one, Maggie, Miriam and even Gwenllian had come to try to persuade her to hold the baby. But how could she? Maggie gave the baby a bottle of milk in the chair beside the bed, and then changed her nappy, and all the while Norma faced the wall, refusing to give in to her longings.

Every time the baby cried, her breasts tingled uncomfortably. By the time dusk fell, they were hard and painful.

Miriam put up the blackout and tried again to persuade her, shaking her head with disappointment as she tiptoed past the sleeping baby. "You'll always regret it if you don't hold her at least once," she said. The words were a knife in her gut, but still Norma knew she couldn't let herself do it.

At last Aneurin came. He sat beside her on the bed and stroked her hair back from her face with gentle fingers.

"Maggie's gone now, but she says she'll come back in the morning to check on you."

She nodded, unable to tear her gaze from his face. There was a healthy, ruddy glow to his cheeks, and he'd had a fresh haircut. His blue-grey flannel army shirt made him look different. To Norma's eye, the white collar band gaped around his neck, and the shoulder seams sat too low, as if he'd been given a uniform a couple of inches too big. No wonder he wore braces to keep his khaki trousers up, if they fitted as badly as the shirt.

"Everyone's worried about you, *cariad*. They say you won't hold your little girl or give her a name. And I was surprised when they told me you hadn't made her anything to wear."

Norma swallowed the lump that had risen in her throat. Although his tone was puzzled, rather than accusing, the assumptions still hurt.

"It ain't true that I never made her nothing. I left it late, I'll grant you, but I knew your gran was knitting for her. I made her a nightgown with satin ribbons. It's in the suitcase under the bed."

He nodded, a smile softening the corners of his eyes, as if he was pleased with her.

"Will you tell me why won't you hold her? I'd like to try to understand."

"What's the point of holding her, when I can't keep her?"

He blinked, drawing his brows together.

"I'll have to give her away, Nye. And if I hold her, it will just make it harder for her and for me."

The dismay in his eyes was too much. She tried to turn her face away, but he tipped her chin back, refusing to allow her to avoid his gaze.

"Don't you start judging me now," she cried. "You're the only person I've ever met who doesn't wear their judgement like a badge of honour."

"I'm not, I promise. It's only that... how will you bear it, if you give up your child?"

Her breast heaved with the effort of maintaining control. She'd cried a sea of tears today, and it hadn't changed a thing. The moment was fast approaching when she'd have to be strong – she might as well start now.

"Life sometimes makes people choose the most impossible things, don't it? How could a gentle soul like you bear to choose between either prison or killing? But you had to, and one way or another, you'll have to learn to live with it. That's what I'll have to do, isn't it? I can't look after a baby and work, and if I don't work, we won't eat. I don't want that for her. She needs to be with a family who'll love her and give her everything I can't, even if it shreds my heart into rags."

"But you're her mother." He reached for her hand.

"She deserves a better one. If you'd known my mother you'd understand. How can someone like me look after a baby and give it what it needs? I never had love as a kid."

"Then give your baby the love you never had."

"What if I don't know how? What if I turn out to be as bad as my mum was, and she turns out like me? I couldn't forgive myself."

"We'll help you. You can stay for as long as you need to."

"I don't want to live on charity. I want my own life, not depending on strangers forever. And if I kept her, and lived like that, let's face it – who'd want to marry me and take on Dickie Tucker's child?"

"I will." It was said without hesitation. But she knew he was only being kind.

She mustered an attempt at a smile. "Oh, Nye darlin'. You have the best, most generous heart of anyone I've ever known. It's so kind of you to offer to save me. But I can't do that to you. Your dad would never accept us. And besides, I need to move on. I have to save meself."

In a rush of love and regret for what they might have had if things were different, she sat up and flung her arms around him. She'd stay in his embrace forever if she could. But real life was hard, and he'd forget her in the end.

"I only want to love you, Norma – if you'll let me. If you do, *you'll* be saving *me*. From a lifetime regretting losing you."

She held him harder, then pushed him away and dashed her hands over her face. "This is pointless," she said.

She'd have to harden herself. It was the only way to survive. Just a few days, and then she'd be well enough to go, and start over again. It would be the hardest thing she'd ever done, but she'd done hard things before and survived. *What doesn't kill you makes you stronger*, as Gran used to say.

Rolling onto her side, she faced the wall. If she couldn't make him see reason, then she'd have to pretend every cell in her body wasn't screaming to take him up on his reckless offer. She couldn't accept a proposal driven by pity. They both deserved better than that.

She squeezed her eyes closed when she felt the mattress shift, realising he'd got up. Now, perhaps, he'd leave her be, and although it would grind her already shattered heart into dust, she'd let him go and set him free to find someone worthy of him.

But he wasn't done. The floorboard creaked, then the mattress dipped again.

"Here's your daughter, Norma. She's perfect. A fresh, new person; a clean slate. And she's beautiful, just like her mam."

With panic rising, Norma couldn't help a frantic glance in his direction. Her heart pounded. He was cradling the baby in his lap, gazing at her with the fondest smile, as if fascinated by her features.

The voice in her head shrieked at her to stop. To look away. She couldn't look at them, these two people who in their different ways meant more to her than anyone ever had.

"Look at her tiny fingernails. They're long! Ah – she's gripping my finger. How can she hold on so hard?" He glanced up, his eyes alight. "She has fair hair – just like yours. Oh, Norma – you should see how lovely she is."

"You're making it worse," she whispered, her voice like gravel in her throat. She wanted to beat her pillow with her fists; to rake her cheeks with her nails; to pull out her hair in clumps. Anything to deflect from the pain tearing her apart.

"Norma, *cariad*. Since the moment I walked away from you, I've longed for you. Every room I've entered has felt empty without you. Whenever someone laughed, it's reminded me how much I've missed your smile. Every night I've dreamed of you. I believed I'd lost you forever. I never dared to imagine I'd see you again and have the chance to tell you how much I wish I'd stayed and tried harder to understand, instead of blaming you for doing what you felt you had to do. Nothing would make me prouder or happier than being at your side for the rest of our lives, if you'll have me. Your love would give me a reason to get through the war. And I want you to know that I'll love you whether you decide to keep your baby or not. If you can't face it after everything you've gone through, then I'll understand, and if you'll let me, I'll support you to recover from the grief of giving her up."

Norma couldn't stop staring as the words poured from him. No one had ever offered her so much. Not only love – though that would be remarkable enough – but also understanding. He'd lifted the weight of a lifetime of harsh judgement from her back. It was more than she could ever have expected or hoped for.

"Whatever path you choose, Norma, I want to walk it with

you. So if you want her, this little baby who looks so much like you, I vow here and now that I will not only provide you with the means to keep her, but I will also give you both every ounce of love that's in my heart."

Awkwardly, he brushed at one of his eyes with his thumb, then quickly moved his hand back to cradle the bundle in his arms.

"You told me once that you want to be somebody. To me, you already are. And to this child, you are. You're the blood in her veins, the voice in her ears that will be forever lodged in her heart. You're her mother, for better or worse. And if you'll allow it, I would count it an honour to be her father."

He paused, running his tongue around his lips as if they'd gone dry, then rose to his feet and carried the baby back to lay her in the nest of towels as if she were made of porcelain.

Norma watched, dumbstruck. He was offering her the world.

"It's your choice, *cariad*. You encouraged me to make my own choice when I enlisted. You deserve the chance to choose your future, too. If you marry me, I'll always do my best to make sure you're looked after. You'll never have to worry. I'll send you money, and, God willing, when the war is over and I go back to the bank, I'll take out a mortgage and buy us a house. Or, if I don't come through it... then you'll have a widow's pension and my savings. You can still sew, if that's what you want. I know how much you love to make things."

With a couple of swift steps he was back at her side. He knelt on the bare floorboards, his face full of uncertainty and love. "I'm not telling you any of this to push you into a decision," he said. "Just so you know that everything I have to offer is yours, if you want it. My heart, most of all."

She thought she might burst. "Oh, Aneurin," she murmured, reaching for his hand and holding it to her lips to kiss it. If his heart was all he had, she would take it and be more than content.

"Don't give me your answer now. About marrying me, or about the baby. You're exhausted, and I don't want to rush you into making a choice you can't be sure about. But I'll have to go back soon, Norma, so don't leave it too long."

She nodded. She'd decide later what to do about the baby. To have the choice... It was something she'd never been offered before. It was dizzying and terrifying all at once.

He took her in his arms as if he was afraid she might break. "You've no idea how desperately I've missed you," he whispered against her ear.

FIFTY-SIX

Miriam

Candles twinkled on the Christmas tree, and the parlour was rich with the comforting smells of pine and burning coal. Miriam reached beneath the tree for the family's Christmas presents. They'd been too busy all day to open them.

"What about Aneurin?" Emrys asked as she handed the gifts around.

"He can open his later. We can still open ours now, while he's upstairs."

"At least we didn't have to eat late, thanks to Norma cooking the turkey," Gwenllian said, tearing open her first gift. "Ah – she's made me some slippers. Look, Emrys. See how soft they are?"

Emrys grunted, his face impassive. He opened a small gift from Norma of a handkerchief monogrammed with a capital E, then laid it on the arm of his chair without comment.

Idwal, too, had received an embroidered handkerchief. "That'll come in handy," he said, and Miriam smiled, grateful to him for always trying to maintain a cheerful demeanour despite everything he faced in the days ahead.

"What has she given you, then?" Gwenllian asked, peering eagerly at the package in Miriam's lap.

Heat rose in Miriam's cheeks as she held up an exquisite camisole of pink satin and delicate lace. What would it feel like to wear something so silky and daring against her skin? She would never buy such a garment for herself.

Idwal cleared his throat and looked away.

Gwenllian's lips had pursed in a manner that might indicate disapproval or an attempt to disguise amusement – Miriam wasn't sure which.

"That's pretty," Gwenllian said. "Isn't it pretty, Emrys? Even when I could sew, I couldn't have made anything like that."

"I'm sure you wouldn't have wanted to," he said, his mouth in a thin line.

Miriam folded her present back into its wrappings and tucked it under her chair before joining in with opening the next gifts. Gwenllian was right: the camisole was lovely. She'd never worn anything like it. It couldn't have been more different from the sensible brown knitted cardigan Gwenllian had made for her, or the apron from Idwal, or the recipe book from Aneurin, or the leather-bound Bible concordance from Emrys.

They had just finished opening their gifts when Aneurin came in, dressed once more in his civilian clothes.

"I have something to tell you," he said, hovering near the doorway.

"Come in and sit down, *bach*," Gwenllian said, patting the arm of the sofa beside her.

"No thanks – I'll stand, if that's alright." He straightened his shoulders, looking squarely at his father.

"I've asked Norma to marry me," he said, then carried on as if the colour hadn't left Emrys's face. "I know it might seem sudden, but in the days we're living in, I don't see the point of waiting. If she'll have me, I'll buy a ring and marry her as soon as I can get enough leave to get a licence and arrange the ceremony."

Emrys struggled to his feet, but before he could speak, Aneurin addressed him directly.

"I'd like your blessing, Dad, but as you know I'm old enough now not to need it. It would be a great joy to me and, I'm sure, to Norma if you'd give it. But if you decide you can't..." He swallowed hard, taking a deep breath before continuing. "If you won't, then you should know I will marry her anyway. We'll go to the register office if we can't marry in Chapel. I love her. And I've told her that if she decides to keep her baby, I'd be honoured to adopt her and bring her up as my own daughter."

"Aneurin, even allowing for the foolishness of youth, how can you not see that marrying the girl would be madness? What you're feeling is infatuation, not love," Emrys said.

"You're wrong, Dad," Aneurin snapped back, his fists clenching. "And please, don't try to tell me what I feel. Not a day has gone by since I left here that I haven't regretted my decision."

"There's still time to change that decision! You could still refuse to fight, register as a conscientious objector if they won't give you a non-combatant role..."

"I don't mean deciding to serve. I mean my decision to leave Norma. I shouldn't have abandoned her like that. I should have tried harder to understand what it was like for her. She hasn't had the advantages we've had, of a loving family, or a safe place to go. She did the only thing she could to try to give herself and her a child a secure future. I should have forgiven her. We *all* should have forgiven her, and understood, instead of jumping to condemn her because we felt we'd been gullible. We cared more about how we were feeling than what she had gone through." Passion had made his voice rise.

Miriam's hands twisted. She looked away, hating this conflict, hating herself for having been too slow to understand the need to forgive. Aneurin was right. She should have shown Norma more understanding. She'd been judgemental and unkind. They all had.

"If I'd known she was here, I would have come back sooner – but then you knew that, didn't you? That's why you didn't tell me."

Gwenllian spoke up, her sharp tone startling them out of their combative stance. "Aneurin – go upstairs to my room, please. In my wardrobe there's a wooden box. I'd like you to bring it down to me."

"Now, Mam-gu? Can't it wait?"

"No, it can't. I'd like to look in it now, if you don't mind."

She'd barely finished speaking when the doorbell rang.

Aneurin's face turned putty-grey. He turned anxious eyes towards Emrys, like a rabbit poised to run after hearing the bark of a fox.

"Who could that be at this time on Christmas night?" Emrys muttered, scowling.

"Dad. There's something else I should have told you." Aneurin's Adam's apple bobbed in his throat.

Emrys's eyes narrowed. "Go upstairs and fetch that box Mam asked you for," he said. "I'll see to the door."

Bewildered, Miriam followed as Emrys limped slowly into the hallway, giving Aneurin plenty of time to take the stairs two at a time and vanish into Gwenllian's bedroom. The bell rang again before they'd had time to pull back the blackout curtain.

"Alright, alright," Emrys grumbled, pulling the door open as if he had all the time in the world.

A middle-aged man in a policeman's uniform stood outside, the light of the moon making the silvered badges on his ink-blue helmet gleam.

"Good evening, Constable Todd. Have you come to wish us a happy Christmas?"

"Ah. No, but a happy Christmas to you, of course, Reverend. And to you, Mrs Powell." The man's suspicious gaze scanned them, and he leaned to look past them into the hallway.

"How can I help you?" Emrys asked, shifting to block the man's view.

"I'm afraid we find ourselves with a bit of a tricky situation, Reverend. We've had a telephone call from the barracks in Brecon. It appears that your son is absent without leave. I'm sure it's just a misunderstanding, but I've been asked to call by and see if he's with you."

Miriam put a hand to her breast. She'd assumed Aneurin had been granted leave to come home. It hadn't occurred to her that he might have absconded.

"Why do they imagine he would have come here?" Emrys's eyes flashed dangerously.

Todd frowned. "Well, it's Christmas, isn't it? It's natural enough for them to suppose that he'd go home, isn't it?"

"Hasn't the army caused enough pain to my family by evicting my mother and brother and all my flock on the mountain from their homes, without sending you to my house on Christmas night? We have a newborn baby in the house, with a sick mother who mustn't be disturbed. And as for my son – I'll have you know, Constable, that he and I have been at odds ever since the day he went against my express wishes and beliefs to enlist. Do you imagine, after that, that he'd be so eager to seek me out, knowing he'd betrayed everything I stand for?"

Todd gaped. "I'm sorry, Reverend. I didn't know..."

"He was born at Pant Glas, on Moel Carnau. If what you say is true, that would be the first place he'd want to go, before the military blows it up. If I see him, I'll tell him you're looking for him. But you can tell the officers in Brecon that if they bring any further trouble to disturb the peace of this family, I shall call the wrath of God down upon their heads," Emrys thundered.

Embarrassment made Todd's cheeks turn as red as his nose. Mumbling apologies, he hastened back down the path, making a show of shutting the gate carefully behind him.

Miriam dashed a hand over her forehead. While the policeman's visit had frightened her, presenting the possibility of poor Aneurin being dragged away in disgrace, Emrys seemed almost to have relished the chance to defy the authorities. As she moved back into the hallway, tucking her hands under her armpits to steady them, he cocked an eye at the leaden sky and inhaled deeply.

"I'd say we're in for snow," he said, pushing the door closed and sweeping the blackout curtain back into place.

Behind them, a footstep creaked on the stairs.

Emrys looked up at Aneurin and raised an eyebrow. "I expect you heard all that," he said.

"I'm sorry, Dad. I should have warned you. I didn't want to risk them not letting me go to the last Plygain. I had to be there to support you and Mam-gu." He followed them back into the parlour, carrying a small wooden box and a piece of folded cloth.

Emrys sank into his armchair, rubbing his chin.

Gwenllian laid the box on her lap and lifted the lid to peer inside. "Ah, good," she said. "There's something in here that I'd like to give you... Yes, here it is."

Aneurin reached to take something from her palm, then closed his fist around it, staring back at her with eyes wide.

"It's my engagement ring," Gwenllian said, calmly closing the box. "I can't get it over my knuckle these days. It's just going to waste shut up in this box. So if she likes it, you can give it to Norma."

Emrys cut across the boy's murmurs of thanks. "Am I the only member of this family with a grain of sense?" he demanded.

Undaunted, Gwenllian glared back with equal ferocity. "Might I remind you, Emrys, that you have been blessed to have your chance of love, not once, but twice. Oh, I had some doubts about Miriam at first..." She flapped a hand towards Miriam as if to lessen the impact of this criticism, then ploughed on while Emrys stared at her, slack-jawed. "But I hope you know how fortunate you are to have her. She's been a good wife to you, despite the language difference and her being so much younger. Let Aneurin have his choice. Any fool can see by the light in his eyes when he talks about Norma that he loves her. And he's as stubborn as you are when something really matters to him, in case you hadn't noticed. If you stand in his way it will cost you dearly. A strong tree must bend when the wind is blowing."

Emrys rocked back as if she'd struck him.

"Norma made me this, Dad. Look – it might help you understand," Aneurin said. He held out the piece of cloth he'd been carrying, and after a moment's hesitation, Emrys took it and shook it out.

"It's Pant Glas," Aneurin explained, looking around the room at each of them in turn. "She wanted me to have a picture of it, knowing how much it means to us all. That's the woman I love, Dad. The one whose tender, generous heart and creative imagination fashioned something so beautiful for someone she thought she'd never see again. She did this for me, even though I'd let her down, because she hoped it would bring me joy. Because she loves me. Now, can you understand why I can't lose her again?"

Miriam stepped forward. "She stitched a picture of Moel Carnau for us, too," she murmured.

Emrys tore his gaze from the picture to her face. "You never told me."

"I should have. Aneurin, would you fetch it, please?" Quickly, she told him where to find it, and he ran back upstairs.

Emrys spread the embroidered panel out over the footstool before the fire. He blinked rapidly as he stared at it, a muscle working in his cheek.

"It's beautiful," Gwenllian breathed, reaching out to stroke the picture. "There's the farmhouse, look. And the barn. And even some sheep up on the hill."

Idwal put his arm around his mother's shoulder as they took in the details of the scene Norma had recreated in cloth and silk threads.

Breathless, Aneurin burst back in with the other panel and handed it over. Laid side by side, they showed very different scenes, but both were so evocative that Miriam wasn't surprised to see tearful smiles light Gwenllian and Idwal's faces. They nodded at each other, smiling as Gwenllian wiped her eyes and Idwal blew his nose with his new handkerchief.

"It's the view from our picnic, isn't it?" Aneurin said. "She's so clever. Looking at that, I can almost taste the cheese sandwiches and feel the sunshine on my face."

"So many tiny scraps, making up the whole," Emrys murmured, tracing the lines of patchwork with a finger. "A perfect metaphor."

Miriam moved to stand behind him and laid a hand on his shoulder. "A metaphor for what, *cariad*?"

"For life. Not only that, but for *cymdogaeth* – community, as you would say. When all we have left of our dreams is torn and fragmented pieces... When every individual is different, some maybe even unwanted or seemingly useless... The hand of the artist can put them together and create something lovely. Side by side, with their complementary and contrasting textures and colours, they make up a work of beauty that's infinitely greater than the sum of its parts."

There was a moment's silence while everyone absorbed the words, still gazing at Norma's remarkable handiwork.

"She'll be happy when I tell her you like it," Aneurin said.

Emrys sent a rueful look his way. "You won't need to," he said. "I'll tell her myself."

FIFTY-SEVEN

Norma

Norma's thoughts were still whirling over Aneurin's proposal when a knock sounded at the bedroom door. Sitting up, she almost swore aloud at the sight of Emrys entering the room. Her heart thumped wildly.

Flamin' Nora. He's not come to make me sling my hook tonight, of all nights?

"My apologies for disturbing your rest," he said, silhouetted by light spilling in from behind him.

"I wasn't asleep anyway," she said warily, easing her aching body upright against her pillow. If he'd come to throw her out, starting with an apology was a funny way of going about it.

He turned towards the baby tucked up in the drawer at the foot of the bed. "May I pray for your daughter?"

"Suit yourself."

"Have you given her a name?"

She shook her head, watching him hitch his trouser legs to kneel awkwardly beside the child. Gradually her pulse slowed as it dawned on her that even Emrys wouldn't be so cruel as to put a newborn baby and its mother out onto the street. Especially not on Christmas night.

In the half-light, he leaned over the baby, his deep voice soft and remarkably unlike the haranguing tone she'd so often battled against.

"Heavenly Father, we thank you for this new life. In your mercy and wisdom, grant your blessing on this child. Surround her with your unfailing love and grace, and guide her footsteps always." Gently, he laid a hand on the blankets covering the baby. "The Lord bless thee, and keep thee. The Lord make his face shine upon thee, and be gracious unto thee. The Lord lift up the light of his countenance upon thee, and grant thee peace. In Jesus's name. Amen."

In the silence that followed, Norma dashed a stray tear from her cheek, unwilling to let him see that a prayer to a God she couldn't believe in had such power to move her.

"I owe you an apology, Norma," he said after struggling to his feet.

Her eyebrows flew upwards. Praying for a new baby wasn't out of character, whatever his views on the circumstances of its birth. But an apology was the last thing she'd expected.

He took a halting step, then knotted his hands in front of him as if trying to stop them twisting with nerves. "I'm sorry if I've appeared lacking in Christian charity, on occasions. Although my intentions were always to help you along the right path, and to protect my family, I realise I've fallen short of the— the pastoral care you needed. I hope you can find it in your heart to forgive me."

His shoulders shifted, and she had the sense that the words were being wrung from him.

"It's become clear to me that Aneurin will be happier if you and I can... If we can move forward on a more amicable footing from now on. Especially as I understand he hopes to marry you and to bring up your child as his own."

Norma absorbed this sudden change. It wouldn't be like Emrys to lie, so the apology must have been genuine. But she couldn't believe he'd ever be happy to have her as a daughter-in-law.

"I ain't said yes to him yet, Emrys. My gran always used to say that fools rush in where angels fear to tread. So it wouldn't be right to let him go charging into a decision as big as that, when emotions are running high. I wouldn't want him to—" She broke off, swallowing the lump in her throat that threatened to choke her. "I wouldn't want him to come to regret asking me."

There was a pause, as if Emrys was weighing his words carefully. "If it helps – I believe he is certain of his choice." His head bowed and he moved as if to go, then looked back. "He's shown me the cloth pictures you made. It takes a rare talent and vision to bring out the beauty in such small, tattered remnants. Put together, they become remarkable. By joining them as you did, you created something beautiful. I believe that when the right people are joined together, something beautiful is created then, too."

Biting her lip, reeling from this unanticipated encouragement, she watched him limp back to the open doorway.

"Whatever you decide, Norma, I wish you every blessing." He let out his breath in a rush as he left the room, as if he'd done what he'd set out to do and had been left exhausted.

Afterwards, her mind was too dazed and confused to sleep soundly. She drifted in and out of a restless, troubled slumber through the night, grateful when Miriam came in twice to tend to the baby. By the time morning came, she was almost giddy from the constant tumbling thoughts that sped out of control like a wild horse galloping downhill.

Up to now, she'd had almost no choices in her life. Not in her most outlandish dreams could she ever have imagined having the possibility of a future with a man like Aneurin. A man who was as considerate, kind-hearted and tender as he was handsome and passionate, who still wanted her even though he'd seen her at her ugliest and weakest and most vulnerable. It was surely too good to be true. It was as if the fairy godmother she'd once wished for had suddenly and inexplicably waved a magic wand, transforming everything. Aneurin's return and proposal. Miriam pregnant. And as if that wasn't enough, Emrys asking for her forgiveness.

Most incredible of all, after nine months of denying herself any thought of being a mother, the possibility of being able to keep her baby had been laid before her. Most girls in her situation would be turning cartwheels and whooping for joy. So why did the prospect seem more terrifying than wonderful? What was wrong with her?

In the past, the way forward had always been more or less clear, even if it had often been strewn with yet more potential pitfalls. There had always been the hope that things could only get better.

But now... They could get horribly worse. All these remarkable gains could be lost. What if she made the wrong choice? She wouldn't only wreck her own life. She'd hurt Aneurin and her baby.

What if she married Nye and he realised, after the initial excitement, that he didn't love her after all? What if he started to regret choosing a wife with a past, who wasn't a virgin bride and who'd never read the Bible; who didn't even go to church for Christmas or Easter, never mind the rest of the year? A girl who sometimes used coarse language and who liked to get dressed up in her glad rags and sing down the pub, and maybe even have a little tipple of gin now and then. A girl who dreamed of having her own business and who'd be bored stiff if her days were filled with nothing more exciting than cooking and cleaning up for him and a baby. A girl whose own mother had set her the worst possible example.

Worse, what if neither of them found they could love the baby? *The road to hell is paved with good intentions*, Gran used to say. Aneurin hadn't stopped to think about what it would mean, at the age of twenty-one, to take on another man's child. And if he was sent away to fight, he wouldn't even be around most of the time. He'd probably have to go abroad soon, and the last war had dragged on for four years. What if he hardly saw his wife and daughter for that long, and came home a changed man, as so many had before?

Soldiers weren't paid much. How would they manage financially with him gone? What if people in Pontybrenin couldn't accept her as the minister's daughter-in-law? What if Nye came to regret saddling himself with responsibilities at such an early age? They could both be twenty-five by the time he returned, and she'd look nothing like the pretty girl he'd first set eyes on back in September.

So many what ifs. So much could go disastrously wrong. And it would be all her fault for making a wrong decision today. That's what everyone would think. No one would think any the worse of Nye for being generous enough to want to support her. All the blame would fall upon her for taking advantage of his good nature and his soft heart.

FIFTY-EIGHT

Miriam

At last, they were alone. Emrys had hesitated at the door to the bedroom, almost as if he needed her permission to come in. Miriam reached up: his jaw felt rough in her hands.

"Come to bed," she said. "Mind, I don't know how much sleep we'll all get, with a newborn baby in the house. And I doubt Idwal will get much sleep on the sofa, poor thing."

"Until he starts at the farm in Chepstow, he's just grateful to have a roof over his head." Emrys sighed, closing the door and rubbing his tired eyes with the heels of his hands.

No doubt it was true. She hoped Idwal would be happy. There wouldn't be much call to speak Welsh so close to the border with England, but at least he'd found a tenancy.

"I'm grateful to you, too," she said. "More than you'll ever know." Her voice caught on the words.

His brown eyes were soft. Humble, even. "Why?" he asked, starting to unbutton his cuffs.

"For giving Aneurin your blessing. And for buying him some time, protecting him when Constable Todd came. It was clever, the way you made him think Aneurin would be at Pant Glas, without telling lies."

"It isn't in me to practise deceit. But he's my son, and the army doesn't deserve my loyalty."

"Will he be alright? They'll punish him, won't they?"

Emrys raised a weary eyebrow. "He'll lose a few days' pay and maybe some privileges. The most he'll face is a stint in the guard-room when he gets back to the barracks. They're too desperate for men to do anything worse."

She let out her breath. "That's a relief. Emrys, I hope you know I'm proud of you. For helping him, and for finding room in your heart to consider his happiness. We need to learn to see the Norma Aneurin sees, and forget the one who's made mistakes, don't we?"

She helped as he shrugged off his shirt, tugging at the sleeves and then folding it while he reached under his pillow for his pyjamas.

"I underestimated him. I thought he was a fool, but in the ways that matter, I've realised this evening that perhaps he's the wisest of us all. Which of us, after all, can say we've never slipped? I don't tell lies, but I have let people down. Time will tell if he's making a mistake... but I'm willing to give her a chance if it makes him happy. I couldn't bear to be estranged from him when he's sent overseas. Not when there's a chance that..." He stopped, too overcome to continue.

Miriam moved to stand in front of him, catching hold of his wrists. It was time.

"Our children are blessed to have you as their father," she said, holding his gaze.

Her heart leaped as a question dawned in his face.

"Our children?"

"I've been wanting to tell you. I wasn't sure for a while, but... I think I must be."

"God be praised!"

She laughed softly as he seized her in his arms, then promptly let go, as if she might break.

"We should probably keep it quiet for now. It's early days."

"Yes, but... Oh, Miriam, *cariad*. I never thought... I thought I was too old. A *baby*!" He shook his head with joy and disbelief, then kissed her with the kind of passion and tenderness he hadn't shown her in weeks. There was a glow of hope in his eyes such as she hadn't seen since before the war began.

"It's our own Christmas miracle. In spite of everything else that's happening in the world. And you'll be able to help Aneurin. He'll want to be a good father. You can show him how."

Emotions streaked across his face. She sensed there was still a part of him that feared Aneurin might have rushed in too quickly, but at least now he was willing to give his son and Norma a chance.

"We should tell him. And Mam, too." He reached for the doorknob, but she stopped him.

"Tomorrow," she said, and drew him close. "There's plenty of time."

FIFTY-NINE

Norma

Norma gathered the bedclothes in her fists, wishing her whirling thoughts would stop. There wasn't much point lying in bed wide awake and tying herself in knots with worry. Perhaps getting up would help her start to rebuild her strength. Gingerly, she slid her legs out of bed and sat up, pushing her feet into her slippers, which were mercifully dry now thanks to Miriam. They fitted comfortably again: that was good. Her body might be aching almost as badly as if she'd been thrown into the road all over again, and her breasts felt fit to burst, but her feet, at least, must be beginning to shrink back to their former size.

With the blackout curtains still closed, it was too dark to tell if her sausage fingers were looking better. She moved to the window and pulled the curtains back, stunned to see a dazzling, white brightness through the condensation on the pane. Rubbing the moisture off the icy glass revealed that the road and houses all along Ebenezer Street were blanketed in a layer of snow. Fat, fresh snowflakes were plummeting from a sky dense with cloud.

The light disturbed the baby, who squawked out a cry.

"Oh, Gawd." Milk started seeping into Norma's borrowed winceyette nightdress, leaking down her front and onto her tummy, where it cooled rapidly in the frigid air seeping through the windowpane. She grimaced and dabbed at herself with a handkerchief.

"Shhh..." she said from across the room. If the kid didn't stop crying, she'd end up soaked. But she couldn't go and pick her up. She wasn't ready for that. She might never be.

Two tiny fists waved in the air, visible above the wooden sides of the drawer. The volume of the cries rose.

"Alright, shush now. I'll fetch Miriam. She'll sort you out."

But to get to Miriam, she'd have to pass the baby. And Miriam had already been up to her twice in the night. Pregnant herself, she deserved the chance of a rest.

"Gawd," Norma said again under her breath.

With her hands over her mouth, hardly daring to breathe, she moved closer and peered at the child. She was so small! Her tiny, scrunched-up face was turning from peachy to crimson as she started to squall, and she thrashed from side to side with surprising strength, knees lifting the shawl that Miriam had tucked so carefully around her. It would be too cruel to leave her to cry.

Terrified of hurting her, Norma bent and picked her up. The baby's head lolled alarmingly, and Norma plopped down with her on the foot of the bed, holding her against her chest for fear of dropping her or inadvertently doing her some other kind of harm. As her cries turned to snuffles, the child's eyes opened, and her mouth moved against Norma's wet nightgown. Her determined grunts made the tingling even worse.

Paralysed by indecision, Norma sat and stared, wide-eyed, at the fractious bundle in her arms. The world had shifted under her so much since yesterday morning, she felt dizzy with it.

A soft knock at the bedroom door made her gasp with relief. Miriam came in, yawning and rubbing eyes heavy with fatigue. A step or two behind her was Gwenllian, wrapped up warmly in a dressing gown covered by a paisley shawl. Both faces lit up at the sight of her holding the baby.

"Oh, how lovely," Miriam exclaimed, her kind smile like a beacon. "I knew you wouldn't be able to resist her. She's such a beautiful little flower, aren't you, poppet?" She bent to stroke the baby's soft downy head.

"Don't go jumping to conclusions just because I've picked her up. It was only that I couldn't stand to hear her crying."

"Have you decided on a name for her, yet?" Gwenllian asked, gazing fondly at the child.

"I ain't had a chance to think about anything like that. Look, I ain't no good at this. The way she's fretting, I think she must want feeding or changing or something – I don't know what. I don't think she likes me," she added, her heart rate racing as the horrible crying started again.

Miriam clicked her tongue impatiently.

Struggling to her feet with her awkward burden, Norma pushed the baby into Miriam's arms. "Let's face it, if she could walk, she'd run a mile from a mother like me. Here, take her, will you? I'm no use to her."

"Hush, now, little one. Let's take you downstairs and warm up a bottle of milk, shall we? You can see your mammy again in a little while, when she's had time to calm down. While the milk is warming, we'll change your nappy, get you nice and clean and comfortable." Miriam cooed into the baby's ear, rocking her and carrying her out of the room with such confidence it was enough to take Norma's breath away.

"That just proves it, doesn't it? I'll never be like that. Miriam's everything I'm not. The baby needs someone like her, not someone like me."

As she buried her face in her hands, Gwenllian grasped her arms and shook her.

"Silly girl," she said.

"It's not silly. I'll never be good enough."

"It's silly to ever imagine any one of us is good enough to be a parent. We all just muddle along. Miriam's had more practice with babies, that's all. All you have to do is let yourself love the child. The rest you can learn, just like you learned to sew. You weren't born knowing how to use a needle and thread, were you? So come on, where's the girl who never let anyone or anything get the better of her?"

"I think that girl's gone," Norma whispered.

"I never heard such nonsense." With a stifled grunt of pain as her joints clicked, Gwenllian sat beside her on the bed and gripped her hand with surprising strength. "Being a mother... It's like walking a tightrope wearing a blindfold. You just feel your way along, step by terrifying step, until the day comes when you look up and see there's a mile of rope behind you. And if you think caring for a baby is hard, wait till they grow up a bit, and they think they no longer need you. Then, all your years of hard-won experience will count for nothing because they imagine they know much, much more than you do."

Norma wiped away tears. For several heartbeats Gwenllian stared at her, one white eyebrow arched disdainfully. "It's a shame to think I misjudged you, Norma. There I was, encouraging Aneurin to follow his heart. I told my Emrys to give you both his blessing. I was even willing to give up my own engagement ring. And yet now it turns out, after all that, I've let my boy throw his heart away on a coward. Surely you're not going to turn down the best chance of happiness you ever had just because you're scared?"

With a shiver, Norma looked away. "I don't want to ruin everything for them," she said. "I don't know how to be a good wife, or a mother. Aneurin deserves better, and so does she."

"So that's that, then. That's your decision made. Tsk."

Miriam nudged the door open with her foot, cradling the baby with one arm and holding a bottle in her mouth with the other. "Everything alright?" she asked, pausing as if she could sense the tension in the room.

Norma gazed at her hands. Her fingers had almost returned to their usual size. At least they felt normal and familiar.

"Give me the baby," Gwenllian said, hobbling over towards her daughter-in-law and taking hold of the child with her bottle before pushing her into Norma's arms. "There you go," she said, refusing to accept Norma's protests. "She won't break unless you do something really daft like dropping her. She doesn't need much from you yet. Just milk poured in at one end and the waste wiped off the other end. Even stupid girls can do it. I've told you before – that sewing machine of yours is more complicated. And whatever she needs, or however hard it gets, we'll help you. Won't we, Miriam?"

Miriam nodded.

Taking care to prop up the bottle and to support the baby's head, Norma watched her determined suckling while the level of milk gradually drained. After a while, realising the baby seemed to be content, she risked a glance up at Miriam and Gwenllian. Their eyes were warm with approval, as if she was already doing well. They both looked as if they truly believed she could do this.

The baby stopped sucking, and milk started to flood out of the corner of her mouth. Instinctively, Norma pulled the teat clear and used the bib around her neck to wipe away the milk dribbling towards her ear.

Gwenllian nodded encouragingly. "No one can be a good mother by themselves; we all need others to cheer us along the tightrope, to hold our hands when we wobble and to make us get right back on when we fall. That's what we women do."

"You'll have us to help you," Miriam murmured, nodding along. Norma had never seen them so united. "And Maggie, of course, and Ceinwen. And Miss Proudfoot, come to that. But the best part about it is that we'll also have you, Norma. The girl who saved little Audrey even though it meant putting herself at risk."

"The girl who was ready to give up her own chance of happiness for fear that she'd spoil Aneurin's," Gwenllian added.

Norma thought back to the summer, when she'd thought Dickie would save her from ruin. She'd learned so much since then. She'd made mistakes, of course. Plenty of those. But she'd come so far.

Perhaps there were no guarantees. But the baby seemed content in her arms now, pleasantly heavy in the crook of her elbow. A rush of feeling flooded over her as she gazed, fascinated, at her daughter's perfect button nose and delicate, sandy eyelashes. Extraordinary, to think she'd carried this tiny person inside her for nine months. Could she really let go of her now that she didn't have to?

Her own mother had abandoned her without an explanation. How could she do the same to her own child? Knowing, as she did, what it was to grow up wondering if she'd done something wrong. If she'd been so wicked, so awful, that she'd driven her own mother away. Feeling unwanted. Unloved. How could she condemn this perfect, innocent baby to the same fate, when she'd been offered not only Aneurin's love and support, but the care of these two women who'd been the closest thing she'd had to a family since her gran died?

Perhaps, with help, she could at least try. Nye would make a better dad than Dickie could ever have been. And perhaps she could make a mum after all. Maybe not a great one. Not as good as Miriam would be – but maybe things like knowledge and experience didn't matter so much, as long as love was there?

With Aneurin and his family at her side, she could still be a thousand times better than her own poor mother had been. And she could still sew. This would be the best dressed little girl in Wales.

"You were right about her being beautiful, Miriam. She's like a little angel, ain't she?" Her heart seemed to swell, as if the hard shell she had constructed around it out of fear of having to give the child up was beginning to crumble. For the first time, she was daring to imagine a future that included her baby. A baby she'd protect with all the ferocity she'd felt when she lobbed the gnome through Mr Arthur's front door.

She handed the glass bottle to Miriam and stroked a wisp of hair that curled onto the baby's forehead. Greedily, she took in every feature of her squished, pink face, making up for the wasted hours since she'd been born. It dawned on her that she was free. Free to love her daughter. Free to enjoy her. To delight in her, even. With tears welling, she infused her smile with all the emotion she'd been denying herself, and made a vow deep in her heart. *I'll always do my best for you. I'll always be on your side. And you'll always know you're loved. I'll never give you cause to doubt it.*

Barely noticed, Gwenllian nudged Miriam towards the door. Before they reached it, it opened.

Aneurin peeped into the room. "I woke up and saw the snow. Looks as if I might be able to stay another day or two," he said. "Is everything alright in here?" His gaze fell upon Norma and the baby, and the love she read in his eyes sent any last fears about his commitment fleeing away.

"It is now," Norma replied. "I think I'll call her Ivy, after my gran. It seems a good name for a Christmas baby."

"It does. I'm glad you've given her a name. Does that mean...?" He caught his lower lip with his teeth, as if he hardly dared to ask.

She nodded, her mouth curving. "It does. My answer to your question is yes... *Os gwelwch yn dda.*"

His answering whoop of joy was so loud, Ivy's arms flew out, her hands outstretched like little starfish. Gwenllian and Miriam both hushed him before discreetly leaving the room.

Rocking Ivy gently to soothe her back to sleep, Norma soaked up the happiness in Nye's wide smile, glad to know she had the power to bring him such delight that it threatened to make his face split in two.

"You remembered how to say please in Welsh," he said in an exaggerated whisper, tiptoeing towards her.

"I had a good teacher. I still don't know what you said to me that afternoon in the bandstand, though. Are you ever going to tell me?"

"Haven't you guessed yet?" He sat beside her on the bed and stroked her hair back from her cheek. "I said that I loved your beautiful smile. But what I should have said – what I really wanted to say – was *rwy'n dy garu di*. I love you, Norma."

He kissed her as if it didn't matter that her hair was a mess and her breath must smell of sleep and her nightie was damp with milk. He kissed her as if he'd happily go on kissing her forever.

Not so long ago, she'd felt alone. But now, wrapped in the warmth and safety of Nye's arms, with Ivy sleeping peacefully on her lap, she knew everything she needed was right here.

EPILOGUE
SPRING, 1940

Norma

In all her girlish dreams of her wedding day, not once had Norma Sparrow ever imagined that she'd marry a preacher's son in a small Welsh chapel, with the muffled boom of artillery fire from the mountain a mile away making the minister twitch as he pronounced them married. Yet here she was with her new husband in a slightly shabby room in Pontybrenin's Station Hotel.

Aneurin stared at the double bed and shoved his hands into his trouser pockets.

"Don't look so terrified," Norma said, tilting her head to one side and sending him a wink. "I promise to be gentle with you."

It worked: the tension in his shoulders seemed to relax as he laughed and began unfastening the brass buttons on his khaki tunic. She caught his hand to stop him, noting the tremor betraying his nerves.

"Hold on a tick. I'd like to do those for you. And then, you can do mine. We can take our time – we've got all night. I'll just nip to the bathroom first, if that's alright?"

He nodded, keen to please as always.

She slipped out of the room and along the dingy corridor. The bathroom was occupied, so she waited a few feet away, next to a heavy chest of drawers with a potted aspidistra on top. The Station Hotel was hardly swanky. The old-fashioned prints of landscape paintings on the walls were faded, the threadbare carpet even more so. But it had been kind of the Powells to pay for a room for them there. Spending their wedding night at the manse would have been embarrassing, knowing every squeak of the mattress might be overheard. And if she'd heard Ivy crying, it would have thrown her into a terrible fret. Here, she and Nye could focus on each other, to the exclusion of everything else.

Her thoughts ran through the events of the day. Putting on her pretty underwear after her bath first thing, then the real silk stockings and blue garter that Miss Proudfoot had sent along with a note offering Norma some work turning a wedding dress into a christening gown. She'd enjoy doing that once Nye had gone back to his regiment.

The awed, adoring expression on her bridegroom's sweet face when he turned and saw her walking up the chapel's narrow aisle on Joe's arm, wearing her new frock.

Audrey's delight at being a bridesmaid and having a pretty dress to wear.

Gwenllian's pride at seeing her son marrying her grandson to the girl she'd taken under her wing.

Ceinwen's calm assurance as she held Ivy in her arms. Beside her, Miriam positively glowing, her gloved hands resting proudly on her swollen stomach.

And Emrys's voice, dark as treacle as he led them through their vows. He'd seemed more resigned than enthusiastic, but even his dour features had softened at Aneurin's unabashed joy.

Most faces had worn smiles, with the notable exception of Hilda Hughes, who had pouted miserably from her pew at the back. Norma hadn't found it hard to be gracious in victory, though. It was easy enough to sympathise with a girl whose dreams had been dashed. Hopefully one day Hilda would find a feller who looked at her the way Nye looked at his new bride.

They hadn't had a fancy wedding breakfast. Sugar rationing had meant the cake was tiny, hidden underneath a box covered in piped plaster to resemble royal icing, but Emrys's congregation had rallied round to provide finger sandwiches and dainty sausage rolls. And now here they were, legally married, thanks to a special licence and Aneurin's sympathetic commanding officer, who had granted him forty-eight hours' leave before his deployment.

It had been so much better than her wedding day last year could ever have been, even if she hadn't been jilted by Dickie. That night, she'd thought her chance of happiness was over. What a relief to look back now and realise she'd had a lucky escape. Dickie could never have made her feel the way Nye did, like a precious treasure. He wouldn't have given her the freedom to choose her own path, or encouraged her to pursue her dreams. He'd have resented Ivy and spent his evenings down the pub with his pals, pissing away what little money he earned instead of making sure he set his wife and child up securely. If he were sent away to fight, he wouldn't write tender letters home telling her how much he loved her and how he couldn't wait to see her smile and hold her in his arms again.

Aneurin was a husband she could be proud to walk beside. He'd help her stay true to her promise to her daughter. With his help, and the help of his family – her family too, now, she supposed – she wouldn't repeat her mum's mistakes. Already she was doing better than her poor mum had. Every time Ivy smiled one of her gummy grins or reached out a chubby hand, Norma's love and pride grew stronger. The little girl's name had been well chosen, for she'd woven tendrils around Norma's heart that could never be broken. For the first time in years, Norma had a family. She knew she was loved, and it made her feel ten feet tall.

"Oh dear, is there a queue?" A smartly dressed woman had emerged from one of the doorways along the corridor.

"'Fraid so," Norma confirmed.

"My goodness, what a charming frock you're wearing. So elegant. Is that pleating on the bodice?"

"Ruching," Norma said, preening at the woman's rapt examination of her handiwork. "I made it myself, based on a photo clipping I kept from a magazine. Some viscountess or other had a bodice a bit like it."

"You have an exceptional talent, my dear. Do you take commissions? My niece recently got engaged and is looking for a seamstress. There won't be much time to make a gown, though. Her fiancé will be deployed soon."

"My feller, too." Norma's mouth snapped shut. She didn't want to think about how little time she and Nye had, or the dangers he might face. "I made this dress in less than a week, so yes, I can do it quickly. Depends on what she wants, of course. Tell her to telephone the manse in Ebenezer Street and ask for Norma. Or she can visit, if she wants. Bring some pictures if she's seen a dress she likes."

They chatted until the bathroom was vacated, and then, having freshened up, Norma returned to the room where Nye was sitting on the bed waiting.

He scrubbed his palms on his thighs and rose to greet her.

We have so little time. Just one night, and then he'll be gone. One night to convince him he made the right choice.

Her mouth went dry. If she tried to seem more confident than she was by acting knowledgeable and experienced, would it reassure him or disgust him? She wasn't confident at all. It might as well be her first time all over again. But she wanted so much for this night to be perfect.

Aneurin stood before her. He watched in silence, his chest rising and falling shallowly as she unfastened the buttons on his tunic. She paused after each one to rest her fingers on his chest, taking it slowly to steady her nerves.

"Will you tell me what you like?" he asked, his voice husky.

Her hands stilled. "Oh, Nye, darlin'. I don't really know what I like. I ain't never been asked before." She risked a peep upwards to see how he'd received this admission.

His mouth was soft and warm, parting her lips. She leaned towards him and clung.

"Shall we find out together?" he murmured, once they were both breathless and the air between them felt charged.

"There's nothing I'd like more... *Os gwelwch yn dda.*"

Turning in the circle of his arms, she lifted her hair off the back of her neck, where a line of buttons traced her spine all the way down to her bottom. She'd relished every fiddly moment of covering those buttons with the same artificial silk she'd used to make the dress, anticipating this moment. Imagining his fingers moving down her back, half an inch at a time, his breath a whisper against her nape.

A shiver of anticipation rippled over her skin.

For tonight, she'd forget everything that had gone before. She'd forget the war; pretend he'd never have to go away. Tonight, they'd hold on to the hope that they'd have a lifetime.

AUTHOR'S NOTE

In the spring of 1940, an entire community in Mid Wales was shattered. Fifty-four farms, a school, two chapels and a pub on the mountain of Mynydd Epynt were evicted and 30,000 acres of its fertile, productive agricultural land taken over for military use. It's hard to imagine how devastating it must be for any community to be forced to leave the homes in which they have dwelled, in many cases, for generations. The people of Epynt lost their rootedness in a place where family members had been born, lived and died. Permitted only a few weeks to find suitable alternative accommodation, they were severed from the neighbours with whom they shared a profound bond, as well as from their places of worship, school and pub. They also lost their livelihoods, and the animals they reared, which had to be hurriedly sold for whatever price they could get. Their knowledge of the land, its rhythms and its needs, built over generations, was rendered worthless by the impersonal stroke of a pen in faraway London. As many were tenant farmers and shepherds, not landowners, they received little or no compensation. There was no consultation, and those who asked what would happen if they refused to move out were told they would be thrown out onto the road.

Other areas across the British mainland were also requisitioned for military use between 1938–1940. Over 6,000 acres in Scotland and nearly 57,000 acres in England were also taken over at that time. However, the much smaller country of Wales lost 70,000 acres in the same period. Consequently, Welsh Nationalists felt that the impact on the country was disproportionately brutal. For the people of Mynydd Epynt, whose mother tongue was the Welsh language, the impact was especially damaging. Having to scatter usually meant moving to places where their own language was not widely spoken. This *chwalfa* (meaning in English a shattering, dispersal or disintegration) was a severe blow to a precious culture, to an identity, and to a way of life. The last Christmas Plygain service and the last Eisteddfod were noted as particularly poignant occasions for a community which had celebrated these cultural events for generations. To many of the 200-plus people who lived on the mountain, being forced to move was the end of the world. So great was their grief, a few died not long after being evicted.

I've taken inspiration for my fictional mountain, Moel Carnau, from this shattering event. In doing so I hope I can raise awareness of its impact on the people who were affected by the real-life events, and its importance to Welsh history. However, when writing my fictionalised account, I made the decision not to keep strictly to the historical timeline. For Moel Carnau, I set the evictions to happen at the end of 1939 to suit the timeline of events in Norma's story. In the case of the real-life events on Mynydd Epynt, most sources state that eviction notices were first given to the farmers in early 1940, with a subsequent extension of several weeks grudgingly allowed to enable the farmers to deal with the lambing period. All the land, with its farms, school, tavern and chapels, was taken over in June for military use. Even now, nearly ninety years later, the mountain and its valleys are still owned and used by the British military, with access to the public strictly limited.

It was a joy to create my fictional evacuee Norma and drop her into a completely different world. When we think of evacuees at the beginning of the Second World War, we tend to think of children like those in my previous book *What We Left Behind*, labelled like parcels and despatched far from their parents to unfamiliar families. It's not as well known that pregnant women and mothers of young children were also given the opportunity to leave the potential dangers of the city, where they might be exposed to enemy air raids. Unmarried pregnant women might work for their keep in maternity homes set up for evacuees, while married women who could afford maternity care were treated much more kindly.

As difficult as it was to find billets for unaccompanied children, it was still more difficult to find them for young women whose expectations and previous way of life were often quite different from their hosts'. It's easy to think that the so-called "Blitz spirit" made everyone pull together, when in fact many evacuees thought rural life primitive, and many rural folk thought evacuees were dirty and ill-behaved. Class differences and snobbery on either side might, of course, have added an extra spice to this potentially tricky mixing of cultural backgrounds. Some country folk disapproved of city women drinking alcohol, swearing, or going into pubs. Clashes could easily arise from differences in approaches to child-rearing. Rural housewives might have resented sharing a kitchen with another woman, and some insisted that evacuee mothers and their children stayed out of the house during the day.

On the other hand, some adult evacuees were horrified at the lack of facilities in countryside villages and homes. Evacuees were cut off from their former support networks and most of their possessions; many might not have even been able to take a pram with them when embarking upon their new life. They missed regular public transport, cinemas, shops like Woolworths, and ready access to cafés where they could buy familiar foods like pie and mash or fish and chips. The cost of living tended to be higher in the countryside. No wonder many found the transition challenging. Although some stayed, it wasn't unusual for women to decide they'd prefer to take their chances with the bombs.

A LETTER FROM THE AUTHOR

Dear reader,

Huge thanks for reading *Before the Mountain Falls*. I hope you were hooked on Norma and Miriam's journey. If you want to join other readers in hearing all about my new releases and bonus content from Storm Publishing, you can sign up here:

www.stormpublishing.co/luisa-a-jones

You can also sign up to my personal author newsletter and receive a free short story at www.luisaajones.com.

If you enjoyed this book and could spare a few moments to leave a review that would be hugely appreciated. Even a short review can make all the difference in encouraging a reader to discover my books for the first time. Thank you so much!

As so often in my historical novels, I was inspired by a snippet of Welsh history. Even many Welsh people I speak to have never heard of Mynydd Epynt and the evictions which took place there during the Second World War, to take the land over for military use. I couldn't resist bringing this history into my tale of a pregnant, unmarried evacuee trying to make a new life for herself in Wales.

Thanks again for being part of this amazing journey with me and I hope you'll stay in touch – I have so many more stories and ideas to entertain you with!

Luisa A. Jones

KEEP IN TOUCH WITH THE AUTHOR

www.luisaajones.com

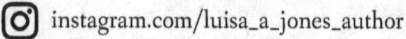 instagram.com/luisa_a_jones_author
facebook.com/Luisa-A-Jones-232663650757721
bsky.app/profile/luisaajones.bsky.social

ACKNOWLEDGMENTS

Just as it takes a village to raise a child, a writer can't create their book alone. For this book, I'm grateful to many people for their help and support, most especially to those mentioned below.

First and foremost, my thanks go to my husband, Martin, and to my family. Your support and belief in me mean everything. Thank you for cheering me on all the way. Thank you, Mum, for casting your eye over the final proofread, to help spot those last few wayward typos.

As always, the team at Storm Publishing have been brilliant. Thanks for believing in this book and helping me make it better. My editors Naomi Knox, Kathryn Taussig, Natasha Hodgson and Becca Allen are simply the best. Thank you also to Eileen Carey for the beautiful cover design.

Thank you to my first beta reader, David Hobday, who gave insightful comments on my very rough first draft, and helped with research into enlistment and the military in 1939.

I'm grateful to my author friends Jenny O'Brien and Jan Baynham for sharing their generous feedback on an early draft.

My Welsh tutor, Ruth Lloyd, shared an extract from her late father's memoir about Mynydd Epynt and gave up her time to read a pre-publication copy of the book, generously going far beyond the call of duty. Any errors in the Welsh language used in the book are, of course my own. *Diolch o galon*, Ruth!

My friends in the Cariad Chapter of the Romantic Novelists' Association have been an unfailing source of support, encouragement and laughs. I wouldn't have made it this far as a writer without them.

My research into Mynydd Epynt was aided by Sioned Williams of Amgueddfa Cymru, Ydwena Jones of the Atgofion Epynt Facebook group, and Euros Lewis, who kindly responded to my queries. I'm particularly indebted to Euros for taking the time to chat to me over a video call, and for explaining the Welsh word *cymdogaeth*. *Diolch yn fawr*.

Thanks are also due to Catrin Lewis for confirming details about pre-eclampsia and labour, and to Janine Davies for information about Welsh sheep farming, while staff at The Royal Welsh Regimental Museum in Brecon helped with research into conscription in 1939.

Rowena Tasker shared information and pictures to help with my research into hairdressers in 1939. I later decided Norma would be a seamstress, but I've kept the hairdressing details for future reference. Who knows when they might come in handy?

Lastly, but certainly not least, a heartfelt *diolch yn fawr* to Ruth Jones and Elaine Williams for their patience and help as I tried to invent plausible Welsh place names. I'm particularly thankful to Ruth for her suggestion of Moel Carnau, making a link to the horses of Mynydd Epynt. *Mae'n enw perffaith!*

www.ingramcontent.com/pod-product-compliance
Lightning Source LLC
LaVergne TN
LVHW031536060526
838200LV00056B/4516